MW01138668

The Actuary

K T BOWES

DISCLAIMER

DEDICATION

It's gratifying when someone likes my work enough to want to be part of it. Although I have invented the character of Allaine, I have used her real name with her permission and I'm grateful for her ceaseless encouragement.

I also want to acknowledge Dave Carson, UK, who helped me with some particularly difficult chapters relating to the main character, Rohan Andreyev. His help was based on his own painful experience and I'm grateful for his openness and honesty with me. I sincerely hope I've managed to do his daily struggle justice.

CHAPTER ONE

"Congratulations, Susan!" The dark haired woman leaned in and kissed her friend on the cheek, her pretty skin flushed with the heat of the room. "You look so content at last, I'm pleased for you."

"Oh, Emma! It's been a long time coming. I finally feel lucky."

Emma wrapped her arms around her friend, trying not to get lipstick on the delicate fabric of her ivory wedding dress. Over her shoulder she saw Susan's new husband, Frederik. He was handsome and sophisticated, his salt and pepper hair suiting his courtly appearance. "He's pretty fit," Emma whispered in her friend's ear, laughing at Susan's squeal of delight.

"My sister says he is," she sniggered, covering her mouth with her hand.

Emma felt hot breath on her leg and looked down. She smiled and offered her hand to the fluffy white retriever at Susan's side. He smiled back, his tongue lolling sideways from his mouth and he sat abruptly on his backside, yanking the harness from his blind mistress' hand. "Oh Jay!" Susan complained. "I know you've had enough but this is my wedding day!"

"He did a good job of escorting you down the aisle," Emma joked, stroking the soft, downy hair on the top of Jay's head. She smoothed her thumb down the bridge of his nose and the dog closed his eyes with a dreamy expression on his face. "You're such a flirt!" she chastised him, ruffling his feathery ears and shaking her head. Dark curls cascaded down her back and bounced with the movement.

"It's been a beautiful day," Susan sighed. The strobe lights caught her red hair giving her an ethereal glow. "You'll stay a bit longer, won't you?" She couldn't see the uncomfortable look on Emma's face as the other woman battled with issues Susan could not contemplate. The borrowed green silk dress bit into Emma's waist and the rental car outside needed to be back at the hire company by midnight. The three hour drive south in the dark was daunting.

"Just a little while," Emma promised. "But then I have to get Nicky home. We had an early start this morning."

"Well come and say goodbye before you go, won't you?" Susan's face pleaded with her as Emma nodded and squeezed her hand. "I wanted to talk to you about your work in the school archives. I need to tell you what we've been doing with ours. I thought it might help."

"I'd love to, but I do have to go soon." Emma winced as the band started up after their intermission, deafening everyone nearby. The guide dog whined and looked like he wanted to stick his paws over his ears. "Would you like me to take you to Frederik?" Emma yelled over the din and Susan nodded.

"Yes please. I think if I ask Jay to take me, I'll end up at the car."

Emma laughed. "Oh gosh, yeah. Remember the time you told him to take you to the vets and he walked you around for hours and then took you home?"

"Pardon?" Susan shrieked back and Emma shook her head, leading her friend by the hand towards her tall new husband over at the bar.

The place was crowded with bodies and Emma sighed as she recognised one of them. Her six year old son stood at the side of the buffet table, paper plate towering with food. His blonde wavy hair spilled over a face covered in chocolate. He grinned displaying brown teeth covered in goo and waved, his bright blue eyes sparkling with mischief. His plate tipped and a sausage roll bounced to the floor. Not realising it fell from his plate, he looked up at the ceiling to see where it came from and then back at his mother. She held her free hand up in the air, fingers splayed and mouthed, "Five more minutes."

The child nodded with enthusiasm and began cramming delicacies into his mouth, making use of the time left to get his fill. Emma cringed. *Definitely time to leave.* She weaved through the bodies, navigating Susan and Jay towards the landmark of Frederik's head, standing high above everyone else's. As Jay realised he was going back into the throng, his feet ceased their happy padding along the wooden dance floor and he stopped dead. Susan yanked on Emma's arm in warning but Jay made a valiant rush for the open door, hauling the two women after him. He cut through the dancing crowd like a heat seeking missile, making his bid for freedom with the women as ballast. Susan had no choice with her wrist caught in the strap of his leash and her fingers clamped around the handle of the harness, but Emma held onto her friend's other hand for dear life, clopping along in the borrowed heels.

From the corner of her eye, Emma saw Susan stop sharply as Frederik's capable hand seized the harness and halted Jay's unauthorised kidnapping of his bride. Unable to stop, Emma sped past the knot of man, woman and dog, feeling herself tilt dangerously in the open doorway as Susan let go of her hand. Too late, Emma remembered the stairs down to the entrance. She let out a strangled scream as a body stepped in the way, taking the full brunt of her hasty exit. The male figure grunted and grabbed her upper arms, keeping her upright and allowing Emma the dignity of a few seconds in which to collect herself. "Thank you," she gulped, spying with horror the awful sight of her buttons undoing themselves over her cleavage.

"Are you all right, Emma?" Susan's voice sounded concerned and Emma nodded as she fumbled with the fiddly pearl buttons, failing miserably to get them closed.

"Yep, yep. I'm fine thanks. Just catching my breath." She heard Susan behind her, admonishing her furry companion.

"You made it!" came Frederik's voice and his hand appeared next to Emma, shaking her saviour's with enthusiasm. "Awesome! I'll just sit my wife down and then we'll catch up."

"Oh, bloody hell!" Emma breathed as another button sidled out of its hole as soon as she put the one above it back in. A male snort made Emma's head whip up as familiar fingers brushed her shaking hands away.

"Here, let me, *dorogaya*."

Emma gulped and closed her eyes. If she didn't look up, then it couldn't be true. *It's not him*, she told herself. *It can't be. It's someone else with a Russian accent. You're tired and imagining things.* An unexpected flare of disappointment took her by surprise and her cheeks flamed with embarrassment. "I'm fine. I'm leaving anyway." She pushed the fingers away as their buttoning action brushed the soft flesh of her exposed

4

breasts. Emma dared to look up with indignation in her eyes and her heart bounced in her chest.

The tall blonde man in front of her was every bit as striking as she remembered, a strand of the disobedient blonde fringe flipping over his left eye, bumped sexily by the action of his long eyelashes. Vibrant blue eyes stared at her with question, bright like azure diamonds. "Hi, Em," he said, his voice seeming to touch the deeper, buried parts of her soul.

"I don't think we know each other," Emma ventured, drawing her shoulders back and looking sideways at possible escape routes. To her irritation, the blonde man threw his head back and laughed.

"I think I know you better than you know yourself." He smiled but the expression failed to reach his eyes.

"I need to go!" Emma stated firmly and stepped sideways, desperately looking for help. Frederik and a disgraced Jay were busily settling a shaken Susan on an armchair in a seating area. Susan wagged her finger at the wilful dog who looked around the room and purposely ignored her.

Emma took another step sideways and the blonde man blocked her. "If you want to dance, we need to be over there." He pointed at the dance floor. Foolishly Emma looked and while she was distracted, he seized her wrist in a vice-like grip and led her to the throng of gyrating couples. Emma groaned as the music dropped to a slow dance and the man smiled, settling his hands either side of Emma's neat waist. He fixed his penetrating blue eyes on her face and pulled her in close. Emma stood in front of him like a log and he sighed and grasped one of her hands in each of his, placing them carefully around his neck.

"Just like old times." He smiled. "So, how have you

been?" His voice was raised against the music, his mouth very close to her ear and Emma closed her eyes against the rising flood of emotions which fought for dominance in her heart.

"Good," she lied. "Lovely to see you, Rohan, but I really should be going."

"Stay." He fingered a lock of her hair, watching in fascination as it wound round and round his finger and then plummeted down her back. He selected another one and repeated the exercise. Emma whipped her head from side to side, trying to locate her son. She didn't have to search far. He sat on a chair next to the deserted buffet table with a half-eaten mountain on his plate. He looked sick. *Fantastic. A three hour drive with a vomiting child.*

"I really need to go." Emma withdrew her hands from around the man's neck and turned her body to block the amazing sensation of his groin so close to hers.

"Ok." He sounded sad and resigned and Emma's breath caught in her chest. He gave her a tiny smile, revealing the dent from a scar above his lip and another under his eye. Emma's brown eyes made the mistake of straying from his brilliant blue ones, to his full lips and back again. His smirk was instant. He caught her up in one easy movement and put his hand at the back of Emma's neck. His lips on hers were gentle and paralysing. Emma opened her mouth and his tongue slid in like it was only yesterday, familiar and dangerous. She reached up and put her arms either side of his chest, feeling the rippling muscles under her hand. He felt taller, stronger, older and definitely different. But then so was she. With a huge act of will, Emma broke the connection, inhaling sharply as she put the back of her hand to lips swollen by the familiar kiss.

"Em!" she heard him shout at she fled the dance floor. She gripped her son by his wrist and ran for the toilets, remembering another exit at the end of that corridor.

"Night, miss," the doorman said and she nodded in acknowledgement and ran, dragging the small boy after her.

"Mum!" the child complained. "Don't bounce me. I'm gonna puke!"

"I've got a bag," Emma insisted, hurling her stiletto shoes onto the back seat of the car. "Get in the front and you won't feel so bad. I'll put the cold air on."

"But my booster seat's in the back!" he grumbled and Emma uncharacteristically snapped.

"As soon as we get away from here, I'll pull over and sort everything out," she promised. "Please, Nicky, just do as I ask."

"Ok then!" he complained. "But if a policeman tells you off, it's coming out of your pocket money, not mine! I was havin' fun talking to Harley Man before you ruined it!"

"Nicky!" Emma exclaimed, panic making her cruel. "Harley Man isn't real! He's just a character you've seen in a comic or on TV. He can't talk to you."

"He can, Mum. My friends have seen 'im. He stops and talks to me back home and he was here tonight!"

"Ok, Nick, ok." Emma fumbled with the car key and ignition in the darkness, banishing talk of her son's imaginary friend to the back of her mind as she dealt with the more immediate issue of escape. She started the engine on the rented saloon car and spun the wheels. The lights glared on at the last minute as she sped by the front doors of the hotel, blinding the doorman. The handsome blonde Russian emerged from the doors at a run, his suit jacket hanging open and his tie flapping in the breeze. His face was ashen and distraught.

"That's your friend what you was kissin'," Nicky informed his mother as they careened past. "Harley Man saw him kissin' ya and he said, '*Uh oh, that's not gonna end well.*' Funny hey?" The child lifted his tiny hand and waved at the blonde man, who stopped and gaped. His face was a mask of agony at the sight of the small carbon copy of himself on the front seat. Bile leaped into Emma's throat as she navigated the minor roads until the motorway, feeling sicker than she thought possible. Her hands shook on the steering wheel and she gripped it until her knuckles shone white against the lights of oncoming cars. Emma glanced sideways at her small son, hoping he didn't notice her anxiety.

"There he is!" Nicky squealed and dipped forward in his seat, craning his neck to look in the side mirror. Emma swerved and swore.

"Don't do that!"

"But he's behind us, Mummy, look."

"Who is, Nicky, who?" *Please, not Rohan?*

"Harley Man! Who else?" Emma peered in the rear view mirror at the motorcyclist two vehicles behind. He kept a steady pace, his visor blocking out any facial features. He stayed where he was, keeping a neat line in the centre of his lane, unconcerned with passing either vehicle. Emma kept an eye on him, cursing herself for buying into Nicky's overactive imaginary world, but then the bike took off at the next roundabout, taking the outside lane and moving off ahead. Nicky sat back in his seat looking disappointed. "You scared 'im off! Coz you kept starin'. It's rude to stare!"

Emma sighed as her petulant son sulked in the oversize seatbelt next to her. Thoughts of the blonde man overrode any feelings about Nicky's grumpy mood and she battled with images of his soft hands caressing her skin. Stifling an involuntary sob, Emma pressed her fingers either side of the bridge of her nose and Nicky was instantly contrite. "Sorry, Mummy. I'm sorry. S'not your fault. Harley Man will come back, he always does."

"Yeah, he certainly seems to." Emma kept the sarcasm out of her voice as she fought the inner tide of misery, focussing on the road and grateful for the tiny hand which stretched over and gently rubbed her thigh.

At the first service station they stopped and used the bathrooms. "I can go in the big boy ones," Nicky insisted, veering off towards the men's toilets.

"Er, I don't think so, buddy!" Emma grabbed the back of his shirt and pushed him towards the door adorned with a female silhouette. Nicky turned to face the door while Emma used the facilities, disgusted with his demotion to child status.

"It's oomiliatin'," he complained.

"It's life!" Emma retorted. "Did you really think I was gonna let you go into a gents' toilets in the back end of nowhere in a service station, with every nomad weirdo passing through?"

"I can take care of myself," Nicky said, his voice filled with touching sincerity. "When Big Jason jumped me last week, I kicked him in the jewels." He turned around as Emma flushed, his blue eyes alight with victory.

Emma righted her dress and looked down on her son. "Big Jason is a forty year old midget!" she said. "I could defend myself against him!"

"He's not a midget!" Nicky insisted with indignation. "He's just got delicate bones."

Emma bought Nicky a bottle of mineral water to help him look a little less green around the gills, although much of his sickness had passed. She topped up the car with petrol and prayed it would still look full when she dropped it off at the rental place. More excitement ensued at the counter, as Nicky spotted a leather clad motorcyclist in the other queue. He smiled and waved and Emma looked away, embarrassed. The male had a neat physique and looked as though he was poured into his protective leather gear. He stood at the till with his legs slightly splayed and Emma found herself staring at the outline of his pert backside. He kept his helmet on but the visor raised and Emma looked guiltily away as he turned. "See ya later," Nicky intoned with a beautiful smile and a wave.

Emma cringed, ignoring the tugging on her skirt from the small boy. "He ruffled my hair," Nicky said confidentially and Emma smiled and nodded, her mortification complete. Her son's fixation with Harley Man was bordering on the need for a psychologist, not that his underfunded, forgotten primary school had access to such professionals.

Emma fixed Nicky's booster seat into the front of the vehicle, settled him in and left, heading south to Lincoln and the government owned house on the notorious Greyfriars Estate.

CHAPTER TWO

"Mum!"

"I'm just upstairs, love."

Emma heard her son clumping up the stairs in his trainers. There was no point getting him to take his shoes off indoors. The bare wooden floors played hell with the soles of delicate socks. "Mum!" He yelled from the top of the stairs and Emma poked her head out of her bedroom. "Oh, there you are. I took your dress back to Marie's house but she's not there. Kane said his dad gave her a slap last night and she's in the hospital."

"Really?" Emma looked ashen and Nicky nodded at the enthusiastic response to his news flash. "And I saw Big Jason McArthur outside their house smokin' weed. He said he's gonna come round and give you one." Nicky licked his lips and looked worried. "Is he gonna give you a slap or a weed stick?"

"Neither, Nicky. We don't take anything off Big Jason."

Nicky followed her from one side of the room to the other, tripping over the sleeping bag serving as Emma's bed. "Mum, if he tries to give you something you don't want, do you think I could give 'im a slap?"

Emma squatted down next to her son's loyal face. He oozed concern for her in his sad blue eyes. "No babe. He's a forty four year old smack addict and a patched gang member. You're a beautiful six year old boy with a big heart and it won't go well for either of us."

"Well, I've been thinking 'bout it and I reckon me an' Mo can probably pop the tyres on his Harley."

"Seriously Nicky, if you want us in big trouble, that's the way to go. And anyway, it's not really a Harley, he just thinks it is."

"Ok then." He looked happy.

Emma's brow furrowed in fear. "Don't do it, Nicky. I'm telling you. I'll be really cross!"

"Oh." He looked disappointed. "Mum?" He fixed intelligent eyes on her face. "That man last night was kissin' you a real long time. And he was enjoyin' it. Why was he kissin' you?"

Emma gulped. "He was giving me a new year's kiss."

Nicky rolled his eyes. "Well that's dumb! It's only November!"

"He's Russian," Emma said, biting her top lip and transferring clean washing from the black bin liner into the suitcase balanced on a rickety cupboard. "Everything's upside down there."

"What even Christmas?" Nicky sounded indignant. "That's sucky!"

"Yep," Emma answered. "Now please could you wheel your suitcase here for me? Then I can put your clean clothes back in it."

The child skipped off to his room and brought back his wardrobe on wheels. "I miss Nana Lucya's house," he said softly. "With proper beds and wardrobes and stuff. Can we go back there?"

"Nana Lucya died, remember?" Emma's heart constricted in her chest and she rested her hands on her son's slumped shoulders. He face planted roughly into her stomach and put his free hand around her waist.

"But I still miss her, Mummy," he sniffed.

"Me too," Emma whispered. "Me too."

Nicky balanced his chin on the belt of Emma's jeans. "Mum? Nana was Russian too, wasn't she? But she had Christmas and New Year at the right time. Maybe the man got mixed up."

"Clever boy!" Emma faked her joviality, realising her mistake too late with this highly intelligent child. Each year it got harder and harder to deflect his questions. "It must be me getting mixed up. Silly Mummy."

Nicky laughed and repeated the label. "Silly Mummy," he chortled, placing his neatly rolled clothes in the suitcase and wheeling it back to his bedroom.

Emma breathed a sigh of relief and suppressed the sick feeling in her stomach. "Damn! Susan!" The sudden flash of realisation bit into her consciousness and Emma grappled in her jeans pocket for her mobile phone. She needed to text her friend to apologise for her hasty exit but also to stop her passing on Emma's contact details to Frederik's handsome friend. She typed in the hurried text and pressed 'send'. The phone bleeped immediately and Emma peered at the screen. '*This phone has insufficient credit,*' the message stated and her text flashed back on screen with an option to, '*Try again.*' "Not much point really, is there?" she grumbled, knowing the last of her money went on refuelling the hire car before she returned it the night before and then the taxi home.

"I'm not driving on that estate," the taxi driver scoffed and Emma had argued with him.

"It's literally down there!" she said. "I can see the house from here!"

"Well you bloody walk there then," he replied grumpily.

"So you won't drive onto the estate, but it's ok for me to walk there in the dark with a sleeping child?" Emma bit.

The man shrugged. "You chose to live there," he said in an irritating sing-song voice. "Ten quid please."

Emma threw the money onto the passenger seat and hitched the sleeping Nicky higher over her shoulder. She kept a stiletto in either hand to defend herself. "Actually," she said through the open passenger window at the smug man behind the steering wheel. "Nobody chooses to live on this estate. God forbid you ever hit hard times!"

"Oh sod off!" he replied and pulled away from the curb, activating his central locking at the same time as closing the electric windows tightly.

It was a five minute walk through the darkened no-go area. Most of the street lamps were smashed and Emma walked barefoot, listening out for sounds that might indicate danger. Many pairs of eyes watched but she arrived home unharmed, with sore feet from the frozen ground and a hole in both soles of her work tights.

She stood in her empty bedroom and contemplated the calamity of no phone credit. Susan wouldn't divulge her contact details. They went through university, struggling together, one with a toddler and the other with progressive blindness, both robbed of aspects of life but for different reasons. "She won't give him it," Emma concluded with a nod of satisfaction.

"I hope you don't either!" Nicky said with austerity, kneeling down next to the black bag and reaching inside for his freshly laundered school shorts.

"You hope I don't what?" Emma asked her son, switching her mind back to the present.

"I hope you don't give Big Jason *it!*" He grunted as he found his faded sports shirt and flicked it in the air, inspecting it for clumps of the cheap washing powder Emma was forced to use.

"I definitely won't!" Emma promised, shivering at the thought.

"Marie did!" Nicky piped up. "That's why Kane's dad gave 'er a slap and put 'er in the hospital."

Emma shook her head and exhaled. She stared around her at the near derelict house and wondered what the hell she was doing.

CHAPTER THREE

The insistent knocking on the front door didn't sound like anyone Emma knew and she stood just inside the hallway door, waiting.

"What ya waitin' for, Mum?" Nicky whispered. "Is it the repo man?"

Emma snorted and held her arms out. "There's nothing to take! Just go and hide in the cupboard in case it's trouble."

Nicky kissed the bottom of Emma's back and skipped down the hallway, shutting himself quietly in the cupboard under the stairs. Emma watched as he closed the door tightly and then braced herself to open the front door.

The watery mid-afternoon sun glinted off the broken glass in the street, contrasting with the expensive black Mercedes Benz parked on her cracked driveway. Emma looked at the vehicle currently inviting much interest from her curious neighbours and swore. A crowd of people gathered around the pristine piece of engineering perfection, like zombies around a corpse.

"Nice welcome," her visitor commented, leaning against the door frame with his hands in his pockets.

Emma paled and stared at Rohan open mouthed. "What the hell are you doing here?" she squeaked. "Are you trying to get me killed?"

"I'll karate chop 'im!" Nicky burst from the cupboard under the stairs waving his arms and kicking out with his legs.

"Bloody hell, it's Harry Potter!" Rohan looked astounded.

Nicky stopped dead when he saw Rohan. "Oh. Are you a bit simple?"

"Pardon me?" Rohan's brow knitted.

"Eugh. Did you fart?" Nicky stood next to Emma, putting his arm in front of her in a protective motion.

"Er, no." The tall blonde man looked completely wrong footed. He stood up straight and took his hands out of his pockets. Half the rotten doorframe tumbled on to the frayed door mat and the rest stuck to the back of Rohan's sweatshirt.

"I think he's a bit simple, Mum. Look, he broke the door frame. Will I get Fat Brian to beat 'im up?"

"No! Nobody needs to beat anyone up."

"But he thinks Christmas is upside down and that I'm a magic boy. He can't be normal. I'll get Fat Brian."

Nicky took a step towards the door and Emma grabbed hold of the back of his sweater. Nicky made exaggerated choking sounds. "Pack it in!" Emma warned him. "But yes, go and get Fat Brian, please. Tell him I've got a problem."

"Seriously?" Rohan stood up to his full height, another piece of crumbling wood falling from the back of his clothing and landing on the floor. Emma counted four woodlice running for their lives. She knew how they felt. Rohan looked angry and the tell-tale vein pulsed in his neck. "I turn up to talk to you and you want someone called Fat Brian to beat me up?" He looked a mixture of dismayed and irritated.

Emma shook her head. "No! Don't be ridiculous! How much cash have you got on you?"

Rohan's jaw dropped. "What?"

"Rohan, will you just answer me?" Emma watched the crowd of onlookers edge closer to the shiny black car. He followed her gaze and opened his mouth to speak as a skinny man completely tattooed from forehead to waistband, tried the locked passenger door.

"About fifty quid," he replied, sounding stunned. "Why?"

Nicky appeared at the end of the driveway, flanked by an elderly man with gang tattoos on his bare chest and swear words on his cheeks. Rohan hid a smirk at the unfortunate spelling mistake on his forehead. *Fork off,* was written in a beautiful font, but at the violence on the man's face, the tall blonde man wiped all expression from his eyes, leaving a regimental nondescript mask.

"You all right, girl?" Fat Brian was so fat, he couldn't get on the front step at the same time as Rohan and pushed past him, ridges of hairy flesh smelling of lager and cigarettes. His flaccid face and bulging eyes were inches from Emma's delicate features. Rohan's eyes widened in amazement as Emma kissed the man gently on the cheek.

"Thanks for coming, Brian." She smiled. "I have a visitor and his car is becoming something of a problem. I wondered if you'd take care of it for me. He won't be staying long."

Fat Brian smiled, displaying two pink rows of gums. "Hell yeah!" He held his hand out towards Rohan with enthusiasm and the blonde man looked at Emma for a clue.

"Brian will take your car to his house until you want to leave," Emma informed him helpfully. She jerked her head towards the wallet she knew he kept in the front pocket of his trousers and Rohan rolled his eyes and drew out a fifty pound note. He handed it reluctantly over and Brian put out his other hand.

"Erm...I..."

"Give Brian your keys," Emma said nicely and smirked with enjoyment at the horror on Rohan's face.

Rohan drew out the key fob and seemed to choke as he placed it carefully on the sweaty pink palm. "I'm assuming you've got a full licence?" he asked the man in front of him and Brian gave a beautiful smile.

"I don't believe in corrupt political certification," Brian stated with complete seriousness and Rohan watched him set off towards the crowd of forty people, all touching the expensive motor car.

Speechless, Rohan watched Brian start his car, rev it loudly a few times and screech off down the street. He opened his mouth numerous times but nothing came out. He shook his head at Emma and stayed on the step, looking in the direction his car was last seen.

"You might as well come in," she sighed. "Turn around first though. You're wearing half my dry rot on your sweater."

"I really liked that car!" Rohan sounded heart broken and Emma laughed.

"You'll get it back when you leave. I'll send Nicky round and he'll bring it back. That's what the fifty quid was for. Safe keeping. Nobody will touch it on Fat Brian's driveway."

"Fat Brian likes my mum," Nicky added helpfully. "When 'is missus beats him up, he sleeps on our living room floor. Lots of people with nowhere to go do that, sleep on our living room floor. That's why we're protected by Fat Brian and lots of other people. Cause my mum's right kind." Nicky smiled in approval at

Emma and she felt her heart give a little flip flop in her chest. The child observed the tall blonde man with open curiosity and his next question sent Emma's brain scrambling. "Where're you from? Your accent sounds like my..."

"Nicky?" Emma interrupted, jerking her head towards the hallway. "Please would you go and play in your room for a while, while I talk to the man?"

The six year old scoffed like an old man. "What wiv, Mum? Me sleepin' bag?"

"Try, your homework!" she chided him and the boy pulled a face.

"Ok," he said cheerfully. "Then will you test me?"

Emma smiled and nodded and the child climbed the rickety stairs, hands stuffed deep in his pockets. He stopped at the top and opened his mouth. Emma winced. "Oh, Big Jason said..."

"Thanks!" Emma stopped his repetition of something vile and waved him away.

Rohan looked utterly horrified by everything around him and Emma felt pity at the sight of his wide eyes and pale complexion. "You ok?" she asked kindly.

He shook his head. "You're bringing up a child in a freakin' war zone, Em! I was in the Helmand Province in Afghanistan and this makes it look like a bloody suburb of London!"

Emma laughed. "You get used to it eventually." She turned away and walked towards the kitchen, muttering under her breath, "Or you kill yourself!"

Rohan stuck close to Emma down the hallway, almost walking on her heels. He did a lot of head shaking but to her relief, kept his extensive opinions to himself. Emma placed water into a saucepan and lit the gas hob. While she waited for it to boil, she put instant coffee into two mugs with a spoon left over from a spoon bending competition by the looks of the handle. She took a carton of milk off the windowsill and sniffed it, pulling a face and then adding it to the mugs. When the water boiled she added it to the mixture and handed Rohan the mug with less chips in the rim. He took it, his blue eyes never leaving her face. "How did you find me?" she asked, leaning her backside against the battered work surface behind her. Rohan looked around for somewhere to sit, quickly realising there was no furniture.

"Do you not own anything?" he asked, disbelief in his voice.

Emma shrugged. "Things come and go really. Sometimes other people need things more. I owned a dining table for a while, but Marie up the road borrowed it for a family party. The party turned a bit nasty and it was collateral damage."

Rohan gaped for a second and then closed his mouth, running his free hand across the lower half of his face. Emma heard the scratching sound of his blonde stubble on the palm of his hand and it sent a curious shiver through her body. "I asked how you found me." An edge appeared in her voice and it made Rohan jump and bring himself back to the situation in hand.

"Frederik got your address from Susan," he replied and Emma looked shocked.

"I don't believe you!" She sounded aggressive and he looked surprised.

"Oh, she doesn't know. He was my sergeant at Camp Bastion. It was a favour."

"Great!" Emma plonked her mug down on the work surface, looking at the handle in surprise as it came off in her hand.

"Em, talk to me. What the hell happened? I got back and you were gone..."

Emma took a step away from Rohan, hardening her face and her heart. "Well, thanks for stopping by. Fat Brian lives at number forty-three. It's only a three minute walk on foot and he'll have put the word out. You should be fine." Emma backed away further and Rohan put his mug down, ready for a fight.

He jumped when the sharp tapping came on the kitchen window. "What's going on in there?" a muffled voice called through the curtainless glass. Rohan bridled at the sight of the tattooed face peering through the window, readying his fists and recalling his military drill.

"Go away, Big Jason!" Emma called to the ridiculously small man. "And I've told you to stop standing on my flower pots to see in the window!"

"Just looking out for ya, darlin'," the tattooed mouth called, stepping back and disappearing with a cry of pain.

"He keeps doing that," Emma sniggered and Rohan shook his head in disbelief.

"It's a bloody circus for weirdoes," he breathed and Emma laughed out loud.

"It kinda is, hey?" she snorted. "There's Fat Brian and Big Jason. I'm the Bearded Lady!" She burst into raucous laughter and Rohan halted at her beauty in the incongruous surroundings. He shook his head in confusion.

Emma wiped her eyes and stared at Rohan. "Well, this is...awkward." She sniggered again at the inappropriateness of the situation and he stared at her.

"Just come in here!" He seized her arm and led her

out into the hallway, checking there were no windows they could be viewed through. Then he crushed her into his chest and stroked her hair. It caught Emma off guard and she forgot to resist, caught up in the moment and the heady sense of comfort she hadn't felt for far too long. She smelled the clean scent of fresh linen and deodorant on Rohan, satiating herself with the essence of him before the God who surely hated her, snatched him away again and left her alone with her tiny son to fend for. Emma gasped as Rohan tilted her chin upwards and kissed her, wasting no time in turning her on and making her hot and bothered.

"No!" She pushed him away, leaning back against the plaster wall and hearing the clink as a piece of the lath behind fell into the cavity.

"Emma, is he my son?"

"Rohan, leave things the way they are, please?" Emma's inner panic showed in the dilation of her pupils and the way she worried at her lower lip.

"No, I can't. Why did you run away? My mother said..."

"Don't talk to me about *her!*" Emma shouted, pushing at Rohan's broad chest. "Don't mention her name, not now! It's taken me years to...to..." Emma's breath caught and she lifted her hands to her face, covering her eyes in misery. She writhed with an inner agony and felt Rohan's arms draw her in again, strong and comforting. "Please go," she whispered. "I need you to go."

Rohan lifted Emma's chin and his face was a mask of confusion. "I don't understand, Em. Please explain what the hell happened?"

"No." Emma inhaled and wiped her weeping eyes with the sleeve of her ratty fleece. "It's in my past and

I'm not going there again. It's best if you just leave. I don't want to upset Nicky."

"I'm already upset." Nicky's voice echoed in the empty hallway. He peeked around the top spindle, his face ashen. Emma exhaled as she heard a clunk on the wood above.

"Put the baseball bat down, Nicky!" she told him, running her sleeve across her eyes and nose before facing him properly. "I'm fine. Go back to your room, please."

"No, I'm not going 'cause you're cryin'."

"I'm not, baby, I'm absolutely fine. Honestly. Go and put the bat away and I'll see if there's anything nice in the cupboard for tea."

"There isn't." Nicky stood up and dragged the bat slowly across the bare floorboards above. "I'll put it back, but in a minute I'm comin' down and if that man's being mean to ya, I'm gonna chop 'im."

Rohan watched the space where Nicky had been and then dropped his gaze to Emma's face. Emma saw the reflection of her empty house in his irises and bit her lip. "Em, come away with me?" he begged. "I've got room for you and the boy. Please? You can't stay here."

"No! I've got a job here and responsibilities. I can't just leave on a whim."

Rohan stuck out his chin and postured in front of her, his six feet and four inch bearing casting a shadow over Emma. "Well, I'm not leaving without you!" he stated with determination.

Emma giggled despite herself. "Don't be ridiculous. There's nowhere for you to stay."

"I'm not leaving." Rohan set his jaw, his blue eyes flashing dangerously.

Emma shrugged, tired with the battle. "Then you should probably visit a cash machine. Because if you don't give Fat Brian another fifty tomorrow, he'll start selling your car piece by piece!"

CHAPTER FOUR

"I'm gutted about my car," Rohan whispered into the darkness. Emma rolled her eyes and sighed loudly.

"It'll be fine for tonight. But Sunday's not a great day to leave town. Everyone gets drunk after tea. Brian will be rat-faced and probably forget who you are if you turn up wanting your car. Last weekend his wife clouted him round the head with a frying pan and he was senseless until Tuesday."

"I'm astounded you noticed!" Rohan breathed and Emma giggled.

"You sound so stuck up. I don't remember you being like this."

Rohan turned on his stomach on the sleeping mat, grunting in annoyance as Emma's fleece and coat slipped off his body and left him uncovered in the freezing cold room.

"You're such a baby!" she complained. She opened out her sleeping bag and shuffled her sleeping mat next to his. The draught was unbearable as Emma flapped the bag into a wide rectangle and draped it over the two of them. Rohan lifted his head off the foam mat and scooted over, groaning as he buried his face in Emma's pillow.

"It smells of you," he whispered, sounding pleased.

"In what way?" Emma's voice betrayed her nervousness. It was her greatest fear that her living conditions made her and Nicky smell, but nobody had the courage to tell her.

Rohan inhaled loudly. "Shampoo and perfume. I've missed you so much."

Emma smiled in the darkness and felt wistful. She wanted to thank him for the compliment but couldn't face the idea of where it might take them. "Just get some sleep," she whispered. "Sometimes they kick off breaking windows and stuff after midnight and then you'll be awake until morning. The cops and the council won't come out here at night so we're on our own." Emma turned on her side facing away from him, stunned when Rohan moved across behind her. He fitted his long body into hers, perfectly placed and snugly tight against Emma's back. She inhaled slowly and tried to stop the intense feeling in her stomach from blossoming into full blown attraction. She couldn't be with this man, not ever.

"I didn't know it was possible to be so creative with such a tiny amount of food," Rohan whispered and Emma heard the smile in his voice. "It was like the feeding of the five thousand. Jesus couldn't have done better with a few slices of a bread and tin of tuna." She chose to ignore it and the silence poured in between them. "Night," he breathed finally into the back of her neck. Rohan planted a single, tender kiss on her hair and inhaled deeply. Emma bit her lip, not sure what to do. She remembered every single inch of his beautiful body, ingrained on her mind from their stolen moments in the Gretna Green motel and then at his mother's house. She writhed inwardly and tried to detach from his crushing embrace. Fully dressed, Rohan slipped his left hand around her waist and separated her pyjama top from the trousers. Emma breathed in as his fingers settled gently over her stomach. She waited for his hand to rove further but it didn't. Rohan sighed in satisfaction and rested his cheek against the top of her head.

Emma swallowed as the memory reluctantly surfaced, the same hand resting on her bare stomach. She was sixteen and in love, her stomach still childishly flat and her pregnancy not yet evident. Emma felt suddenly embarrassed by the ridged silver stretch marks on her flesh and tried to push Rohan's hand away. He sighed into her hair and clamped his fingers over her hand, making it part of his strange embrace. He was strong and Emma gave up eventually, succumbing to the feeling of safety, Rohan's body cupping hers in a comforting encirclement.

Emma woke when night was at its darkest, her body tense and instantly alert. She stopped and listened, taking her bearings and readying herself to defend her son. She groped above her for the cricket bat, panicking when it wasn't in its usual spot behind her pillow. The street sounded silent, no wandering troublemaker calling out in drunken shouts, no sound of distant breaking glass. Emma lay and listened, noticing the clammy warmth at her back and remembering her guest. She shifted slightly on the mat, realising the back of her pyjamas were soaked and uncomfortable. Then Rohan shuddered and she heard him make a choking sound which sounded incongruous in the silence of the night.

"Ro?" Emma whispered, managing to turn herself in the small space he allowed her. His body felt slumped over hers and he tightened his grip. Then he whimpered and gripped her even harder.

"He's dead," he hissed.

"Who?" Panic lit a fire underneath her and she pushed at Rohan's body. "Who's dead, Rohan, who?"

He muttered a name she didn't know and Emma relaxed. "Not Nicky?"

Rohan's grip constricted so her body was pressed hard into his rigid frame. Her back arched and it felt painful. His hand slid up to the back of her neck and he mashed her face into his chest. Emma felt the coarse hair against her cheek and began to struggle. Something cold with a sharp edge cut into her shin and she moved her leg away. Rohan's hand slid over her hair and he gasped, "Where's your helmet?" There was panic in his voice. "Don't move, there's shrapnel everywhere."

Emma knew then. Rohan was trapped in some hideous nightmare filled with the monsters of unreasonable men and destructive weapons manned by sons, brothers and fathers. She stilled in his arms and heard him whimper, his chin wedged painfully on the top of her head. "My legs," he let out a tiny wail. "I can't feel my legs."

"Ssshh, Rohan. It's ok, babe." Emma worked her arms free from the vice around her and used her weight to tip him onto his back so she was half on top. She rubbed at his left thigh and tried to soothe him. "Your legs are fine." She reached under herself and rubbed at his other leg, managing to reach only his hip. "It's just a dream, see?"

Rohan felt soaked, sweat dripping down the sides of his face and underneath his hair. He groaned and Emma knew she needed to wake him up and release him from the nightmare. Her heart flickered with fear of what the trained killer might do if left in his war scenario. "Ro! Wake up, babe. Ro!" Emma stroked his face, feeling his taut, frightened body underneath her. Nothing. He inhaled as though there wasn't enough oxygen in his nightmare and as Emma heard the sharp intake of breath, she kissed him.

She wasn't sure why. As soon as her lips contacted his, she knew it was a huge mistake because she wanted it so badly. It was like putting on a familiar, comfortable pair of favourite shoes and Emma was instantly sunk.

Rohan jumped from hell to heaven with breathtaking speed. There were no soft kisses in the terrifying dream places which sleep forced him back to and Emma felt his body jerk awake. He was stronger than she remembered and as he kissed her in a frenzy of instant need, she doubted she could make him stop. His strong arms crossed over her back and pressed her into him and Emma felt every part of him wake up fully. She cursed her own body which responded with practiced haste and tried desperately to halt this new road to destruction.

Rohan's lips caressed hers and they struggled for breath between them. One hand released her but made its way to the bottom of her pyjama top and began the journey under the hem and up the inside. Emma's brain played hideous games with her. *Yes. No. Yes. No. No.*

"Stop!" she cried, breaking her lips from Rohan's and his sensuous activity ceased. His body felt like a furnace and he panted under her. Emma felt his heart through their combined chest walls as he plummeted back to earth after visiting dizzying extremes of emotion.

"Em?" He sounded tearful and confused, driving a stab of sorrow into her heart. The material from his trousers felt rough against Emma's stomach and his belt buckle dug into her flesh.

"Yes," she whispered. "You were having a nightmare about something and I couldn't wake you. Everything's fine now."

Rohan exhaled and Emma felt him under her, struggling to control his breathing and gain control. "Did I hurt you?" he asked and his voice was numb. His fingers shifted against her soft back, ticklish and guilty.

"No," she whispered. "I think we both just defaulted to...what we were."

Rohan sighed and the hand against Emma's silky skin moved slowly across her back, stroking and sampling before being ordered to leave the comfort of her pyjama top. Emma felt the electricity between them and resisted. It was a bitter road and she couldn't go back. For Nicky's sake.

She slid off Rohan's body and slumped to the side of him, tumbling into the gap between the two sleeping mats and contacting the cold floorboards. Rohan's palm slid with her, lingering on Emma's side and sweeping across her stomach as she pulled away and lay on her back. The clink of metal attracted her attention and Emma reached up, feeling around Rohan's shoulder until she found what she wanted. She seized the dog tags in her fingers, rubbing the familiar surface and reciting what was written there in her head. The chain felt just the same, tiny links made of metal balls, strong and unbreakable until snapped a certain way by the hand of another soldier, collecting a dead man's identity for his family.

Emma sighed and let it drop down the side of Rohan's neck, hearing the clink of the two metal rectangles. "You're still serving?" she asked with interest and waited for him to answer.

"No."

"Oh. When did you come out?"

"Six years ago."

Emma leaned up on her elbow and looked at the space where she knew his face should be. Her hip fitted uncomfortably in the gap between the mats and tipped her so her breasts touched Rohan's side through her clothing. "Why don't you take them off then?" She knew as she asked it, the question was a dumb one. Who knew the inner workings and complications of a soldier's mind? In the absence of her pillow, Emma balanced her head in the crook of her arm. "It's ok. It's none of my business."

"It's fine." Rohan stretched his arm out and laid the back of his hand on Emma's hip. "I keep it on because it reminds me I'm alive. In a practical way, it identifies my body for the authorities if something happens. Mum's not reliable and...Anton's...well, it feels like part of me, I suppose."

Emma nodded slowly, not really understanding, pushing her nose close to Rohan's shoulder. She sniffed quietly and smelled his familiar scent, breathing it in and trying to satiate more than six years of craving. He snuffed and gave a small laugh. "That's ticklish, Em."

"Sorry." She got up and shifted the mats together again, making Rohan lift his head off the pillow so she could turn it over and move some onto her side. Dragging her coat and fleece over them and the damp sleeping bag, Emma finally settled down after a trip to the dilapidated bathroom, shifting around to get comfortable.

"Here." Rohan lifted his arm and put it around Emma, pulling her into him in the darkness. She scooted across with surprising speed, pressing her nose into the downy fluff of his armpit. "I don't know why you always did that," he chuckled, his voice light.

"Mmmnnn," Emma sighed and felt Rohan's chest jerk as he laughed again.

In the silence as she drifted off to sleep, she sensed the veil of sadness drape itself over her head. "I missed you too much, Em," Rohan whispered, so softly it was almost inaudible. She tried to rouse herself again, wondering in her sleep fuddled state what it was about his brother, Anton that was unreliable. Or did he say it was his mother, who wouldn't be able to identify his corpse.

They woke at six in the morning with the sound of the dawn chorus. Emma loved how the birds didn't distinguish between the Greyfriars housing estate and Buckingham Palace, trilling for them all with equal enthusiasm. Rohan's arm felt heavy over her left side, pinning her to the floor. As he stirred and yawned, his fingers flexed against her skin, invoking an erotic tickling sensation. Emma gasped.

"Morning," Rohan whispered and kissed the side of her head. "I haven't slept on the floor since the army. I actually feel ok." He sounded surprised, withdrawing his hand from Emma's back and rolling over. He swore. "Forget that last comment. My body disagrees."

"Welcome to my world," Emma smiled. "Mine feels like that every morning." She shifted onto her back and sat up, hugging her knees. Rohan touched the bare spot between the pieces of her pyjamas, caressing the soft skin at the bottom of her back and Emma closed her eyes, deliberately staying silent. She felt strangely disappointed when he withdrew his hand.

"How long have you been here?" he asked, his voice

tightening as he used his stomach muscles to sit up.

"Almost two years," Emma replied, glancing back at Rohan. Her hair was a tangle of black curls and he pulled them away from her face and tucked them behind her ear.

"Why?"

Emma bit her lip and shrugged. "Nowhere else to go really. I got the job at the school and this was the only thing on offer. I can't really afford anything else and because the school's on the estate, you kinda have to live here to be accepted. It just made sense."

"I get that." Rohan rested his chin on her shoulder and Emma felt his stubble through her sleeve. It caused a plunging sensation to start in the pit of her stomach and she fought it valiantly. It was as though Rohan sensed it and he grazed the side of her face with his, seeing her close her eyes in defiance and exhale slowly through full, pink lips. "Em," he whispered, kissing the space under her ear which used to drive her mad for him. Emma shivered.

Rohan carefully moved her long curls out of the way, placing them gently down her spine. Emma was like a scorpion, tail coiled in threat and body rigid. Rohan willingly diced with death, waiting for her to strike as he snuffed sensuously in her ear and nibbled the soft skin of her neck. When she attacked, she saw he still felt stunned, even though her rejection hung over him like a cudgel. "I'm not doing this!" Emma pushed herself away from him, sitting at the end of her thin sleeping mat and running her hands down her face. "Why are you here, Ro? What do you want?"

"You." His face was straight and full of determination. There was no edge to it. He spoke the truth.

"For a divorce?" Emma asked, dreading the answer. Her body tensed as she waited for the defining blow.

"No, Em. Never," Rohan answered, his face more confident than he felt. "I told you all those years ago when we married, I'm Russian Orthodox; I won't divorce you. You agreed to it so you're stuck with me. You might want to live like this..." he cast his hand around him, taking in the peeling wallpaper and the damp patch in the corner of the room from a roof leak. "But we'll stay married until one of us dies." He smiled pensively at her. "And hopefully that won't be any time soon, unless one of us catches pneumonia in this shit hole. It's always funny until someone croaks."

Emma closed her mouth with a snap and looked offended. "Nicky caught pneumonia last winter and spent a week in hospital." Emma was allowed to stay on the children's ward with him and they ate well and slept warmly. But when they returned home, there were squatters in the downstairs rooms and Emma stood on the front lawn and cried through sheer exhaustion. Fat Brian sorted it out for her, ejecting the uninvited guests from the dining room window face first. Then he boarded up their unfortunate exit point with graffitied chip board.

"Sorry, that was tactless." Rohan looked down and bit his lip.

"It's fine. *Chto sdelano, to sdelano.*"

Rohan's jaw dropped and he looked at Emma with sudden alertness. His blue eyes narrowed. "My father used to say that. *What's done is done.*"

"Did he?" Emma smiled brightly and brushed the moment aside as inconsequential. *Damn!*

Rohan watched her with a soldier's intensity as Emma fluffed around the empty bedroom, grabbing clean clothes from her suitcase and fleeing to the bathroom. She showered without peace, the sound of the pipe-clanking orchestra dulling her pain until the boiler chucked a fit and she was doused with freezing water.

CHAPTER FIVE

"What do you mean? I don't understand." Emma stood in front of the headmaster with a look of incredulity on her face. Nicky stopped dead in the corridor, holding Rohan's hand as he showed him a piece of his artwork clinging to a corridor display. The males looked towards the site of the trouble and Nicky turned his body and tensed.

"Is he shoutin' at my mum?" he spat and Rohan shook his head.

"No mate. Hold on. I think she's shouting at him."

"My mum dun't shout," Nicky replied and tried to shuck Rohan's hand.

"Wait!" Rohan sounded irritated and Nicky squeezed his face into a scowl.

Emma postured at the end of the corridor and saw the headmaster sweep her appearance with approval. Black hair curled down her back in sedate ringlets and her figure was still trim. Emma's body was stiff under smart grey trousers and white blouse and her brown eyes flashed with danger. Paul Brown let his lascivious glance wander down her neat figure and Emma felt bile stir in her stomach. "We can't afford to keep you on," he smirked, his expression as oily as his greying hair.

Emma took a threatening step towards him. "Is this because I knocked you back?" she hissed. "You're firing me because I wouldn't let you cheat on your wife with me?" Her voice climbed at the end of her sentence and Brown shot a look at Rohan and Nicky. He blanched at the sight of Rohan's tall, muscular frame and his firm grip on Emma's son. Realisation dawned and he took a step away from the vitriolic woman.

"I don't want any trouble." He gulped. "You're not permanent staff, so put in a timesheet for the last few weeks and I'll pay you out as normal."

"You're a disgrace of a man!" Emma raised her voice and scorn filled her eyes. "You're a dirty, sexual harassing piece of..."

"Problem, Em?" Rohan stood next to her suddenly and Emma halted in her tirade. Nicky clutched Rohan's big hand and his blue eyes were wide and terrified.

Paul Brown bent like a spindly reed in the face of Rohan's masculinity and Emma sneered. She leaned in close to his face. "One day, you'll bite off more than you can chew, you pathetic little man!"

Rohan's eyes moved from Emma to the cowed, skinny man and back again, but the headmaster cut his losses and backed away. "Off the premises, Miss Harrington, or I'll call...someone." He suffered a moment of confusion, knowing the police would take ages, turning up reluctantly if at all.

Emma's cheeks were flushed and angry, her brown eyes on fire behind her beautiful face. She turned to Rohan with disbelief. "What an ars..." She thought better of it, seeing the distress on her son's face.

"I don't think I want to go into class." Nicky's bottom lip wobbled and the machoism disappeared like water down a drain. "What we gonna do, Mum? How we gonna eat and pay for stuff?" Panic lit in the boy's eyes and he pressed the flat of his hand to Emma's stomach. "Mummy?"

"Hey, enough!" Rohan bent from the waist and scooped Nicky up into his arms. The child was too big for pick-ups but he clung to the former soldier like a drowning man to driftwood. Rohan put a firm arm around Emma's shoulders, feeling her heave with shock. He leaned close to her ear and whispered, "Unless you want me to smack him hard enough to make his head fall off, we should probably leave."

Emma glanced up at the sound of small children bouncing into the building and disgorging themselves from outdoor clothing. "Hello, Miss Harrington," they chorused as they passed her. Emma gulped and forced a smile onto her face as a boy with beautiful brown eyes and skin the colour of melted chocolate pressed a piece of paper into her hand.

"I done this for you, Miss H. Nicky said he dun't mind if I marry you." The child beamed, his wide eyes searching for approval. Emma smiled, fighting tears as she patted him on his afro.

"Bless you, Mohammed." She smiled.

The child glanced up at Nicky, whose face was buried in Rohan's neck. He yanked on Nicky's shoe. "Is this your dad?" The brown eyes roved with approval over Rohan's impressive physique and he edged closer and yanked on Nicky's foot again. "Share 'im, Nick? Can he be my dad too?"

Nicky popped out of Rohan's neck and his face was streaked with tears. He opened his mouth and certain he was about to blurt out her unfortunate circumstances, Emma stopped the touching moment from progressing. "We're just heading out, Mo. See you later."

Taking her lead, Rohan strode from the building

carrying Emma's son like an army kit bag over his shoulder, his other arm resting protectively around her. Going against the tide of people was painful for Emma. Everyone acknowledged her with a wave or a greeting. "Day off? All right for some," one woman joked with a smile and Emma didn't put her straight. Every single pair of eyes stared warily at Rohan and by the time they reached the peeling front door, he felt rattled.

"I think they've stared holes in me!" he commented, trying to stand Nicky up on the hall floor. The child clung to his neck and refused to get down.

"Nicky, stop!" Emma snapped. "I'll sort it all out, don't worry! When have you ever gone hungry?" She stalked through to the kitchen muttering, feeling upset with herself for attacking her son. He hadn't gone hungry, but she often did. Emma flicked the kettle on to boil and leaned her backside against the work surface. She blew out slowly through pursed lips and heard Rohan whispering something to Nicky in the hall. She thought about Mohammed's cute face and his desperation for a male role model in his life. "*Is this your dad?*" His question punished Emma and she shook her head and wished life had taken different turns for her. His love letter was folded in her pocket and she pulled it out and smiled at the drawing of a small brown stick man holding hands with a fat stick woman drawn in yellow. '*Can yoo b mi wif?*' he'd written, presumably without help. Emma folded it and put it back in her pocket. "No point crying over spilt milk," she whispered to herself, jumping as Rohan strode past her into the room. He lifted the milk carton from the windowsill and poked his nose into the hole.

"Ugh!" He held it at arm's length and pulled a face. "I dunno, Em. I think this could get pretty close to crying." He tipped it down the sink, swilling it away and washing the carton out under the tap.

"I'll get some more after you leave," Emma replied, knowing full well she wouldn't have any money for another few days, not until she could get into town and sign on at the benefit office. She groaned and shook her head, feeling sick at the thought of begging for handouts once again. She heard Nicky's footsteps clomping overhead and raised an eyebrow at Rohan in question.

"He's a bit upset," Rohan commented, understatement of the year. He spun round looking for the dustbin.

"Just leave it on the side. I'll deal with everything once we've got your car back and you're safely on your way." Emma smiled woodenly, panicking inside, her brain doing flips and cartwheels as she tried to work out how to salvage her situation.

Rohan walked towards the door, stopping at the last minute to enfold Emma in a tight hug. "Don't be nice to me," she muttered into his sweater. "It'll make me feel worse."

Rohan sniffed and kissed the top of her head. "Idiot! I'll be nice to you if I want to. You can't stop me, *dorogaya*."

Emma pressed her face against his chest and closed her eyes. Her hands strayed to his waist and she allowed herself to fantasise about how different life could have been if Rohan hadn't been sent to Afghanistan and she hadn't ended up left alone with...

"Em," Rohan whispered. "Why did that guy fire

you? Was it because he came onto you and you refused?"

Emma nodded. "Yeah. He's a total sleaze. You're only safe if you're over fifty and sometimes, not even then. He's been working up to it for a while but then he actually tried to touch me on Friday. I told him no and at the time he seemed ok. I thought I'd got away with it. Most women just leave but a couple have been desperate enough to go there - just to keep their jobs." She inhaled and looked around the derelict kitchen. "The question is; how desperate is *that* desperate?"

"I wanted to knock him into next week!" Rohan spat and Emma grinned and squeezed herself into him closer, feeling a wave of gratitude from her toes to the top of her head.

"Then he'd delight in having you arrested and ruining your life too. And as for complaining about him, don't even go there. It's been tried. His brother's the chairman of the board of governors so nothing sticks."

Emma jumped at the awful banging sound coming from the front of the house, realising it was inside. She wriggled out of Rohan's clutches and walked into the hallway. "What are you doing?" she asked Nicky, furrowing her brow as he thumped his suitcase down every single stair.

"Movin' out!" he said stubbornly.

Emma's face fell and she panicked. "No, Nicky!"

The child ran to the top of the stairs and began the operation again, this time banging her case down every step until it got too heavy half way and he let go, watching in dismay as it plummeted to the bottom and took a dent out of the wall. "Oops!" he said, his hand over his mouth. "Sorry."

Emma intercepted her son half way up the staircase, pulling him down to sit on the step with her. She lowered her voice so Rohan couldn't hear. "Nicky, we've nowhere to go, baby. Let Rohan leave and then I'll try and sort this mess out. Ok?"

Nicky shook his head with certainty. "No Mum, we're leaving now." As Rohan's handsome face appeared at the bottom of the stairs, Nicky pointed at him. "We're goin' wiv him. He said so. I'll just grab the sleepin' bags and mats." The child stood up and trotted up the stairs, leaving Emma with her head in her hands. She glared at Rohan through her fingers.

"I can sort my own life out, thanks!" she bit and he shrugged and smiled cheekily, a cute dimple appearing on his right cheek.

"I didn't say you couldn't. But I do think you need a break, even for a couple of weeks." He jerked his head at their surroundings. "Come away from here for a little while and things will feel less...desperate." He held his hand out towards her and Emma closed her eyes and ignored it.

"Nicky has school," she replied stiffly.

"We'll enrol him at the school near me and before you say it, I'll pay for his uniform. It's not a big deal there anyway. He can keep his black trousers and shoes and it's just a royal blue jumper or sweatshirt. It won't hurt him to be somewhere different for a while."

"I don't know!" Emma sounded agonised.

Rohan grinned as Nicky appeared at the top. He threw the sleeping bags down the stairs, remembering at the last minute that Emma was sitting half way down. "Sorry Mummy!"

His mother shook her head from under the coverings which smelled slightly damp. She heard both males sniggering at her. Nicky's shoes clumped down next to her and Emma felt his spindly arms around what he thought was her neck but was actually her face. "I'm taking Uncle Ro to Fat Brian's to get his car. Then we'll go. Everyfink's gonna be ok, Mummy. I'll take care of you."

Emma was released and Nicky thudded down the remainder of the stairs. By the time Emma fought her way out of the sleeping bags, both males were gone and the front door rocked back and forth on its hinges in the breeze. It was far too late for her to object, but her heart quivered at the thought of coming face to face with her stepmother again. She would never be safe around Alanya Harrington but worse, nor would her son. The woman would find a way to hurt them, just like all the times before.

CHAPTER SIX

"What do you do for a living now?" Emma tried to make conversation as Rohan indicated and pulled out onto the main highway, moving south through the English countryside.

"I'm an actuary," he replied, knitting his brow at a transit van following too close behind. "Em, just look behind us, will you? Did you notice that transit anywhere around your house over the last twenty-four hours?"

Emma turned her head, taking a cursory look out the back window but mainly checking on Nicky. He slept on the back seat, his cheeks pink and his blonde hair tousled. A line of dribble worked its way down his chin. "Nope. I don't remember it. It can't have been on our estate. It's still got wheels."

Rohan snorted with laughter and then realised she was serious. "It was pretty bad there," he agreed. "Thank goodness for Fat Brian and his protection racket!"

"He's actually quite a good bloke," Emma sighed. "They all are really, just stuck in a bad rut. Like me." She looked out of the window at the green fields rolling by and stretched her body out, feeling the tension leave her spine. "You always liked maths at school, so I guess an actuary was your kind of thing."

"You know what one is?" He sounded impressed.

"Isn't it someone who works out risk for major corporations? So if there's a massive earthquake and buildings get damaged, you work out how much to put everyone's insurance premiums up by next year to cover the debt and ensure the company doesn't suffer a loss?"

"Kind of," Rohan answered. "That's basically it, yeah." Rohan turned the indicator on and moved into the outside lane as a light rain began to speckle the windscreen. "Ok, so, say a disgruntled employee at a bank steals a list of highly sensitive information, well, knowledge is power and he can potentially use it in a number of ways."

"Like the bank teller recently, who stole information about customers involved in tax evasion and handed it over to the British government?"

"Yeah, sort of like that. So the company he worked for would have got actuaries crunching the numbers straight away, working out the financial risks involved with each possible outcome. The employee could have held them to ransom or published the information on a blog or public forum. Or he could do what he did and hand it over to Her Majesty's Revenue and Customs. He's out of a job the second he acted, but an actuary works out the significant risks of different situations based on mathematical calculation and in my case, experience. Each of those scenarios carries a level of threat and the bank needed to know what each one entailed; how every single one would affect them as a corporate, right from the financial hit they could potentially take on the stock market, to the cost in terms of customer perception and goodwill. Ultimately, they'll pass the risk on to the customer, so an actuary works out how much it can be spread across a particular set of clients without disrupting business or sending customers to find another bank. If it's so obvious it makes customers leave, it's counterproductive, because the bank ends up paying for the risk anyway. It's a complicated business and the bank would have brought in heaps of people with different skill sets to sort it out from public relations to operations managers. I'm part of that whole process, but I'm brought in usually when it's all gone a bit too far."

Emma watched the concentration on Rohan's face as he changed lanes again, increasing the speed of the wipers to cope with the deluge. "Do you work for a bank then?"

Rohan shook his head. "No, I'm...free-lance, I guess. I work for whoever pays me at the time. Ultimately I work for myself."

"Is that what you did in the army? Her voice sounded small and far away, hurt creeping into her tone. "Calculated risk with mathematical formulae?"

"It was broader than that." Rohan glanced sideways at her, picking up on her perception of something he hadn't actually said. "I monitored security systems and worked out logistics." He scuffed over a role he still couldn't discuss. "In my down time I did university papers and by the end of my army career, I only needed a year's worth of papers left to finish a degree. I had plenty of time to do them because..." Rohan paused and bit his lip, causing Emma to peer at him covertly, disarmed when he continued. "So I graduated with honours. I started working for a major bank which underwrites insurers when I was twenty-two and did more exams fairly continuously for two years. I guess my army experience gave me a route into other kinds of actuary work."

"I remember you doing university papers when you

came home on leave." Emma sounded wistful. "I thought you were so clever; I hated maths. I'm glad you carried on. I'm pleased your life didn't stop..." She almost said, *like mine*, but prevented the words escaping. It wasn't true anyway. She did well under the circumstances. She glanced back at Nicky again and smiled. His eyes were still shut and his head lolled forward. Emma reached round and pushed on his forehead to take the pressure off his neck. The boy grunted and shifted position.

Emma sat round in her seat again, brushing Rohan's arm with her face as she turned. He looked at her and smiled, his blue eyes twinkling. "My job title is an actuary, but I've strayed more into the area of risk management so it makes me more money than friends."

"Hence the expensive car," Emma smiled and Rohan narrowed his eyes. "I'm not criticising," Emma added. "It's just my jealousy talking."

Rohan laughed. "That's what I love about you. Your honesty. When we get home, I'll put you on the insurance."

"Don't! I would be too scared to drive it! I'm sure there's buses and I've got perfectly good legs."

Rohan smirked across at Emma, winking like a dodgy second hand car salesman. "You sure have, *dorogaya*."

Emma slapped his thigh playfully. "Dirty old Russian sailor!" She turned in her seat, curling her legs underneath her. Her eyes were wide and frightened and she leaned forward as she spoke. "Ro, on the subject of risk management, how close to your house does your mother live? I cannot afford to run into her. Our last parting was...not good."

"It's been years, Em. I'm sure she'll have got over it."

"No, Rohan! You have to promise me this. It's important. If she turns up, we're gone!"

"Oh." Rohan frowned and looked confused. "I'll have to think about how to manage it then. She normally rings me before she walks over to the house. She's been unwell recently with her arthritis and much worse ever since...well, she's been ill. She doesn't tend to just turn up because she needs to sit down before she walks home. Don't worry. I'll sort it out." Rohan reached across with his left hand and caressed Emma's writhing fingers with his. "Just promise me one thing, Em?"

"What?" Stubbornness shrouded her face and Rohan chuckled.

"Don't just run off without telling me, please?"

"What like going to the shops or down to the park."

"You know exactly what I mean!" Rohan's tone was sharp and Emma sighed.

"Fine! If I can find you, I'll tell you."

"No Emma! Find me *and* tell me! And if you can't find me, you don't get to leave."

"That's not fair!" Emma argued. She lifted one of her hands out from under Rohan's and smoothed the knuckles of his left index finger softly. His hand was dotted with white lined scars, one across the back of his hand looked rugged and pink. On an impulse she kissed it, hearing the tiny gasp which escaped through Rohan's pursed lips.

"Emma!" his tone was sharp. "After what I just told you, are you seriously going to defy me and make me find you?"

"No." She pouted like a sulky teenager. "Fine then!

I'll tell you before I go missing. Unless it's because the wicked stepmother's appeared. Then I won't have time. I'll be grabbing my son and running like hell!"

Rohan sighed and blew out an exasperated breath. "Do you ever give a straight answer?"

Emma laughed sadly. "I did once." She fixed sultry brown eyes on his face and Rohan knitted his brow and looked stern. "And it ended so badly for me, I don't want a repeat of it, thanks." She shifted so she faced forward, watching the windscreen wipers slapping from side to side.

"Of all the things in my life I'd change, it wouldn't be that." Rohan drove past a town sign that said 'Corby', his face serious and his blue eyes dulled. "I'm glad I married you, Em, whatever you might think. I'd do it again as well."

Emma felt his eyes wander to her face, flushing with the awkwardness of the moment. "What about you? Would you change that part of your life? Marrying me?"

"Fifth amendment," Emma said, salvaging her coy answer with a cheeky smile. Her dark eyes glinted with veiled threat and her hair hung in drapes around her tired face.

"You can't plead the fifth!" Rohan snorted. "This is Britain, not America!"

"It works for me." She grinned at him and Rohan gave in, sensing she wouldn't answer anyway.

"Not far now," he sighed. "Probably about twenty minutes in this weather. Then you'll officially be a resident of Market Harborough, home of the king's army during the Civil War and proud owner of a school house in the centre of town on stilts."

"Oh, goody," Emma remarked with sarcasm and

Rohan shook his head.

"I've missed some parts of your humour more than others," he sighed.

Emma shrugged and looked out of the window at the bright green grass and the bare trees. "Hello Market Harborough," she whispered. "Please be kind with me?"

CHAPTER SEVEN

"I'll get in touch with Social Security and they'll hopefully sort out my money so I can pay something towards our keep for the next two weeks." Emma breathed out a sigh of frustration and stroked the black dog's soft ears.

"I don't need you to pay rent. You're house sitting for me. Technically you're working for me."

"It's fine. I'll still pay my way. It's so annoying though. I felt I was really getting somewhere with the school's archives and then they just fire me overnight. I didn't do anything wrong."

"The guy's an idiot. He needs a slap."

"True, but I hadn't finished the task. Which means they'll damage things for their centennial and probably use the originals. I didn't get to finish scanning them all and the teacher in charge won't know how."

Emma knitted her brow and slumped onto the couch in the corner of the kitchen. The dog sidled towards her with a dopey look on his face and sat next to her, pressing his furry body against her legs. "I didn't think you were the doggie sort." She smiled at Rohan and he gave her a rude gesture. Emma laughed. Then she remembered her dire circumstances and shook her head in irritation at herself. "I really enjoyed using my degree..." Emma bit her lip and abruptly grew silent.

Rohan stirred the tea with a teaspoon and put the lid on the pot with a clink. He poured brown, steeped liquid into two mugs and added milk. "Sugar?" His blue eyes fixed on Emma's troubled face and waited for her answer. The dog sneezed on Emma's foot and she pulled a face and wrinkled her nose.

"Yuk!"

"Farrell, get away!" Rohan sounded stern and the dog sloped off and threw himself into a bed next to the conservatory door. "That's not how you make friends," his master complained and the dog gave an exaggerated sigh, possibly in agreement. "Em, do you want sugar?" Rohan asked again, lifting one corner of his mouth in a wistful smile.

"Oh, no thanks." Emma flushed pink with embarrassment at her sudden surge in hormones. There was something quite comfortable about being in Rohan's house and it consumed her. *Don't get comfortable*, she warned herself.

Rohan padded over to her in his socks, offering the steaming mug to her handle first. She took it with a lame smile, almost slopping it over herself as Rohan sat down heavily next to her. The sofa was a two-seater and Emma pressed herself into the corner, wishing she was sitting at the breakfast bar instead. Her drink was hot and burned her lips as she sipped, needing a distraction from Rohan's powerful presence. His jeans brushed against her thigh and he rested his left ankle on his right knee, bracing his leg against hers. He exhaled and looked uncomfortable. "Long day." He smiled at Emma sideways and she looked away, taking it as a rebuke.

"Sorry," she offered and Rohan tutted.

"I wasn't looking to blame you," he said gently, his voice soothing and lyrical. He rested his drink on the arm of the sofa and stretched out his other arm behind Emma. She sensed it at the back of her neck and felt a slight tug as Rohan twirled one of her curls in his fingers. She pulled her head forward and the curl slipped from his fingers. Rohan looked at her with mischief in his eyes and selected another one.

"Nothing's changed! You're still such a pain!" Emma huffed and he smirked, a handsome lopsided grin which revealed the dimple in his cheek caused by a fall from an apple tree when he was thirteen. His eyes sparkled dangerously and he tilted his head to one side. Emma tried not to look at him, diverting her attention to her drink.

"Where did you get your degree?"

"Wales." Emma boxed clever, deliberately not naming the university town and Rohan didn't pick up on her subterfuge. "The work at the school was my first proper job. I started making a dent in my student loan."

"Couldn't have been easy, studying with a little boy."

Emma shook her head and twisted her mug in her hands. "No."

"What did you study?"

"History and librarianship with archives papers. It was a conjoint degree."

Rohan nodded and watched Emma with interest. "Why did you leave Wales? Was there no work there?"

"Only cafe work and that wasn't getting rid of the debt. I felt like I needed to go back to...where I started and slay my demons. I got the job at the school but it was in a rough area so paid surprisingly well. I guess nobody else wanted to go near the place. I can't believe they just finished me like that. It sucks!" Emma sighed and patted her hand on her jeans in frustration. Rohan put his large hand over Emma's writhing fingers and stilled them.

"I really admire you."

Emma's head whipped round and she stared at him, waiting for the catch, aggression ready in her flashing brown eyes.

"No, really." Rohan stroked her fingers. "You've done amazingly well, *devotchka*. I'm proud of you."

Emma gulped and her face crumpled. She pulled her hand from under Rohan's and squeezed the bridge of her nose to stop the ready tears escaping. Only one other person ever told her they were proud of her and sadly, Lucya was unable to tell her anymore. Emma focussed on the good things in her life, remembering how Nicky entered the world with a healthy gargantuan squall, surrounded by strangers, a great grandmother and one very relieved teen mother. His first years of life were a blur of part time schooling, breast feeding and extreme tiredness, interspersed by the odd highlights of his first smile, his first word and the first time he told her he loved her. Emma breathed out slowly through pursed lips and grappled for control over her emotions.

"I hope you'll be happy here," Rohan said, patting her hand and reaching behind her. He twirled another curl and watched it arch around his fingers.

Emma shrugged. "It's only temporary," she replied, putting an unaccustomed hardness into her voice. Rohan let go of her hair and it slithered down her neck and settled over her breast. His hand brushed her shoulder and ran seductively along her back as he withdrew it. Emma shivered and closed her eyes. "If we're here to look after Farrell while you're away, when do you leave?" she asked him, desperate to change the subject.

"I'll head off in a couple of days once you've settled. I'll go spec some things out. Then if all goes well, I'll have a few days in the office finalising arrangements and then I'll be gone."

"How long will you be away?" Emma asked, risking a look at his profile. Her heart hammered at the sight of downy blonde hair dusting his strong chest. It was thicker than she remembered. Rohan's open shirt displayed a honey coloured tan and Emma battled with the memory of his skin sliding under her fingers. His hair was short at the back but long on top, cut into layers and pushed back over his head in blonde waves. Rohan's looks were classically Russian, a strong profile with a thin nose which arched gracefully over soft lips. His vibrant blue eyes were striking, guaranteed to captivate whomever he spoke to. Rohan turned them on her suddenly and Emma quailed under the force of his personality.

"I don't know. I never do. I have a job to do and it takes as long as it takes unfortunately. It hasn't really mattered before, but this time's different."

"Why?" Emma asked, tipping forward with interest.

"Because of him." Rohan nodded towards the dog, who sat up straight and cocked his head in his master's direction. "I never kept pets before. I just locked up the house and left."

"Why did you get him then? Doesn't it make life harder for you?" Emma smiled, showing no harm in her enquiry but Rohan's face darkened.

"He belonged to Anton," he said quietly and Emma's face lit up with enthusiasm.

"Oh, wow. So that's the famous dog! Of course it is; I see now." She corrected herself quickly, masking the thing she shouldn't have said. "How is your brother? I remember him saying he wanted to travel. I guess he finally got his wish to go home to *Mother Russia*." Emma giggled at her poor impression of her stepbrother. Anton was wiry and endowed with a beautifully clown-like nature. Apart from her abiding love for Rohan, Anton was the other bright spot in a situation where two selfish adults blended their respective families without considering the wishes of any of the other members. Emma sniggered. "Remember when your mum told us we couldn't have any tea until we picked every last apple on that damn tree? And Anton fell out of the branch above you and landed on your head." Emma rubbed her eyes, feeling the scratchiness of exhaustion. She yawned. "They would call Social Services now if a parent treated a child the way your mother..." She stopped herself just in time. The cruel Russian matriarch she fled from at sixteen, confused and pregnant, was no longer in her sphere of consideration. Rohan's face darkened.

"You've been talking to Anton, but not me!"

"Oh." Emma's cheeks flushed at her betrayal and she considered lying.

"How do you know about the dog?" Rohan's face tightened with stress, wrinkles appearing around his eyes.

"We emailed and messaged each other." She stared at her hands in shame, the dog's brown eyes watching her from across the room. Farrell sat up and whined. "Please don't be mad at Anton. We just chatted over social media and sometimes he visited. He sent me jokes and enjoyed my photos. I missed you guys..." Emma couldn't look at Rohan. His blue eyes were like fathomless lagoons in his face.

"He died."

"What?" Emma gaped, her mascara spread under her eyes like a panda bear from her rubbing. She must have misheard.

"Anton died. Farrell was his dog. Nobody else wanted him."

Emma's jaw worked but no sound came out. An image of her vibrant stepbrother doing an impression of the more serious, studious Rohan, danced unbidden across her inner vision. He wore one of his mother's voluminous nightdresses and chased his older brother across the garden with the hosepipe. Rohan lashed out and the fabric ripped, condemning them all to yet another night with no dinner. Anton climbed down the drainpipe and stole crab apples which made them all sick. "No!" Emma said, sounding certain Rohan was lying to her. "No. Anton can't be dead. I talked to him just a few weeks ago. He's coming to see us on Boxing Day."

Rohan watched her with pity in his blue eyes. The sheen of tears glittered their surface. "I'm sorry. He died last month. I didn't know he'd seen you...so often." He gulped and took a sip of his drink, simultaneously rubbing at a spot on his right thigh which evidently pained him. He massaged the skin through his jeans but the action brought him no comfort. "I miss him." Rohan turned his face and smiled at Emma but there was no mirth in the expression. "He loved you very much and sent his regards." Rohan looked away and Emma saw his jawbone showing through his skin, tight and wooden as he held onto his emotions. "He told me I didn't understand some stuff but...I didn't know he'd seen you." He stopped rubbing his thigh and left his hand there, a hard fist encasing his fingers.

"Ro, you're lying! He can't be dead." Emma's voice was a whisper which ended in a sniff. Rohan leaned forward and dumped his mug on the tiled floor at the same moment as Emma's fell from her hand, cascading tea with it and smashing on the hard surface.

"Shhh," he soothed, wrapping her in a firm embrace. "It's fine. He's gone home. He's at peace. He told me to say, *"Mother Russia salutes you, printsessa Emma,"* in that frickin' stupid accent he did. It was bad, Em. He was in agony. It's better this way."

The first of Emma's sobs was delicate, quickly followed by a wail of misery. Her body constricted into a small ball and Rohan pulled her onto his knee and held her, rocking and soothing her until her tears ceased. "It's ok," he whispered and the catch in his voice bonded them again in a common grief as Emma cried enough for the both of them. She sat sideways in his lap for ages, sniffing into his shirt and feeling his chest hair against her cheek, comforting and familiar. Rohan stroked her hair and breathed light kisses onto the side of her head.

"I didn't know he was sick." Emma's sentence was punctuated by a hiccough as her lungs complained about the crying. She wiped her nose with the back of her hand.

"Nor did I until it was too late." Rohan kept his lips against her damp temple, making a kissing sound as he pulled away. "He was sad about what happened between us. He told me to find you. It was the last thing he asked me to do." Rohan sighed and his chest heaved against Emma's side. She sat up.

"Is that why you brought me here?"

Rohan smiled at her with fondness, using the cuff of his expensive shirt to wipe the snot and tears from her flushed face. It was black with make-up when he finished. "No, *devotchka*. Meeting you at the wedding was pure chance. I hadn't started looking for you yet."

"But you were going to?" Emma's face clouded, her brow knitted in lines of concentration. She looked like a five-year-old and accentuated the image, running her hand up and down her face, far too uncouth for a lady. Rohan pulled her hand away.

"Yeah, I was going to. As soon as I got back from this job."

"Do you think Anton knew he wouldn't visit us on Boxing Day?" Emma asked in a small voice.

"Em, he lived two weeks longer than they gave him. He definitely knew. He'd written your address down on a piece of paper and I should have looked properly at it then, because when I read it later, his hand shook so much it was illegible. I was due to visit the next day but his heart gave out that night and I couldn't ask him for it verbally." Rohan's breath caught in his chest.

A light began in Emma's eyes like the rekindling of a fire which held the appearance of being extinguished, but simmered beneath the ash. *Rohan was planning to search for her, after all this time*. Rohan studied her with intensity and Emma felt him stir underneath her. He put his hand behind her head and pulled her forward, resting his forehead against hers. She felt his breath softly stroking her face and relaxed, waiting for his lips to crush hers and knowing she wanted it. Rohan patted her bottom with the flat of his hand. "Up ya get. I'm getting a dead leg."

Disappointment coursed through Emma's psyche, making her waspish and cross. She retrieved the biggest shards of her broken cup from the soaked tiles and stalked over to the dustbin in the corner. Then she grappled with the kitchen roll, tearing some off to deal with the spill and the smaller broken pieces. Turning she saw the black dog lapping at the mess between the lumps of cup, having admirably bided his time. *Anton's black dog.* Rohan remained seated but moved the dog away with his foot, rubbing his right knee at the same time. He looked tired and careworn. "Sorry, was I too heavy?" Emma asked, bending to retrieve Rohan's cup of cooled tea from the floor next to him and gathering the tiny shards of her broken mug.

"No," he replied, sounding exhausted. "You're not heavy, you're gorgeous." His words made Emma falter in confusion but he dismissed the moment, hauling himself to his feet unsteadily.

"How did Anton die?" Emma asked, her voice small in the large kitchen.

"Cancer." Rohan brushed a strand of hair from her cheek as he said the terrible word. "He was diagnosed in the summer and died in September. He left it too late to get help; too busy having fun. He must have known for ages though."

Emma shook her head at the speed of her stepbrother's death. Rohan looked wrung out, dark circles appearing under his eyes and she squashed her endless questions back into her brain.

A knock on the front door made her jump and Rohan smiled in amusement at her overreaction, before walking into the hallway and peering through the glass. "You're fine down here. I don't think there's a Fat Brian in the town." When he opened the door, Emma heard a female voice echoing in the porch outside, then the click of heels as someone entered. She steeled herself to meet the visitor, hoping and praying it wouldn't be Rohan's mother as her fists clenched involuntarily and her heart rate sped up. It wasn't Alanya, but this visitor's entrance felt just as devastating.

"Oh, hi." The pretty woman stripped off her long black coat and draped it over the arm of the sofa, kicking off her stiletto shoes with accomplished ease. "I'm Felicity." She extended a manicured hand and Emma reached out and shook the cold fingers. "How was your trip, darling?" She stood on tip toes next to Rohan and kissed his cheek, leaving a line of pink lipstick like a stamp of ownership.

Rohan shrugged and then yawned. "Yeah, good thanks. Tiring. But I found a house sitter for Farrell. This is Emma, my..." The pause sounded awkward to Emma. "Stepsister." Rohan struggled for a label and settled on the more obvious one. Felicity looked and sounded relieved, her face softening at the edges and the threat leaving her body language.

"Oh that's great! How wonderful."

Emma narrowed her brown eyes at the inflection in the other woman's voice. Somehow she'd managed to make it sound anything *but* wonderful. Emma swallowed at Rohan's casual dismissal of her to step sibling status, confusion knitting her brow. His earlier affection seemed dirtied by the entrance of someone who behaved like his girlfriend.

"I would have happily stayed here for you," Felicity simpered, running light fingers up and down Rohan's bicep. "I'm here most of the time anyway so I might as well."

"You don't like dogs." It was a simple statement, but dismissive by implication and he moved his arm away from her. Emma watched Rohan with interest, concerned by the numbness in his eyes. He left the room without saying anything else, leaving the women standing awkwardly opposite each other. Farrell finished his clean-up operation and sauntered over to Emma, sitting affectionately on her foot. They both fixed their gaze on Felicity. She was beautiful in a teenage doll kind of way and Emma felt her heart sink at the idea of ever competing with her, resolving not to bother. It wasn't why she was here. *It's temporary*, she reminded herself. *There can't be anything between us thanks to his spiteful mother!*

Farrell sneezed again, not once but twice, letting out a whoosh of doggy spit that sprayed Felicity's bare legs with frightening accuracy. "Bloody hell!" she complained, dabbing at her catwalk couture skirt with red nailed hands. Emma reached behind her to the kitchen roll and offered it to Felicity. "Thanks." She took it with grace and resumed her dabbing. Giving up on the skirt, she ran the tissue down her shins with a look of disgust on her face.

"Dog snot's awful, isn't it?" Emma sympathised, looking down at her jeans with Farrell's crusty decorations dotted around the ankles. He looked up at the mention of his bodily fluid, smiling and lolling his tongue, an uncanny look of Anton about him. At the thought of her stepbrother's vibrant nature so easily extinguished, Emma took a sharp intake of breath and tried to imagine a world without his exuberance. She couldn't. He died so suddenly it explained why he didn't acknowledge receipt of her last email, containing Nicky's latest school photo.

Rohan reappeared, clumping down the stairs and smiling at the tail wag the dog gave him. He ignored the women as though they weren't there. "Come on, Faz," he patted his side and the dog lurched forward.

"Last go round the garden and then it's bed time." Rohan slipped his feet into a pair of trainers by the back door, struggling with his right foot. The door clicked shut behind him and the women heard a tennis ball bounce on the paving slabs outside, accompanied by a happy woof.

"It's a bit early for bed, isn't it?" Felicity asked, watching Rohan's strong frame throw the ball outside, backlit by the conservatory light. She bit a cherry coloured lip with sensuous poise.

"Not for me. I'm knackered. It's been a very long weekend!" Emma smiled a painful, wooden expression and left the room, jealousy rising to dangerous levels. She gritted her teeth against its slippery embrace, reminding herself she had no claim on Rohan anymore. A final glance saw Felicity standing in the centre of the kitchen, pirouetting like a graceful ballerina, tissue in hand as she searched for the dustbin.

Emma looked in on Nicky. He lay snuggled up in one corner of the double bed, hugging his favourite Action Man. He snored lightly and Emma retrieved the decongestant oil from her suitcase, spotting a few drops onto his pillow in the half light. "Night baby," she whispered, placing a kiss on his warm cheek. "Don't need you getting sick now." She stood in the doorway and watched her son with love in her eyes, unable to imagine the grief of losing a child. For the first time in her life, she sent vibes of sympathy to Rohan's spiteful mother, not as the inconvenient daughter of a cash rich meal ticket, but from one mother to another.

CHAPTER EIGHT

Emma lay awake in the pre-dawn, contemplating her life and feeling displeased with the dreadful turn in circumstances. She was jobless and by the time Rohan got fed up and took her back to Lincoln, she would probably be homeless as well. The little furniture she owned before Nicky's stay in the hospital the previous year, was ruined by the time she got home. In less than a week, her house had turned into the local crack convention and Emma shivered at the memory of facing the stoned occupants.

"We thought you weren't coming back," her neighbours muttered guiltily, helping her rid the house of ruined carpets and a two seater sofa. Someone had put their foot through the ancient tube television, but Nicky sobbed for hours at the state of his bed.

"Ugh!" Emma rolled over in the comfy double bed and covered her face with her hands. She felt sickened at the thought of returning. She reached for her usually unwavering sense of optimism and felt it gone. She could start again, find work and a place to rent but it would probably be on yet another government housing estate and she lacked the energy to push through. She heard a strange sound in the darkness, an odd clicking noise which was strangely familiar. Emma listened through the closed bedroom door. She knew the noise but couldn't place it. "Crutches," she said finally to the darkness. "But it can't be." The house felt suddenly unfamiliar and threatening. Failing to draw comfort from her depleted inner reserves, Emma sought the next best source.

She slipped from the warm bed and padded across the floorboards in her socks. Light streamed out from underneath Rohan's bedroom door and she heard his ensuite toilet flush as she pushed into Nicky's room. The suitcase was against the door and groaned on the floorboards as Emma sneaked through. He sat up immediately. "Mummy?"

"Hey baby," she whispered back. "Why's all this stuff against the door? I checked on you last night and it wasn't here." Emma slipped under the covers and pulled her rigid son into her, rubbing at his stiff back.

"I waked up and got scared," he grumbled. "I found the bathroom but was too scared to flush. You was snoring so I set a trap so they couldn't get me."

"Who couldn't get you?" Emma whispered. "There's only us and Uncle Ro here. Nobody else. And I don't snore!"

"Yeah you do," Nicky said, matter-of-factly. "You sound like a gremlin. I heard noises. My trap didn't work though."

"Yes it did. The suitcase made it hard to get in." Emma rubbed her son's warm back and kissed the top of his head. She jumped at the sound of a loud twang and a clunk as something hit the wall behind her head. "What was that?"

"Oh, it did work then. It was late."

"What did you do? Please don't damage anything, Nick, we'll probably have to leave if that happens." Emma heard the fear in her own voice and worked to quell it, for the child's sake.

"I set up Action Man bungee jumper. I used his twangy rope like a sling shot and put Lego in it. It should've whacked you in the face but it sounded too low. I'll have to reset it."

"It might have hit a midget in the face, but only if they moved like a tortoise!" Emma sniggered. "Don't reset it, Nicky. We're safe here. It's not like...home."

"But there's funny noises," Nicky maintained.

"I didn't hear any."

"I think Uncle Ro makes them," the boy whispered. "Through this wall." Nicky raised his arm and tapped the wall behind his head with a forefinger. His blue eyes glinted in the semi-darkness. "It's like this." The child made a whimpering sound and Emma hugged him tighter, knowing what it was.

She made her voice light and unperturbed so Nicky wouldn't detect her sadness. "He's dreaming, Nick. He can't help it. He saw upsetting things when he was a soldier and it comes out when he sleeps. It's not his fault."

"Ok. Should I pray for him like Father Delaney said?" Nicky asked earnestly and Emma nodded.

"That would be really kind. It would definitely help him."

"Mum? Can I go to school today? I want to go to the one Uncle Ro talked 'bout. In the park."

"I don't think it's actually *in* the park. I think it's near the park."

"No, they play on it. Uncle Ro said they do rugby training on it and games. There's swings and stuff. He knows somebody there."

"We can maybe look," Emma ventured. "I'm not really sure what the plan is. I don't know if Uncle Ro has work today."

"He doesn't."

"How do you know?" Emma nudged at her child,

amazed how he always seemed to know everything. She chided herself about the one thing he *didn't* know and hoped he didn't ask.

"I heard him tell that screechy woman last night. She came up 'ere after you went to bed and did talking wiv 'im. They didn't do...other things. She finks she's 'is girlfriend." Nicky yawned and pushed his face into Emma's chest.

"She is his girlfriend." Emma heard her voice sounding flat and tinged with disappointment.

"Whatever." Nicky giggled as Emma patted his bottom with the palm of her hand. He pushed his tiny fingers under her ribs and tickled her. Emma's laughter rang like tinkling bells and she snorted and tickled him back.

A knock came on the bedroom door and the giggling pair froze in position. Emma missed her opportunity to clamp her hand over Nicky's mouth and he yelled, "Come in, Uncle Ro!" at the top of his voice, wafting Emma's hair with his breath. She groaned and buried her face under the covers.

Rohan pushed the door slowly open and put a foot across the threshold. There was a more forceful twang and another Lego flew through the air, narrowly missing his head. Rohan swore and Nicky giggled.

"Nicky!" Emma blew, horrified. "You didn't say there were two!" She turned over in the bed and sat up, her hair tumbling around her breasts and down her back. "I'm so sorry," she gushed, her eyes wide and frightened.

"*Yerunda!*" Nicky exclaimed and Emma drew in a huge intake of breath.

"How does he know Russian swearwords? Not from Anton." Rohan's voice sounded suspicious.

"Nana Lucya said it heaps," Nicky replied. Emma felt him cringe in her arms, obstinacy radiating from his tiny body.

"It's rude!" she chastised. "If you knew what it meant, you wouldn't say it."

"I do know what it means," Nicky said, matter of factly. "I taught Mo it."

Emma sighed but Rohan remained pensive, hovering in the doorway. "Who's Lucya?"

"She died," Nicky said, a catch in his voice. "We loved her so much, didn't we Mummy?"

"Yeah," she replied, her tone wooden. Clearly Rohan had no knowledge of his paternal grandmother; a sad fact, but an incredible blessing for Emma and her son. It made it easier to avoid awkward questions.

Rohan sighed. "How'd you make that trap?" He directed his question at the child and Emma let out her waiting breath.

Nicky tumbled from the bed and scuttled round to a space behind the door. He produced two dilapidated Action Men which were third hand by the time he got them as a birthday gift. Emma felt embarrassed in a way she never had before and hung her head in shame at their torn, faded outfits. Action Man bungee jumper's face was redrawn in biro, giving him the resemblance of an orc. "I maked 'em into slingshots," the child expounded, preening himself at his success. "The parachute one worked better though and I don't get why." He turned huge blue eyes on Rohan, looking for an explanation. Rohan took the battered parachutist from Nicky's outstretched hands and turned him over a few times, holding his silken accessory out behind him.

"This is why, look." He pulled the material and let

it twang back again. "This has more elasticity than the bungee jumper's cable. It shouldn't have, but the cable's frayed and at some point, it's been pulled past its capacity. But this," he twanged the parachute again, "this is still really elastic. It's physics." Rohan looked around the room. "How did you trigger it?"

The boys grappled around in the corner of the bedroom with Lego pieces and Action Man paraphernalia. Emma looked with misery at the sight of their blonde heads close together and cringed inwardly at the coming storm. *You've let desperation push you where you didn't want to go*, she chastised herself. *Emma, what have you done?*

CHAPTER NINE

The house was old but beautifully renovated. A 1930's semi-detached town house, it formed the other half of the only pair like it in the entire street. The inside was decorated in period fittings and colours with modern fittings and appliances. Emma stood under the shower in ecstasy as the boiler pumped genuine hot water over her head without a single trace of brown flecking from dirty pipes. It was heaven.

"So why do I feel so bloody miserable?" Emma asked herself, drawing a sad face on the glass of the shower cubicle with her index finger, stopping the water with her other hand.

"Why do you then?" Rohan's voice made her jump and Emma squeaked in shock.

"What are you doing, you weirdo? Get out!" She banged on the glass with her hand and saw him casually turn, hands in jeans pockets. He strolled through the open doorway into her bedroom and sat on the bed. Emma fumed, opening the cubicle door and almost breaking her neck on the tiles in her efforts to commandeer her towel. Safely ensconced in the sumptuous towelling, Emma faced him, her hair leaking water down her face and back in uncomfortable rivers smelling of shower gel. She slipped again on her way from the ensuite to the bedroom and saw him look away and bite his lip in amusement.

"You can't do stuff like this, Ro! Otherwise we're

gone, ok? What if Nicky walked in and saw you ogling me like that? He knows you're his uncle. It's too weird."

Rohan's jaw set hard and his eyes narrowed, glistening with a myriad of internal emotions. "It's not like I haven't seen it all before." His voice held an edge of stubbornness and the likeness to Emma's son was overpowering.

She knelt on the floor, keeping the towel closed over her breasts and rifled through her suitcase, pulling out underwear and a pair of cleanish jeans. "My body's very different to how it was at sixteen!" she snapped. "It's gone so far south, half my stretch marks could end up in London if I turned quick enough."

Rohan didn't respond to her forced humour. He sat stiffly on the edge of the bed, his face a mask of misery. His tanned fingers picked at a loose thread in the bedspread and his eyes were glazed as he sifted through old memories.

"Ro?" He jumped as Emma spoke to him, turning his attention on her again and pulling himself away from his past. His blue eyes looked dulled as he waited for the inevitable telling off. "Sweetheart, you've got Felicity now. Anton's gone and I'm just your stepsister...like you said last night." Emma watched him swallow and pressed the knife home. "She seems nice, your girlfriend. You should focus on that relationship. I'll sign any paperwork you want to release you. Just say when you're ready."

Emma retreated to the bathroom with her clothes. She pressed her forehead against the steamed up mirror, feeling the tears of agony stream silently down her face. Her heart felt huge in her chest as she gulped for air, resorting to opening the small window and standing underneath the freezing blast of air gasping for oxygen. She took a long time getting dressed, applying make-up which she then cried off and reapplied. "You look like a frog!" she told herself in the mirror, patting her cheeks with cold water for the fifth time. Emma piled her hair on top of her head, allowing the riot of wet curls to detract from her blotchy face.

"Come on, Mummy!" Nicky burst in the door, finding her patting her face with the last dregs of compact powder. "I'll be late for my new school."

Emma turned and fixed a smile on her face, admiring her son in his old school uniform. The trousers weren't too bad and he had a hole in his sock. The polo shirt was passable and his coat at least was a newer second-hand. "Ok, I'm ready," she steeled herself. "I kinda thought you'd start tomorrow and spend today with me."

"Na. You've got Uncle Ro," Nicky said, fixing his blue eyes on her face. "He says this new school does woodwork. I'd like to make a proper slingshot with wooden parts. Me an' Ro's gonna do a plan one night. He's got a shed wiv proper tools in it what nobody nicks." He beamed and shrugged. "Mum, do you love Uncle Ro? I think he loves you."

Emma's face paled at the child's perception and she shook her head in denial.

"Yeah he does," Nicky reiterated firmly. "And I don't mind. But Mohammed will be pissed off. When he married yer, 'e was gettin' me a PlayStation to make up for it."

After a lengthy conversation about not swearing at his new school and actually, not swearing anyway, Emma clumped down the stairs with her son. At the turn they stopped and Nicky looked annoyed about something she said. "That's a low blow, Mum. I never thought about that. You've ruined it now."

Emma rolled her eyes. Rohan looked up from his position on the two seater sofa in the huge downstairs hall. "What's up?" He placed an envelope carefully on his knee, removed his reading glasses and popped them in his top pocket, while Nicky thudded down the staircase in his socks, shaking the whole house.

"Mummy said, right..." *clump, clump, clump*, "that ya can't get married till yer sixteen!" Nicky's indignation continued down the last turn to the three steps to ground level. "But Mohammed's only six! So that's another ten years wivout a PlayStation. By the time I get one, I'll be an old man!"

Emma bit her lip as Nicky stood in front of Rohan with his hands on his hips, indignation pouring out of every nerve and sinew. Rohan smiled and held his gaze. "Mohammed's not marrying your mum anyway," he stated calmly. "I'm not gonna let him. You shouldn't let your most precious things go, not for anything. You'll always regret it."

The two males locked identical blue eyes and Emma held her breath, standing frozen half way down the stairs. She watched Nicky's body language from the side as he visibly relaxed and put his hands out in front of him. "Ok," he capitulated easily. "So are we goin' then, or what?"

CHAPTER TEN

The school was a hub of activity, right from the start of the recreation ground to the playground itself. The school building dated back to the late 1800s, a Victorian structure with huge sash windows and an imposing presence on the landscape. The play areas were enclosed behind a six foot brick wall which ran around the perimeter. The park spread beyond it, attractive green trees and wide open spaces. Nicky walked down the long concrete pavement underneath laden conker trees, clutching Emma's hand and sticking close to her body. Other children bobbed around them, rucksacks bumping on their backs and lunch boxes swinging from their hands. Mothers pushed buggies with other pre-schoolers wrapped up warm against the biting breeze which whipped eagerly at coats and scarves.

"It's a pretty park, isn't it?" Emma smiled and wiggled her son's hand. The confidence left his gait with each passing moment and his blue eyes projected fear as he nodded.

"When you get to Year 3, you get to play soccer in those tennis courts," Rohan said, pointing at the wire fence adjacent to the school. He strutted along next to them, his black coat collar turned up against the cold. Emma's thin fleece flapped around her body and she smiled at him with gratitude.

"I'm Year 2," Nicky said. "Next year's a long way away. Lots can happen in a year." He took a sharp inward breath filled with biting cold. "I looked forward to going to my school in Aber for ages and then my gran died, we lost our house and had to move to Lincoln." He turned wide blue eyes on Rohan in accusation. "That's why you can't make promises like that. I might not ever get in there." He jabbed a small finger at the tennis courts. Rohan looked at Emma for help, his face grieved and his eyes showing confusion.

"Nick, we can't live like that. We have to enjoy today and look forward to tomorrow," she said.

Nicky nodded and Emma looked relieved. They came to a large step up to a tall gate and Emma pushed her son up first. A bottle neck formed behind Rohan as Nicky stood in the gateway, eyeing his new life with disdain. He turned to Emma, her face level with his as she pivoted with one foot on the high threshold between park and school. She looked up at him with her trusting brown eyes showing sudden realisation. Her hand wasn't quick enough to cover his pouting mouth as pure Big Jason came volleying out from between the rosebud lips. "Love today because today is *it*, don't think about tomorrow 'cause it's probably shit."

Emma closed her eyes and felt the hush behind her in the growing knot of people. Then she heard Rohan snort and pushed her backside into him in reprimand. He gave a little, "Oof," in response and by the time Emma collected herself enough to turn around, she caught him wiping the smile off his handsome face.

"Not helpful!" she mouthed to him.

Large wooden planters decorated one corner of the playground and Emma took Nicky behind them to give him the no swearing rule again. "I mean it," she said forcefully. "It's not that kind of place and you'll end up with no friends if you swear. Nobody will want to know us and it will become impossible to stay here."

Nicky came out from behind the planters looking sorry and Emma gripped his hand as Rohan led them through a main door into the building. Everyone else watched them go in with open curiosity as the children lined up in designated groups outside. The ceilings were high, reaching up in the corridor to touch an apex above their heads. Enormous doors opened on the right hand side, showing classrooms with orderly desks and chairs. Artwork lined the walls of the corridor and created a cheery atmosphere against the gloom showing through the windows. Hands in pockets, Rohan led them to the end of the wide corridor and Emma got a great view of his bum with the denim pulled tightly over his physique. She looked away and sighed. They turned down another smaller passage and Rohan knocked on an office door.

Emma whipped round and spoke quickly to Nicky. "Why don't you take Uncle Ro to look at the displays?" she asked, begging him with her eyes. He shook his head and looked horrified.

"Noooo! I wanna stay wiv you." Panic infused his body language and he sidled closer, all trace of the confident Greyfriars child swallowed up in this terrifying new life.

Rohan jerked his head in the doorway, stepping back so Emma could enter the small office. Her heart sank as Felicity rose to greet her. "Oh, hi, Emma! I didn't know you had children. How cool."

Emma smiled woodenly and tried to occupy the doorway to stop Rohan coming in behind her. Nicky pushed his curious face between her leg and the doorframe and peered at Felicity. "Oh great!" Emma heard him mutter. "It's the screechy voice lady with the weird laugh."

Emma batted him lightly with her thigh, squishing him against the doorframe and chastised, Nicky turned doleful puppy dog eyes on her in apology.

"You're fortunately in zone, so we've definitely got a place for your son," Felicity intoned as though Emma was a bit thick. "Here's a form to fill in and I'll need an original birth certificate to copy. Then we can find your little chap a sweatshirt with the school logo on and some shorts for sports classes. After that, I'll take you to his new class."

"Mum, it's ok. I don't need a sweatshirt and stuff," Nicky stage whispered and Emma cringed. She saw Rohan ruffle Nicky's hair with his large hand in her peripheral vision as she concentrated on taking the form from Felicity's outstretched hand.

"I'll buy it," Rohan said quietly and Nicky grinned with relief and patted Emma's leg, to reassure her she wasn't about to be financially embarrassed. Felicity gave Rohan a curious look, eyeing the likeness between him and Nicky nervously. "Nicky would like school dinners too, please," Rohan stated and Emma exhaled in a whoosh.

Nicky's eyes were huge in his small head as he twisted his neck round to stare at Rohan. "Really? What, like proper dinners?"

Rohan laughed and Emma squeaked in protest at the cost. Rohan drew his wallet out of his pocket and held out his Visa card. Nicky held onto his wrist in a momentary flash of magnanimity. "You don't have to pay for pudding if you don't want to."

Rohan handed his card over to Felicity and with the other hand, stroked Nicky's hair back from his forehead. "It's fine, mate. I figure it costs the same whether you have it or not."

Emma's silence left it too late for her to back out of the terrible situation unfolding in front of her. Until Rohan produced the money, it was on the tip of her tongue to say they were just enquiring and perhaps sneak back later. She glanced down at the form which shook in her fingers, seeing the boxes in which she was to write the name of Nicky's mother...and father. Her breath came in huge gulps as Felicity processed the payment and handed the card back, stroking against Rohan's fingers on purpose. Emma glanced at his face as it remained impassive and unaffected.

"You need to fill the form in," Felicity stated, watching Emma with curiosity.

"Can I bring it back later?" Emma asked, working hard to keep the pleading from her voice.

"No, sorry. You need to do it before your son starts. Do you have his birth certificate here with you?"

Emma nodded, her neck feeling wooden as she bobbed her chin. She seized a pen from Felicity's desk and turned her back on the males, feeling Nicky's arms hugging her thigh in excitement as his mind strayed no further than his promised hot lunch. She filled in every box apart from Nicky's full name and the name of Nicky's father. The required sighting of his birth certificate denied her the option of writing 'Nicky' under the child's name and the damning word 'unknown' in the accusing rectangle demanding his father's. She took a deep breath and scribbled in the words, keeping the sheets hidden as she handed them over to Felicity.

The woman made a pretence of scanning the sheet, but Emma watched her eyes fix on the declaration of

Nicky's parentage, the likeness to Rohan making her suspicious. She heaved a visible sigh of relief and beamed. "That all looks in order," she gushed. "I'll just make a copy of this and be right back." She flapped the birth certificate in her red nailed hand and smiled at Rohan. "You never said your brother had a son." Then having dropped her bombshell, she clip clopped from the room in her high shoes.

Rohan watched her retreating back in confusion. "What does she mean?" His eyes clouded in fury. The look he gave Emma was enough to make her want to wither on the spot. She met his eyes with burning intensity, seeing surprise there as he expected her to look away first. "Anton? No, tell me you didn't?"

When Emma held her ground and kept her face impassive, Rohan's cheeks flushed and he stepped back towards the door, retreating from the room and sitting in the corridor.

Emma smiled reassuringly at her son as he was placed into his new class of Year 2 children. Poor Nicky looked terrified.

"Who else has school dinners?" the pretty blonde teacher asked the children assembled on the carpet in front of her. A little brown boy put his hand up high into the air. "Thank you, Mohammed." She smiled in gratitude. "Please will you be responsible for Nicky today and show him everything he needs to know?"

The dark-skinned child fixed beautiful liquid brown eyes on Emma's son and beamed. "Yes Mrs Clarke," he intoned in a formal voice. Then he patted the space next to him on the carpet and flapped his hand so the other children moved outwards to make room.

Nicky turned amused blue eyes on his mother and lifted his face for a kiss. As she pulled back, he grabbed at the lapels of her fleece and yanked her forwards so he could whisper in her ear. "I've been prayin' like Father Delaney said and God sent me another Mo!" He squeezed his face into a look of pure pleasure and shrugged happily.

Emma backed reluctantly from the doorway and Felicity closed it behind them. The silence in the corridor as school got underway caused them to whisper. "School ends at 3.15 pm and we keep the younger children lined up by the rails outside the playground door. We won't let them go unless their carer is there."

Emma nodded and headed back the way they came. It felt like hours ago instead of minutes, her heart enduring agonies in her chest as she strode towards the large red door. Rohan's face was hard to look at and Emma didn't have the energy to explain her son's parentage to her extremely angry husband.

Felicity hissed a warning to her. "Oh, the park gate gets locked until playtime. Then the juniors go into the ball courts. You'll have to use the front gate." She raised her delicate arm and pointed towards her office, making sure Emma understood, before slipping it seductively around Rohan's waist in one fluid motion.

Emma felt the awful moan rage inside her chest, bursting to get out. It overwhelmed her with its intensity and she lurched for the exit, leaving Rohan staring after her. Outside in the fresh air, Emma gasped and heaved huge breaths into lungs which ached as though starved. She fumbled with the gate, reading the notice ordering her to '*push the red button*,' numerous times before actually understanding. Out on the street she experienced momentary panic. She didn't recognise anything about the neat road or ancient towering trees and halted, calming herself by an act of will. She set off left, striding around the perimeter wall and following it as it turned a corner. Emma found herself on the wide concrete path through the park and on an impulse, broke into a run.

She ran past the gate opposite the ball courts and found the play park beyond, the space empty and the swings moving slightly in the breeze as though ridden by invisible children. Emma ran towards them and sank onto a swing, feeling the wet seeping through the hole between her boot and its worn sole. "Damn you, Anton!" she sobbed, hugging her arms around herself in misery. "I warned you it would come back to bite me, didn't I?" She heard the rustle of Nicky's birth certificate in her pocket and groaned.

Emma cried herself empty, watching the tears splash onto the rubbery black surface underneath the swing. She reached into her pocket for a tissue, feeling the rough paper against her fingers. A fresh wave of grief washed over her and Emma pulled it out, smoothing out the creases and pressing it against her forehead.

"When were you gonna tell me?" Rohan restrained his bitterness as he slumped onto the swing next to her, sitting heavily and stretching one leg out in front of him.

"Nothing to tell." Emma folded the certificate and stuffed it back into her pocket. "It's none of your business."

Rohan's blue eyes fixed on her, flickering with anger. "Like hell it isn't! So when I was getting shot to shit in a war I didn't want to be in, you were shagging my brother!"

Emma turned to face him, recognising the sense of

betrayal and disappointment she saw in the mirror every morning. It reflected back at her, Rohan's agony raw and open. She held his gaze with steady eyes that wore no guilt and saw him flinch under her stare. "I loved you, Em!" he spat.

She smiled sadly, blinking away tears that fluttered to her cheeks, glittering there like diamonds. "And I loved you. I always loved you."

"So why?" Rohan's jaw worked in anger and he wiped the back of his hand across his eyes. Emma reached out to touch him and then withdrew her hand.

"There're things you don't understand. I'm not ready to explain them yet. You can think what you like of me, but don't you dare drag Anton's name through the mud. Everything he did was out of kindness and he doesn't deserve your hatred!"

Rohan shook his head and leaned his elbows on his knees. His eyes bore into the ground as he swallowed all the terrible things he wanted to say. "What does it matter? My brother's dead."

Emma stood up and offered him her hand. He stared at it for a moment as though it was distasteful to him. As Emma gave up and withdrew it, Rohan's hands shot out and seized her fingers and her wrist. He pulled her hand into him and kissed her fingers. He pressed his cheek against them, his face hot against her cold flesh. "Do you want us to leave now?" Emma asked, keeping her voice level. "We can go."

"No! Don't be stupid! I asked you here; I'm not going to kick you out." Rohan stood up and pulled her into him, his eyes filled with unreadable emotions. They walked back to his house, his arm heavy around her shoulders. His hand caressed the curls at her neck and Emma shivered as his fingers brushed her skin.

Occasionally he kissed her temple with slow, deliberate touches of his lips which seemed to turn her inside out with misery. He sighed many times in the fifteen minute walk and Emma bit her lip and wished for the millionth time, she could go back and do things differently. Nicky's birth certificate nestled in her pocket, not a symbol of accusation, but proof there were still kind, good men in the world. Anton Andreyev had been one of them. Now even he was gone.

CHAPTER ELEVEN

"Ro, who's that man across the street?"

Rohan whipped his reading glasses off his nose and stood up, instantly alert. The sofa cushions rose up like inflatables in his wake. "What man?"

Emma baulked in the dining room doorway, her brown eyes widening in fear at his reaction. "Just a man. He's been sitting across the street next to the Georgian looking house. He gets out occasionally and goes for a walk but he always comes back."

"What made you notice him?" Rohan walked to the window and peered into the street, careful not to disturb the voile drapes which offered the room privacy.

"Er..." Emma hesitated, not wanting admit she'd spent the last hour crying, sitting in the bay window in her bedroom with her backside on the built in dressing table. "I was just looking out the window."

Rohan looked at her again, noticing her puffy eyes and the sad slump of her shoulders. "Come here," he said softly, opening his arms out to her.

Emma sniffed and ran round the dining table to him, burying her face in his armpit and resuming her miserable crying. "Sshhh," Rohan soothed. "Let's not dwell on what we can't change, hey? It's all in the past now."

Emma muttered something into his armpit and Rohan lifted her chin so he could look at her. His blue eyes were kind. "Say that again, *devotchka?*"

Emma couldn't repeat the soft denial again, grief at Anton's death gripping her throat in a vice. So she hesitated, before changing the subject. "It's that white transit you were talking about last night on the motorway. I didn't see it when you asked me to look but after that, I saw it in the side mirror a few times. I've been watching it for the last hour. The driver's the same man." Emma sniffed and wiped her nose on her tatty sweater sleeve.

"Shit!" Rohan exclaimed. "Are you sure?"

Emma nodded. "Who is he? What does he want?"

Rohan kissed the top of her head. "I don't know. Get cleaned up and we'll take the dog for a walk. I wanna show you the town. We'll see if he follows." He pointed at her stained sweater with the big pulls in the shoulder and her jeans which were frayed at the bottom. "And you're going clothes shopping."

Emma cleaned her face up yet again and donned one of Rohan's spare jackets for the walk into town. It was too big for her but the scent of his aftershave and his unique musky smell provided much needed comfort. Rohan strode next to her with the dog on a leash, Farrell trotting happily next to his leg. Neither of them mentioned Anton, or the birth certificate bearing his name. When they came to road crossings, the dog sat down at the curb without being told. "He's a good boy, isn't he?" Emma commented.

Rohan smiled and clicked his tongue so the dog knew to stand up and walk. "Should be. I trained him for Anton. He was useless with anything involving discipline. He got you as a pup, didn't he?" Rohan spoke to the dog and Farrell looked up at him and opened his mouth in a doggy smile, his flowing black tail giving a little wave of pleasure. "Treated him like a baby instead of a dog. I don't think he realised what he'd got."

"What kind of dog is he?" Emma kept pace with Rohan, finding it hard not to drop into old habits and hold his hand, not that public displays of affection played much part in their history; his mother might have found out.

"He's a working cocker spaniel," Rohan said. "They make excellent search and sniffer dogs. Customs use them heaps in airports. My brother would have been better off with a poodle he could keep in his man bag."

Emma snorted. "That's so true. I can't believe I'll never see him again. It's like this hole where I think he should be."

Rohan looked down at her and nodded. "I know, *devotchka*. It's left an ache in my soul. Nothing takes the pain away. He was my only *brat*, my brother and I loved him."

"Did he live in this town?" Emma asked and Rohan stared at her with a curious look on his face.

"I actually don't know."

"You don't know?" Emma repeated the odd sentence and bit her lip. "So where did you train the dog?"

"He brought him to me. He said it was easier. I never questioned it. I get really busy with work so I accepted him always travelling to see me. Does that make me a bad person? I didn't know where my own brother lived?"

Emma shook her head. "I didn't know either." She let shame blush her soft cheeks. "He always came to see us, too." She saw too late how desperate Rohan was to ask about Anton's relationship with Nicky. The idea of a man so openly gay with a son by his stepsister seemed so utterly incongruous, he struggled with the words and then thought better of it.

"Let's not talk about him now, hey?" Rohan smiled sadly and changed the subject. "Is that man still following?"

Emma made a show of dropping something onto the pavement while Rohan walked ahead. She sank to her haunches and picked up the conker Nicky gave her that morning for safekeeping. Rohan halted the dog to wait for her and Emma gave a worried nod, too slight for the man behind to see. "Yes. He's keeping his distance but he's still there. Why would he be following us?"

"Me, *devotchka*. He's following me. I don't know. I mess with some dodgy people in my line of work sometimes and when I crunch the numbers, someone has to lose out."

"What are you going to do?" Emma sounded panicked and Rohan grabbed hold of her hand, wincing at the electrical current of familiarity and attraction which passed between them. "Is he going to hurt you?"

Rohan snorted as though the idea was stupid and gave a tight smile as they crossed a car park and entered the back of a bustling market hall, filled with stalls selling everything from sausages to cheese under the one roof. Shoe sellers mixed with craft stands and knitting patterns in the front half of the building, alongside vegetable stalls, sewing accessories and ribbons. Farrell kept so close to Rohan's left leg it was as though he was grafted on, clearly not comfortable around the throngs of bodies and feet. Nobody yelled at them to take the dog away and they passed through unseen.

In a particularly busy crush near the front doors, Rohan pressed Emma's hand and smoothed her fingers with his. It was comforting and she squeezed back, navigating a dose of pensioner road rage as two elderly people in disability scooters got their handles locked together by accident in the overcrowded aisle. Rohan cut a clear path through, his imposing height making it easy for him and Emma forged through behind, using his wake to cut through the crowds. They popped out of the front doors in a rush and Rohan dragged Emma to the left and round the corner.

"Take the dog!" he hissed at her, shoving Farrell's leash into her hands. Stunned, Emma looked down at the animal's enormous brown eyes, rimmed by half-moons of white. "Guard!" Rohan told the dog and Farrell sat down firmly on Emma's foot. Rohan blocked her view of the road and he waited for a moment, his body tense and poised. In a split second he was gone.

Emma peeked around the corner to the front of the market hall in time to see the small man emerge and look around him in confusion. Rohan pounced, fixing his hands firmly on the man's shoulders. "Hi my vriend!" he announced with feigned conviviality, accentuating his Russian accent for effect. "Long time, no see!" He steered the surprised pursuer round the corner to Emma and thumped him up against the wall with his forearm underneath the man's chin. "Long time, too much see, actually!" Rohan's eyes flashed with danger and Emma saw the soldier in him rise to the surface in an ecstasy of glee, his purpose as a killing machine revived and renewed. She opened her mouth to stop him and then swallowed instead, trusting him.

Emma's eyes widened as Rohan produced a flick

knife and released the blade in an ease of motion, holding it up to the man's skinny throat. "Come on," he said in a deceptively friendly voice, "you're crap at tracking so you may as well tell me what you're up to."

"Just making a few quid guvnor," the man hissed as the blade pressed against his skin. He was wiry, neatly dressed with an unfortunate comb over which had the unenviable job of spreading twelve frail looking dark hairs across his receding hairline.

Rohan's eyes flicked all around him, ensuring the little scene went unwitnessed by anyone passing. He pressed the man harder against the wall, shielded by the huge sign advising the pay and display car park. Emma watched as Rohan glanced towards the dog. "Warn!" he told Farrell.

The dog jumped to life, standing square with the man. His top lip peeled back in a dreadful snarl displaying sharp, pointed teeth. A low growl emitted from his throat and Emma kept hold of the leash, fascinated by the dog's still waving tail. It was a game to him. She gulped and felt sick.

The man feigned ignorance and complained and griped he didn't know who paid him to follow the big Russian. His voice held an irritating whinge, not helped by the dog's enjoyment of the game. Farrell edged closer and closer to the man's hand as it hung limply by his side. "Please mate, just lemme go!" the man begged. "I ain't done nuffin!"

As the knife blade drew a pebble of blood, the dog took a few slavering snaps at the man's hand and Emma lost patience. "For goodness sake!" she exclaimed and dropped Farrell's leash. She pulled a crumpled face of sheer distaste as she reached between the man's legs and seized hold of his crown jewels. She wasn't sure who was more surprised, the man, Rohan or the dog. "Just tell him!" she hissed and squeezed. The little man squeaked out a sound which would have delighted St Di's Church choir master and tried to bat Emma's hand away with grappling hands. Rohan increased his pressure with the knife and the arms returned to their raised position, although the hands clenched in fear.

"I'm a private investigator," he trilled in alarm. "My client's a woman. She emails me and transfers expenses into my account when I invoice her. I'm paid to follow *him* and take photos!" He jerked his head towards Rohan but spoke to Emma. "Please let go of my nads now? If I can't get my missus pregnant she'll dump me!"

Emma winced at the greasy hair, the acne pocked middle-aged face and pitied the poor woman who was prepared to breed from this type of low grade stock. "No!" She pouted and took a step closer to the man, gripping harder and trying not to look at Rohan's amused expression. "*Why* are you following him?"

"I have to email her where he's been and what he's done. Like, he went to a meeting in Falkirk on Friday and arrived in Leeds late on Saturday at some kind of wedding. He went to Lincoln on Sunday and arrived home Monday. I have to tell her who he saw as well." The man let out a wail of pain as Emma squeezed harder and yanked painfully upwards at an unnatural angle for testicles.

"How do you know it's a woman?" she asked him. Bored, the dog licked the man's hand and he felt tongue and teeth and screeched.

"Shut up!" Emma said in disgust. "Or I'll make sure you never have children."

"The phone! The phone! She rang me the first time and it was a woman's voice."

"Is she local?" Rohan interjected, stepping back from the man and flicking the blade away with his thumb in a fluid motion."

"I don't know!" The man sweated as Emma maintained her death grip on his private parts. His thin hair stuck to his head and he looked sick.

"If you ever follow this man again," Emma pointed with her free hand towards Rohan, "I'll tear them off! Do you understand?"

"Yes!" the man agreed emphatically. "I've seen where you live. I know you mean it."

With a final yank of devilment, Emma let go and the man clasped both hands over his nether regions and rubbed, as though checking it was all still intact. Emma pulled a disgusted face and wiped her hand on her jeans. "Sod off and leave us alone. Forever!" she threatened and the man nodded.

"Fine. It was getting too long distance anyway, although the expenses were good. It must have been costin' her a fortune in petrol alone." He stood up straight and brushed himself down, out of date jeans with a slight flare to their bottoms and a pale flasher-type mac, tidy but stuck in a previous century. His disguise was about as subtle as a fart in an astronaut suit. His final comment was aimed at Rohan and delivered with an air of victory. "You've got rid of me but you won't be able to ditch the other one so easily. He's been tailin' you on and off for the last month, ever since I started and you didn't even notice!" The wiry man strode quickly away, blending seamlessly into a crowd of elderly shoppers heading south on the Northampton Road. Emma looked at Rohan and bit her lip as he watched the man walk away. He looked at her in total bemusement and then caught the obedient dog's leash up into his hand.

"What the hell's going on here?" he asked her.

Emma shrugged. "I have no idea, Ro, but please can we go somewhere so I can wash my hands?"

CHAPTER TWELVE

They found a public house with tables outside the front and Emma sat with the dog while Rohan went inside and ordered food and drinks. "So is it always this exciting in the Andreyev household, Faz?" Emma asked the black dog as he laid his chin on her knee. She fondled his ears and he closed his eyes, only raising his head again when Rohan appeared.

"Where's the toilet?" Emma asked, peering at her palms and pulling a face. Rohan pointed back into the bar and laughed, shaking his head.

"What you did to that guy was so left field it was totally out of the ball park," he snorted. "It reminded me of that fight you got into at school once. I remember now why I never wanted to upset you!"

"Yeah well I had to learn to take care of myself," Emma said wistfully. "I'll be back in a second."

Farrell stood up and wagged his tail as Emma returned and she stroked his ears with gentle fingers and sat down. Her coffee appeared not long afterwards. Rohan smiled appraisingly at her and laid his mobile phone on the table after disconnecting the call. A waitress appeared with a bowl of fries and laid them down, snatching up the table marker and offering a flirtatious smile at Rohan. Emma glared at her with a flash of jealousy and then stopped herself. When she looked up, Rohan's eyes danced with humour.

Emma fought to contain the flush that lit up her cheeks. She grimaced, taking a chip and dabbing it in the runny red sauce. "Why would someone be following you, Ro?"

"No idea." He sat back in his seat and looked at her.

"Whatever!" Emma scoffed. She watched him from narrowed eyes hooded by long black lashes and saw Rohan's lips twitch, knowing instinctively he wanted to kiss her. He shifted uncomfortably in his seat and crossed his legs, disturbing the dog next to him. Farrell sighed in disgust and Emma threw him a chip which he snapped up. "Just pretend it's a crappy PI's finger," she told the dog and he yawned and whined at the same time.

"So come on! Who would be following you and why the hell do you carry a knife?" Emma kicked Rohan under the table and he almost spilled coffee down himself.

"Well, I've never seen the *testicle twist* in action but next time, I'll bear it in mind instead of the knife."

"Whatever! Keep your secrets," Emma smirked.

Rohan's face softened. "You worried about me, *devotchka?*"

"Not really," she grinned. "But I have a child to take care of and if you're attracting criminals, I need to think about moving on."

Rohan shrugged. "Attracting criminals? Do me a favour! I saw where you lived, remember."

"I still live there," Emma said, tight lipped with warning in her tone.

Rohan looked uneasy and shifted in his seat. "Look, I'm sorry." He bit his lip as though fear of her leaving was more prevalent than the weird little man following him. "I saw the guy you...disposed of... a while ago but I needed him to play his hand a bit more openly. He did that today. I don't get the feeling it's about work.

His client's a woman." Rohan shrugged. "I don't know any women who would go to the expense of setting an investigator on me. He was crap. Whoever *she* is, she found him in the Yellow Pages."

The colour drained suddenly from Emma's face and she looked around her in terror. "Oh no!" In her panic, Emma stood up, the adoring dog rising too and watching her with his fluffy ears pricked, ready to go wherever she led. Her coffee spewed onto the table and she cast around aimlessly, dread burgeoning in her heart. "It's *her*. It's your mother."

"Where?" Rohan re-examined the quiet street, looking up and down the pedestrianised area in confusion, his blue eyes searching over and over. He snatched at Emma's coat sleeve as she got ready to bolt and it swung her around towards him. Emma listed heavily into the side of Rohan's chair and the sound of her buttons popping seemed to deafen them both. "Hey, hey!" Rohan seized her by the shoulders at the same time as standing and he shook her gently. The dog growled and Rohan looked down at him with betrayal in his face. "Shut it!" he told the dog with indignation in his voice. The dog continued to glare at him. "Em, you can't just run blindly. Where is she? Show me?"

Emma screwed her face up in irritation and grabbed the front of Rohan's warm jacket. "Not here! She put the investigator on you! She must know Anton told you to find me and she didn't want you to. Now that man will quit and she'll know I'm here and that I hurt him! She'll come after me." Emma's words came in furious bursts and people passing by stopped to watch with interest.

"Em!" Rohan pulled her into his chest and buried

her head in his coat. He spoke to her in a calm, level tone full of healing and safety. "Em, people are staring, *devotchka*. The last thing you need is to draw attention to yourself here. It's a small town. Mama doesn't know you're here but if you carry this on, someone will tell her they saw me with a distraught female and she'll rush straight round. She's desperate for me to marry and give her *vnuchata*."

"No, no, no," Emma moaned. "Not that." She kept her head against Rohan's chest, letting her heart beat slow to a more stable pace. Her head pounded as though oxygen deprived and she took big breaths filled with Rohan's gorgeous smell. Giving in for a moment of pure madness, she put her arms around his waist and held on, splatting herself against his chest wall like a mascot. It was ungainly and undignified but at least people stopped staring and the tension in the street dissipated.

"You feel ok now, *dorogaya?*" Rohan whispered and Emma nodded, her dark curls bouncing along her shoulders and down her back. He kissed her on the forehead and let her go.

Emma couldn't sit down again, rattled by the thought that Rohan's mother knew where she was. She stood in front of him, head bowed and body rigid, while the concerned spaniel sat on her feet and pushed so hard on her shins he almost overbalanced her. "Can we go? Please?" Emma's speech was stilted, her confidence robbed in an instant of overreaction.

"Ok. Let me just pay the bill." Rohan left the dog leash in Emma's stiff fingers and disappeared inside to settle up, emerging to find her stroking Farrell's long sleek body and sniffing. Her nose was red with cold and unhappiness leaked from every pore of her body.

Outside, Rohan pulled Emma under his arm, securing her against his body as he took the leash from her. "It's all gonna be ok," he promised and Emma kept her face buried into him, aware he told her the same thing once before as they lay tangled together in bed, hours before he left for Afghanistan. Nothing had been ok since.

Rohan walked Emma around town, insisting she buy new clothes. She refused to visit the shops on the High Street selling new fashions, reluctant at first to do anything other than run straight back to the house. Eventually he persuaded her and subsequently spent an hour standing in the corner of the second hand stores. Emma bought things from Age Concern and the Salvation Army Store, mainly for Nicky and by the time it was school pick up, Rohan was left scratching his head. "Well, that's the most interesting shop I've ever seen a woman do. I think you spent less than twenty quid all up!"

Emma looked up at him as they walked, her voice toneless and flat. "It'll be easier to pay you back then."

Rohan's face registered hurt and an unhealthy mixture of fear. He carried the bags and Emma held the dog leash. Farrell slipped along next to her easily, sticking to her left leg as though glued on. "Why does he walk on the left of me?" she asked, trying to persuade him to move to the right.

"No, don't do that." Rohan grabbed her fingers and pushed the leash so the bewildered dog returned to her left. "Stick with what he's been trained to do or you'll confuse him. I need to show you all the commands so you can take care of him while I'm gone."

"Ok." Emma reached down and stroked the glossy black body and hid her sadness at the thought of

Rohan's absence.

"Hey, you'll be fine." He smiled, picking up her mood with scary precision.

"I always am," Emma said, not looking at him. Rohan tutted and slipped his arm around her shoulders, pulling her into him and kissing her temple. It felt so right and Emma pulled away with great reluctance as they climbed the step into the school playground, aware of other parents watching the couple with interest. When Rohan reached for her, Emma pushed his hand away. "You've got a girlfriend!" she reprimanded him, the pique escaping from her voice. Rohan shoved his hand into his pocket and frowned, saying nothing more.

CHAPTER THIRTEEN

"Please can we do that fing wiv the slingshot tonight?" Nicky asked, bouncing along next to Rohan and holding his hand.

"See what Mummy says." Rohan smiled down at him. "She's the boss lady."

Emma held onto Farrell and shook her head at Rohan's deference to her, enjoying the sense of family and wishing it were permanent.

"Excuse me," the voice called from behind and Emma stopped and turned. A beautiful dark-skinned woman hurried through the park behind them, dragging the newest version of little Mohammed behind her.

Emma fixed a wooden smile on her face and steeled herself for trouble. "Hi," she faltered.

"I'm glad I caught you," the woman said, catching up with them. Rohan hovered nearby, clutching Nicky's hand. "I wondered if your son would like to play at our house one evening. Mo seems quite taken with him. He hasn't made many friends since we moved down here so it's nice to hear him speak with enthusiasm about another kid." She looked around her cautiously. "It's quite a *white* area."

Emma looked around her in surprise and pulled a face at the bodies moving past them as they clogged up the centre of the walkway. "I suppose you're right," she said. "I guess we didn't really think about it like that."

The woman looked relieved and stuck her hand out.

"I'm Mel. Nice to meet you."

"Emma." Their hands clasped in friendship. Emma glanced at Rohan and opened her mouth to speak. Mel smiled and pushed her frozen hand towards him.

"Well, you're obviously Nicky's dad. He's a gorgeous little boy."

Nicky's ego fluffed visibly and he put his arm around Mohammed. "This is our dog. He's called Farrell."

Mohammed stroked the silky tail and the dog tolerated the imposition with good grace and the slightest look of disgust at Emma for allowing the atrocity. Rohan shook Mel's hand and smiled at her. He looked at Nicky and then back at Emma with an odd look on his face. She gulped. *Back to square one. That didn't take long.*

"We can't 'ave a dog at the shelter for battered women," Mohammed said sadly.

"Battered?" Nicky patted his friend's shoulder and clung onto Rohan's hand. The man quailed as Nicky looked at him for explanation. Rohan feigned selective hearing and Nicky drew his own conclusions. "What, like battered fish? Sometimes if Mummy had pennies left over after the rent and the electric and the money for Fat Brian to protect our 'ouse, she'd get me battered fish as a special treat. It came in a van with a big pot of hot fat in it and it would sizzle and cook in the back of 'is van. Mummy 'ad to go off the estate to get it for me. The van weren't allowed on the estate because the fish and chip man wouldn't pay Fat Brian's fee. I like battered fish," Nicky added.

"We 'ad a Fat Brian on our estate in Manchester," Mo said with childish enthusiasm. "Only 'ee were a Fat Abdul and 'ee was my dad."

Emma gulped and looked back at Mel. The other woman stared at her oversized man's coat with the popped buttons and the threadbare sweatshirt underneath. The white of Emma's sock poked through the hole between her boot and its worn sole and Emma's fingers clutching the dog leash were frozen in position. Mel's eyes strayed to the handsome man bearing clothing bags from second hand shops in the town and visibly relaxed. She smiled with genuine relief at Emma. "Thank God for that!" she gushed. "I started to feel like I 'ad two heads down 'ere."

The group trailed slowly home after the boys enjoyed a run around the park with the dog. Farrell was the best behaved of them all, at least coming when he was called. Rohan stood on the edge of the grass, legs slightly splayed and his hands wedged deep into his pockets while the women chatted quietly behind him. Emma's eyes strayed to the neat backside enclosed in the tight material and saw Rohan glance back at her with a smirk. She closed her eyes, knowing he was doing it on purpose.

"He's gorgeous," Mel whispered and Emma shook her head.

"And he knows it. Don't fluff his ego for him, for goodness sake. He's hard enough to live with as it is."

"Well, you're very lucky. He obviously only has eyes for you," Mel commented, patting Emma's hand. Her fingers felt frozen. Emma swiped one of the plastic bags from Rohan's hand. He ignored her, putting his fingers in his mouth to summon the dog with an impressively piercing whistle.

"Here." Emma felt around in the bag until her hand closed over what she wanted. She pulled out the second hand pair of woollen gloves. "They need a wash but they'll be warm." She held them out to Mel.

"I don't need..."

Emma stopped her with a shake of her head. "I know you don't. We never do." The gloves flapped from her outstretched hand, the tag the charity shop worker stuck on still holding the woolly wrists together. A handwritten cardboard label fluttered in the breeze which whipped around the park, declaring the gloves cost the grand total of twenty pence. A fifth of a pound coin; the difference between comfort and unending misery. Emma jerked her head and watched the woman's agonised brown eyes look at them with naked covetousness, before fingers with blue tinged nails reached out for them.

"Thank you," Mel replied.

Emma smiled and shrugged. "It's fine. Let's call it a trade."

Mel's eyes lit up, hearing something she understood as fully as breathing in and out. "Done!" she said with enthusiasm. "One day I'll give you something you didn't even know you needed."

Children and dog rounded up and back under control, if a little muddy, the group parted company on Northampton Road. Mel walked back to the women's shelter, discreetly hidden in an old Victorian house at the end of a long row. Rohan put his arm around Emma's cold body and held Nicky's hand and with the dog trotting along beside them, they walked home as a family.

CHAPTER FOURTEEN

"You!" The voice was vitriolic, like the scraping of nails down a blackboard, the accent still thickly Slavic in origin. Emma dropped her glass, feeling the sharp shards pierce the skin of her instep as it shattered on the tiles. The tiny cuts stung from the liquid which was fortunately only water.

Rohan's mother stood in the hall, her immaculate figure framed in the kitchen doorway and a front door key gripped in her raised hand. "Vot are you doing here?" she snapped, thinning her lips in a habitual pout. "Vy are you at my son's house? Ver is he?"

Alanya was still beautiful, her straight blonde hair pulled back into a tight bun, the ballerina's poise still slight and graceful. Age had attacked the top half of her body since they last met, bending her slightly forward like a weathered tree, but her lips were still straight and unsmiling and her blue eyes terrifyingly perceptive.

Emma gulped and stared at the mess on the floor and then the terrifying woman in the doorway. She became sixteen again, tousled curly dark hair and a skip in her step, reduced to cowering before this vicious matriarch who seized possession of her father and home. At almost twenty three, the urge to cower was overwhelming. Emma resisted. With poise and dignity, she crunched across the glass, feeling jagged edges press into the soles of her feet. "Rohan's nipped out, he won't be long. Excuse me," she said politely to the woman, pushing past her and walking carefully up the stairs. Behind the safety of her bedroom door she tip toed across to the bed and hurled herself face down. "Shit, shit, shit!" she exclaimed, examining the myriad tiny cuts oozing from both feet, staining her socks. Emma carefully stripped the socks off so they were inside out. She dabbed at her bleeding flesh with a tissue from the bedside table and crawled over to the ensuite on her knees, keen not to stain the light coloured rug.

"Why me?" she complained. With shaking hands, she locked the bathroom door and then blocked the plug hole in the shower tray with a flannel and set it running. "I'm an idiot! It was inevitable I'd see her. What was I thinking? Rohan, please hurry up and come home. Why didn't I just go with you?"

When there was enough water for her to stand in, Emma climbed in and soothed her poor feet with the cold water, sloshing them around to get rid of the glass. She cursed again as it stung over and over. The flannel was ineffective and the water drained away, stained pink and speckled with glass. She sat on the bathroom floor and dabbed at the cuts with toilet paper, making a damp mountain of tissue next to her. The sound of her stepmother's raised voice drifted upstairs to her and Emma felt sick to her stomach. "Shouting at yourself, you horrid old woman!" she hissed, channelling the pain as anger. The woman shouted again in her jerky speech and Emma heard the echo of a male voice, raised in reply. "Fantastic!" Emma complained, as yet another piece of tissue stuck to a weeping cut. She looked at her watch in panic. "Noooo!" She had to leave in half an hour to fetch Nicky from school and it was a fifteen minute walk on cut, bleeding feet.

"Em!" The knock on the bathroom door was accompanied by Rohan's concerned voice. "Are you ok? What the hell happened?"

"My syn," came his mother's argumentative voice from close behind him. "Throw ze bitch out. She is trouble, *beda*, garbage!"

"Stop!" Rohan sounded determined as Emma froze in her futile ministrations. She heard his footsteps as he ushered his mother out into the hall. "Get and clear up the mess, Mama. You don't need to be involved in this. *Ukhodi!*"

Emma heard the severe woman chunter to herself down the wooden split landing, clumping down the stairs in her high heeled boots. She heard Rohan exhale and translate a version of the Russian word under his breath. "Bugger off, woman." He knocked again. "She's gone downstairs, Em. Open the bloody door, please?"

Emma shuffled onto her knees and clicked the lock, sitting down heavily on her bottom and hiding her trembling hands underneath her.

"What the hell?" Rohan stared at the blood spotted tissue and the soaked floor. "She did this to you? Is this why you won't let her see Nicky?" His jaw tightened and an angry flush began on his neck.

Emma shook her head. "No. She let herself in with a key and frightened me. I dropped a glass and...I needed to get away from her." She sniggered as a nervous reaction. "It was a bit kamikaze walking over it. I knew what was going to happen but it was the lesser of two evils."

Rohan tutted and knelt awkwardly on the ground next to her. She pushed him away with force and he wobbled and clutched at the glass shower door. "No!"

she exclaimed. "You've got your work trousers on. You'll ruin them. I'll be fine!"

He stood up crossly and walked away, leaving Emma to her dabbing. She folded some wads of tissue with shaking fingers, wondering if she could limp to school with them in her sock. Nicky was the priority, even if she had to crawl there. Emma struggled with the vision of the woman downstairs, biting down the wave of sickness which accompanied her terror. She took deep breaths and tried to work out how to get out of the house without being seen again. Under no circumstances could the woman know about Nicky.

Rohan clumped back up the stairs with a first aid kit after more shouting in the downstairs hallway. He sighed as he handed over a pack of plasters. His blue eyes fixed on Emma's face making her feel in disgrace. As her reaction to pressure made her want to giggle, it wasn't helpful. She sniggered and snorted through the operation, knowing it wound Rohan up even more. "Stop staring at me!" she spluttered, accidentally sticking the wiggling plaster to the floor. She snorted as she tried to lift it off the tiles with her thumbnail.

"Bloody hell, Em!" Rohan snatched the packet from her hand and ripped the cardboard to shreds, showering Emma with plasters of all shapes and sizes. She burst into hysterical giggles and shook her head, seeing two round pimple plasters cascade from her hair. She put her hand up to her mouth and sniggered behind it as Rohan hefted himself awkwardly on the floor next to her. "Keep still!" he ordered, roughly gripping her ankle in his fingers. One handed, he peeled the backing off a long plaster with his teeth and spat the white paper onto the floor. He aimed it over the worst of Emma's cuts and she squealed and pulled her foot away so he stuck it to her jeans.

"No! I don't want it on my foot when you've had it in your mouth!" Emma punctuated her protest with a peel of laughter.

"It was the bloody paper! I'm so gonna kill you in a minute!" he threatened, but the smirk lifted one side of his mouth and Emma snorted again.

"*Durak*," she whispered and Rohan looked up in surprise. He tore the protective backing from another plaster in absolute silence and Emma's mirth lessened as she waited for his reaction to her calling him a fool in his own language. Rohan held up the biggest plaster in his fingers and lurched for her mouth, sealing it firmly over her lips. Emma squeaked and fell backwards onto the tiles. Rohan overbalanced and unable to save himself with his arms, plunged on top of her. Emma grunted in pain as his strong body crushed her and Rohan came to rest with his face close to hers. Emma squeezed her eyes tight shut and her body rocked with her effort at keeping her giggles to herself. Rohan's lips turned up and he whispered something in Russian and then moved his long fingers to her waist. With her successfully gagged, he set about tickling Emma until tears ran freely from her eyes and snot coursed down her face. "Enough?" he asked her and she nodded enthusiastically, squeaking again as he resumed his tickling. "Tough, you little troublemaker," he smirked.

Emma licked at the plaster over her lips, successfully pushing it off with her tongue and wrinkling her nose at the dreadful taste. "I have to get Nick," she groaned, freeing her hands enough to push Rohan's chest.

"I'll get him in the car." He couldn't resist the urge

to tickle her twice more. Emma grunted.

"Stop! You can't do that. He loves to play in the park with Mo after school. And there's no way you're leaving me here with Cruella de Vil by myself!"

Rohan laughed and used his sleeve to rub the snot and tears from Emma's face. He completed the action with such care and gentleness that she held her breath and studied his handsome face. He caught her watching him and on an impulse pressed his lips to hers. He pulled away with an act of will, clearly not wanting to. His eyes were dark, his pupils huge in his glittering eyes. Rohan leaned on one elbow and brushed Emma's fringe back from her forehead. "Are you getting up then, or what?" he asked, his breath stroking her face. His lips tasted of coffee and Emma nodded slowly and then smirked again.

"I've got a bit of clearing up to do first. This big *durak* made a right mess of my ensuite."

"Sort yourself out woman," Rohan smiled, his eyes sultry and alluring. "I'll clear up your mess downstairs and then we'll go." He shifted his weight onto his hands and knees and tickled Emma one last time as he hauled himself upright.

"Ro!" Emma's voice held panic as she sat up quickly and seized hold of the side of his smart pinstriped work trousers.

"What's wrong?" The fingers of his right hand closed over hers.

"Please don't let *her* near me? And she can never know about Nicky!" Emma looked truly terrified and Rohan nodded with doubt in his eyes.

"Ok." He smiled without surety and nodded again, exiting the room with a heavy gait.

Emma fanned her hot face with a flapping hand and

used more toilet roll to dab her cuts dry. Then she used the scattered plasters to patch up her feet enough to stand. She cleared the remaining plasters into a pile which she left on the side of the sink and put the rubbish in the bathroom bin. She donned two pairs of less holey socks and limped into the hallway, closing Nicky's bedroom door against prying eyes on impulse.

"You can come down, Em. She's left," Rohan said, peering up the stairs at Emma as she lurked on the first landing. "I sent her home in a taxi. Come on, let's get Nicky." He held his hand out to her and reluctantly, Emma stepped down, wrinkling her nose at the pain in her feet. When she was still two steps from the bottom, Rohan wrapped his arms around her waist and pulled her into him. He pressed his cheek against her soft breasts and sighed, wrapping his arms around her waist. Emma suffered a bout of confusion as she fondled the skin on the back of his neck and pushed her face into his hair. "Everything's gonna be ok," he whispered. "I promise."

Emma closed her eyes, remembering the same promise spoken from his lips in another time. Hours after he said it, Rohan left his teenage wife, broken and terrified, nursing her dreadful secret alone. "You can't promise me that," she replied with sadness. "You never could. Now she knows I'm here, I have to leave. She can't see my son."

CHAPTER FIFTEEN

"I've asked her not to come round to the house," Rohan said as they walked through the park to school, the dog plodding at their side, occasionally sniffing the ground.

Emma eyed him sideways. "It won't last, Ro. You were always a soft touch where your mother was concerned. I know you don't believe she's capable of hurting anyone, but I don't want her near me or my son!" She punctuated her sentence with a determined glare and Rohan looked conflicted, hands in pockets and a sad slump to his shoulders.

"I'm not sure what you think she's done, Em, but she's just a very unwell lady struggling with a miserable disease. Arthritis is..."

Emma stopped dead. "Don't you dare defend her, Ro! This is about more than her attempting to murder me or my baby, it's about other things too."

"What?" Rohan looked shocked, his brow knitted in disbelief. "She did what?" He shook his head in confusion and then something else lit his eyes. "Ok, ok. Now you sound like my crazy brother." Rohan pulled Emma in close to him as they found somewhere to stand opposite the school door where Nicky would blast out with Mo like a cyclone. He kissed Emma's temple and squeezed her. "Nothing's more important than you and Nicky, Em. Please believe me?"

"No! I don't believe you, Ro." Emma pushed at Rohan's chest as her heart constricted with the truth of

Anton's complaint. Rohan wouldn't, or couldn't believe his mother was a cold blooded murderess.

"Oh, Emma!" Felicity clicked out into the playground in her high heels, drawing the attention of the waiting parents. She looked at Rohan with fear in her eyes but when she turned to face Emma, it was with an expression of hatred. Rohan made no attempt to let go of her and embarrassed, Emma wriggled free.

She swallowed and tried to keep the guilt from her expression. "Hi, Felicity." She distracted herself inwardly with the thought that every time she said the woman's name, she felt it should be accompanied by some kind of loose limbed John Travolta move. Emma worked hard to disguise the jealousy in her eyes at the way Felicity looked adoringly at Rohan. She wanted to scream and stamp and punch Felicity in the head, but knew she couldn't. If she didn't want him, it was cruel to engineer his life so he would be alone. *But I do want him*, the confused little voice whispered in Emma's head and she beat it down with gritted teeth and determination.

Felicity smiled up at Rohan and he nodded, a small upward gesture which betrayed extreme disinterest. Emma felt sorry for the glitzy woman as she battled valiantly for her boyfriend's attention, failing to raise even a smile in the very public forum. *Boyfriend*, Emma reminded herself. *Felicity's boyfriend, not yours.*

"Have you got a minute?" Felicity successfully shed Emma away from the herd, taking her over to a section of wall where she wouldn't be overheard. She faced Emma with a precision of movement which made the other woman clench her fists in her pockets just in case. "The headmaster wants to see you," she said coldly. "He's got some work you might be interested in. I vouched for you, thinking Rohan might be grateful if I helped his *stepsister* out. Now I'm regretting it." Felicity leaned in conspiratorially towards Emma. "Are you and my boyfriend having an affair?"

"Er, no." Emma regretted the doubt in her voice.

Felicity postured in front of her, tapping the toe of a red stiletto on the concrete playground. Emma gulped as the happy smile painted onto the ground under her foot was pounded in the face. "Well you're looking pretty cosy," *tap, tap, tap*, "but I don't have any choice but to believe you." She shot a look across at Rohan as he watched the exit for Nicky with an air of excited anticipation. "You know he's..." she looked around her and lowered her voice. "You know he's impotent, don't you?"

Emma's eyes widened in shock at Felicity's revelation. Then she shook her head in denial. "I don't think..."

"He is!" Felicity hissed, darting a look at Rohan, filled suddenly more with nervous tension than spite. "Every time we get anywhere near the point of..."

"La, la, la!" Everyone stared as Emma wedged her fingers into her ears to dull out the personal details of Rohan's inner workings. "That's really none of my business! And if that's the case, why are you asking me..." she lowered her voice and shot an agonised look towards the beautiful blonde Russian man who stood in the playground, legs slightly splayed and his hands shoved into his pockets. His eyes were trained on the doors with furious intensity. "Why are you asking me a stupid question like, are we having an affair? What's wrong with you?"

Felicity heaved out a sigh of exasperation. "Ok, fine. I'm just losing patience, I guess and wanted someone to blame. He's definitely been a lot more distracted since you turned up, not that he was particularly attentive before! I apologise. It was a stupid question really because you're related. That would be so yuk!"

Emma paused, speechless as Felicity clip clopped away in the direction of the front office, expecting her to follow. A bell sounded, pealing into the concrete and brick space like a claxon. Children clad in woolly scarves, hats and warm clothes poured from the building and congregated round the entrance, looking for their responsible adult before charging forwards with pictures, library bags and spare or soiled clothing. Teachers kept head counts and nodded to parents as they handed over their charges and then suddenly in the doorway was Nicky. He cast around for Emma through huge blue eyes which glittered in the smattering of winter sun. The colour of a calm lake, they settled on Emma and turned up at the corners in an effortless smile. He raked the playground and then patted his teacher on the leg and spoke to her. She smiled and nodded at Emma's little boy. His faded puffer jacket was open and his white polo shirt hung out of trousers a bit too big for him. His library bag bashed his kneecaps as he skipped down the stairs. He tripped a little on his spindly legs and Emma held her breath but it wasn't to her that he rushed.

Rohan scooped him up with a grin and swung him round, much to Nicky's delight and the jealousy of every other child in their vicinity. Farrell whined and wagged his tail so hard his bum came up off the floor a few inches and leaves and bits of gravel swam around his back end like the detritus from a road sweeper. Emma's brow knitted and the brown eyes in her pretty face grew dark as coals.

"Come on!" Felicity walked back for her, curiosity piquing her soft lips and cold blue eyes. The wind ruffled her perfectly curled blonde hair and she frowned. "Mr Dalton's waiting to see you. He has important things to do."

Emma pulled herself away from the sight of her son enjoying Rohan's company, recognising the green snakelike fingers of jealousy settling in her soul. Mel smiled and waved at her from the exit and Emma smiled and acknowledged her with a roll of her eyes. *I'm becoming a nasty person*, Emma chided herself sadly, no longer feeling the prevalent sense of optimism she usually did. She felt lonely without it and had nothing but bitterness to fill the gap.

"Ah, Mrs Harrington," the headmaster intoned in a deep baritone. His cauliflower ears and twisted nose on an otherwise handsome face, bore testament to his rugby career. His diarrhoea brown suit had seen better days but the man exuded enough confidence for it not to matter. He was someone who got up each morning and went to work for the thrill of seeing the children in his care and satisfaction emanated from him like a cannabis haze.

The urge to correct him on her marital status came and went as Emma remembered the lecherous employer from her last school. Felicity looked at her again with a sideways pout and Emma hid her smirk. Even if the woman ran back to her filing cabinet and checked Nicky's enrolment form, Emma knew she hadn't ticked the box which betrayed her as *married, single* or somewhat worryingly...*other*. The headmaster beamed as though Emma was the giver of a fine present he had always coveted. A missing side tooth made the experience a little freaky. "Walk with me!" he said with great excitement.

The journey down the corridor was not easy. The school population of four hundred tiny, fragile bodies should have left the premises by now, but once the word went out that their halo wearing headmaster was on walkabout, all hell broke loose. Children appeared on every side of him as his small stature bustled along the corridor towards a staircase Emma hadn't noticed previously.

"Mr D, I done this picture for you!"

"Mr D, is your wife all better now after her hystericalectomy? Mum got sweets for her but the dog ate them."

"Mr D, look at my new shoes."

"What ya doin' Mr D?"

"Where ya goin' Mr D?"

Emma surged along in the bodies which thronged around her like floodwaters. The man was like a demigod to this miniature fan crowd. At the bottom of the stairs to the mezzanine floor he stopped and turned, holding out his arms like a televangelist about to ask for money. "Well, children," he said in a sing-song storyteller's voice. "See you all tomorrow."

There was a hum of disappointment and the bodies dribbled away like flotsam, back to their bewildered parents outside in the cold. Mr Dalton beamed at Emma. "I love this job." He skipped up the stairs ahead of her. Emma followed, but at the sound of Felicity's high heels clipping up the stairs behind them, the headmaster turned and bestowed a look of utter benevolence on her. "You can leave early, Miss Prince. I'll just show Mrs Harrington the *artifacts*." He said the last word as though summoning up an air of mystery and his eyes popped with excitement. He skipped up the fifteen stairs like a mountain goat and entered the door at the top.

The upper level was packed wall to wall with computers and Emma waited patiently while the man opened a door which seemed to disappear into the roof cavity. His voice echoed oddly as Mr Dalton continued to speak inside the cavernous space. "Your son tells me you're looking for work and amazing at this!" he boomed. Emma heard the sound of boxes shifting about and her heart sank. *Lunch monitor, kitchen hand, chief stapler, anything but...*

"Oof!" The headmaster emerged from the half-height doorway in a rush, bringing with him a cloud of dust, a damp cardboard box and the smell which every good archivist dreads. *Mildew.* Undeterred, Mr Dalton got up and went back in for more. "It's paid work," his voice came again, repeating itself as it reverberated off beams and slate tiles Emma couldn't see. "Let's start at fifteen hours a week and see how we go." He emerged with a nasty looking cobweb hanging over his left ear. Then he spoke the familiar but terrible words which had suddenly placed the neglected boxes firmly in the spotlight. "It's our hundred and fiftieth celebration next year."

"When next year?" Emma's voice sounded flat next to the man's exuberance.

"December," he replied. "So that gives you a year to get it ready. That's plenty of time."

Emma eyed the box of tarnished trophies, mouldy photographs and cracked frames. Her eyes flicked back to the hopeful man in front of her. She couldn't raise a child on fifteen hours a week at minimum wage and she couldn't impose on Rohan any longer. Emma bit her lip and looked doubtful. Mr Dalton smiled at her and her eyes widened as a spider trotted up the side of his head and sat on top of his ear. She swallowed and to her dismay, the man clapped his hands. "Fantastic!" He reached forward with filthy hands and clasped hers in a bearlike grip. "Welcome to the team! I'll get our caretaker to bring the rest out."

"How many are there?" Emma heard the wobble in her voice.

"Oh heaps!" he said, sounding thrilled. "Look!" He opened his arms like a circus master and Emma poked her head under the dusty lintel. A dim light bulb lit the whole area which resembled something off an Indiana Jones movie. The makeshift room was covered in brown cardboard boxes in various states of decay and Emma's heart sank to her toes. The life and history of this treasured landmark lay in a field of neglect, far more than a year's work.

"I'll need a budget if I'm to sort this lot out," she said. "Are you sure you can afford it?"

"Oh yes!" Mr D grinned like an epitome of the Cheshire Cat. "We've got a committee and everything."

Emma emerged from the school door feeling daunted. The playground was empty and she felt like the last prisoner to emerge from a third world jail, greeted by almost nobody. Almost, because three people and a tail wagging dog waited patiently for her arrival. Rohan sat on the bench which lined the playground, its surface worn down by years of small bottoms and naughty, clambering feet. His elbows rested on his knees and his head hung low, peering at the floor with an intense expression. Cuddled up tightly next to him in a furry coat which doubled her size, was Felicity. Nicky ran around a small court painted onto the concrete, intent on his mind numbing activity; having shut himself off from the world.

As Emma walked towards them, Rohan stood quickly and Nicky deviated his pattern to include her in its new trajectory. Felicity stood and slipped her arm through Rohan's, eyeing Emma with enough curiosity to make her feel like a butterfly pinned to a collector's board. "Did you take the job?" she asked.

Emma nodded. "Yeah. It'll be a start."

"We stayin' down here?" Nicky asked, jumping up and down next to her.

"I'd like to." Emma squatted down next to him. "But it doesn't pay very well so I'll need to get another job in the afternoons so I can afford to get us a house."

Nicky's face dropped into a sad pout. "But we live with Ro and Farrell."

"Not forever, sweetheart. You know that. Only when he goes away, so we can look after Faz. He won't want us there indefinitely. He has his own life and he's been kind enough already." Emma refused to look at Rohan's blue eyes, feeling his stare fixed on her face. She flushed with guilt and embarrassment. "Come on, let's go home. It's cold."

The little party progressed through the park, sneaking out of the playground just before the smiling, elderly caretaker closed and locked the side gate. Rohan walked ahead with the dog, Felicity clamped to his arm, dragging her heels in a sexy-don't-care kind of way. Nicky held Emma's hand and sulked. She dropped back to talk to her son, noticing how the dog kept trying to turn to be with her. Darkness crept around them, extending its long fingers out to touch them as the lamps in the park flicked on overhead. "What's up, baby?" Emma asked quietly, seeing Nicky shrug. "I thought you'd be pleased I'd got a job. Don't you want to stay here? Would you rather go back up north?"

"No." He didn't sound sure.

Emma sighed. "Maybe have a little think about what the problem might be, then we'll talk it out." She squeezed his hand, not pushing him to rationalise or explain something clearly too big to describe. It usually worked. As they crossed the Northampton Road, delaying so they ended up in the centre aisle with Rohan and Felicity strolling ahead, Nicky tugged on Emma's hand.

"Mummy, I don't like her. I don't like it when she cuddles Uncle Ro. He belongs to us, not her."

Emma breathed out heavily and picked her words as they dodged traffic to make it to the other side. "She's his girlfriend, babe. That's what they do. When you get a girlfriend, she'll hang off you like that and keep kissing your face."

"Yuk!" Nicky screwed his handsome features into a horrible squished mess. "I won't be doing kissings and stuff. She can climb trees wiv me and play soccer. I ain't doin' none of that sloppy crap!"

"Language, Nicky..."

"I know, I know. I'm sorry. It just popped out. I wanted to say, shit, but I chose that one instead. I didn't wanna say shit out loud."

"You just said it twice, to me!" Emma complained and Nicky tugged on her hand.

"Yeah but you don't count, Mummy. I can be myself wiv you, can't I?" The child's earnest face was so open and honest, Emma found it hard to reprimand him but knew she had to. They spent the rest of the walk home along narrow streets and lit pathways, discussing the merits and drawbacks of the dictionary according to Fat Brian and Big Jason.

CHAPTER SIXTEEN

Felicity hung around so Emma dished up the casserole she prepared earlier in the day and waited for Nicky to eat at the breakfast bar. Rohan looked disappointed when Emma brought portions for him and Felicity into the dining room. "You aren't eating with us?" he asked and Emma shook her head and eyed Felicity sideways.

Nicky picked, but didn't seem to enjoy it. His behaviour seemed edgy and not like him and Emma grew concerned. "What's wrong, sweetheart? Don't you like it?"

"I love it," Nicky replied, absentmindedly torturing a carrot. "That woman makes my hunger go away."

"Felicity? Why?"

"No reason." Nicky pursed his lips and pushed his fork into the remains of his casserole, before lying the handle on the side of the dish with a sigh.

"Hop in the shower, baby," Emma said as he carried his dish to the sink. "I'll come up and read your library book to you."

"Ok." His sweet little face brightened and he padded off upstairs. Emma heard him trip over his own feet half way up and waited. He picked himself up and carried on.

"That was gorgeous." Rohan sidled up behind her as Emma rinsed Nicky's plate and put it in the dishwasher. "I could get used to having a housekeeper." He pushed her long hair away from her neck and kissed the soft pink flesh.

Emma pushed him away instantly with a frantic glance at the kitchen door. "Stop it!" she told him. "Your girlfriend's already asking if we're having an affair. I don't need this, Ro. We'll be out of your hair as soon as we can."

"I don't want you out of my hair." Rohan reached for Emma's waist and she jabbed him in the privates with her elbow as she stood up after settling Nicky's plate in the rack. Rohan grimaced and grabbed his crotch through his pants. "Ow!"

"Oh my gosh, sorry. Do you have to be careful with…you know?"

"With what?" Rohan frowned and looked confused, rubbing between his legs with great care.

"Nothing." Emma slammed the dishwasher closed and stood up. "I'll sort Nicky out and then stay with him for a while so you can have some alone time with…thingy in there. It must be awkward with us around all the time."

"It's not awkward!" Rohan huffed angrily and put his hand behind Emma's neck. His grip was rough and he pulled her into him and kissed her on the lips. It wasn't a gentle action and Emma slapped him round the face.

"Everything all right in there," Felicity called, gliding into the kitchen. Rohan's face went immediately blank, leaving Emma flushed and upset.

"All fine, thanks," she replied woodenly, shooting a nasty look at Rohan. "I'm just off to bed. Thanks for sorting out the job for me, I'm really grateful." Emma plastered the smile onto her face. "Mr Dalton wants me to start next term so I've got about seven weeks to sort myself out." She sidled past the pretty woman, who leaned against the doorframe as though pole dancing. "Have a good night!" Emma sauntered up the stairs with affected casualness, shuddering as she reached the first landing.

"They make you wanna puke, don't they?" Nicky said, standing outside his bedroom door completely naked.

"A bit," Emma admitted. "What's the matter?"

"You took my pyjamas to wash and I don't have no more to put on."

Emma groaned. "Sorry, baby. I did buy you some more from the shops but they're still wet too."

"I can sleep in the nudd," Nicky giggled.

"No, you can't sleep nuddy," Emma told him, smirking behind his back. "You might scare Farrell." She rifled around in her suitcase and found an old tee shirt of hers. "Here you go, wear this for tonight."

Nicky slipped it over his skinny body and grinned at his mother. "Ta, Mum. You're doin' a good job ya know?"

"I wish I felt like it," she said sadly and the child put his arms around her, hugging her protectively.

"Can't be helped," he said, sounding just like her and Emma smiled, hearing her own words coming back to her.

"Right then, mister. Story time!"

Emma woke at midnight to find the lamp still on and her clothes cutting into her body. She slipped her bra off from underneath her tee shirt, a skill she never rued learning and left her knickers on. Pulling the curtains closed, she spied the dark shape of a man in the garden and held her breath. For a second she wondered what Rohan would be doing outside in the darkness but the shape was less muscular than his. The figure moved and the urge to cry out was instant, but

Emma clapped her hand over her mouth. *What if Felicity was in Rohan's bed? That would be awkward if they came rushing out together.* Emma knew inwardly she wouldn't be able to bear it; the thought of the perfectly manicured hands moving over her husband's lithe body. She choked back the involuntary vision and took a deep breath, not dwelling on the irony that the stranger outside posed less threat than the blonde bombshell inside.

Emma watched as the masculine shape moved away down the garden. She closed the curtains with a swish, choosing not to care. *You're imagining things*, she told herself. The dog made no sound from downstairs and Emma climbed into bed with her son, cuddling his small body from behind and falling asleep with his downy blonde hair in her face.

Rohan went to work the next day, dressing in a crisp white shirt and suit pants and donning a smart matching jacket over the top. He looked like some kind of tall, handsome superhero. "*Do svidaniya*," he said to Nicky as he left, ruffling the child's hair under tender fingers.

"*Do svidaniya, dorogaya*," Nicky replied in an instinctive reflex and Rohan stopped sharply, his hand still on the child's soft blonde hair.

Emma kept very still, knowing Rohan's eyes bored into the back of her head as she pushed a packet of crisps and a chocolate bar into Nicky's library bag for his snack. She shoved an apple in there as an afterthought, her fingers shaking as she tipped her cap at the healthy snack brigade.

Rohan took Emma gently in his arms and held her tightly, crushing her face into his chest. Feeling grateful she hadn't put lipstick on yet, Emma synced her body with his in an old, timeless dance and exhaled. Rohan tipped her head back with his fingers on her chin and kissed her lips, a soft caress that expressed more than his words ever would. "*Izvinite*," he whispered, apologising, presumably for his behaviour the previous night. "How does Nicky know the Russian word for darling?" His lips were very close to her ear and his breath kissed it sensuously.

"No idea," Emma lied. "He's a bright kid." She pushed Rohan away and he released her with obvious reluctance. "Are you back tonight?"

He nodded. "Yeah. I'll walk to the station and leave you the car. The keys are hanging up in the hall cupboard. Don't ding it! Oh and if you need the computer, the password is *neudachnik*."

Nicky snorted behind him and whipped his library bag from the worktop. "Loser! That's funny." He made an 'L' shape with his index finger and thumb and giggled. "Mummy, Uncle Ro's password is *loser!*" He skipped through to the hallway to put his shoes on, singing softly to himself.

Rohan pushed his fingers up the side of Emma's cheek and round underneath her hair. She closed her eyes against familiar, enticing sensations. He leaned in close to her face and pressed his forehead against hers. "Anton never spoke Russian, Em. He hated it. You're not telling me the truth about anything, are you? We'll talk about this later."

"Whatever!" Emma thought she managed to escape until she felt Rohan's strong hands around her waist, pulling her in from behind. His body felt good pressed against her back and she quashed the soft moan.

"We *will* talk later, *lyubovnik!*"

Emma shuddered at the connotations of the word,

lover and headed quickly to the door as Rohan released her. She watched him stride down the garden to the parking area beyond the orchard and saw him opening the huge wooden gate out onto the lane behind the house.

"Come on, Mum!" Nicky complained, clinking the dog's lead. Farrell dashed around the hallway in excitement, eager to walk through the park and chase squirrels.

Emma stuffed her feet into her holey boots, wincing at her healing soles as she took her son's hand, carefully locking up and setting the burglar alarm. She dreaded the questions Rohan might ask her later, knowing it would mean she had to leave.

CHAPTER SEVENTEEN

Rohan was late home and Emma managed to feign sleep when he finally knocked on her door after ten o'clock. She heaved a sigh of relief as she heard him moving around his room next door, grateful for the loss of his interrogation hanging over her head. *This was the stupidest thing you ever did*, Emma Harrington, she rebuked herself. *Why would you come here? All these years of staying safe from her. You're a fool!* She agonised, tossing and turning until sleep claimed her.

Emma's dreams were tortured. Alanya stood before her clutching Nicky's arm and laughing victoriously. Emma screamed at her son to come back to her but the thunder drowned her out and a cruel wind stole her words from her mouth. Nicky smiled and waved at her, as gullible and foolish as his father. In front of Emma's face, Alanya produced a steaming mug of greenish liquid and held it out to Nicky. She looked Emma in the eyes as the child cupped the mug in his tiny hands and drank.

"No!" Emma's gasp woke her up. Sweat ran down the side of her face and the sheet underneath her felt soaked. Her breath came in oxygen-less pants and she hugged her knees into her chest. Mrs Clarke's enquiring face wafted past Emma's inner vision, a remnant of the embarrassing conversation that morning.

"So nobody else is allowed to collect your son from school?" she asked, writing something in the margin of the register, next to Nicky's name.

"No, nobody." Emma stood stiffly, holding her body rigid and praying the dog would sit nicely by her left leg and not do something silly in the classroom filled with exciting scents. "Only me. I don't want anyone else taking him home, not even..." She sighed and raised her eyes to the ceiling. *Not even Rohan.*

"That's perfectly fine, Miss Harrington. We have lots of mothers in the same position. Please don't feel embarrassed about it. We have to protect our children, don't we?"

Emma nodded as the kindness made her eyes fill with tears. "Yes," she whispered. "Please tell me, will the school secretary be able to see that note?"

Mrs Clarke knitted her brow and took a step back. "Well, potentially, yes. But to be honest, there's another four children in this class with exactly the same note next to their name, so it's unlikely she'd bother to look. And even if she did, she wouldn't be allowed to discuss it with anyone outside the school."

Emma raised her eyebrows in disbelief and picked up an odd look from the pretty teacher. Mrs Clarke doubted the ability of her colleague to keep secrets too. It was written on her very professional face and it terrified Emma. With wide, brown eyes and a frightened face, Emma leaned in closer to the teacher, avoiding the influx of excited children pouring into the room behind her. "Nobody's allowed to talk to the children at playtimes, are they?" she asked quietly and Mrs Clarke shook her head with a definite, confident movement.

"Absolutely not. All the smaller children are in the courtyard and only the juniors are allowed into the ball courts. A teacher supervises them both in and out at all times. So please don't worry about that. Is there someone in particular we need to be aware of?"

Emma gulped. Alanya's murders were undetected as yet and Emma realised her accusations would seem little more than slanderous when said out loud. Rohan never believed Anton's theories about his father's mysterious death and had been disturbed by the sudden death of Emma's. He refused to hear any discussions implicating his mother and so the teenagers gave up eventually, whispering in corners and finding no evidence with which to prove their case. Emma shook her head. "I just don't want strangers having access to my son," she said, her voice sounding a little huffy. "Sorry," she added.

"It's fine," Mrs Clarke had said, patting Emma's hand in sympathy.

A clap of thunder overhead shocked Emma out of her cringe worthy memory. She jumped and counted the seconds between the second growl from the sky and the first flash of lightning which lit up the bedroom. It gave context to her weird dreams and she relaxed a little and remained sitting up in bed, watching the fireworks unfold over her street view.

The storm was terrible, edging nearer with each flash and roar until it raged directly overhead. It rocked the house with horrific rumbles and lightning shone like a strobe every few seconds. Emma heard a muted woof from Farrell downstairs in the kitchen and then the house was silent against the backdrop of the pyrotechnics outside. Fear drove Emma to Nicky's room for comfort, jumping at a particularly big crash from the swollen sky while the next bolt of lightning lit up her son's bedroom and his beautiful, sleeping face.

Emma sighed and pulled the threadbare cardigan

more closely around her shoulders. She peered into the gloom of the long back garden, enduring yet another floodlit moment. Emma froze. Her breath felt caught as everything stopped, adrenaline coursing through her blood. The same man stood in the garden looking up at the window. He was tall and well built, dressed entirely in black. Another flash of lightning backlit his slender silhouette and Emma gasped. The usually silent dog barked again, not at the storm but at the intruder.

Emma stepped back from the window and glanced at her son. *I didn't imagine it!* Nicky slept peacefully despite the din, comfortable and safe in his new surroundings. She peeped from behind the curtains and watched the man turn. He left the flat area of concrete outside the back door and used the stepping stones to make his way down the lawn. The previous moonless night had allowed him to slink around the property like a spectre, but the lightning show robbed him of the cover of darkness. Emma listened but couldn't distinguish his footsteps on the crunchy pea gravel from the sudden, pounding rain. He hovered for a moment under the archway leading to the orchard and looked back up at the window. And her.

Emma couldn't see his eyes. They were shrouded in the blackness of his figure but she felt them on her face, burning like lit matches held too close to the skin. He turned and walked away, trudging steadily through Rohan's property as though out for a stroll, his hands swinging gently by his sides. Emma lost him as he blended into the darkness near the large glasshouse, half way down the property and she jumped as another thunderous groan tore the atmosphere apart. Farrell barked again as another flash of lightning lit up the shiny metal of Rohan's car in its car port beyond the orchard.

Closing the curtains to keep Nicky undisturbed by the pyrotechnics outside, Emma left the bedroom and knocked softly on Rohan's door. Two sightings couldn't be the result of an overactive imagination. The man had to be the one referred to by the useless private detective. Hearing no sound from Rohan's room, Emma ventured in. The fear of disturbing Felicity and him in bed overrode her alarm at the stranger, whom she decided must be stealing Rohan's expensive black car. The room was silent and the floorboards slippery and polished under Emma's worn socks. The curtains were partly open, displaying the impressive flashes outside. As Emma approached the side of the bed where a lumpy shape lay still, a beautiful bolt of lightning leaped from the blackness and licked the earth. Emma stood next to the bed and gasped at the zig-zagging thing of pure wonder, at the same time as the house shook again with the aching of the sky.

A small squeak escaped her as a hard vice closed around her throat, instantly choking her. Emma's fingers clawed as her lungs screamed for air and she found herself pulled downwards until she contacted something knotty. Her body arced painfully backwards and she was denied the ability to even cry out, her windpipe crushed under strong fingers. The voice swearing in Russian was husky and low and Emma's panic abated as she recognised Rohan. But the problem of her asphyxiation remained. She let go of the hand at her throat and lashed out at the face above her as the lightning betrayed its position. She felt bone underneath her knuckles and heard the impact. Her fingers smarted as though broken and an ache ran up her arm and into her shoulder. There was a groan and the choke hold ended with an abruptness that left her sliding down the side of the bed and onto the floor.

"Shit!" Rohan's voice contained a mixture of irritation and horror. The bedside light snapped on as Emma took rasping breaths and clutched her throat. In the intrusive yellow light, she saw Rohan's face staring down on her, a line of blood dribbling from one nostril. "Em! What the hell are you doing?"

Emma coughed and choked, unable to answer. Rohan leaned further out of the bed and she felt a stab of fury that he didn't even bother getting up. Regaining control of her bodily functions, Emma kept one hand at her throat and put the other on the ground to push herself up. Her fingers contacted something shiny and hard which rolled sideways and clinked against the leg of the bed. She quested for it, sensing the surface of a hollow metal bar. *I am so gonna hurt him*, came the instant thought as she gripped it.

"Don't you dare!" Rohan spoke through gritted teeth and Emma forgot the ready weapon in her indignation.

"You just tried to throttle me!" Her voice sounded croaky and strained.

"Never creep up on a soldier!" Rohan bit back, leaning further over the side and hauling Emma up two handed. His biceps flexed in the lamp light, fed by ridged veins carrying blood and oxygen to the muscular chest and shoulders. Emma clawed her throat and used the other free hand to slap Rohan. Her aim was off and the blow landed, futile and empty against his defined pectorals. His skin felt warm and welcoming. "*Svin'ya!*" she taunted him in his mother tongue. *Pig!*

Rohan snorted like one and pulled Emma into him. He lay on his back, his breathing heavy, his heartbeat thunderous against her ear. He felt so alive. "I came to tell you there was someone in the garden," she hissed, sitting up and smoothing her fingers over her throat.

"No way!" He dismissed it to her overactive imagination and Emma's sense of injustice flared.

"There was! He looked right at me. The lightning lit him up really well! Why do you never believe anything I say?" A rumble of thunder moved overhead, competing with the end of Emma's sentence. The storm began to move off and a sheet of rain pounded the window behind Rohan's head.

"Well, he'll be getting wet, whoever he is and I'm not going out there now." Rohan exhaled and fixed his arms around Emma's waist. She experienced a rush of hormones at the way his fingers stroked her flesh in the gap between her too-small top and her flimsy pyjama bottoms. The retreating adrenaline left an unclaimed void which quickly filled with desire. Rohan wiped the blood on his bicep, a regal dip of his head which only smudged it across his cheek.

"Ro!" Emma turned and reached for his face, running her soft pads across his full, expressive lips. She felt his stubble under her fingers and imagined it on the tender places of her neck and shoulders. His naked torso, warm and inviting called to her, blurring the lines which made Emma fear his mother and the stranger outside. Suddenly there didn't seem any harm in satiating a need. *They were still married.*

With a sigh, Emma dipped forward to kiss him, wishing she'd cleaned her teeth before she went on her nighttime wanderings. Her eyes were shrouded in the darkness but Rohan's were lit spectacularly by the bulb next to him. His pupils dilated with lust and Emma held her breath, desperate for him to begin his lovemaking. Her body remembered how they learned the art together and she yearned for him to touch her.

Then Rohan's face clouded and something else took over, claiming and replacing it with a latent fear. "No, Em." He put his hand out and halted her downward progress, making her feel embarrassed and foolish. Rohan's fingers splayed against her chest, pushing on her ribcage as though fending off something awful. His face closed to her, encased in an agonising numbness and Emma bit her lip and sat up. "Go back to bed," Rohan said coldly. "Get some sleep."

Emma fled from the room, closing the door quietly against her humiliation. A muted flash lit up her room as the storm moved off east, highlighting her messy, unmade bed, the sheets pulled back and the mattress cold and lonely. She turned her back on it, refusing to accept her aloneness and padded down the hallway to Nicky's room. Emma snuggled in her son's bed, comforted by the small sighs escaping his rosebud lips. *Screw you, Rohan Andreyev*, Emma sulked in the darkness, knowing she would have and not comforted by the realisation of how much she still wanted to.

CHAPTER EIGHTEEN

"Mummy, why are there other letters in my name?" Nicky scrawled his name on the top of the plan for the slingshot.

"Sorry, darling. What do you mean?"

Nicky sat back in his seat as though contemplating the mysteries of life. Rohan smirked and watched him out of the corner of his eye, pushing his dinner plate away and loosening his tie. Emma avoided his studious gaze, last night's awkwardness hanging over her like a curtain of barbed wire. "Well, you call me Nicky which is my short name and it has a *curly ker* in it and a *yer*, but there isn't any of them in my proper name. So how did they get in there?" He studied Emma with a seriousness beyond his years.

His mother shrugged and looked down at the shorts she darned. She really didn't want to have this conversation in front of Rohan. "It's just your calling name. I called you it when you were a baby and when I had to write it down, I wrote it how it sounded.

Nicky watched her with his eyes narrowed. Then he tapped his pencil on the name he had scrawled on the top of his homework in large, uneven letters. "But the letters aren't the same," he persisted. "My new friend is called Mohammed and his short name is *M-o*, so he can fit his names together." His brow wrinkled in concentration. "Mine don't fit."

"I don't know, Nicky," Emma let the held breath out slowly, keeping her eyes down. "Get rid of them if you don't want them there."

Her son placed a skinny finger over the offending two letters of his name and pulled a face. "No! It looks funny."

"It's because you're used to seeing it that way," Emma soothed. "It really doesn't matter."

Rohan pulled his laptop towards him, watching the exchange with obvious interest. Emma cringed, trying to think of ways to head her son off without making a big scene.

"Write my other name then. Do it on my spellings," Nicky said and pushed his paper and pencil across to Emma. She eyed the paper nervously and shook her head.

"I'll do it later, but not on your homework. Mrs Clarke won't know who did it."

"Yes she will! It's got my other name on the register. She keeps reading it out by mistake and all the other children laugh at me. I've got four names and they've only got three. And why's my last name different on the register too? What if the school burns down and the fireman don't know to shout for Nicky Harrington and shout for..."

"Nicky!" Emma snapped. "Stop prevaricating. It's nearly bedtime so get on with your spellings, please."

Nicky postured. "But I want you to write it. Fine! Will you do it if I get some other paper then?" he pleaded, with a whine in his voice. He slipped off the chair and pattered into the hallway. Emma heard the Velcro on his library bag make its distinctive ripping noise as Nicky pulled it open. "Here you go." The paper fluttered from his hand onto the table in front of Emma and he leaned across her to retrieve the pencil.

"Nicky! I said later. I have to sew your name label

back into your shorts seeing as you managed to rip it off already."

The small boy pouted. "Sorry Mummy. You're a fast writer. Do it really quickly."

Emma steeled herself, placing the shorts on the table to block Rohan's view of the paper. She rapidly scribbled Nicky's full name onto the rumpled sheet and pushed it into the boy's chest. "Here. Now go and get ready for bed."

Nicky peered at the paper and formed the letters silently with his rosebud lips. Emma glanced at Rohan and saw him remove his reading glasses and lay them on the table. He rubbed his eyes and fixed his gaze on the child. He looked intrigued and Emma controlled her breathing, knowing she was the problem. Nicky's antics were vaguely entertaining, but Emma's reaction caused Rohan's antenna for trouble to perk up with curiosity. "Bed, Nicky!"

"Ok. But can I do my homework upstairs when I'm in my pyjamas? I'll get told off by the teacher if I haven't done it. She said she'll sell us down the market." Nicky rolled his blue eyes and postured, drawing a sigh from Emma.

"Fine. Hurry up."

The boy gathered his pencil crayons and books together, hefting them under his arm with a grunt. "Oh, I got that book you like out of the library, Mummy. I know you love reading it."

"Cool, thanks. What's one more time on top of four hundred and fifty?" Emma lifted herself from the chair, feeling her legs wobble underneath her. "Hop upstairs and I'll come now." She gathered her sewing and walked towards the door without looking back at Rohan. As Nicky skipped from the room in his underpants, the paper slithered from his arms and he stopped so quickly, Emma nearly ran up the back of him.

"Oops!"

"Leave it, Nicky. I'll get it. Please stop fluffing around and delaying. I'll end up cross and there'll be no story time."

"Fine!" He humphed, comical with his pale skinny legs sticking out of his tiny pants and his arms full. "It doesn't matter. You can put it in the rubbish. I like Nicky best anyway. Sid says it's a cool name."

"Ok. Now go!" Emma balanced the needle and thread in her left hand, bundling the shorts under her arm. She sighed as Nicky cascaded coloured pencils from his open wallet, oblivious as he skipped into the hallway and up the stairs. She bent, retrieving a blue crayon and a green one before lurching for an orange one near the skirting board. Emma heard the scrape of Rohan's chair legs on the floor and dropped all three crayons in her attempt to snatch up the fallen paper before he got to it. In the fracas, Emma banged the dining room door shut with her bottom. "Leave it!" she snapped and the shorts tumbled to the floorboards, joining the crayons.

Rohan grabbed the paper and lifted it above his head, his tall body and long arms easily defeating Emma. She jumped up and down on the spot with her arm outstretched, banging her breasts into his chest. As Rohan brought the paper lower to read Emma's writing, she fought with dirty tactics and unable to reach, covered his eyes with her hands. "Stop being an idiot!" she complained. "Just give it here. I need to get upstairs before Nicky floods the bathroom."

Rohan laughed and jabbed Emma in the ribs on the

ticklish spot he knew so well. She squeaked and covered her mouth with her hand, freeing up one eye for Rohan. "What's the big deal?" he chuckled, sensing the anxiety coming off her in waves.

"Please Ro, just give it to me," she begged, her voice growing hoarse.

"Ok." He lowered the paper and handed it to Emma, who withdrew her remaining hand from his face.

"Thanks." She snatched it from him and balled it up tightly in her fist. Her neck bore a red flush that was more from nerves than exertion and she looked wrong footed. "I'll go and sort Nicky out," she said, bending to pick up the dropped items and scurrying from the room with haste. At the dog-leg on the stairs where the wooden balustrade curved up to the left, Emma looked down and saw Rohan standing where she left him. His head was bowed, his blonde hair flipped forward into his eyes and his hands were stuffed deep into his pockets. She felt a wave of sadness at her own cruelty and intercepted her naked son at his bedroom door. "How come you're not dressed yet?" she asked in annoyance and he gave her a coy grin.

"Just doin' a surprise," he beamed.

"Yeah? That's nice. Now get that bare bum in the bathroom or I might just surprise it with a slap," Emma joked, using the shared joviality to ground herself.

While Nicky splashed around in the bathroom sink in a pretence at washing for bed, Emma tore the paper into small pieces and flushed it down the ensuite toilet. "Coming here was a big mistake," she whispered to herself as the torn pieces swirled away. "Thank goodness our time's nearly up." She bit her lip and knew she didn't mean it.

Nicky looked cute in the huge bed as Emma tucked him in. "How did you get wet hair?" she asked him, tucking the buoyant curls behind his ear and smoothing them back from his damp forehead.

"It's annoying me now. I don't wanna be surf bum anymore. I want Uncle Ro to take me to the barber shop and get it snipped."

"I'll cut it," Emma volunteered but the child shook his head.

"No. I want boy-time with Uncle Ro."

Emma snorted. "Boy-time? Have you been reading women's magazines or something?"

"No!" Nicky pouted. "Sid has boy-time wiv his dad every Friday and the girls do nails and stuff. Can you ask him for me, please?"

"Look Nicky," Emma rested her chin on the pillow next to his. "We're just staying here for a little while to help Uncle Ro out with Farrell. It's probably best you don't get your hopes up. We won't be here long enough."

"But I luff 'im." The small boy's vibrant blue eyes lost their mischief and filled with the sheen of tears.

"That's awesome, mate. But it's not for keeps, ok? We have our own life and he has his. We can't push into his too much or he'll get fed up of us."

"Ok, Mummy. Please will you help me wiv my spellings and then read the story?"

Emma smiled and kissed her son, settling down into the bed with him. They made songs out of the spellings so Nicky could remember them for his test the next day and they sniggered and giggled at the ridiculousness of the sentences they made up to include the random root words. Then Emma read the story picture book, doing all the voices for the familiar characters, including a Scots pirate and a Russian teddy bear. When she closed the book finally, Nicky's eyelids drooped and his lips gripped his tiny thumb between them. In his hand he clutched an old blue teddy and Emma hunted surreptitiously for his favourite Action Man. Unable to find it, she hoped the boy didn't wake up crying for it and left the room, leaving the door slightly ajar.

Outside in the light of a small lamp, she almost fell over Rohan's legs. "Bloody hell!" she hissed. "What are you doing?"

"Just listening to you being a great mother," he said, keeping his voice low. He held his hands out, asking without words for her to pull him up and Emma bridled but did it anyway, almost overbalancing when he was upright. Rohan caught her, his hands in the small of her back, his eyes looking hard into hers. "I need to talk to you," he said, seriousness in his voice and Emma shoved at his firm chest until he let go of her.

"Can we do this tomorrow?" she asked, cringing. "I've still got four name tags to sew into Nick's clothes and two that fell off. I'm knackered."

"Get them. I'll help you," Rohan offered and Emma snorted.

"You're actually going to sew name tags into my son's sports kit?" she scoffed and he cocked an eyebrow at her.

"I can sew really good, thanks. I learned in the army, so there!"

"Ok." Emma smirked. "I'm not going to turn down good help. But I'm really not interested in talking so please don't start." She flounced off to fetch the abandoned clothing and the packet of labels, determined to shut any awkward conversations down instantly. Back in the hallway, Emma grew anxious as Rohan jerked his head towards the huge master bedroom. She followed him reluctantly in.

The room was very masculine, a blank canvas of grey, white and black, but it was very much Rohan's imprint on the decoration. The heavy furniture was stylish, black in colour but striking. Rohan indicated the bed and opened his hand to tell Emma to sit down. She eyed an armchair in the corner covetously but Rohan plumped the pillows up on one side of the bed and pushed her gently into a seated position.

"We can sit together and share the cotton and the labels," he said, lying next to her on the bed with his legs out straight in front of him. "Here, give me the stuff." He held his hand out.

Emma watched Rohan thread the needle, fascinated with the concentration on his chiselled face. He sucked the very end of the cotton and poked it at the eye of the sharp needle, smiling with satisfaction as it slipped easily through. He seized a pair of sports shorts and a label, marrying the two on the elasticated waistband. "No, not there," Emma said quickly, placing a restraining hand over Rohan's. She felt him shiver at her touch. "It's too stretchy on the waistband. The first time he puts them on, all the stitching will go. That's what happened before. Put it on the seam or the bottom of the leg. Then I'll write his name on it in pen."

Rohan turned the shorts the other way and started stitching. He was quick and neat and Emma raised an eyebrow in surprise. "How come you're stitching socks?" he asked, jerking his head towards her deftly moving fingers.

"He lost a sock already and the tags popped out of his shorts. His uniform back home was second hand so I guess the elastic wasn't so enthusiastic." Emma smiled a tight little movement of the lips, dreading the thought of returning to the dilapidated house on the dreadful little estate, especially without a job. She bit her lip against the unwanted tide of emotion and changed the subject. "What did you do at work today?"

"Nothing important. I wanted to talk to you about this." Rohan stopped sewing and reached sideways, producing a scrappy piece of paper from his bedside cupboard. He handed it to Emma. She read it and put her hand over her mouth as a wave of sickness pushed up her throat and took her breath away. The bed shuddered as she swung her legs over the side and thudded her feet to the floor, flinging the garments to one side.

"Whoa!" Rohan retrieved the fleeing needle, stabbing it into the uppermost sock, still managing to grab Emma one handed around the waist before she gathered herself enough to run.

"Let go of me!" she hissed, desperation leaking from her core.

"No!" Rohan dragged her backwards onto the bed, hauling her until she lay with her head on his thighs, both of them panting with the exertion. "You stay and talk about this! Stop running from me, Em. Do you hate me that much? What did you think I'd do?"

Emma felt like a fool laid on her back looking up at Rohan. His cheeks were flushed, blue eyes glittering in the unnatural light from the overhead bulb. His arm felt strong around her waist, pushing her breasts upwards like a freaky boob job and his biceps bulged as they strained against his work shirt. She covered her face with her hands to give her time and Rohan relaxed, his stomach muscles less firm against the side of Emma's head as he lay back against the pillows. She knew he watched her with intensity. She could feel it.

"Why do you always have to run?" Rohan's voice was soft, soothing and full of sadness. Emma couldn't bring herself to answer. "I don't think he means anything by it," he said, referring to the letter.

Emma groaned heavily from behind her hands. "Yes he does! He's saying I'm not enough for him."

Rohan released his arm from around her waist and Emma felt the coolness of its lack. To her surprise, he put both hands under her armpits and lifted her like a child, cradling her in his chest and stroking her face. "You can't think like that, *devotchka*. You're an amazing mother; I've seen you with him. Listening to you tonight reading that story was humbling."

"So why's he writing things like that to you?" she sniffed, fighting back tears of disappointment and guilt. "You're just some random male to him. Is he doing this without my knowledge to every guy he meets? That's dangerous as well as insulting!"

Emma pushed herself upright, kneeling on the bed with her legs touching the side of Rohan's thigh. She reached for the letter, casting agonised eyes over it again. '*Wil you b my daddy?*' She flapped the paper, channelling a heady mix of emotions through her dark eyes. Rohan wrenched the paper from her hand, leaving Emma holding a tiny corner of it.

"He'll hear you!" he chastised, looking at the childish scrawl again and biting his lip. He looked at Emma with defiance and shrugged. "What's so bad about this?"

She postured angrily and rolled her eyes, the teenage

girl not far below the surface after all. "Well firstly, he doesn't know you well enough to be asking things like that. It makes him vulnerable. Secondly, I don't want him getting attached to you because it will make it harder for us to leave. And thirdly..." Emma rubbed her eyes feeling suddenly exhausted.

"What's thirdly?" Rohan reached out and pulled her hand away from her face. He didn't let go of her wrist. "Thirdly?"

Emma shrugged. "He spelled things wrong. Look, he's only put one 'L' in will." She lurched for the paper but Rohan kept it away from her, holding it out to the other side of him.

"No." He shook his head. "Thirdly, he's my son and he and I both know it. I feel it in my chest every time I look at him so he must too. It makes me feel so confused..." Rohan raised his eyes to the ceiling and then closed them. "I dread to think what it's doing to his little heart." He opened sparkling blue eyes and fixed them on Emma's flaming cheeks. Rohan maintained his grip on her wrist and held the letter away from her, squinting slightly as he read it out loud.

'*Deer Ro. Pleez wil you b my daddy??? Can we do fings togevver? Can you tak me for hare snips like yors??? Love Nikolai xxx*'

Emma refused to look at Rohan as he repeated Nicky's full name. She kept her eyes closed and her jaw clenched hard to keep her silence. Her whole body felt stiff and unyielding and the silence in the room condemned her. "I think we should go," she said woodenly and tried to move. Rohan's grip on her wrist tightened.

"Nikolai? No wonder you didn't want me to see that bloody birth certificate. For what it's worth, Em, I worked it out the minute I saw him with you at Fred's wedding. I didn't need to see my family name handed down to my eldest son to realise it, Em. The drama at the school was a wobble but that's all. Don't you understand? It's more than biology, Em. It's like his spirit called out to me in this incredible connection. I just *knew*. Anton's handed down name was Stepanovich. He would never use mine, not under any circumstances. It's just not done. Now can we drop this whole pretence thing and work it out?"

Emma gulped. "No, I can't do this."

Rohan flexed his fingers on her wrist and it shook her arm. "I don't care, Em. I don't want to start talking about rights and lawyers. You might not love me like I love you but I want a relationship with my son. I've missed...so much, Em. I want to make it up to him."

Emma shook her head again. "I'm going home. Please leave us alone?" Her eyes begged as she turned them on him, the fear so prevalent it took Rohan's breath away.

"Em, what the hell's wrong?"

"You know! You always knew!" Emma exploded. She tried to jerk away and Rohan clasped her round the waist again. "Please, Ro, just let us go?"

"What is it Emma? What?" Bemusement and frustration creased Rohan's face as he grappled with Emma. She ended up underneath him. Her foot contacted Rohan's right shin and feeling a sharp sensation and thinking it was his switchblade, she panicked.

Rohan roared as she brought her knee up and connected with his groin. Curling into a ball, he let go of her. He groaned and rolled around on the bed in pain and Emma felt a stab of guilt as she backed away, hearing him hiss every curse word she had ever heard in a bilingual mix of English and Russian. He wiped at his watering eyes and Emma heard him exhale slowly as she reached the door. "Please, Emma? If it's not me, then who are you hiding him from?"

Emma turned the handle slowly and pulled the door towards her, ready to escape. Rohan sat up, one hand clamped firmly between his legs without shame. He wasn't coming after her. Emma licked her lips and took a steadying breath. "Your mother; Alanya. She's a murderer and you know that in your heart. After you went back to Afghanistan and I started throwing up, she took me to the doctor. She made me say I wanted an abortion but the doctor wouldn't agree to it without me having counselling."

Rohan's jaw dropped and his eyes widened in horror. Emma bit her lip and got ready for his dismissal. It didn't come. "Your mother knew someone who would abort my child without asking questions and she arranged to take me there. She locked me in my room to make sure I couldn't get out and Anton came home from university unexpectedly with Glandular Fever. Alanya was at the bank getting the cash for the...operation and Anton drove me to a friend's. He was so unwell he could hardly stay awake at the wheel and it was a five hour journey. I had nothing with me and I didn't know where he was taking me." The sob caught in Emma's throat and she yanked the door open. She pointed an accusing finger at Rohan's prone body. "Your mother tried to kill my baby! And now you know he's your son, you won't be able to stop yourself telling her. Anton knew what she was, but you always tried to see the best in her. *You wouldn't listen to Anton!* First thing tomorrow, me and

Nicky are leaving and you're not stopping us."

She backed out of the door and closed it behind her, slipping quickly into Nicky's bedroom and closing the door behind her. She dragged Nicky's suitcase back across and pushed it against the door

"Mummy, what was that noise?" Nicky sat up in bed, his eyes glinting in the light from the moon through his open curtains.

"You just had a bad dream," Emma lied. "Lay back down and I'll cuddle you." She moved across the room and pulled the curtains closed, slipping her clothes off down to her tee shirt and underwear. Nicky's body was warm and soft as he snuggled willingly into his mother's chest, bringing his knees up and pushing his bare feet onto her thighs. Emma released the ragged breath she held and sniffed her child's downy hair, letting the stray strands irritate her nose and force her back to reality. Vengeance made her want to tell her son the truth but maternalism squashed the urge as it had many times before, especially in these last few weeks.

Emma cried without making any sound as her tears soaked the pillow beneath her head. Growing too hot, Nicky turned away and slept deeply as his mother walked through dreadful memories. Anton drove the five hours to his dead father's family, needing to be shaken awake as he dozed at the wheel in his fever. Emma remembered his reddened eyes and shivering body, slumped in the driver's seat of the rickety old vehicle as he navigated the narrow, breakneck Welsh mountain roads. "I can never tell her I was there," he said in terror, more than once, fearing the consequences of his mother finding out his part in Emma's escape. "Does she know it's Rohan's?" Anton turned frantic eyes on Emma and she screamed as he veered across the road.

"No! No, she doesn't!"

"Then Rohan can't know either, Emma. You can't tell him. He doesn't understand about her. He doesn't know what I know. She poisoned my father, Em and we know she did the same to yours. We just don't know how yet. Stay away from her, promise me? Do you promise, Em? That means you have to stay away from *him*. Ok?"

Emma nodded in terror as a lorry honked its horn and Anton swerved out of its way on the inadequate road. A sign whipped past, declaring in the wavering headlights that it was twelve more miles to Aberystwyth. Those few miles felt like a hundred as Anton struggled with the exertion, pulling over to vomit in a layby in a tiny town called Machynlleth. Emma felt numb as she rubbed his stiff back, and stroked his blonde hair away from his soaked forehead. The numbness took root in her heart and stayed, shattering only with the angry wail of her newborn son.

"Here you are, *cariad*," the gentle Welsh midwife whispered, using the soft word for *love* as she placed the wriggling boy on Emma's chest. "What you callin' 'im?" she asked.

Emma looked across at her birth partner and felt a rush of affection slowly replacing the nothing. The wizened old lady sat with bowed head, pushing prayer beads through gnarled fingers. She looked up once with vibrant, sparkling blue eyes and smiled and nodded at Emma. "Nikolai," Emma breathed as the midwife kept her pen poised above the tiny wristband.

"Aw, *bach*," the portly midwife chuckled. "Youse gonna 'ave to spell that for me."

The old lady nodded and a single tear rolled down her crinkled cheek. "Nikolai Rohan Davidovich Andreyev," she said with deeply accented English. She pursed her lips and searched the ceiling for other words that wouldn't seem to come. Emma spelled out the familiar names and Rohan's grandmother cried without shame, remembering the naming of her own newborn, years before. She reached across and stroked Emma's forehead in gratitude. "*Da*," she said through her tears in broken English. "*Da*. Thank you child. Is old family name passed through eldest son. Nikolai my son. Rohan Nikolai Davidovich, *mal'chika* father." With a bent, arthritic thumb, the elderly Russian made the sign of the cross on Nicky's pink forehead, smiling at the crease of skin above blonde eyebrows. "One day," she predicted. "One day, Rohan Nikolai Davidovich Andreyev will see what he cannot now."

CHAPTER NINETEEN

Emma slept fitfully and woke before Nicky. She crept from the bed and sneaked into the hallway, cursing the creaking floorboards in the darkness. The open space felt cool on her naked thighs and she let out a gasp of fear as her feet contacted something soft.

"Sorry, sorry." Rohan's voice was a frantic whisper as he stopped her falling, placing his palms on her stomach. Emma pushed herself back upright using his broad shoulders and stalked to her bedroom, shoving the door closed behind her. When she emerged from her ensuite bathroom having got rid of the uncomfortable ache in her bladder, Rohan sat on her bed in his pyjama bottoms and socks. His head hung miserably and his eyes were red rimmed and tired.

"Oh, sod off, Rohan!" Emma bit, tiredness staining her nature and making her spiteful. He clutched a sleeping bag in his hand, a khaki coloured swathe of squashy material which draped over the bed and touched the floor boards. "You seriously slept on the hall floor outside Nicky's bedroom?" Her voice held scorn.

Rohan shrugged. "I finished the name tags."

"You laid out there all night to tell me that?"

"No." Rohan narrowed his eyes and pouted. Emma struggled not to find him adorable, sitting on her bed, his chest bare and his blonde hair tousled. "I didn't put it past you to do a runner. You did it once before."

Emma's eyes flashed and she rounded on him,

152

trying to keep her voice from a shout. "Are you for real? Were you not listening to me last night? Your mother's evil and she tried to force me to get rid of my son. I don't want her near me or *him*. We're leaving today!"

"Please don't." Rohan stood up and Emma saw his difficulty with the action. When he took a step forward, he winced, his legs tangled in the sleeping bag. Emma looked at his eyes in the eerie light and they shone from his face in an agony of wordless pleading. Up close in the light from the small hall lamp, Rohan's muscular chest was a myriad of wounds across his torso of varying length and ugliness. In the dull light they looked red and shadowed. A huge tattoo depicted a cross on his right arm. "Please don't take him away from me, Em. I don't want to lose either of you, not again."

Emma exhaled loudly in frustration and shivered in the breath of the cold morning. She heard the central heating kick in, pumping hot water through the radiators which clicked and clanked around the house, accompanied by the familiar whooshing sound. "What's the time?" she asked, mentally calculating her escape.

"Five," Rohan answered, the mechanical timetable of the house meaning he didn't need to check the sports watch on his wrist. He reached out and touched her arm. "Get into bed for a minute. You're freezing."

Emma looked behind him at the soft pillows and duvet, a final shudder driving her into its comfort. She shifted across to the window side as far away from Rohan as possible, realising her mistake when he got in next to her. But he didn't touch her and she ached with an internal agony she didn't understand.

"Talk to me?" he begged. "Explain. I won't say anything, I promise. I'll just listen."

Emma let out a scoffing sound and her face if he could have seen it, was a mask of bitterness. "Really, Ro? So this one time, you'll listen to me? That'll be a first. You've never listened to anyone in your life. That's been the whole problem." She lay still in the darkness and heard the sound of Rohan running his hands through his hair and scratching his scalp in his classic stress tell. Nicky did it too and Emma's inner self squeezed harder on her heart until she wanted to gasp out loud.

"Please?" he pleaded.

Emma waited a few minutes, ordering her thoughts and allowing the painful memories to surface. Her voice wobbled with the effort of releasing them, when she finally began. "Anton said the man your mother organised was a Ukrainian butcher who performed back street abortions to order. We left straight away. He drove me to Aberystwyth and took me to Lucya, your father's mother." Emma heard Rohan exhale and waited, but he kept his promise and said nothing. "Lucya was with me in the hospital when Nicky was born, during my first term in sixth form. She looked after him while I went to classes and helped me in every way possible. It was a good school and allowed me to come and go as I needed. I did well there, despite everything. Anton smuggled things from Alanya's house so I could start again - my birth certificate, passport, results and certificates from my old school. He visited often but found it hard to carry on the pretence with you and I could see how much it cost him. He tried so hard to prove your mother killed both our fathers but he never could. There was something else he wouldn't talk to me about; another death which upset him and he made me promise never to let Alanya see Nicky. He was certain she used some kind of poison but she was too clever and covered her tracks. I did a three year degree at the university in the town and worked part time in a cafe to supplement our benefits. I got a job at the National Library of Wales and worked there for four months in the summer before Nicky started school. I received a call from his playschool one afternoon to say Lucya hadn't arrive to collect him." Emma stopped and gulped painfully.

"I picked him up and rushed home and...she lay in the hallway in her shoes and coat with her handbag still over her arm." Emma hiccoughed through the tears, seeing the heart breaking vision in the secret compartment of her mind where she kept her worst memories. "She looked so peaceful. In her hand were cookies in a little pot for Nicky; his favourite chocolate ones. She said the energy helped him walk home and she'd baked them that morning. I was too late to help her and it was worse...even worse than you leaving me when I needed you most." Emma's hands shook and writhed on the mattress and she bit her lip hard enough to taste blood. She felt the warm sensation of Rohan's fingers covering hers and was grateful. Still he said nothing.

"I had no-one then and a son to raise. I should have stayed because I had a job, but council workers turned up a few days after the funeral. The council owned Lucya's house and had no idea we lived there with her. Her death ended the lease and they wanted to renovate it and put another family in, so I was homeless. They gave us a week to get out. I felt so shocked. I grew to love Aberystwyth but suddenly everywhere I turned, I saw her smiling face and it became like a noose around my neck. I had nobody to mind Nicky for me in the holidays and I couldn't think straight. I wish now I'd gone to my employer and asked for time off, found somewhere else to live and asked for help. But I didn't. Anton was lovely. He stuck around after the funeral and tried to convince me to stay in Wales. When I wouldn't listen, he drove Nicky and me to Lincoln and rented a cottage for a few weeks. I got the job at the school and secured the council house. I let him think I was sorted, but when he saw the house and the estate and...Fat Brian...he went crazy. He tried to give me money but I wouldn't take it so he visited us every few months. I suspect he paid people on the estate to make sure Nicky and I were ok. We settled into a routine and I was safe there. Until Susan's wedding..."

Emma heard Rohan rustle in the sheets next to her, digesting his private agony. He sighed. "I had no idea. I wrote you so many letters from Afghanistan; all my hopes and dreams. I organised a married quarter for us on camp and had this image of you feeling excited about moving into our own house. I never heard from you and then I...there was an explosion and I was injured. I have this memory of calling for you over and over. The army kept telling me they couldn't find you. When I got back to the UK, I asked for you and Mum turned up instead. She said you'd run away with some other guy. At first I refused to believe her, but as time went on and you didn't come I had to accept it. I was devastated. Still am really." His voice was low and laden with misery.

"Do you think *she* read the letters?" Emma asked, squeezing his fingers in fear. "She'll know we got married and she'll guess that Nicky..."

"Hey, don't worry." Rohan turned onto his side and put his other arm across Emma's stomach. "Anton gave them all back to me at the hospital, unopened. I was furious at him because I thought he took them out of jealousy. I shouted at him and he handed me a piece of paper and said I had to find you. I figured it was your address. The alarms sounded on his monitors and the doctors shooed me out of the room. We never got to talk about any of it. He died later that night and I never got to say sorry." Rohan gulped and Emma closed her eyes in the darkness, sensing the waves of pain reaching out towards her. "I've been such an idiot."

"Did you know Anton was gay?" Emma asked and felt Rohan nod by the vibration on the bed.

"Yeah. I actually found that more believable than the thought of Mama being a serial killer." He snuffed, but not in humour. "If you were both so sure, why did you never go to the cops?"

"Anton tried. I've got the case number somewhere. There was no evidence and certainly not enough to start exhuming bodies and doing extra post-mortems. He was convinced she did it and that's why he stayed away from her all these years." Emma sat up in bed with a gasp. "You don't think she killed Anton, do you?"

"No, Em! Not unless she's worked out a way of giving people bowel cancer without them realising. I'm not sure what to think about all this."

"Oh. Ok, sorry, but you must understand why Nicky's not safe around her now. Or you." Emma shifted down in the bed and shivered.

They were quiet for what felt like ages. Then Rohan spoke. "Em?"

She shifted on her side to see his face expression by the orange glow coming through the window. He let go of her fingers and held both arms out. "Can I hold you, please?" His voice sounded too small for a man over six feet tall and her maternalism overrode any other resistant thought process. Emma inched slowly across the bed, her cold hands contacting Rohan's firm stomach first as she edged towards him. Emma sank her head into his armpit, overwhelmed by the comforting familiarity of his smell, the same deodorant and the same musky-Rohan-scent. The old army sleeping bag had left the faint institutional tinge on his skin and it was exactly as Emma remembered with the ache of fondness. Devilment made her run her fingers over his taut muscles and she felt him tighten underneath her and groan. "Rohan?" she whispered, her breath tickling his pectoral muscle under her lips. "I'm sorry I wasn't there for you when you got hurt. Nobody told me."

"It's fine," he replied softly in the darkness.

"Rohan?" Emma's voice came again, a hushed confidence. "Anton registered Nicky's birth for me. I was really unwell afterwards. I was young and I lost a lot of blood. He signed as the child's father and I was so mad. He said he was only trying to help." She felt Rohan's body deflate underneath her and didn't know when to leave things alone; her one defining flaw. She let her fingers wander over his stomach to the line of hair disappearing into his pants, playing around the waistband. "Ro?" she whispered and leaned up on one elbow.

Rohan turned towards her and dragged her into him. "Emma, shut up!" he hissed, crushing her lips with his. His hand in the small of her back felt good and she arched into him, yanking her knickers down under the covers. Emma pushed herself on top of Rohan's firm body and heard the bed groan underneath them as she took control, kissing her husband and reminding herself who she really was. Gone were the two fumbling teenagers in a secret marriage bed as Emma ran her hands through Rohan's hair, her breasts pressed hard into his chest. She heard him take quick breaths through his nose as her tongue danced with his and she felt his hardness against her hip, his cotton pyjama pants bruising her skin. Rohan put one hand firmly behind Emma's head and the other stroked the soft flesh of her bare bottom as she kissed him with maniacal force.

"Mummy?" Nicky's voice cut into the darkness from the hallway, drifting through the closed bedroom door. "I'm lost!"

Emma froze in horror, her heart plummeting from its soaring high. She pushed with trembling hands off Rohan's body and ran to the door on shaking legs, pulling it open at the same time as yanking her tee shirt down around her bum. "Hey baby, what's the matter?"

"I waked up and you was gone. I couldn't remember the way and I need the toilet."

"It's here, Nick, come on. I'll take you." Emma glanced over her shoulder as she led her son in the opposite direction from her bedroom, down onto the split level landing and then up the next flight of stairs to the bathroom.

"Wait for me?" he pleaded as Emma agreed and sank onto the cold wooden stairs, listening to the bathroom sounds inside.

"Flush!" she reminded him as she heard the tap running and the soap falling into the basin. The belated wooshing of water congratulated her on her prompting.

"Can I get a shower!" Nicky called happily. "I'm waked up now."

"Well, I'm not sitting here all morning!" Emma called back grumpily. "I'll turn the hall light on and I'm sure you'll be fine now you're properly awake."

"Fanks Mum!" came the reply as the shower spurted to life.

Emma laid her head back against the wall and groaned. She jumped as Rohan's strong hand appeared in her peripheral vision and she took hold of it, letting him pull her to her feet. The stairs made her higher than him by a head and he pulled her in close to him, winding her hand behind his neck. He buried his face in her breasts and turned his head sideways, gripping her around the waist. "Please stay, Em?" he whispered. "I'll do whatever it takes. She won't come near you or my son again. I'll make sure of it." Rohan tipped his head back and Emma watched the coloured prisms from the stained glass window to his right, speckle his face with pretty shades of sunlight as the day began. She felt the tracksuit pants he had hastily donned, tickling the skin on her thighs and enjoyed the feeling of his strong body wrapped around hers. Emma rested her chin on his shoulder and ran her hands up the back of his hair, feeling him shiver under her touch.

"How can you ban your own mother from your house and your life? It won't work."

Rohan gripped Emma's forearms and pushed her upright, staring into her eyes with fearful intensity. "Just watch me!" he told her. He reached up and placed a burning kiss on her lips which left them feeling swollen. He flicked his tongue into her mouth just enough to leave her wanting more and then let go, striding down the stairs in front of her. Emma heard a happy bark from the kitchen as Farrell cranked up his anticipation levels to seriously excited in the kitchen. She smiled and shook her head.

"Are you going to London again today?" she called after him, trying to control her raging hormones.

Rohan nodded. "Just for the day. I'm back later."

"Hurry up, Nicky!" Emma warned, her voice betraying her emotional turmoil. "Don't use all the hot water."

CHAPTER TWENTY

"Where's my fiancé?" Felicity postured in the entrance to Nicky's classroom, hands on hips as the children divided around her.

"Work," Emma replied, blushing with guilt at the memory of their early morning romp. Felicity saw the emotion in her eyes and honed in on it.

"You dirty little whore!" she hissed. "I know your game. That's disgusting! He's your brother! If you've done anything to seduce him, I'll make you sorry!"

Emma opened her mouth to retort, halted by a tug on the bottom of Rohan's borrowed jacket. She looked down, appalled to see her son's white face. Nicky looked sick. "Mummy, I don't want to go to school today. I don't feel well." He flicked his eyes towards Felicity and the dislike was apparent.

"Come on, Nick," Mo urged, yanking on his friend's arm. "Sid's brought his footy ball for playtime. It's gonna be radical!"

Nicky looked conflicted and Emma's eyes flashed with anger. "Come on baby," she said to her son, ignoring the woman in front of her. "Let's get your coat hung up and go in. I'll stay with you for a minute."

Nicky looked doubtful and walked into the classroom, clinging onto Emma's hand. It took a while for him to settle and Mrs Clarke was so kind, it brought tears to Emma's eyes. The teacher even ignored the black dog, who flopped down in a corner and went to sleep, much to the amusement of the children. Emma emerged from the classroom an hour into the day, having been allowed to stay for show-and-tell time. Sid showed his soccer ball with extreme pride, autographed by his uncle who used to play as the goal keeper for Chelsea. The ball looked a little worse for wear, but Nicky and Mo seemed keen to get their hands on it so Sid was thrilled. He swayed cutely from side to side and kept his ball on the carpet in front of him during story time and Farrell cast a propitious eye over it occasionally.

Escaping through the front doors, Emma was amazed to hear Felicity calling her name. She whirled round on the spot, aware that any exchange would be viewed by all the Year 3 classrooms. "Leave me alone!" she hissed. "You're crazy."

"And you're a dirty little tramp!" Felicity bit back, her eyes blazing. "I don't know where you came from, but you need to go back there. I met with Alanya yesterday. She was most interested in your sudden appearance. She knows what you are; nothing but a filthy hooker. She told me how she threw you out when you got pregnant with your precious son. You got knocked up by some spotty teenager and then ran off with him. I told her you listed Rohan's brother as the father and she was very intrigued. You make me sick. Stay away from my future husband; he's not interested in you, bitch!"

Emma's breath seemed to lodge in her chest, failing to release oxygen to her brain. She felt lightheaded. "You set Alanya on me?" Her voice had an edge of hysteria. Farrell growled low in his chest and Felicity took a precautionary look in his direction before speaking.

"Of course I did. She likes me. We meet for coffee.

She said you were always a troublemaker and led her boys astray. She blames you for her broken relationship with Rohan's brother. If it wasn't for you, she could have been with him when he died. You're poisonous and I'm going to make you pay!" Felicity stepped back, huffing slightly. Emma was obviously stunned by the bile in the other woman's voice and failed to reach for her usual retorts. She raised her hand to slap Felicity round the face but restrained herself.

"You set Alanya on me?" she repeated, defeat in her voice. "I can't believe even you would do that to a child."

"You're pathetic, bitch. What are you talking about; setting her on a child? You're everything my mother-in-law says. You're crazy. Why don't you go back to where you came from and drop dead!" Felicity's eyes flashed with something akin to insanity. Her face was a ghoulish mask of fury and Emma took a step back, knowing she would lose a physical battle with this crazy woman. There was little fleshly restraint for the clinically insane. A few faces popped over the window sills of the Year 3 classrooms and Emma backed down.

"Leave me alone," she said, her voice strong but cold. "Don't speak to me again." She turned once to make her message clear. "And if you ever speak to my son, I'll kill you."

Felicity blanched and then laughed, as though Emma had confirmed everything Alanya said about her. Emma walked home feeling sick and ill, determined to resist all Rohan's advances from now on. His girlfriend was seriously unhinged and Emma's priority was Nicky. As soon as her money came through from the benefits office, she and her son would head north again, to reclaim her council house from the smack heads.

The handsome stranger was waiting for her when she returned home, standing outside the green front gate and resting his backside on the picket fence. Emma saw him from a distance away, mistaking him for someone else's guest until she got closer and realised. He gazed at her with a lazy smile, all six feet in height of him, dark hair cropped close to his head and the brownest eyes she had ever seen.

"Hallo, how are ye?" He smiled. His eyes flashed like glowering coals and Emma couldn't help the ready smile she returned him. "I was after yer man, Rohan, but I guess you'll do instead." His strong Irish brogue was distinctly Belfast in the way he dragged his vowels out.

"He's not back until later. I can take a message." Emma watched as the dog strained on his leash to get to the man, wagging his tail and greeting him like an old friend. He smiled his wide, doggy grin and let his pink tongue slip from the side of his face.

"Hey there, Farrell," the visitor said. "How're you doin'?" He looked up at Emma from his position smoothing the excited dog and gave her a lazy grin from underneath sweeping black eyelashes. Upright he seemed even taller as he stuck his hand out towards her. "Christopher," he said politely.

Emma reached out and touched his skin with her cold palm, feeling the flare of attraction arc between them. It was unexpected and she beat it down. "Emma," she replied, recognising a man rarely denied what he wanted. "It's freezing out here. You should probably come in."

Emma stripped off Rohan's borrowed jacket and left it on the arm of the sofa in the hallway. Christopher removed his shoes as she kicked off her boots. "Drink?" she asked him, playing the bountiful hostess in her borrowed abode. Farrell rushed through to his bowl and checked for food, before ploughing his face into his water dish. Emma laughed and pushed at his tail with her toe. "You just run a marathon or something, boy?"

The tail wagged like a sail and water slopped in the vicinity of his bowl. When he was finished, the dog took himself off into the corner of the kitchen and hurled himself down in his squashy bed with an enormous sigh and something of a grumble. When Christopher turned laughing eyes in his direction, the tail thumped on the tiled floor in a staccato beat, while Farrell's brown eyes smiled his pleasure.

"He really likes you," Emma commented, busying herself with the kettle and mugs.

"Sure yeah." Christopher bobbed down next to Farrell's bed and the dog moaned and rolled over on his side, hinting heavily that a belly scratch would be in order. The man obliged and the dog looked disappointed when he stopped rubbing and stood up. "Na, that's your lot," he said, his dark eyes smiling seductively at Emma. She felt a rush of blood and recognised it as a response to flattery, difficult to ignore. *No, no, no*, she told herself. *I'm not going there! My life is complicated enough with Rohan.* Thoughts of Felicity's possessive kisses dared Emma to trifle with the Irishman out of spite.

Christopher kept his eyes trained on Emma's face as she fumbled around with coffee and handed his to him. He deliberately brushed her fingers in a way which caused her to almost drop the mug and then he smiled openly.

"Are you trying to seduce me?" she asked him, putting a defiant tilt into her chin.

"Absolutely!" he replied.

"But you met me five minutes ago. Have you no shame?" Emma sounded scandalised.

"Rohan said he had a kid sister so I thought you were probably fair game. Although you know he'd kill me for trying."

"Kid sister?" Emma sighed and shook her head, Felicity's bile colouring her view of life.

"Are you not then?" Christopher's Irish accent was lyrical and soft, lulling Emma into a dangerous state of *don't-care*.

"I'm his stepsister." The word tasted nasty on her lips.

Christopher blinked, long black lashes grazing his cheeks as he sized her up. "You're very beautiful. Anyone ever told you that?"

Emma let out a snort of spontaneous laughter. "You are dreadful. Has anyone ever told you that?"

"Hell yeah! Me mammy says it often to me." He raised his voice to do an impression of a high pitched older woman. "She says, 'Chris! You're a feckin' eejit!' Only I can't do her exact voice as she's deeper, like a man who's smoked fifty a day since his third birthday..."

Emma laughed and put her hand over her mouth. "Is there no end to your wit?"

"Na, I have to say not."

Emma shook her head and sipped her hot drink, the moment turning suddenly awkward. Christopher observed her from under his eyelashes with a frightening astuteness. "So, can I sit down or do I have to stand on ceremony the whole time?" He smiled and

Emma pointed to the two seater couch at the end of the kitchen.

"No, sorry. Sit down. It's not my house and I'm not used to having...it doesn't matter." She followed him to the seat and squashed herself into the corner of it, avoiding the tantalising touch of his thigh against hers in the small space. Guilt seized her chest at the sight of Rohan's blue sweater lying across the seat of one of the stools at the breakfast bar. She knew without touching it what it smelled like and how its rough, woolly surface might feel. It condemned her sudden need for physical contact and Emma frowned without realising. She looked up, finding Christopher watching her.

"I don't know when Ro will be back," Emma smiled apologetically. "Was he expecting you?"

Christopher shook his head. "Not here, no."

"Oh. Do you want me to try and get in touch with him?"

"Do ya know his number?"

"Er...no, sorry."

The man stretched out his long legs and sipped his drink. Emma observed him covertly from under her lashes, admiring the smooth shaven skin and the neat dark hair which barely touched the top of his shirt collar. He wore clothes that were smart casual, exuding a confidence which left her in awe. "Tell me about yerself, Emma," he said soothingly and she felt herself tighten, not wanting to betray her poverty stricken lifestyle to a stranger.

"Not much to tell." She closed down, her face shutting like a portcullis, desperate to keep this attractive man out of her head. She slammed a gate on Felicity's accusations.

"Tell me about you. How do you know Ro and what

was your meeting about?"

Christopher turned towards Emma, shifting himself in his seat so he half-faced her. He smiled with veiled approval at her fencing tactics and nodded. "Ok, have it your way. I've known Andreyev three years and worked on the same projects as him quite a few times. He's a good man, sharp as a knife and knows how to use one. We have a healthy respect for one another. Will ya come on a date wit' me whilst I'm in town?"

"Pardon?" Emma's face registered her surprise. "How did we get from you telling me how long you've known Rohan, to you asking me out?"

"Easy." Christopher placed his drink carefully on the floorboards and leaned across to stroke Emma's cheek. "I like you. Come on a date wit' me."

"No! Don't be ridiculous." Emma's emotions flip flopped with confusion and fear. Christopher edged closer to her and Emma felt her heart beginning to pound in her chest. "I'm not going anywhere with a total stranger!" She resisted as his arms edged around her shoulders. Christopher pulled her towards him and she smelled aftershave and mint as he leaned forward. She didn't expect him to follow through but his lips on hers were firm, different to Rohan's soft kisses. Emma felt a flush of excitement, followed quickly by anger. "Get off me! This is stupid; I don't even know you!" Emma slid off the sofa, putting a safe distance between her and the confident male.

Christopher sat forward and seemed to rethink his game plan. He stood up. "Sorry. I've imposed on ya. It was stupid. You're gorgeous and it made me forget my head." He took a step forward and Emma reversed further until her backside rested against the dishwasher. "I'm not married. I'm not in a relationship and I am real interested in you. Come on a date with me tomorrow night. We'll go for dinner and see how it goes."

Emma looked indignant and Christopher carried on with his gentle persuasion, moving towards her at a slow pace. *One step, two steps.* He stood in front of her, forcing her to crick her neck to look up at him. "Meet me tomorrow night," he breathed, leaning in and kissing her neck. "Seven o'clock at the motel on the corner of Welland Park Road. If yer show up, we'll go for dinner. If you don't, I'll be heartbroken about our missed opportunity." He stood up and winked at her. "But I'll live."

Emma lifted her knee to give Christopher a well-deserved whack in the groin. He blocked her with his thigh and laughed out loud. Then he stroked the dog's curly head in a circular motion and walked through to the hallway. She listened to him slip his shoes on, do up the laces and leave, blowing her breath through pursed lips. "What the hell just happened?" she asked the dog. Farrell sat up with his fluffy ears pricked and glanced hopefully at his leash. "Who was that guy and how come you're such a rubbish guard dog?"

Farrell snooshed a horrid wet sneeze from his nostrils and wiped his nose on his paw. "Useless!" Emma grunted and went out to the hall to lock the front door. Her hand shook as she pushed the lock down on the Yale, not sure why she did that. "Bloody hell!" she exclaimed, leaning back against the door, bemused by the small smirk which turned her lips upwards and sparkled in her eyes. "Ro's marrying a crazy who wants me dead and I've just come home to her twin."

CHAPTER TWENTY ONE

Emma walked head down, chatting to the dog and kicking the rotting conkers for him to chase. The low sun twinkled through the trees, speckling the pavement with dapple and blinding eyes accustomed to the grey of winter. Emma squinted and looked at the bell tower of the school, seeing it as a black silhouette against the orange sun.

"So, you return at last?" The old woman blocked Emma's route along the footpath, terrifying her.

"Get away from me!" Emma spat, looking frantically around for help. She came early to let Farrell off his leash and the path was deserted. Picking up her tension, the dog growled and snorted in warning. Emma worked out her options. Tempting as it was to turn around and run home, she still had to fetch Nicky from school. The other alternative would be to tramp through the muddy field and use the school's rear gate, but it would mean she needed to find another way home. Rohan's mother was relentless and would never give up.

"My son has...how you say? Banned me from his house. Because of you. Always when there is trouble, there is you!"

"Yeah that's right. It's always because of me," Emma retorted. "Everything was great until you got landed with me. I'm like the family albatross aren't I?" Emma gathered the lead tightly into her fingers and hauled the dog closer to her for protection. "You kill my father and then try and kill my unborn child. Is it just me you hate, or anyone connected with me?"

"Do not say dat! I loved your father. He vas sick. I try to heal him."

"He was fine until you met him! He was a good man in a good church. He was your pastor for goodness sake! We were happy! Of all the women batting their eyelashes at the recently widowed reverend, he had to pick you, a poisonous, spiteful child hater. You make me sick!" Tears sprang into Emma's eyes.

"I vatch you, Emma; you have the child, a boy."

"Mind your own business! He'll never know you. Stay away from us."

"But Emma. I do for best. I think I help. Let me see child?"

"No!" Emma's temper reached explosion point, filling her head with hot blood and glazing her eyes with a red mist. She stood and eyed the slightly stooped Russian woman, feeling herself summon up all the latent hatred she spent the last seven years fostering and nurturing. "You ruined my life!" Emma felt surprised at the sentence, realising as she said it, how sad it sounded; how self-pitying and pathetic. She took a step back and the dog moved with her as though synced with her left leg.

Emma conjured up Nicky's sweet face, his father's unruly blonde locks and the stunning blue eyes. She thought of all the times he told her he loved her and the way his tiny feet felt against her thighs when she crawled into bed with him. He was more than worth the last six years of struggle. Much more. And this foolish old woman had missed out on all of it.

Emma fixed her eyes on Alanya's sharply hooked nose and fading blonde hair. Her blue eyes were wary and filled with an uncharacteristic fear. Rohan's mother had passed her beauty onto Nicky, but not her nature. "Leave us alone!" Emma felt the sense of blessedness in her heart and afforded herself a smirk. "Don't ever talk to me again!" She pushed past Alanya and took a few steps into the park. But just as she thought she was victorious, the monster of her childhood reared its face again and thwarted Emma's quest for security.

"You vill not have my son, girl!" Alanya sneered, pointing a twisted finger in her face. "You always coveted his affection. I vill not let you taint him vis your sin like you did other boy. I lost Anton because of you and I do not forgive!"

Emma gulped and turned to face her stepmother. Alanya had morphed back into the terror of Emma's youth and gone was the old lady guise. "Leave Rohan Andreyev!" Alanya ordered her. "Or I vill make you vish you had!" She took a menacing step forward. "His real girl knows what you are, nothing but a whore. You pedaled your flesh to both my sons and I vill see Anton's *syn*, whether you like it or not! My *nevestka* vill see to it that you are punished."

Emma turned and moved quickly down the path towards the school, refusing to compromise her dignity by running away. Her fingers quaked on the dog leash and Farrell stuck close to her leg, looking up at her with wide, brown eyes of sympathy. By the swings, Emma unhooked the leash and threw sticks for Farrell to fetch in his tireless enthusiasm. In her peripheral vision, the old woman turned and shuffled away, leaving the park and moving along the pathway into town.

Emma shook her head as bile rose into her chest with the withdrawal of adrenaline. Alanya knew how much Emma idolised Rohan. She warned her off repeatedly, the rant always followed by a bout of illness for Emma. "*Nevestka*, daughter-in-law! So it's true and Rohan's lying to me," she hissed and ran a shaking hand over her face as Farrell dropped a stick at her feet. "She knows Felicity. I can't fight against both of them. I need to get away from here." Emma shuddered at the thought of the Russian woman plying her son with poisoned sweets or drinks. Felicity worked in the school and could potentially help get her access to Nicky. Emma glanced around her, relieved to find the park empty but her own words came back to taunt her. '*You ruined my life.*' How could anything to do with that sweet child ever be considered ruinous. Nicky was a blessing, not a curse.

Emma looked at the apex of the school building, rising above the red brick barrier; an unshakable landmark in the gathering gloom. Her son was in there, chewing his pencil as he learned and struggling to keep his jiffling bottom on the flat seat of his tiny plastic chair. "Oh, Nicky, I don't deserve you," she whispered to the surrounding trees.

"Talking to yerself?" Mel laughed as she appeared behind Emma. Farrell dashed up for a stroke and a head rub before hurtling after another flying stick.

"Yep. Just slaying some demons." Emma grunted as she bent to pick up another blunted piece of wood, cast down by the gargantuan oak trees around the park.

"Can you do my ex at the same time?" Mel snorted. "Then maybe me an' Mo could go back to Manchester."

"There's no point. I failed." Emma's voice sounded flat.

A blonde woman stood next to Mel, silently

contemplating the dog. She smiled at Emma, an inner confidence lighting her face with ethereal beauty. Then she poked a mittened hand out. "Hi, I'm Allaine. I live along the street from you. I've seen you walking with your husband and meant to say hello."

"I'm Emma." She put her freezing fingers into the warm gloved hand and nodded. "Ro's my...oh look it's complicated. Probably a story for another day." Emma stopped, watching the dog with a big stick he'd found. It was way too long to retrieve, so he entertained himself by spinning in a circle without apparent aim. He looked thrilled, so it obviously fulfilled a base desire to get dizzyingly doggy-sick. "Faz, come here," Emma laughed and the dog stopped his stick twirling and padded over, looking dazed. Emma clipped the leash onto his collar and he dropped instantly into well behaved pooch, walking sedately on her left side.

"Nice dog," Allaine said. "I've seen him out walking with...what did you say his name was?"

"Rohan," Emma said, caressing his name on her tongue. A world of possibility opened up in front of her and then slammed shut on her fingers. The thought of Felicity and Alanya conspiring against her brought only nausea. They were two hags plotting her downfall and it made her feel hopeless. Her home in Lincoln would be occupied already and she didn't have the train fare anyway. Christopher's proffered date seemed to offer hope and a way out. Perhaps she could confide in him and tell him the truth. Emma groaned inwardly. Of course she couldn't go to his juvenile tryst; he'd think she was a crazy.

"I just call him 'The Demigod,' Mel squawked, referring to Rohan and sending them all into giggles. "He's hot property, woman! If you're not interested, I might make a lurch for him. I could probably keep him busy for half an hour if you mind the kids!"

You might need a bit longer than that, Emma smirked lecherously, her memories doing an inappropriate dance before her eyes. Then she remembered Felicity's accusations and the blackness descended over her head again like a mask. Rohan's promises fell like ash to the ground and the spectre of Alanya returned to haunt Emma in the peace of the park. She felt hunted, not helped by Mel adding suddenly, "Oh yeah, damn! He's with that scary secretary from the school, isn't he?"

If total strangers could see it, it had to be true. Emma knew with surety that her time at Rohan's and possibly in Market Harborough was at an end and quietly contemplated leaving and going somewhere other than her former address.

Nicky was his usual effervescent self, running through the park with a whole entourage of willing worshippers. The women walked behind the gang of miniature tree huggers, loaded down with book bags and lunches. Emma's son exhibited all the charisma of his deceased uncle, drawing people to him like a magnet. His laughing eyes and ready smile were pure Anton and it made Emma's heart clench, knowing she would never get to hear his wicked snort at some inappropriate joke again. *Find Emma*, he told Rohan in his dying breaths. *But what had he possibly hoped to achieve?*

Mel and Mohammed parted from the little group at the bottom of their street, avoiding the sweet shop on the corner with the same wariness as Emma. Neither of them had money to waste on sugar which would last only seconds anyway. Nicky smushed his face into Emma's stomach after Mo left, his words filling her heart with dismay. "I love it in Harborough, Mummy.

Can we stay here forever? I love my new school and I love Mrs Clarke so much."

Allaine stayed with Emma until a little way along Newcombe Street from the alley, chatting while the children watched a group of ants carry a leaf along a wall.

"Nicky's very tall for his age, isn't he?" Allaine commented, her short blonde hair poking out from under a woolly hat.

"His dad's tall," Emma replied, realising her error as the shutters crashed down over her wistful expression. Allaine made an obvious pretence of not noticing.

"Nicky's a beautiful person," Allaine said, smiling. "Kaylee told me he shared some of his lunch with Mohammed the other day when Mo had very little."

"But Rohan paid for him to have hot lunches..." Emma stopped and shook her head. "Oh that makes sense now. The peas in his trouser pockets. Thank goodness they didn't have gravy!"

Allaine snorted and indicated her three storey town house with an outstretched arm. "Well, I'm here if you need me."

"Thanks," Emma said, feeling the kinship of a budding connection. She turned to leave and then twisted her body to face Allaine as the other woman fumbled with the latch on her front gate. "Hey, you wouldn't know where I could go to find out about places for rent, do you?"

"Yeah sure. Why don't we meet up after we drop the children tomorrow? I'll take you into town and show you the sights."

Emma smiled with genuine gratitude. "Thank you! I'd love that." She walked home slowly, her heart filled with misgiving and the mantra sounded in her head, *this is a mistake, you need to leave this town.*

Back at Rohan's house, she struggled with the door key and dog leash, the dog prancing up and down on her toes and the child pressed close against her bottom. The library bag fell to earth with a crash. "Can't you take something from me?" Emma snapped at her son, falling forward with a yelp as the door gave way in front of her. She staggered, tripping over the doorstep from the porch, feeling Rohan's strong arms underneath her as her knees went. She felt a fool, her feet still outside and her whole body leaned into his. Embarrassment made her snippy. "I'm fine!"

"Yeah, you looked it," Rohan replied with a wooden smile. He didn't seem himself somehow, his body rigid and his eyes betraying an inner nervousness. "Why are you so late? I was getting worried."

"We were just talking with a lady down the street!" Emma's tone was filled with aggression. "I wasn't aware we were on a time limit."

Nicky rolled his eyes and smirked at Rohan, lighting the fuse on Emma's patience. "Don't start that eye rolling thing between you! Get upstairs and get undressed." Emma pointed to Nicky, who lurched off up the wooden stairs to his bedroom, his footsteps thundering overhead.

"Does that include me? Should I go upstairs and get undressed?" Humour touched Rohan's full lips and Emma felt lost for words. *What's wrong with me?*

The feel of Christopher's brown eyes on her face answered the question, the memory lighting her cheeks with a soft blush. Guilt could do that to a person. Christopher was looking for Rohan, not her and she needed to tell him his friend had been round. "Ro..."

"Yep?" He looked back at her as the sharp knock came on the front door and he stepped forward to open it. Emma's words were swallowed back into her gullet as Felicity bounded across the threshold, threw her arms around Rohan's neck and kissed him full on the lips. Emma gulped and squashed an instinctive jealousy. Rohan looked surprised, pulling back with something like confusion on his face. He glanced at Emma, embarrassment in his eyes.

"I got take out," Felicity simpered, dangling the white carrier bag higher so he could see. "Your favourite."

"But Emma made tea," Rohan replied, shaking his head. "It's in the oven cooking."

Emma watched Felicity as she breathed in the Shepherd's Pie which was almost ready, browning itself off in Rohan's kitchen. Her nose wrinkled at the meal Emma lovingly created with ingredients from his copious pantry. "I hate mince," she replied rudely. "And anyway, I only brought enough for two. We'll eat it in your room." Without removing her stilettos, Felicity bounded upstairs with all the grace of a cat walk model.

"Bloody hell!" Rohan spat at her retreating bottom, swishing under a designer skirt. He said something far more unrepeatable in Russian and Emma was forced to smile.

"Go on. You should go," she said, forcing an element of joviality into her voice.

"But I need to talk to you." Rohan moved closer to Emma, keeping one eye on the top of the stairs and sidling near enough to whisper. "It's important. Today didn't go well at all. I tried to pull the plug on this current job because I've lost my back up. They won't let me. It's too far in. The contact's been made and if I don't go now, I'll miss the window of opportunity. It means there'll be consequences, bad ones. It's how it works. I need to..."

Emma looked confused. "What? I don't understand. You're a number cruncher. What kind of mathematician's job requires back up?"

"Rohan!" Felicity appeared at the top of the stairs and sidled down the first few steps to peer through the bannister rails. "The food's going cold." The blonde woman glared at her adversary and bared her teeth in a threatening grimace which made Emma's flesh creep and reminded her of Alanya. Felicity put on a baby voice which Rohan might have liked, but it made Emma want to smash her face into the wall. A glance at Rohan revealed the same reaction. "I've got things to show you." Felicity smirked and Emma felt a violent flash of green eyed monster at what those things could possibly be. "I want to talk to you about a sexy weekend away too."

Emma couldn't help it. She looked at Rohan with such horror, she saw him wince. Her jaw dropped open with dismay and he saw it. Too late, she covered her misery and disappeared into the kitchen. Nicky appeared close behind her, winding his arms around her waist and burying his face into the small of her back. "It's ok, Mummy. I still love you."

"You were listening?" Emma's voice sounded flat even to herself.

"Yeah. I don't like her. I wish she'd stop talking to me in the corridor. Mrs Clarke got cross with her today because she made me late to assembly."

"What does she talk to you about?" Emma removed the hot casserole dish from the oven and set it on a wooden board to the side. She reached up and took plates from the overhead plate rack and began spooning some of the mixture onto a plate for Nicky.

"Yummy!" He peeked round her waist at the delicious meal. "She asks me about you and where we came from. Today she asked why we were here. Did you know her and Uncle Ro get married soon?"

Emma dropped the serving spoon into the baking hot mixture, burning herself as she tried to retrieve the handle. "So she told me. She shouldn't be talking to you in school about private things." Tears pricked the back of her eyes and she sucked her finger, the spoon disappearing into the sumptuous folds of meat and potato. "I'll talk to Mrs Clarke."

"No, please Mummy, don't talk to my teacher. I don't want you to. Don't cry Mummy!" Nicky appeared at the front of her, the back of his head dangerously close to the dish. Emma put a protective hand around his soft hair as she struggled to collect herself. Then she looked down.

"Ye gods! Nicky!"

Her naked son giggled. "Well, you told me to go upstairs and get undressed. So I did. You din't say to get dressed again." He pushed his face into Emma's stomach and his tiny arms around her waist offered her comfort as he squeezed her tightly. He lowered his voice. "I thought if *she* saw my willy, it might put her off comin' round. I think it worked."

Emma snorted through her tears at her son's antics, while knowing she should reprimand him. "Flashing's actually not cool, Nick. You can go to prison for doing that outside."

"But I'm not outside," he answered, the point made fairly.

"Hey." Rohan's hand was soft on Emma's shoulder as he leaned over and dangled a pair of pyjamas in Nicky's face. "You left these." He dropped them on the child's head and graced Emma with an open smile. It faded as he noticed the tears on her cheeks and he looked as though he would ask. Nicky burst out of the clothing and let it fall to the floor, ruining the moment for Rohan. "Get them on," he told the child. "We don't want the women falling for you instead of me." He thought about his jibe after he said it and Emma saw him shake his head at his own mistake.

"Was Felicity scared then?" Nicky asked, disappearing inside his tight pyjama top.

"Impressed," Rohan answered, never taking his eyes from Emma's face. She felt the heat of his stare but chose not to meet it.

"Oh shit!" Nicky stamped his foot in anger.

Emma clapped her hand over his mouth in horror and turned to deal with her child's expletive. When she looked up, Rohan was gone.

CHAPTER TWENTY TWO

"Hurry up, Nicky!" Emma called up the stairs, looking around for her holey boots. Fortunately it was only cold outside and not raining. Rohan appeared down the stairs first, dapper in his smart work clothes. Emma smiled nonchalantly at him, keen not to get into any discussions.

"Sorry about last night." He paused at the bottom of the stairs and reached out for her.

Emma backed away. "What about it?" Her voice was clipped and cold.

"Felicity. She was being loud on purpose. I kept asking her to be quiet. I don't know why she..."

"Too much information, thanks." Emma's face betrayed her distaste. "Your sex life is your business."

"No, I meant..."

"Nicky! Last call for Nicky!" Emma yelled like an airport tannoy, over speaking Rohan in her anxiety to get away from him.

"Whatever!" Rohan sighed heavily and opened the front door. A cold wintry blast rushed in as he forced his way out, slamming the door behind him.

"We takin' Faz?" Nicky looked eager.

"No, I've got some stuff to do in town."

"But he looks sad," Nicky interjected. "Will I give him my crisps to cheer him up?"

"No! You'll make him fat and he'll get health problems. It's cruelty dressed as kindness to overfeed them."

"Like Uncle Anton?"

"What?" Emma's head whipped round so fast, she hurt her neck. "What about him?"

"About him bein' sick."

"How do you know he was sick?" *How did I know he wasn't?*

"You could just tell the last time he came to the estate. He didn't wanna play wiv me. When's he comin' again? Does he know we're here and not in Lincoln?" Nicky looked worried. "I wanna see 'im."

"I'm sure he knows exactly where we are," Emma soothed, knowing she would need to have the very difficult conversation soon.

"Like God?"

"Nicky, shoes!"

"God knows everything. Kaylee says he really *does* know everything."

"I hope he doesn't!"

"Why Mummy? Why do you hope that?"

Emma sighed. "Because if he did, he probably wouldn't like me very much."

"Yeah he would." Nicky sounded confident. "I like ya, so he would. Else I'd bash 'im."

"I don't think that would be a good idea. Let's go."

Allaine and Kaylee emerged from their gate as Emma and Nicky got close to their house. Kaylee bounced out looking thrilled to see Nicky. They skipped off ahead, Nicky looking back towards Emma for security, as he always did. "You look a bit down today," Allaine commented softly as they followed the children down the street towards Nithsdale Avenue. Emma pushed her hands further into the pockets of Rohan's jacket, which she borrowed from the coat cupboard again.

"Yeah, I feel it," she replied.

"Is there anything I can do to help?"

"Not really." Emma smiled at her new friend. "Just by helping me find somewhere to live."

"Are you looking forward to your job at the school? That starts soon, doesn't it?"

"Yep, first day of next term. Hopefully the benefits office will have sorted everything else so I can move out and start my new life with Nicky. Just him and me again." Emma sounded wistful and saw Allaine look at her with curiosity. If she had questions, she tactfully kept them to herself.

They walked to the end of Nithsdale Avenue and turned right, heading for the lollipop lady and her safe passage across the treacherous Northampton Road. "Actually, there might be something else you can do to help me," Emma said at the beginning of the park. The children skipped off ahead, joined by other bouncing friends of varying height. "I've got a date tonight and I don't have anything to wear." Emma bit her lip. "I don't even know if I should be going." Felicity's behaviour the previous night had strengthened Emma's resolve to cut Rohan out of her life, for her own safety and Nicky's. This would be the first step; seeing someone else romantically.

Allaine considered for a moment, walking in silence while she mentally sifted through her wardrobe. "Yes, I'm sure I have something you can borrow, but if you're not sure whether to go or not, then maybe you shouldn't."

"Yeah, I know. I met him yesterday and he's very...alluring. I feel like I need something to lift my spirits and a night out with a handsome bloke would definitely do that. Trouble is, he's a friend of Rohan's and I'm not sure it's a good idea from that point of view."

"What does Rohan say?"

Emma tutted. "Well, I was about to tell him when his girlfriend arrived. Christopher was actually looking for him, not me, but we kinda hit it off and he left. I'm meant to be meeting him tonight at seven at his hotel."

"Can you tell Rohan tonight?"

"We're not communicating." Emma bit her lip in a flash of guilt. "It's my fault really. He has his own life and I need to stop putting my expectations on him. I'm hoping he'll babysit Nicky tonight for me and don't want to upset him by telling him it's a date."

"Well definitely don't tell him lies," Allaine said without reprimand. "Believe me, that's when it gets messy! Tell you what, how about I give you my mobile number and then at least you can call for help if you need it?"

"Thanks, that's a great idea." Emma went through the pretence of exchanging phone numbers, knowing she had no credit and even if a lion sat on her chest, she would never be able to summon Allaine's very genuine help.

"I've got a job interview!" Mel hugged Allaine and Emma from behind. "Thanks for lending me the suit, Allaine. What do you think?" She did a twirl.

"Oosh girl! You look like a banker. What job is it?" Emma laughed.

"In the cafe booth inside the market. I'm gonna be a barista." The beautiful woman smiled, flashing perfect white teeth. "Oh, I hope I get the job." She screwed her face up and hugged her body. "I really need a break. Well, one that isn't of the bone fracturing kind, anyway."

"Good luck!" Emma hugged her and wished her well with all her heart. As Mel dashed away in stilettos that looked a little big for her, Emma smiled at Allaine. "You runnin' a clothes shop, lady?"

"Yeah, I think I must be," Allaine laughed, bending to kiss her small daughter goodbye.

"*Do svidaniya, mumiya*," Nicky chimed, planting a wet kiss on Emma's cold lips.

"Bye darling. Remember how much I love you, won't you?" she whispered in his ear. "Don't talk to strangers, Nicky. I mean it!"

Nicky pulled a coy face and shaped a heart with both hands. Emma laughed softly and counted her blessings.

In town, Allaine showed Emma the sights of historical interest which Rohan hadn't bothered with. In the central heart of Market Harborough stood the old school house, a wooden building raised onto stilts. It was breathtakingly beautiful, a piece of engineering brilliance for something constructed in 1614. Emma stroked one of the enormous beams holding it up and sighed, her spirit connecting with the sense of permanence it radiated through its contact with so many others like her. Old or young, rich or poor; it didn't distinguish between them. The words engraved into the beams infused her with sadness. '*He the Lord seeth not as man seeth; for man looketh on the outward appearance, but the Lord looketh on the heart —1 Samuel 16:7b*' Nicky's comment returned to her, filling Emma with fear. If God could see her heart, he would be dreadfully disappointed. "It's dirtier than the outside of me," Emma breathed.

She turned sharply, tears in her eyes. Allaine stood behind her looking up at the words. She made no comment about Emma's whispered confession but sighed heavily. "I love this building." She smiled at Emma, her height advantage making Emma feel tiny next to her. "It oozes history and meaning."

Emma nodded and got control of her face expression. "It's very beautiful."

St Dionysius Church stood proudly next to it like a protector, pale stones and a sun dial which struggled to convey the time in a world overcast by one enormous shadow.

"The estate agent's up here," Allaine said, tugging at Emma's arm. "We can come back another day and I'll show you the museum and library. That's the benefits office in the Symington Building. Have you been in there yet? You said you were going to."

"Not yet. I rang the one in Leicester. They were really helpful. I'll call in there with the details of my new place, once I've got it. I hate asking for help from the state." Emma pulled a face.

Allaine gathered her arm into hers and gave it a squeeze. "Hey, sometimes we all need a bit of help. It's not a crime." She pointed back towards the red brick building. "Do you find it ironic they dish out dole and benefits from an old corset factory?"

Emma snorted. "I don't know why that's so funny, but it is."

Emma was grateful to the level headed woman for her comfort and appreciated her company when it came to looking for properties. The smartly dressed, female agent drove them out to see three in total and Emma felt the weight of difficult decisions resting on her head. One was a little too far for someone with no vehicle and she rejected it for that reason. But the other two were possibilities. One was at the back of the leisure centre but a long walk for a child. "I think Nicky could manage it, although it's quite far," Emma mused, thinking of the benefits of being well away from Rohan, Felicity and Alanya. The other one seemed perfect, a mid-terraced house with three bedrooms and an upstairs bathroom, two downstairs living rooms and a galley kitchen. On Gladstone Street, it was within ideal walking distance of the school and town. Emma's face paled at the size of the rent. "That's my whole wage per week," she panicked. "And if the job's contracted like my last one, I won't get paid in the holidays. I don't know what to do."

"We'll think about it," Allaine told the agent calmly. "Thanks for driving us around. We really appreciate it." She led Emma gently from the shop and down the road to a cafe. "Come on, let's get coffee." At the look of horror on Emma's face she pulled at her arm. "I'm paying!"

Over lattes, Emma picked over her options. "Maybe if Mr Dalton will let me squash all my hours at school into three days, then I could get another job on the last two days a week while Nick's at school. That's another twelve hours possible income. Or if I do three hours a day at school, then I could get another job in the afternoons until school pick up time. That's potentially another fifteen."

"Oh, Emma," Allaine said softly. She reached across and put her hand over Emma's, compassion in her face but pity nowhere to be found. "I'm sure there are things the state can do to help boost your disposable income. And what about Nicky's father? Can't he help out?"

"No." Emma withdrew her hand on pretence of reaching for her drink. "He's...it's complicated."

"You said your arrangement with Rohan was complicated. You sure have a lot of complex things going on. Look, I'm happy to have Nicky before or after school sometimes if you need me to. For free, so don't look at me like that. It's what friends do. But I'm scared of you loading yourself up to breaking point and then snapping. If you've got two jobs, what happens if Nicky gets sick? If it's chickenpox or measles or something highly infectious, there's only you who can really look after him and then you've got two places to call in sick to, two places to miss out on wages from and extra guilt to add to the pile."

"I just don't know what else to do," Emma sighed. "Maybe I should just go back to Lincoln. This was only meant to be temporary for a few weeks and here I am, making it more permanent than perhaps it was ever meant to be. Yesterday I was all set to go and then Nicky told me how happy he was here. I moved him from Aberystwyth just as he was about to start school and he took ages to settle. Today I'm finding work, houses and other things."

"And friends." Allaine winked at her and Emma smiled.

"Yeah, and friends. How dare I, hey?"

They walked back to Allaine's house and she made cold chicken sandwiches while Emma tried on every dress in her wardrobe. "It's no good!" Emma complained. "These are all way too beautiful for me. What did you do before you had children? Were you a supermodel?"

"No. I was a laboratory technician in Leicester."

"What's that exactly?" Emma stood in front of the mirror and twirled. The sheer red material shivered against her shapely legs.

"The lab techs are the ones who actually perform all the tests. The cops and experts are the ones who talk about them and get all the praise for results. It's a behind-the-scenes role and nobody really cares about the techs. But in every movie you watch, there's always someone who has to '*get on to the lab*' for results or shout down the phone at someone in the lab. It's not a role which is portrayed particularly well. We worked damn hard for no recognition."

"A bit like motherhood then?" Emma grinned and swirled the red fabric around her knees. "This is quite nice."

"That's the dress, Emma. You should wear it. It looks beautiful on you." Allaine watched Emma for a moment as she pulled a face in the full length mirror.

"Do you think so?" Emma pushed her plump breasts into the area designated for them and jiggled around a little. "These buttons up the front worry me. If one pops open I could kill someone."

Allaine laughed and laid back on the bed. "You have a gorgeous figure. You look amazing. At least your breasts point in the right direction and you have a waist." Allaine pushed at her flat stomach and Emma scoffed.

"Whatever! For a woman of forty with five children, you look incredible. I've only had one child and earned stretch marks for England."

"I'm sure someone will love them," Allaine yawned.

"Yeah but who? Oh I can't do this." Emma plonked her bottom down on the bed, alarmed at the way her unfettered bosoms wobbled in the red fabric. She put her head in her hands. "How do I start again? I was eight when I fell in love with Nicky's dad. We grew up together and he knew everything about me there was to know."

"How old were you when you got married?" Allaine asked, interested.

"I was sixteen and one month old," Emma smiled, her face taking on a faraway expression. "He was nineteen and in the army. I loved him so much. He applied for a licence to marry me at Gretna Green just inside the Scottish border. We lied to..." Emma realised she was in danger of revealing too much of herself and stopped. Allaine sat up.

"Hey, you don't have to tell me anything if you don't want to. It's none of my business."

"Thanks," Emma replied, feeling relieved. "I'll tell you one day, but it feels a bit raw lately, for lots of reasons."

"You definitely look hot in that dress, though." Allaine leaned forward and scooped Emma's long curls up into her hand and held it off her neck. "Wear your hair up. Do you have clips?"

Emma nodded. "Yeah, I'm fairly sure I do. If not, it won't matter."

"No, it looks better up with the low cut of the dress and the length of it. I've got a red one if you want with a kind of decoration thing on the back. It would match. Do you have shoes?"

CHAPTER TWENTY THREE

At home later, Emma laid the pretty dress on her bed and dealt with Nicky's shower and tea. Rohan wasn't home and she began to feel relieved at the legitimate reason for not going on the date with Christopher. Rohan clattered through the front door at six o'clock, when it was already dark and his face looked haggard and filled with worry. "Hard day?" Emma asked kindly, dishing up a plate of macaroni cheese and laying it down on the counter, next to where Rohan stood emptying his pockets of keys and a train ticket.

"Yeah. Thanks for this." He gave her a tired smile and ran his hands through his hair.

"Did you go to London again?"

Rohan nodded and dragged a fork from the cutlery drawer. "Kensington. It seems warmer in the city than here. There's a big freeze coming." He pushed a forkful of the yellow mixture into his mouth and closed his eyes. "This is nice. I love coming home to you and Nicky and tea on the table." Crow's feet appeared in the corners of his eyes as he smiled. "I really love it."

Emma smiled and went through to the dining room to deal with Nicky. "Sit with me, Mummy," he begged. "After you bring me back some more mac and cheese."

Emma sat and sipped a cup of tea while Nicky polished his plate with a piece of bread. "That was gorgeous, Mummy. I wish we'd had food before when we lived up Lincoln then you could've cooked this for me all the time."

His mother masked her hurt and worried about her son's precarious future in her hands. Rohan scraped out a chair and sat with them, eating as though starving.

"It's nice ain't it, Uncle Ro?" Nicky chattered and Emma flushed with embarrassment and tried to hush him, putting a finger over her lips. Rohan smiled and nodded to the boy as both males shoveled their food into hungry mouths. "I din't know Mummy could do cooking."

"Will you be in tonight or have you got plans?" Emma asked Rohan as he finished his food. He knitted his blonde brows and stared at her.

"Why?"

Emma shifted uncomfortably under his gaze and looked at the grains of life in the wooden table. "I wanted to ask if you'd babysit Nicky so I could go out with some new friends."

Nicky's eyes widened in surprise. "Go out? Wivout me?"

"No, you're right. I don't need to go. I'm probably too tired anyway and I don't have money for drinks and stuff. Ignore me. I'll just clear up the kitchen." Losing her fragile nerve, Emma rushed away with Nicky's plate, loading it into the dishwasher in a fit of activity. Disappointment ate at her, demonstrating her inability to completely squash the desire to get out for a while and be normal.

"I'll look after Nicky." Tiredness made Rohan's speech lazy and his mother tongue heavily accented his sentence. He stood in the doorway and Emma felt his eyes on her.

She fought a rush of hormones as her body heated up at remembered whispered endearments in dark stolen moments, too long ago. The flame in her stomach for him vied with her attraction to Christopher, who at least seemed available. "Just then, you sounded like you did when I first met you," she mused. "A confused nine year old boy who lost his father and thought he was going home to Russia." Emma sounded wistful, clattering the cutlery. "You stood in my father's living room in Lincoln and said, '*I vant to go home!*' I thought your accent was so exotic."

"Then Anton did this huge fart," Rohan smiled, the pain of his grief fresh and unmasked.

"And you stayed."

"Em..."

"No, it's fine. I won't go."

Rohan moved slowly towards her as Emma clanked a saucepan against the metal sink. "Em?" His arms were firm on her shoulders as he turned her, ignoring her wet hands and drawing her body into his. She felt his heartbeat through the thin blouse covering her chest, her breasts pushed up against him. "Emma, *dorogaya...*" *Sweetheart.*

Emma held her breath, waiting for something impossible. When Rohan spoke again, she felt her heart clang in her chest and it hurt so badly. "Emma, I need to sort my affairs out. I have some documents I need you to look at..."

"Oh." Emma jerked herself back, horrified at his casual allusion to their divorce. It had to come, despite what he maintained. Felicity expected a ring and a sexy weekend and clearly Rohan needed to oblige. She didn't look like the kind of girl to hang around while Emma played house with her boyfriend. Felicity and Alanya's combined threats chilled Emma's heart and she pursed her lips. "Can we sort this later? If I'm going out, I need to get ready."

Emma slunk out of the small space between Rohan's body and the sink and skulked off upstairs, seeing the hurt in blue eyes which seemed even bluer as he observed her with a strange look on his face.

She showered in her ensuite, scrunched her hair until it was a mass of damp curls and pushed it off her neck. Allaine's clip mounted it on the top of her head in a cascading waterfall of dark brown ringlets. Emma used the very last dregs of her compact powder, drew thick black lines above her upper eyelids and scraped out some mascara from the ailing tube. In the absence of lipstick, she used an old chap stick to gloss her full mouth. "That will have to do." She wiggled into the dress by stepping into it and pulling it upwards, jumping at the sight of Rohan's long body leaned against the doorframe of her room.

"Stop doing that!" she squeaked at him. "I haven't got a bra on!"

"I know." His lips curved upwards. "I always loved it when you did that little wiggle thing in your school uniform. It still does it for me."

"Do you realise you sound like a pervert?" Emma bit, poking her breasts into place and buttoning the tiny pearl seeds up the front of the dress. She felt naked without a bra, but hers were a manky shade of grey from over washing and did little to prop up her breasts anyway. The red fabric rose from the first button in her cleavage, sliding left and right in a gentle gradient until it brushed the bones of her shoulders. There was no room for dingy grey bra straps. Emma stood in front of her walk in wardrobe door which housed a mirror, peering at her reflection. Her underwear showed through the silky material and made her feel self-conscious. The lines and ridges of her belly knickers left the illusion of a beautiful woman in a stylish red dress, wearing a nappy. With a snort of exasperation, Emma reached under the dress and yanked them down, stepping out of them with ease. She heard Rohan inhale and then hold his breath, enjoying his frustration with an unfair sense of vengeance.

"You can leave the room any time you like," she said, turning and facing the handsome blonde man in her doorway. He watched her with a predatory expression in his eyes but didn't move. Emma shrugged and pulled her suitcase from under the bed, rifling through it by feel rather than sight. Her fingers closed around the G-string her neighbour gave her for Christmas last year as a joke. They were from the *Pound Shop* and she got them all one each. Emma looked at the flimsy dental floss holding the garment together and wondered if it would hold for a full night of dancing and revelry, deciding she actually didn't care. She balled it into her palm and closed her hand, desperate for Rohan not to see the extent of her choice of undies and stood up. "Just get out, please. Ro, you said you didn't mind looking after Nick. I didn't realise it meant watching me get ready."

"You're not going out like that!" He spat the words and stood up straight, his head nearly touching the underside of the door frame. "You've got nothing on underneath that dress."

"I remember you finding it horny once upon a time." Emma's eyes danced with mischief and she watched Rohan struggle. His eyes darkened to an unusual blue and she recognised the signs of a man losing control. She watched with interest and saw unsatisfied desire turn quickly to rage.

"You're not going out like that!"

"And you're not my father!" she shouted. "He's dead, remember?"

Emma heard Nicky run from the living room downstairs and make his way towards the stairs. "Mummy?" he called, sounding alarmed.

"I'm your husband!" Rohan hissed, hearing the boy breach the stairs behind him.

"Yeah, well not for much longer!" Emma bit back.

Nicky pushed around Rohan's body to get to his mother, his little face full of concern. "Why you shoutin'?" he began and then his face broke into a wide smile. "Mummy, you's so bootiful. I didn't know you looked like that!" Childish delight filled his eyes and guilt ate at Emma's heart. *What am I doing?*

Her son's brain switched to more interesting facts, once he fulfilled the criteria of admiration drummed home to him by his teacher at the Lincoln school.

'Always tell a woman she looks beautiful.

Never ask her age.

Never, never ask if she's expecting a baby. Remember that one, children. It's for your own good!'

Nicky gave Emma a hug and smoothed his hand along the soft material from her hip to her thigh. He sniggered. "You're rudey dudey under there!" He looked bashful. "Like Shaz on the estate. She din't wear knickers, remember? The wind blew and she showed her..."

Emma fixed her free hand over her son's mouth and gave him a warning look. He slobbered on her hand and she pulled it away with a look of distaste. "Don't be disgusting! It's nearly time for bed."

"No, me and Uncle Ro is gonna make the slingshot in the tool shed in a minute," Nicky whined, immediately on a different trail altogether. "He promised!" His eyes flicked towards Rohan with hopeful expectation.

"Well give me a kiss and then you can both get on with it. I need to leave now." Emma ignored Rohan as she planted a gentle kiss over her son's lips. Nicky wrinkled his nose.

"Strawberry chap stick. Yuk!"

"Go!" Emma pointed to the door and both males left, one more reluctant than the other. In her ensuite bathroom, Emma wriggled her bum into the G-string, a horrified look planted on her face. The cotton thread was uncomfortable and she looked in the mirror and practiced a face which didn't betray her horror at the need to keep yanking the thing out of her nether regions. She bent down and picked up the bright red stilettos, keeping them in her hand to broach the steep, split level staircase.

As Emma opened the front door, she let out a squeak. Felicity stood in front of her with her hand raised and her mouth open. "You look...amazing!" the other woman conceded, with considerable reluctance. "Where are you going?" She looked behind Emma with suspicion on her face, obviously expecting Rohan to be following her.

"Out," Emma replied, without explanation. "Ro's in the shed with Nicky. They're making something together."

"Oh, damn." Felicity waved a bottle of red wine in Emma's face. "I was hoping for some alone time with him."

Emma shrugged and pushed her way out the door, feeling the frozen concrete underneath her bare feet. "See ya!" she intoned with a smirk, avoiding the splinter laden wood of the front gate as she slipped into the street. She almost laughed out loud at the memory of Rohan's face as he watched her slip into the dress. She knew every twitch and expression of that man's body language and his discomfort filled her with amusement. "Impotent my ass," she sniggered. "He just doesn't fancy you, Felicity darling."

Half way down Newcombe Street, Emma was forced to stop and put the shoes on. The ground made her feet feel numb so at least the shoes didn't hurt initially. "You look like a hooker!" she chastised herself, her shoulders bare to the wintry night. "I hope I don't see anyone...oh, hello."

The dog walkers nodded and stared and Emma cringed. She made an incongruous sight in the depths of November, walking the street in a cocktail dress and high heels. Against her better judgement she used the darkened alley ways to reach Northampton Road, clattering noisily through the most risky places at a run, her heeled feet sounding like gun shots and probably drawing more observers from behind closed curtains than she wanted. At the entrance to the motel, she paused, primped her hair and started up the stairs.

"Hey." Christopher leaned against the door frame with an air of casualness that was instantly calming.

"Hi." Emma felt her heartbeat fighting to return to normal. She stood frozen at the bottom of the steps.

"You look amazin'." His lyrical Irish accent sounded sexy.

"That's good then," Emma allowed herself a smile. "You're the second person to say that tonight."

"Rohan?" Christopher said the name with something of a sneer and Emma shook her head.

"No. He said something very different."

Christopher took a last drag of the thin cigarette and

stubbed it out on the brickwork, before flicking it into the hedge. His confidence shrouded Emma in protection and she admired the close cut of his suit in the lamp light from the motel as it fitted neatly over his trim figure. He strode easily down the stairs and bent to kiss her, his lips tasting of nicotine and gin. Emma didn't expect to like either but surprised herself. "I didn't know if you'd come," he whispered.

"Nor did I," Emma replied, masking a tiny, inappropriate giggle at her daring and courage. The dental floss underwear exacted its revenge and she winced. Christopher's brow knitted and Emma placed her index finger over his lips. "Don't ask." She smiled.

CHAPTER TWENTY FOUR

They walked into town at a slow pace, Emma clinging to Christopher's arm for dear life in her shoes. "Want me to give you a piggy back?" he asked in his slow drawl and Emma let out an unladylike snort.

"I don't think you want to go there! Some parts of me might not survive."

"Sounds interestin'." He eyed her sideways as though wanting to devour her and Emma blossomed under the sense of danger he brought out in her.

Christopher took Emma for dinner in a local bar, where they sat in a booth and talked endlessly about nothing. Emma's agenda of asking for help from a total stranger died without being spoken, under a shroud of awkwardness. Christopher's deep brown eyes bore into her face throughout the meal, like dark holes of nothing into which she felt she could pour herself. Other diners stared at them, both overdressed for the occasion, but neither of them seemed to notice. "D'ya fancy kickin' up yer heels and havin' a dance?" Christopher asked her, as Emma reappeared from the toilet looking more comfortable.

"It sounds brilliant." She smiled, cringing as he got up to pay the bill. Emma tugged on Christopher's arm. "Maybe I can pay next time..." He silenced her with a kiss that took her breath away and momentarily halted a few nearby conversations.

Outside on the pavement, Emma shivered. Christopher easily shucked his jacket and laid it across her shoulders. He wrapped her in two strong arms, allowing one of his hands to stray just below her hip. His face crinkled with mirth. "Geez woman! Have you no shame?" His palm stroked the curve of her buttock and his mouth dropped open a little. "Bloody hell! I've never met a woman like you, so."

"Let's just say, I'd had enough of Shazza's little Christmas gift!" Emma smirked, the G-string now nestled in the dustbin in the ladies' toilets.

"I haven't a clue what you're talkin' about," Christopher snorted. "But it sounds good to me!"

The nightclub thronged with perspiring bodies and the volume was deafening. Christopher kept Emma close as they climbed stairs to an upstairs level, his hand periodically straying to the top of her buttock. A couple of times he shot her a lascivious look full of promise. The bellyful of red wine dulled her senses and helped her towards reckless decisions. They danced until just after midnight. Christopher was entertaining and funny, flowing drinks easily with unlimited wads of cash from his wallet. His kisses on her lips, cheeks and neck felt addictive and she wanted more.

"Come back with me!" he shouted over the music as they gyrated on the dance floor, Emma's curls snaking free of her clip and bouncing around her face.

"To Belfast?" she yelled back and he smirked and pulled a *maybe* face. "Sounds good," she laughed. "Right after I find a contract killer to take out some people."

Christopher looked at her oddly and realising she said too much, Emma indicated she needed another trip to the toilets and clattered down the stairs, feeling drunk and untouchable. In the mirror of the ladies' she looked at herself and beamed, feeling her lost teenage years catching up with her in revelling and debauchery without consequence.

At the top of the stairs to the bar and dance floor, Emma paused in the doorway, seeking out Christopher before attempting to weave her way through the hot, sticky bodies. Her heart skipped in her breast as she saw his tall, dark figure near another exit door, ogling his gorgeous physique and mentally undressing him in her drunken mind. She froze. Something about the rigidity of his stance cut through the alcohol as a warning

Two men stood next to Christopher, thick set like body guards and menacing. Emma felt the waves of tension cross the room and paused in the doorway, jostled by passing revellers keen to get back to the party. Christopher looked ill at ease, but not overly so. He shrugged and kept his hands in his pockets, dipping his dark head towards the mouth of one of the men. He nodded, looked up to get eye contact and nodded again as if in agreement. Then he lifted an index finger and raised it up to the closest man's face. Emma read his lips. "*One hour.*"

The heaviest set man had his back to her, but he leaned his head towards the other and they discussed something, opening their mouths wide to shout. The one speaking was bald, but the other had dark hair slicked back against his head like a throwback from an Elvis Presley impressionist. Emma lived on the council estate in Lincoln for long enough to recognise heavy duty muscle when she saw it, sensing trouble oozing from every pore of their bodies. The men seemed in agreement and turned as one to face Emma's date. Holding his index finger up, the bald man leaned in and shouted into Christopher's face, the words lost in the pulsing music but the meaning evident. "One hour!" Emma couldn't make out the other part of the sentence as the troll turned to his companion. But she saw Christopher wince as spittle from the beefy lips whipped past.

They turned away and strode towards the bar like sumo wrestlers locked into suits, the crowd of drinkers oozing out of the way like reluctant jelly. Emma watched Christopher run his hands through his hair and across his mouth, sitting down at a nearby table with a slump of resignation in his shoulders. *What's happening in an hour? Is he in trouble?*

The answer pounded into her addled brain like a stab of reality. *No! You are. You're the one in trouble, you stupid, pathetic woman!* Reason and good sense banished the alcoholic haze and Emma looked down at her pretty dress and awkward shoes, her body vulnerable and naked underneath. Her hands were empty, testament to her leaving the house without door key, money or phone. She panicked. Christopher was delivering her to the menacing pair; in an hour.

Emma was gone from the doorway before Christopher looked up, running down the street with her shoes in her hands. The frozen pathways stung her feet until she could no longer feel them and tiny stones dug into her numb soles without care. Still she ran. Emma took stupid risks, using alleys and cut throughs which would have made Rohan's hair grey in seconds had he seen her, sobbing and crying as she went. She berated herself for her stupidity over and over, seeing the dreadful danger laid out before her like a muddy cloth. The narrow escape had saved her from dreadful harm but the night would cost her all her dignity.

At the front door, Emma sank onto the prickly

doormat, exhausted and panting. She heard Farrell bark from inside and his nose against the threshold, scenting her and kicking up a fuss.

"Sit! Stay!" Rohan's voice sounded firm and calm from behind the wooden door, the stained glass panel lighting up with colour as he whipped the curtain back and peered out. The door shuddered as he opened it, looking out at the empty street in confusion. Then he looked down and saw Emma.

Her breath heaved as he carried her inside, finally releasing the desperate dog from his position on guard. "Release!" he told him and immediately Farrell jumped at Emma's bare and bleeding feet, whining and concerned. When Rohan laid her on the sofa in the kitchen, the dog put his paw on her knee and peered into her face.

"Emma! Look at me. *Chto sluchilos?* What happened? Did someone hurt you?" Rohan balled his fists on her lap and gritted his teeth, a frenzied, maniacal look in his eyes.

"Oh no! Felicity!" Emma tried to struggle up, prevented by Rohan's strong hands on her wrists.

"What's she got to do with this?"

"Nothing. I don't want to see her, not now. I can't cope. I just want to go to bed. Let me go!" Emma struggled to her feet, hobbling across the cold floor tiles. The dog accompanied her to the bottom of the stairs, worried brown eyes watching her face with doggy intensity. Emma stroked his head and felt the wetness of his comforting lick on her hand. When she climbed the first steps to the landing, she looked down and saw Farrell's concerned face, front two paws on the bottom step. Emma tried to smile reassurance at him, wasting her effort as his face remained the same.

In her bedroom she sank down onto the soft duvet, feeling an ache in her soul she thought she mastered long ago. It burned and stung, bone deep, soul deep, ripping her open along painful, half-healed scars. Emma sank her face into her pillow and sobbed.

CHAPTER TWENTY FIVE

"You bloody did what?" Rohan's face was angrier than Emma had ever seen it, his eyes blazing a peculiar blue like storm waters and his honey coloured face morphing into a furious puce.

"I know, I know. It was reckless and stupid; you don't have to tell me something I already know. I met him yesterday and he seemed nice..."

"Nice?" Rohan shook his head and repeated the word as though trying to understand how it was relevant. "You went on a date with a complete stranger because you thought he was nice!"

"He made me feel good about myself and I thought just one night out wouldn't hurt and..."

"One night out!" Again, Rohan didn't let Emma finish her sentence and she gritted her teeth in temper as guilt and foolishness mixed in her gut. Rohan paced her warm bedroom, his body stiff with rage. "Ah yeah, enjoy one night out and end up running through the town in a ball dress with no shoes. Did it not matter that one night out might lead to you not coming back at all? What about your son? Don't you care about him?" His voice rose an octave and Emma's sense of humiliation overrode her need to sit and listen to his accusations.

"Don't you dare shout at me! He's been my priority since I gave birth to him so don't you start trying to make me feel like a failure!" Emma stood up, the silky material cascading down around her shapely calves.

"You wake Nicky and we'll leave right now!" She wiped her blotchy face on a piece of kitchen roll, wincing at its scratchy surface.

"But I don't want you to go, Em. Don't you get that?"

"Oh, go to hell, Rohan. I'm done with your games. I don't know what you want from me! One minute you're kissing me and the next, you're marrying Felicity and she's threatening me..." Emma's voice broke as she struggled with the swathe of emotions which overwhelmed her. She clutched at her chest and agitated fingers grappled with the buttons at her cleavage.

"What? Please! Just listen to me," Rohan begged. He reached for her and Emma shook her head and turned away from his questing hands.

"No. Ro, please leave me alone. We'll be gone in the morning. I was stupid to think I could ever do this; live here with you like we were brother and sister and not...I let my desperation get the better of me. I should have known." With a mammoth sigh, Emma turned and walked across to the window, looking out at the deserted street down which she performed her frantic hundred metre dash earlier. The floor underfoot made small squeaks as her sore feet passed over the beech wood joins and Emma sighed at her misfortune. The thought of telling Nicky they were going filled her with misery.

Unable to settle mentally, Emma shoved past Rohan and followed the hallway to her son's room. Nicky snored softly and she smiled and pulled his door gently closed, not trusting herself to disturb him in her turmoil. She fought the urge to gather him up and run. That would come tomorrow.

"Please, go!" Emma pushed Rohan from the room with force and closed her bedroom door with her bottom, hearing the reassuring click as the catch snapped shut. She stood for a while with her hands over her eyes, waiting for her heart to slow and reach equilibrium again. Her eyes stayed strangely dry, the wells of her soul all cried out and emptied long ago for Rohan Andreyev. Her earlier tears were for herself and born of shame and disappointment, leaving a stinging tingle in her soul. With a sigh, Emma flung herself onto the iron bedstead, hearing the mattress groan underneath her. "I'm an idiot," she whispered into the darkness, punctuated only by streetlamps. "I knew this would never work."

The sick feeling rose into her chest and she sat up, fighting the urge to gag. Christopher's face drifted past her inner vision, dark and beautiful. Emma shook her head and tutted. His darkness attracted her like a moth to a flame and it frustrated and confused her. Then her heart overruled the musings of her lust and Rohan's bemused face moved into her mind, chastising her with the pain of using Christopher as a distraction. Even as a teenager, it perplexed Emma how desperately she needed Rohan's approval and attention. His physical touch was like a balm in their haphazard world.

Emma groaned and yawned, pushing her hair back from her face. She plucked at the upper buttons of her dress, popping them one by one and feeling her breasts relax as the tight material released them a little. Her skin felt soft against fingers which shook, despite Emma's attempts to control her emotions and a deep sadness snuck in through the cracks in her armour. She pushed the threatening tears away with pure bloody mindedness and allowed her fingers to stray to her slim waist and the stomach that once held the secret of her unborn son. "Damn you, Christopher. And double damn you, Rohan," Emma whispered.

As though in answer, the door clicked open and light from the hall lamp filtered through. Rohan's silhouette was framed in the gap and Emma looked away, her fingers fluttering to hide her exposed chest. He stared at her and waited a moment before sliding through the gap and closing the door behind him. "Em, can we talk?" Rohan's voice held an edge of begging and Emma let the heavy sigh escape her.

"No."

Rohan made the distance from the doorway to the bed in one stride and perched next to Emma without touching her. The familiar electricity arced between them, burning them both in its intensity. Emma closed her eyes as exhaustion claimed the last of her energy but when she opened them, she sensed Rohan's eyes on her face. "Em. I still love you. I haven't stopped..."

"Shut up!" Emma's shout cut through the darkness, louder than she intended. She held her breath, waiting for Nicky to come pounding into the room in terror, but he slept on in the hum of ensuing silence. She exhaled in a rush and anger reclaimed the space vacated by fear.

Rohan's gentle fingers on Emma's shoulders acted like a catalyst. She exploded, venting almost seven years of abandonment and disappointment. "I hate you!" she hissed as she pounded at Rohan's broad chest, feeling his expensive shirt rip under her scratching and clawing. "You destroyed me! I hate you!"

Emma felt her nails contact soft skin and she allowed them to bite into the flesh underneath, venting

211

her disappointment with herself, with him, with life in general. Rohan inhaled in pain and grasped her wrists, holding them out sideways and infuriating Emma further. He wrenched her hands behind her back so she was pinioned and then he eased her body under him, trapping her writhing and squirming on the bed with her hands underneath her. Their combined knuckles dug into the base of her spine, knotty and painful and Emma's anger dissipated as quickly as it came, realising she was beaten. "Let go and you're dead!" she spat.

"I just won't let go then." Rohan's face was close to Emma's and she heard him breathing heavily from their fight and from the other thing Felicity claimed he wasn't able to feel. Emma gritted her teeth and tried to kick him sideways, realising as she felt his warm palm on her thigh that he trapped her wrists one handed. His other roved to the top of her leg under her dress and Emma held her breath as Rohan's fingers traced the line where her knickers should be. "Promise me nobody hurt you...like that?" His voice sounded anguished.

"Nobody did," Emma replied, counting her blessings. Her body burned with the gentleness of Rohan's intimate touch, remembering the former passion of two misguided kids indulging a forbidden love.

"Rohan, don't." Emma's voice was nasal, forgotten tears filling her sinuses and waiting for the order to fall.

"You're still my wife." Rohan's voice was tender and Emma felt him dip towards her. His full lips against hers crumbled her resolve, smoothing away Christopher's ardent kisses and replacing them with ones of love and affection. By the time Rohan's soft tongue flicked between her teeth, Emma had long since given in. Rohan's deft fingers moved up further underneath the dress. She moaned, but the opening of her lips allowed him further access and Rohan made good use of the break in hostilities. "I'm gonna let you go," he breathed. Emma felt his warm breath kiss her skin, laced with wine and the faint scent of mint. He moved and Emma's hands were free. They tingled numbly behind her, feeling as though they belonged to someone else. She groaned as she brought them out in front of her, the blood rushing back into the compressed veins and making them throb. Rohan's free hand strayed to the remaining buttons on her dress and he popped them expertly until Emma lay underneath him with her breasts exposed. The streetlamps dappled the light against the trees outside and cast patterns across Emma's luscious skin.

As the feeling re-entered her numb hands, so it also reactivated her dazed brain and Emma countered. Her battered heart couldn't keep up such a drain on its emotional resources. She dragged her right hand across, aiming to connect with Rohan's head as he kissed the soft, willing breasts which struggled for freedom under the red material hiding the last of her dignity. It met with instant resistance.

"Don't inhale before you hit." His whispers were soft and hypnotic, laced with his sexy Russian accent. "You give yourself away." Rohan clasped the errant wrist again, pushing it above Emma's head.

"Screw you!" she grunted as she fought him, but Rohan laughed and put his lips over hers to silence her.

"That has to be an invitation." He dragged her other wrist above her head and held them both one handed, using his leg across her thighs to prevent any further meting out of justice. His free hand strayed to her waist and then began to lower, raising the soft red material with silken movements. As Emma held her breath, Rohan kissed her just like he used to.

"Don't!" she begged him but only once, her body betraying her as it responded to her husband's forgotten kisses.

"Sshh," he soothed her, lying across her body. "Tell me you don't love me." Passion made him shiver on top of her as fear and anticipation mixed in his blue eyes. Emma gasped as the stitching tore on the dress and Rohan displayed her underneath him, vulnerable and naked like a prize. His shirt and trousers felt scratchy and rough against Emma's skin, but fear paralysed her as he eased the dress back with expert hands.

"We can't do this!" Emma's voice held a rasp of anguish as Rohan's fingers explored and his lips caressed hers, punctuating her sentence and ignoring her weak protest.

"I love you, Emma Andreyev," he whispered, breaking the kiss only to speak and then resuming it.

Emma felt hope blossom within her tired heart at the sound of a married name she never got to use. "I know." The sob caught in her throat. "Hold me, Ro. Please, hold me." She clung to him, no longer restrained but willing, leaning into Rohan and allowing herself to remember his scent, the feel of his skin and the sensation of his chest pressed against hers. Disaster smiled its ghastly grimace as the couple danced with it again, driven by the soul-mate connection and a separation that refused to be brooked.

Rohan wrapped his arm tightly around Emma as though he would never let her go, whispering to her in his lyrical Slavic tongue as he undid the buttons of his shirt.

CHAPTER TWENTY SIX

"Emma, I want to hear you say it, *da*. Promise you'll stay?" Rohan's voice was hushed in the darkness and Emma held her breath. And there it was. *The problem*. Alanya, Christopher, Felicity and Nicky; they pushed into her brain bringing confusion and misery.

"I don't want to talk about it." Emma rolled away from Rohan's warm body, feeling the cold air rush in to occupy the space between them. She lay with her back towards him, cursing the weakness that allowed him dominion over her. Undeterred, Rohan slid over behind her, spooning her with his body.

"You're still gorgeous," he whispered, placing gentle kisses on her bare neck and shoulders.

"Stop it!" Emma shrugged him off and heard Rohan's familiar low chuckle. He ignored her, snuggling in tighter and wrapping his arms firmly around her resistant body. She grunted as she shoved his questing hand away, scratching him deliberately. Rohan hissed with pain but increased the pressure, pinioning her against him.

Something cool and angular touched the back of her knee and Emma reached down to investigate. Rohan batted her hand away. "Leave."

"What is it?" Emma reached her fingers out again and Rohan seized them, drawing them into her chest and clasping them there between her breasts, his hand fixed firmly over the top. He nuzzled into the back of her hair, making her shiver.

"Just the brace for my knee," he said.

"Is that what you meant when you said you were injured? How did you hurt it?" Emma's voice sounded small in the darkness.

"War." Just the single word was enough to condemn her absence.

"When did it happen?"

Rohan's reply left her cold with his naming of the day. Because as Emma cried out, labouring Nicky into the world in a hospital continents away, Rohan rolled around in agony on a battle field. "How bad is it?" Emma whispered and he brushed the question away with a sensuous kiss underneath her hair. She groaned and arched her back, despite herself.

"I don't want to talk about it. I love having you here," Rohan whispered against the back of Emma's head. His breath felt warm and mussed her hair. "I bought this house for you. Anton said you'd like it."

Emma bit her lip, closing her eyes against the guilt burning in her breast. She felt taunted by the memory of Christopher, just a few hours before, working his way into her mind and her tender mouth with his tantalising kisses. "I do like it, but Ro?" She struggled to turn in his arms, wriggling to face him, their bodies becoming tangled. Rohan squeezed her and took the opportunity to kiss her upturned lips. "No, I need to talk to you," she protested, desperate to confess her stupidity with Christopher.

"It's fine. If you're gonna tell me you're leaving, I don't want to hear it." Rohan silenced Emma with another powerful kiss and she temporarily lost the fragile thread of conversation. His deft fingers roved down Emma's back and strayed to the top of her buttocks as an odd sound broke into the room. Rohan swore. "Sorry, *devotchka*. It's probably work. I have to take this." He moved backwards with a heave and pushed himself out of the bed, letting the sheets flutter down in his wake and causing a draught. Emma sighed and pulled the covers around her nakedness, watching Rohan's tall figure in the dim yellow streetlight.

He bent and grappled in his trouser pocket, retrieving his mobile phone. Its screen lit up like a Christmas tree, colourful and garish. "Andreyev." Rohan's answer was clipped and abrupt. Emma watched the outline of his shoulders sag. "Oh, hi Felicity. Why are you ringing this number?"

Emma gasped as guilt washed over her at her hastily forgotten tormentor and she buried her face in the covers. *What have I done?* Rohan cast around for his clothes, pulling the bedroom door open and flooding the room with light from the hallway.

Awkwardness descended like a mantle, shrouding the couple in misery. The usually clipped and capable man looked lost, stepping into the hallway and then halting, boxer shorts and trousers dangling from his hand. He shot a look of desperation towards Emma as she peeked over the sheets. Rohan stared at Nicky's door, obviously not wanting to risk being found naked coming out of Emma's bedroom. He waited another heartbeat and turned once more, his blue eyes filled with confusion. "*Sorry, I'll just get rid of her*," he mouthed.

Emma allowed herself one last, covetous look, taking in Rohan's strong muscular back and shoulders, his swollen biceps and trim waist. Her eyes roved over his neat buttocks and down the back of strong honey coloured thighs covered in downy blonde hair to the sinews of his knees. She gaped.

Rohan's right leg was missing from the knee down,

replaced with a skin coloured cuff and a metal prosthetic leg. Scar tissue covered the leg above, ridging the skin in ugly red wheals. Emma stuffed the sheet into her mouth to dull her reaction of horror as Rohan bent to retrieve his fallen boxer shorts before bolting into his own room and pushing the door behind him.

Rolling onto her back, her hands over her mouth, Emma fought a wave of sickness. *I didn't even know! Why did nobody tell me?* The evidence showed it was more than just an injury; he could have died. "You didn't tell me about this, Anton bloody Andreyev. Would you have even told me if he died?" Emma hissed into the darkness.

Bile and guilt mixed into a foul tasting concoction that threatened to exit without warning and Emma sat up and hugged her knees. The peace and satiation of good sex dissipated as she coped with the double blow. She had trespassed into Rohan's relationship with Felicity, finding once she got there that she knew nothing of her former lover's life since their acrimonious parting. She imagined Rohan in agony, perhaps calling her name and begging someone to fetch her. Was she even listed anywhere as his wife? Tears soaked the bedding at her failure as a wife and a human being and Emma berated herself internally. The heavy feeling between her legs reminded her she was also a failure as a woman. Felicity mistrusted her and clearly with just cause.

Emma heard the steady rumble of Rohan's deep baritone next door as he talked on the phone to his unsuspecting girlfriend. She could hear him keep saying he had to go. Emma slipped from the bed and felt her way to the bedroom door, feeling the fabric of

Rohan's shirt under her toes. Picking it up from its careless abandonment on the carpet, Emma lifted it to her nose and sniffed Rohan's familiar scent, feeling her stomach churn with a myriad of emotions. She dropped it as though it was contaminated and used the ensuite bathroom to wash her swollen face and clean herself up. Then she dressed in her pyjamas and crept out into the lighted hall.

Rohan's lilting voice sounded sexy on the phone as Emma crept past, shielded from view by his partially closed door. She slipped into the room next to his, closing the door behind her and dragging Nicky's suitcase quietly across the floor to block the door. "Move up, baby," she whispered as she pushed into the double bed next to him. Her small son grunted and turned his back on her, rolling away towards the other side of the bed. Emma climbed into the warmed space he vacated, swaddled in his little boy scent of shampoo and washing powder. His soft bare feet were cold as he pushed his tiny soles against Emma's thighs, a habit from babyhood. She sighed with relief and clasped them in hands grateful to be busy. "I love you little boy," she sniffed, wiping her tears on the pillow under her. "I've screwed up everything, but I'll try my best not to screw up being your mum."

Nicky stirred and turned over, his breath smelling of toothpaste and hot chocolate. "Mummy." His voice sounded loud in the silence. "Mummy, cuddle me." He pulled himself into Emma's chest, wrapping his delicate arms around her neck in a throttle hold. "Love you, Mummy," he sighed. Emma kissed his warm forehead and rested her cheek on the top of his fluffy head. She closed her eyes as peace descended over her soul. Her son was all that mattered; nothing else.

Emma heard Rohan disconnect his call from Felicity and move around his room. He went out into the hallway and knocked quietly on her open door, calling her name on discovery of the empty bed. She stiffened as his footsteps stopped outside the child's door and held her breath, listening. She exhaled as Rohan moved away, his gait slightly uneven in his tiredness. At least now, she knew why he listed slightly as he walked.

Emma slept cradling Nicky's skinny body and woke up numerous times in the night. The surety of her child's steady breathing was soporific, until Emma remembered the feel of Rohan's hands on her body and the sounds of their shared ecstasy. The dull ache between her legs provided a constant reminder, infusing her with an unsettling anxiety which made her toss and turn.

By the time the insipid daylight broke through the curtains at dawn, Emma was decided. She needed to go home. *Today.*

CHAPTER TWENTY SEVEN

"Don't do this, Em," Rohan pleaded as Emma rolled up her clothing and stuffed it into the old suitcase. "Not like this. Let's talk about it."

"I can't!" Emma flung another jumper into the battered inner, frustrated as it unrolled itself in protest. She thumped a pair of jeans on top, resisting the urge to start again.

"*Devotchka*, please." Rohan's grip on her wrists was strong and halted her progress.

"Don't call me that!" she snapped. "Don't ever call me that again! I'm not your girl; Felicity is."

"What? No! I thought everything was fine. I don't understand. Nicky's gone to school ok, hasn't he? Don't you like it down here?" Keeping hold of Emma's slender wrists, Rohan sank onto the bed and pulled her down next to him. "Talk to me, Em!"

Emma looked down at his strong fingers, the knuckles white as they encircled her wrists. Rohan wore a white tee shirt which accentuated tanned biceps peeking from under the sleeves. Emma dipped her head forward, unable to meet his perceptive blue eyes and Rohan rested his forehead against hers. Emma's speech came haltingly. "How could you get out of my bed and then talk to Felicity as though nothing wrong? We weren't just chatting, Ro! What we did was wrong!"

"How can it be wrong when we're still married?" Rohan settled his rough, stubbly cheek against Emma's soft skin, enfolding her in an embrace which betrayed his desperation. "You're my wife and I love you. I lost you once. You're not leaving again."

"I can't do this, I'm sorry." Tears spilled from Emma's pretty brown eyes, glistening on her eyelashes like glitter. "I let a desperate need to change my circumstances cloud my judgement and already it's caused so much damage. I need to go back now before I wreck both our lives."

"I won't let you go." Rohan's voice wobbled, the first sign of emotion Emma had seen and it rocked her, strengthening her resolve.

"See." She shook her head. "Now you're upset. We'll just end up destroying each other. Like before..."

"We were kids before!" Rohan's exclamation contained the hint of a sneer. "We were two kids, in love with no support. I'll talk to Felicity, I promise. I'll sort this out. I never made her any promises, Em! She just wanted to tell me about some dress she bought..."

"She'll be devastated! I can't stay here if you do that! I'll keep bumping into her in school and it will be awkward and nasty."

"So what then?" Rohan raised his voice in frustration and his grip on Emma's wrists increased, digging into her soft flesh. "What do you want from me?"

"Nothing!" Emma shook her head and wrenched her hands free. "I want nothing, Ro."

"Where will you go? You can't possibly go back to that shit-hole!"

"Thanks for that!" She stood up, her legs shaking underneath her. Emma took a deep breath and tossed her head in defiance, steeling herself against the mess she made every time she opened her mouth.

"Where will you go?" Rohan repeated, using the bed to stand up. Awareness of his injury made Emma even more attuned to his suffering, the odd wince of pain and the slight imbalance in his movements. *I should have been there for you,* her heart cried but her brain silenced it with an inner forcefulness.

"I don't know." She shrugged and turned, groaning as Rohan wrapped his arms around her from behind. He pressed her shoulders back into his body and pushed his face into her neck, breathing in the perfumed scent of her long hair. "I'll borrow some money from Allaine maybe and go...somewhere. Nicky and I can start over. Perhaps if it works out, he'll forgive me for uprooting him and failing again."

Rohan turned Emma's body gently, resting his hands on her shoulders and staring into her eyes. His shone with an unnatural sheen, misery causing them to glitter with surface tears. "Tell me what to do," he asked, his voice level. "What do you want, Em? Name it and I'll do it. If you stay here, I'll do whatever you want."

Emma looked at the luxurious house, its plush carpets and expensive decoration, more opulent than anywhere else she'd ever stayed. "I don't know."

"Do you like the town?" Rohan asked, allowing himself a smile of relief when Emma nodded.

"Yeah. It's lovely and the people are kind," she replied.

"Nicky likes the school, doesn't he?"

Emma nodded with enthusiasm. "Yeah. He loves his new teacher." She bit her lip. "He's gonna freak when I tell him we're..."

"Then don't. You stay here and I'll find somewhere else to go." Rohan's huge blue eyes were filled with sincerity as he laid everything on the line for her. "Or I'll rent something for you."

"You don't owe me anything!" Emma exclaimed. "We've been separated long enough for you to divorce me, if you want to."

"Emma!" Rohan moved in close so their bodies touched. His hands slipped from her shoulders to settle around her waist, his presence intoxicating. Emma felt her head swim with the effort of not reaching up to kiss him. He smiled sadly. "If I wanted to divorce you, I would have." He plucked at a loose curl and wound it absentmindedly through his fingers, like he used to. Rohan pushed his hands either side of Emma's neck, trailing his fingers through her hair and massaging the back of her neck. Emma managed to keep the groan of ecstasy to herself. Rohan dipped forward and kissed the end of her nose and she closed her eyes. "I don't want a divorce. Stay?" he begged. "I'll be gone again in a few days and you can have the house to yourself. Look after Farrell for me? Please? I promise not to try and seduce you again, I'll keep my hands...and other parts to myself." He smiled wistfully and ran a lazy thumb under her eye, feeling the dampness of her tears.

"How long will you be gone?" she heard herself ask.

"I don't know. I never know. A few weeks, months. I come home when the job's done."

Emma sighed. "And what about when you come back? What then?"

"Let's just cross our bridges one at a time, hey?" He smiled, small crow's feet appearing at the corners of his eyes. His blonde hair flipped forward into his face and in obedience to a gut reaction, Emma reached up and pushed it back. Rohan closed his eyes and when they opened, agony streamed out. Emma gulped and put her hands by her sides.

"Ok," she replied. "Thank you. We'll stay until you get back. But then we should either get our own place or move away completely."

Rohan smiled a sad little smile and nodded. "Good," he said and released her. He walked down the hallway towards the stairs, turning his body slightly to deal with the gradient and Emma felt a click in her heart as it awoke and tortured her with her mistakes.

"Ro!" Emma shouted and he stopped, his brow creased as he looked at her. Emma walked to the top of the stairs, seeing him from above, strong, muscular and capable. "About Felicity...she loves you, anyone can see that."

Rohan's shoulders slumped and he set off down the stairs, his right foot clumping more heavily than the left. "Well I don't love her."

CHAPTER TWENTY EIGHT

Rohan put his phone on the counter as Emma walked into the kitchen and clicked her tongue to Farrell. "School time," she called to him and he rushed towards her, his tail wagging furiously. Rohan bit his lip and stared at her, his eyes unseeing.

"I'm leaving now. I don't know how long this will take. Emma, I need to be straight with you about some stuff, so just listen. It might not go well for me and I can't back out now. Hack is missing and I don't have the information I need to stay safe. If anything should happen to me, all this," he waved his hand around to indicate the house, "it's all yours. My will is with a solicitor in town and his name's on the computer under a file called '*Emma*.' You remember the password for the computer don't you? I wanted you to sign stuff the other night but..."

"Rohan, you're scaring me! I don't understand any of this. You crunch numbers so how is this relevant and who or what the hell is Hack?"

"I need you to be scared, Em! It's important. Don't talk to anyone you don't know, ok? None of the guys I work with know where I live. I've registered everything at a dummy address. But they can find me easily if they want to, so until I find out what's going on, be careful, *dorogaya*."

An image of Christopher's handsome face halted Emma's denials and she blushed a deep red. Rohan was all over her guilt in seconds. "What is it?"

Emma gulped. "A man called Christopher came looking for you a few days ago. He was waiting outside. I let him in for a coffee because it was cold..."

"Shit!" Rohan's hands clamped around her upper arms with painful force. "What did he say? What did he look like?"

"He said he was waiting for you and we chatted a bit. He was tall and dark with brown eyes." Emma paused, terrified by the intensity in Rohan's face. "He was from Belfast and spoke with a strong Irish accent...what?"

Rohan dropped her arms and took a step back. "Are you serious?"

Emma's jaw dropped like a goldfish and she gaped unattractively. "Er...yes and the other thing is..."

"He was Irish?" Rohan interrupted her, fixating on Christopher's nationality.

"Yes and..."

"Definitely from Belfast? He didn't say he was from Ballysillan?"

"No! Belfast. But the thing is..."

"Ok, right. Keep the dog with you at night, Em. Take him upstairs with you and stay with Nicky. Don't separate. Take your mobile phone and keep it charged at all times. Don't mess around if you feel unsafe, just dial the police and tell them it's an emergency."

"But the guy outside, was his name not Christopher then?" Emma's shoulders slumped as foolishness overcame her. "Did he lie about that too?"

Rohan shrugged. "How would I know? I never knew his real name. Guy's a computer genius called *Hack*. I didn't need to know his real name. He was my back up and he went missing a week ago."

"He's Hack?" Emma's voice sounded small and

frightened, even to herself. This was way bigger than a deviant trying to rape her with strangers. He wouldn't have needed to hurt her if it was just him. Emma felt a flush of shame at the knowledge she would have given herself to him willingly, in exchange for a night of freedom. "I don't understand."

"I know, *devotchka*. Come here." Rohan's arms were strong around Emma and she pressed herself into his chest, smelling his clean linen scent and the aftershave he always favoured. She sighed, all enmity forgotten as she wrapped her arms around him and held on tight.

"Please don't go, Ro. Please don't leave me? I'll behave, I'll do whatever you want but don't go?"

Rohan closed his eyes and exhaled. "I should have seen this coming but I didn't. I got distracted by my personal life and I've walked into something really bad."

"I know about you and Felicity getting married and..."

Rohan placed his finger over Emma's pink lips. "I'm not marrying Felicity, sweetheart. I've told her that a million times. We started as friends and it led to more on her side. I don't fancy her and I'm really not interested. She's going to a lot of effort to force me down a road I don't want to go with her and I'll put her straight as soon as I get back. But I need to go now. The car's on its way. I'll leave you the Mercedes. The key to the back gate is in the glove box. Don't park there in the dark because you have to get out and unlock the gate. It's unlit down there and overgrown. Park on the street if it's dark. Don't walk to school anymore, Em. Use the car."

Rohan's lips pressed down on Emma's with a naked hunger and his eyes were pained. They were both consumed by a bitter memory. Rohan's army uniform cut through the years as Emma cried in his arms and bewailed his desertion of their fledgling marriage, to go to a war which had nothing to do with either of them. "Be here when I get back this time?" Rohan's words shocked her back into the present and Emma inhaled and let out a sob of misery.

"I'm sorry," she gasped, tears springing from her brown eyes. "I'm so sorry, Ro. I loved you so much. I couldn't tell you, I needed you and…"

"Sshhh." His arms made Emma feel secure and she cried loudly into Rohan's shirt. "I know, *devotchka*. I know."

"I was pregnant with your son," Emma gulped, sobbing and hiccoughing in misery. "I was so scared."

"*Dorogaya*, I know. Do you think my heart didn't recognise my own son? I know. *Ya lyublyu tebya*, I love you, Em, I love you."

"Please don't go, please, I'm begging you. I don't understand anything."

Rohan smoothed his fingers across Emma's wet cheek and kissed her there. "I've been paid a lot of money to eliminate a risk, sweetheart. I can't back out now, it's not how it's done. But when I get home, we'll sit and talk. Really talk. I'll tell you what I do for a living and we'll tell Nicky I'm his father; together, you and me telling him together."

A loud hammering came on the door and Emma caught at Rohan's clothing as he gave her one last kiss and reached down for his bag by the door. "There's a thousand pounds cash in the safe under the stairs," he said over his shoulder, heels clicking monotonously against the wooden floor in the huge hallway. "I showed Nicky how to get into it last night, just in case we didn't have time. Take care, Emma. Be here when I get back. Promise?"

"Promise," she said, her brown eyes terrified and sincere.

Then Rohan was gone, closing the front door behind him with a dull click.

CHAPTER TWENTY NINE

"How was the date?" Allaine whispered as Emma stepped in close next to her in the playground. Farrell stayed glued to her left leg as though instinctively knowing something was wrong.

"He was a jerk!" Emma commented, misery oozing from her like a tangible thing.

"Oh, I'm sorry!" Allaine sympathised, putting her arm around her friend. Farrell gave a low growl and the woman stepped back in surprise. "Oh. What's wrong with him?"

"Sorry." Emma pulled on the leash as a reprimand. "He's feeling a bit protective over me today. The guy was *that* kind of jerk."

"Oh no, really? He didn't hurt you, did he?" Allaine turned terrified eyes on her friend, searching for hidden pain or anguish.

Emma opened her mouth to answer, silenced by Mel's exuberant appearance. "I got the job!" Mel squealed, throwing her arms around both women in her excitement. "I actually got the job. I start on Monday and I'm so excited!"

The women hugged and congratulated and allowed Mel's happiness to rub off on them. She pulled a paper bag shyly from her pocket as the children poured out, handing it to Emma. "I did a couple of hours practice this morning and my new boss paid me. So I got you these."

Emma took the bag and pulled out the contents. A

brand new pair of knitted black gloves lay in her palm, decorated around the cuffs with tiny pink flowers. Her eyes filled with tears and the last twenty four hours spilled over, leaving her breathless and crying.

Nicky was anxious when he emerged from school and found his mother in tears. He hung around her feet, ignoring his friends' urging to come and play, gripping the material of Emma's jacket in frightened fingers.

Mel left with Mohammed, secretly pleased her gift of a few coins had touched Emma so deeply, but Allaine wasn't fooled. The older woman led Emma to the park and they sat together on a bench under the trees.

Nicky stuck to them but Allaine sent him away to play on the swings with Kaylee. "Here, take the dog." she told him. "Keep him on the lead but give him a little run around. I'll look after Mummy."

Reluctantly, Nicky wandered off, staying within earshot. Allaine sat waiting, exhibiting her great patience while Emma collected herself. When Emma spoke, it was haltingly. "The guy last night didn't like me at all. He was a colleague of Ro's who seems to have double crossed him. Rohan's gone off to do some retrieval job I don't understand, without any of the help he needs and the guy who was meant to support him was pretending to like me. He took me to dinner and then a nightclub. He got me a bit drunk and..." Emma paused in shame at her own stupidity. "I just happened to see him talking with these two heavies as I came out of the toilet. I think they were planning to take me within the hour and I ran home. I thought they were rapists until Rohan became spooked this morning. Something's wrong and he thinks Nicky and

I are danger."

Allaine breathed out. "My husband will know what to do. Will's a policeman..."

"No! Rohan said not to talk to *anyone*. I'm sorry. I don't mean to offend you but he said I should dial emergency only if I felt in real danger. I have to do what he says."

"What a mess!" Allaine breathed. "What will you do?"

Emma turned towards her, her eyes trusting and desperate. "Allaine, if for some reason I don't turn up at school to get Nicky, please will you take him for me?"

Allaine's blue eyes filled with horror. "Emma this is serious! You can't ask me to do this without talking to my husband..."

"Please?" Emma looked desperate. "Please Allaine? Rohan's his father. If he comes home first, please let Nicky go to him. If neither of us turn up...there is nobody else. His mother cannot have Nicky under any circumstances. She killed Ro's father and mine Anton and I know that, we just couldn't work out how. Please Allaine, I've nobody else I can ask. Will you help me? I'll tell Mrs Clarke in the morning that if I'm not here, you can take my son."

Allaine's chin wobbled with stress and her eyes filled with tears. "Of course I will. You didn't need to ask. Let's just pray it doesn't happen."

The women walked back to where Emma had abandoned Rohan's expensive car on the road outside school. The women, children and dog piled into the plush vehicle and Emma kangarooed it home, finding the automatic gearbox a mystery and the indicators on the wrong side. Emma parked on the street ready for the next morning and Allaine gave her a hug before they parted. "Take care," she urged Emma. "We'll hold you in our prayers."

"Allaine?" Emma looked conflicted as the children swung on Rohan's wooden gate. "I need to wash your dress and there's a little rip I have to mend before I give it back. I'm sorry."

"It doesn't matter." Allaine enfolded Emma in a warm hug and whispered in her ear. "Call me if you need me."

Emma locked up the house early and charged her phone. Nicky fiddled with the buttons and she grew cross with him. "There's no credit on it anyway, Mummy. You can't do ringing can you?"

"No," she admitted, sniffing sadly until Nicky cried too.

"I need Uncle Ro," he wailed. "He makes everything better."

"I know, baby," Emma whispered, holding her small son tight against her stomach. "Then pray for him to your friend, God. Pray for him like you never have before."

They went to bed early in Rohan's room, darkening the house against the deepening night. They watched TV on his small portable, Nicky favouring the mindless cartoons and Emma's eyes misting over as she fretted. The doorbell rang at eight o'clock and Emma ran to her room to see who it was, fearing Christopher's dark shape in the street below.

Felicity looked up at the house, stepping backwards to rake the windows with eager eyes. Emma hid behind the curtains and sighed, wishing the pushy woman nothing but ill. "I know you're up there, bitch!" Felicity shouted, drawing attention from the neighbours across the street. "Get downstairs and face me, you whore. Alanya was right about you. We're gonna get you, slut! You and that kid of yours will be sorry!"

"I'm calling the police!" a man's voice shouted from an upstairs window opposite and Felicity took a last look up at the house and clip clopped quickly away.

Farrell slept in his bed next to the door, settling down with groans and padding around the house periodically. He wasn't meant to be upstairs and the well trained dog knew it, needing to be brought up on his leash and looking continually guilty as though Rohan might burst in and tell him off.

In the morning Emma woke feeling as though she hardly slept but Nicky was bouncing and happy. "I like Uncle Ro's bed, Mummy. It's squishy."

"Mmnnnn." Emma was uncommunicative, pressing her face into her husband's pillow and pleading with a God who really didn't seem to like her very much. She contemplated telling Nicky the truth about his father but Rohan said they would do it together, which meant he would return. *He had to.*

For the next three weeks, Emma drove her son to school in the huge car, often going for a drive afterwards. Rohan's house seemed strange without him and she avoided going back to it, exploring the local area in snow, rain and hail from the safety of the vehicle. The surrounding countryside was beautiful; green rolling hills and gentle undulating slopes. Driving out towards Northampton in the first week, Emma chanced upon a layby just past the border sign and parked for a while. On a hill to the left of her sat a red brick manor house with sandstone detail. It was a beautiful piece of architecture but looked run down and spoiled by neglect. Black empty windows blinked back at her and Emma imagined what it would be like to be the lady of such a manor, holding court in her morning room and drinking tea from a delicate china cup. The history of the place called to her and she felt drawn to it, time and time again.

In the middle of the third week, Emma left Nicky at school and drove towards the layby as usual, a wad of drawing paper on the passenger seat. The proportions of the building appeared to predate the Norman Conquest in 1066 and it interested the historian in her. Without access to a camera, Emma decided to sketch it and then get Nicky to help her search on Rohan's computer for details. A dull metal sign on the locked gate gave the name of the house and although the Verdigris staining made it unreadable, she wondered if rubbing one of Nicky's pencils across the paper might leave an impression and give her a clue.

Emma felt a skip of excitement as she crossed the border from Leicestershire into the county of Northamptonshire. It was good to have something to do apart from housework and worrying about Rohan. To her dismay, the layby was full. Even the grass verge either side of the concrete area was filled bumper to bumper with vehicles. Emma cruised by slowly, her brow furrowed with disappointment as she searched for somewhere to pull and allow the cars behind her to pass. She thumped the vehicle wonkily onto the verge and put the handbrake on, wincing at the ratcheting sound it made as she forgot to press the button first. Within seconds, four more cars pulled up in front of her. Emma sighed with defeat and reached across for the drawing pad and soft lead pencil. She emerged from her vehicle and the wind whipped the first few pages off the pad and hurled them up the road.

"Oopsie!" a smartly dressed woman cried, lurching for one of the sheets and missing. "Bad luck. It's so windy up here, isn't it?" Emma smiled wanly as the woman drew level with her, feeling stupid with the pencil clutched between her fingers. "Jade." The woman stuck a manicured hand out towards Emma and she stared at it gormlessly.

"Oh, sorry." Realising she was meant to shake the proffered hand, Emma clasped the warm fingers and smiled.

"Come on then, best get in," Jade said, setting off towards the driveway to the old house, her boot heels making sucking noises as they sunk into the grass verge. Emma shoved the pad and pencil back into the car and locked it up, hurrying after the determined woman.

"What's happening?" she asked, puffing up behind her.

"Oh, aren't you here for the auction?" Jade replied, stopping and staring at Emma differently. She took in Emma's man-sized jacket and the frayed bottoms of her jeans and took a step back, distancing herself. "I guess you're not then."

"Are they selling the house?" Emma struggled to banish the sadness from her voice.

Jade shook her head. "Just contents. Must dash!" She clopped towards the gates, leaving Emma shivering on the verge. As another group of eager purchasers swarmed past Emma, she made a foolish decision and tagged onto the back of a family group, sticking close, hands in pockets and head down against the cold wind. The open gates were blocked to all but pedestrians by four large red orange and white cones, explaining the cars lined up on the verge. The group trudged up a long, tree lined driveway, wide enough for two cars to pass with room to spare. The crowd continued to swell and by the time they reached the top of the driveway and headed towards the open front doors, Emma felt increasingly uncomfortable.

"How did you hear about it?" an elderly lady asked Emma, leaning into her face and smiling sweetly as they formed an orderly queue. "The auction, dear. Was it the papers?" She qualified her question in response to Emma's obvious confusion.

"Oh, somebody told me," Emma replied, noticing Jade moving slowly ahead in her high heels. She grimaced, wishing she could telepathically trip the snobby woman up. Instead, she focussed her attention on the lady next to her. "What do you know about this house?" Emma asked. "I love history and I'm really interested."

The woman fixed a beatific smile on Emma. "Oh that's marvellous, dear. I'm a local historian. I'm not here to buy anything. My mother was in service here as a very young girl between the wars. I visited many times as a child. After she left service, Mother continued taking in washing and ironing for the lady of the house and we called here once a week on the horse and trap." The lady squeezed her wrinkled face into the sweetest smile. "I'm so excited to see inside again." She did a tiny skip which almost overbalanced her and Emma giggled as she caught her arm.

"Oh, that's so wonderful." Emma's brown eyes lit with happiness as the old lady's enthusiasm touched something in her and she felt excited too. The long queue snaked towards the front steps.

"I'm Freda," the old lady said, patting Emma's

elbow and fixing strong, watery blue eyes on her. Emma returned the greeting and they chatted like old friends as Freda regaled her with stories from the servants' quarters below stairs. "The old kitchen's long gone now," Freda said, shouting as she adjusted her hearing aid. "It was at the north end of the house under the existing kitchen. Mother and I used to use the back stairs to the first floor laundry. We packed everything up into baskets, even the master's underwear..." Freda gave a high pitched giggle which drew attention from those around and Emma sniggered.

"Oh, that's so radical! Promise me, you'll walk around with me and tell me everything?"

Freda bounced on the spot and gave Emma a cute smile during which her top set of false teeth crashed down onto her bottoms. Emma giggled. "This is turning into the best day." She linked her arm through the old lady's and they snuggled close in the plummeting temperatures.

The queue up ahead began to grow disquiet and the mood seemed to drop along with the centigrade as people filed back past them looking unhappy. "What's going on?" someone called from behind Emma and Jade turned to answer them.

"It seems to be by invite only. Or you needed to register as a buyer, days ago. My husband registered me." The confidence waned a little from her formerly buoyant self, although she scraped her stiletto heels on the gravel and tossed her hair, giving an illusion of superiority.

"Do you have an invite?" Emma asked Freda and the old lady looked sad, shaking her head and making her hat wobble on her head. "Maybe we should just leave," Emma whispered. "We could go to my house for coffee?"

"Oh, no dear. I want to go in." Freda turned wide, tearful eyes on Emma and she gulped, wondering at what point Freda would realise it wasn't going to happen. Emma clutched the frail arm to her side and felt the carefree sense of fun dissipate. She peered in the windows at the front of the house, seeing flaking, white painted shutters, tired decor and period architecture she would never see up close. Emma's body tensed as she waited to join the other dissatisfied visitors in the ultimate humiliation, as they tramped back down the long driveway in disappointment.

The biggest shock came when Jade was turned away by a man with a black mackintosh over his pinstriped suit. He shivered in the cold, examining names written on a clipboard. "I'm sorry, madam. You're name isn't on the list. You can't have expressed your interest as a buyer."

"But I did!" Jade argued, her voice shrill with indignation. "My husband declared our interest with the executors last week. I want that Queen Anne chair!"

"I'm sorry, madam. You're name's not here. Please make your way back down the driveway."

Emma gulped. If the rich and famous weren't being allowed access, what hope was there for the poor and elderly? She gripped Freda's arm and received a beautiful grin in return. Rohan had some loose change in his ashtray and Emma wondered if Freda would be mollified by a cup of tea in town. She thought Nicky might have used the last of the milk at home. She braced herself for the lady's disappointment when they were inevitably turned away.

A few more people were admitted entrance and

Emma and Freda shuffled forwards, entertained by Jade who made a loud phone call on her mobile and berated the doormen in hysterical tones. "But you promised you'd talk to them, Peter!" she screeched down the handset at her unfortunate husband, who presumably took the call at work whilst trying to fund her lifestyle. Two men in jeans and jackets were granted entry and handed brochures of the items for sale and then Emma and her new friend faced the smartly dressed businessmen at the door.

"Name, madam," one of them said, directing his question at Emma.

Freda fiddled with her hearing aid whilst shouting, "Pardon?" The device behind her left ear made a loud squealing sound which was so piercing it had to be up there with supersonic.

Emma stuck her finger in her ear and whispered her name. "Emma Andreyev." As her married name rolled off her tongue it shocked her, unfamiliar even though it was hers. Emma's face registered surprise at the unpremeditated action. She hadn't known what would come out of her mouth and it rocked her.

The man nodded politely and then looked pointedly at Freda. Emma waited for the hatchet to fall and to be ordered off the premises, dragging the little old lady behind her under Jade's satisfied scrutiny. "Name, madam? Are you with Mrs Andreyev?"

"Yes," Emma said quickly, laying familial claim to the entertaining pensioner.

"I used to come here when I was a little girl, young man," Freda giggled, her hearing aid making a din louder than the incoming Arctic breeze. "My mother was a lady's maid for the eldest Ayers girl until she had me at sixteen." She leaned in to the man's chest and whispered to his neat shirt buttons. "My father was the wayward son and Lady Ayers always took a *very* special interest in me." She tapped the side of her nose. "Everything was kept quiet in those days but my mother had an annual allowance until the day she died."

Emma gasped at the intrigue in the sad little story. She put her arm around the elderly lady next to her and stared at the fluffy white hair peeking out from under a knitted hat. The man smiled and held two neat brochures in his hand. "Go on through ladies and take a look around. The auction begins at ten o'clock sharp. Please help your grandmother on all the stairs, Mrs Andreyev." He looked pointedly at Emma. "They're quite unforgiving." He flashed extremely white teeth at them both and Emma gaped for a moment at his assumption of her married status.

"Come on, dear." Freda tugged at Emma's arm and looked at her expectantly. With a bemused look at Jade, still posturing around on the gravel behind her, Emma walked past the two men and into the peace of the imposing house.

CHAPTER THIRTY

Emma's breath caught in her chest as she passed through the second set of outer doors into an enormous reception hall. "Wow!" she exclaimed, her mind immediately consumed by images of ladies in ball gowns, disrobing from expensive stoles as their skirts swished across the oak floorboards. She glanced down at the brochure in her hand, flicking through the pages to find the floorplan. "This hall is over twelve metres long!" she hissed to Freda. "And it's six metres wide. But this is only the entrance!"

"Yes, dear." Freda's head bobbed up and down and the fluffy woollen pom-pom on her hat wibbled and wobbled with the motion. She stared around happily, her blue eyes bright with happiness. "Oh look, there it is!" She glided across to the far wall and peered at a line of exquisite oak panelling. Emma followed her and focussed on an ugly chip in the wood near the bottom.

"What is it?" she asked, following the line of Freda's outstretched finger.

Freda stood up and hugged herself, her eyes sparkling with memories. "I came with Mother to get the laundry and wandered off, pretending to follow my spinning top." She squeezed her eyes tight shut. "I was a very wilful child and didn't like that Mother was expecting yet another red haired baby to my stepfather. I knew the Lord's family were all in London and I wanted to find my father's room. I'd heard the whispering and rumours. But more than that; I thought if I could stand in his room amongst his things, I might just know. You understand? It's terrible for a child not to know who their father is."

Emma gulped and bit her lip. Oblivious, Freda continued. "It was just before my eighth birthday and I was already working, helping Mother with laundry. I ran off on the pretence of chasing my spinning top and found myself here. Just for a moment, I picked up my skirts and danced, pretending I was a fine lady invited to the house for dinner." Freda seized her corduroy skirt and lifted it high, revealing a pair of wrinkled pop socks and very bare, white knees. She twirled unsteadily on her feet and the little knot of bargain hunters stopped to watch her from a gallery overhead. "I whirled and waltzed...and then I bumped right into my father."

Emma gasped and stared at the little old lady, desperate to hear more of her story. Freda kept her eyes firmly closed as she processed her memory. "Of course I knew who he was. It's so curious how blood calls to blood." She giggled and placed arthritic fingers over her pink lips. "Oh, he was so handsome; dressed in his fine shirt and an expensive suit. He hadn't gone to London at all. He picked me up and swung me around like the most dashing of princes. I laughed and giggled and my spinning top went shooting off towards the wall and took out that chip of oak. I thought he might tell me off, but he didn't. He set me down on the ground and kissed the top of my head. Father never married and I believe he truly loved my mother. I saw him a few more times through the years but then he went off to war and never came back. Like so many others..."

Freda sighed and Emma bit back the choking

feeling in her throat at the thought of Rohan, who so very nearly didn't come home either. Tears of sadness welled up in her eyes at the unfairness of life and the premature death of her own dad; two women deprived of fathers through no fault of their own.

Nicky's beaming face chastised Emma with her secrecy. He never asked about his father, yet his attachment to Rohan demonstrated how badly he needed one. She gulped and gave a little hiccough and Freda opened her eyes and reached out to touch Emma's elbow. "Oh, don't be sad for me, dear. I'm ninety and I've had a good life. I'm satisfied with my lot." She smiled at Emma with a wealth of supernatural perception. "Some wrongs, my dear, just can't be righted."

Emma stood transfixed with the words resounding in her brain. She looked stunned and Freda's brow knitted in concern. The elderly woman's light touch on her arm forced Emma to collect herself and they proceeded to the end of the reception hall and into another enormous room to the right. The brochure announced it as the ballroom and Freda wandered around, examining the threadbare curtains which hung from ceiling to floor and shaking her head sadly. "It used to be so beautiful," she sighed. Resting a gnarled hand on the back of an old chaise lounge which had once been chintz but now resembled something faded and past its day, she stroked the fragile fabric and screwed up her face. "I can see why they're getting rid of it all. It's ruined."

"I'm sure the right buyer can take it all and restore it back to beauty," Emma said, offering hollow reassurance. The furniture would need more than a face lift from an expert. She read the auctioneer's brochure, ticking off the items in the room and shaking her head at the exorbitant cost of it all. Just the Queen Anne chair in the corner of the room would feed Emma and Nicky for a month or two. Emma heaved out a breath and followed Freda to the end of the room and into the one behind, listed as the morning room. The grey light filtered in on dusty furniture which looked scratched and dented. The once polished surfaces would have been slick with wax and the loving touch of a butler's gloved hand as he refreshed the filthy drinks cabinet. It was heart breaking and the atmosphere was oppressive and dark.

Two men whispered in the corner of the room, eyeing a sideboard with covetous eyes. "I can French polish this out," one of them said under his breath. "See how high the bidding starts and then try and get it."

"There's not much here, dear," Freda remarked as they wandered into the drawing room, which matched the size of the reception hall on the other side of it. "I wonder where the rest is."

"The rest?" Emma glanced down at the brochure again. "Yes, I suppose it does look quite empty. Maybe someone else stripped it first."

"Well," Freda began confidentially, "I know when the last Ayers was declared bankrupt four years ago, furnishings were all included. My dear friend wrote to tell me. What a shame. All the best pieces are missing."

Emma walked along, clutching Freda's arm and no longer interested. The woman's words felt like an omen, hanging over her like a cleaver. *Some wrongs just can't be righted.* Emma felt destined never to be happy. They progressed through an unfurnished dining room, a library in which none of the books were for sale and stood in the industrial kitchen while Freda poked around in the old wooden cupboards. "The cook when Mother worked here was Mrs Daventry. She was a slave driver. I had my bottom slapped once by her for stealing cherry tomatoes from the top of a pie." Freda snorted and clapped her hand over her mouth, letting out a squeak of mirth. "Gosh I was a naughty girl!"

The rooms were beautiful but Emma's heart felt too laden to enjoy them. Freda needed help up the back stairs to the rooms on the first floor, taking each step carefully on fragile bones and gnarled, arthritic feet. "I used to run up these!" she exclaimed once, puffing on the middle step and causing a bottle neck behind. "Damn these old bones!"

"Hey!" Emma snapped at a man in a suit who attempted to push past the old lady. "Have some bloody respect!" Her eyes flashed like black coals and he took a step backwards, standing on the toes of the woman who followed in his rude wake. "Serves you right!" Emma told her and the face of disgust was quickly made blank and expressionless. Emma felt like a harpy, taking her anger and disappointment out on everyone around her. *Some wrongs just can't be righted.* Freda's words tortured her, causing a diaphanous void in her gut.

Most of the crowd behind disappeared, using one of the other two staircases up to the first and second floors above. Freda made it to the landing of the first floor, cheering and waving her tiny fists as though she scaled Everest in a tweed jacket and corduroy skirt, one pop sock wrapped round her ankle like a skin coloured, gossamer scarf. Emma hauled it up for her, restoring her dignity just as one of the suited men from the auction company jogged up the steps behind them.

"Er, madam," he said to Emma. "The auctioneer would like to see you, please."

Emma looked at him in horror and Freda giggled inappropriately. "Me?" Emma panicked, her eyes wide with fear as she pointed at her own chest like a schoolgirl. The man nodded and indicated the stairs behind him.

"Yes, madam. Now."

Emma's knees began to shake. She shouldn't be here and now she was about to be unceremoniously expelled. She shot a look of desperation at Freda, who came admirably to meet the challenge. The elderly lady drew herself up to her full shrunken height and fixed an authoritative blue eye on the young man below on the stairs. "My dear," she began. "I'm the bastard daughter of Geoffrey Ayers and I intend to look around his home before it gets chopped up for apartments. My friend and I have just hauled my sorry ass up these stairs at great cost to our sanity. I shall not be going down again in a hurry!" With that, she scuttled off left towards the laundry, giving a squeal of delight from inside. "Oooh! It's still the same! I do believe I was conceived on this very floor. Mother did ramble so as she got older..." Her voice tailed off as she went further into the cavernous room.

The young man gulped, his red curls moving on his head with the motion. He fiddled with the black buttons on an immaculate waistcoat and agonised internally. Then he nodded. "Ok, madam. I'll tell the auctioneer you'll be down in a minute." Reluctantly he left, treading quickly down the stairs but glancing up at Emma twice more. As soon as his feet hit the oak boards of the reception hall, Emma took off after Freda, clattering into the laundry to find the old woman peering into the glass door of a modern washing machine.

"We need to get out of here!" Emma panicked. "We aren't meant to be here and I think we're about to be thrown out."

"I want to see my father's room." Freda's wizened face crumpled like a naughty child. "I want to see Geoffrey's room."

Emma ran her hand through her hair in fear, snagging her index finger on an unruly curl. "Fine!" she said decisively. "But do you know a back way out of this place when we're done?"

Freda's face curved into a beautiful smile and Emma glimpsed the wayward child who spun her top just to dance in the reception hall. She tapped her nose with a crabbed finger and grinned. Freda held Emma's hand and scurried to a room at the south end of the building, next to the huge master suite, dressing room and ensuite, which she would have loved to see. The dilapidated state continued with peeling flock wallpaper hanging in swathes above their heads and a dusting of plaster in patches along the way. "In here, dear. Father slept in here." Freda's steps were urgent rapping against the oak floors like a much younger woman.

The room opened up before them, renovated to perfection. A beautiful four poster bed graced the centre of the room and the walls were decorated in a subtle powder blue. The furniture was all of a French style, chic and white with distressed edges and a golden sheen to the corners. The ensuite was fitted with a modern shower and fitments, a white claw footed bath sat diagonally across one corner. Freda disliked it but confusion showed on Emma's face as she stroked the top of a tallboy leaned against one wall. Something about the decor resonated with her and she shook her head to clear the image. "This isn't right! Father wouldn't like this," Freda commented in disappointment, wrinkling her nose. She sounded upset. "Where's Father's things?"

Emma gulped and took the old lady's arm. Something about the style of the decor pulled at her memory, familiar and unnerving. It irked and jarred in its simplistic beauty and Emma's brow knitted in confusion. Freda began to pull drawers open and then Emma noticed the sign on the bedroom door which the old lady had flung open. No entry.

"Where's his things?" Freda asked again, as a pair of boxer shorts tumbled from a bedside drawer, pulling Emma back to reality. Nearly seventy years had passed since the end of the Second World War and Geoffrey Ayer's personal effects would be long gone. She didn't have the heart to crush Freda's dreams further and cuddled her close. "I'm sure they're somewhere here," she soothed. "But I need you to get us out of here now, like you promised." Emma kept the urgency out of her voice and Freda swiped at her eye with an inaccurate hand and reluctantly nodded.

Down the back stairs they went, at a faster pace than the upward journey. They trotted through the kitchen and storerooms beyond, turning left and skirting underneath a rope barrier which declared the area out of bounds. Freda picked up speed, admirable for a lady in her nineties, forcing Emma to jog to keep up. "This is the old coach house, dear," she called over her shoulder. "We'll go out this way, then they won't see us from the main house."

Fortunately the Yale lock on the front door allowed

them to click it locked behind them and the two unlikely companions hot footed it down the long driveway. Freda was puffing by the time they reached the ornate gates. Emma began to giggle, suppressing the urge to laugh until she cried. Something about the house and the blue room made her sad.

Passing the open gates, Emma stopped and looked at the ruined sign. "What does it say?" she asked Freda. "What's the name of the house?"

"It's Wingate Hall, dear," Freda said proudly. "Owned by the Ayers family for generations, since before the Norman invasion. They were King's men during the civil war and it's rumoured Henry VIII stayed at the house once on a visit from London to the parishes, during the Reformation." She tapped her nose again and peered up and down the long country road.

"How did you get here?" Emma asked, looking at the smattering of vehicles remaining. Most of them looked like transit vans belonging to bespoke furniture companies and antique dealers. It seemed everyone else had been turned away from their rubbernecking adventure. Emma thought of Jade's posh indignation and smirked.

"I came on the bus," Freda announced, looking back up the driveway. "I say, is that young man waving at you?"

Emma glanced back towards the house, seeing the red haired young man running down the driveway with his arm raised above his head. "Oh no! He probably wants to cite us for trespassing!" Emma panicked. "Quick!" she squeaked, running towards Rohan's smart car, parked haphazardly on the grass verge. "Get in!"

Freda shuffled towards the car and struggled with the heavy passenger door. As she lurched into the seat and slapped her handbag onto her knee, Emma put her foot down and screeched off the verge, taking a large slice of juicy turf with her. The auctioneer's assistant reached the end of the driveway and lowered his hand in disappointment as the car sped off towards Northampton and Emma heaved a sigh of relief. "So long, sucker!" Freda called behind her and Emma gaped in horror.

Emma drove towards Northampton and then doubled back to avoid driving past the manor house, in case the young man waited on the road. Freda managed to click her seat belt eventually and halted the dull bell which tolled on the dashboard in warning. Then she sighed and grinned. "That was very enjoyable. I haven't been back to the house since 1946."

Emma gaped. "I though you hadn't been back since you were a girl. That would be what? 1930s?"

Freda wiggled her shoulders and eyed Emma sideways. "Oh, I never actually said that, dear. I came back here in 1946 on the day I eloped with my sweetheart."

Emma swerved as she looked too long at the smug old lady in the passenger seat. "You what?"

Freda huddled herself more snugly into the seat and beamed out the front windscreen. "I eloped with my sweetheart when I was twenty one years old."

Emma felt a shiver down her spine at the sudden similarity with her own life story. "I eloped," she whispered to the gentle woman next to her. "But I was only just sixteen."

"It's exciting, isn't it?" Freda giggled. She turned her

beautiful blue eyes on Emma. "Why did you elope, dear? Didn't your parents approve either?"

"He was my stepbrother." Emma's cheeks flushed with an old embarrassment. "We aren't blood, but Rohan's mother called me *disgusting*. She warned me off when I was fourteen and someone told her they saw me holding her son's hand. She said I'd go to hell." Emma shuddered and concentrated on the country lane zooming past underneath them.

"Ooh, let's go for morning tea!" Freda clapped her hands together in her mittens and Emma laughed.

"Ok, then. There's some cash in the ashtray. But tell me your story. Why didn't your parents approve?" Emma pressed the indicator and turned onto a signposted road which claimed it would take them back towards Market Harborough.

Freda flashed a beatific smile filled with mischief. "My poor mother was horrified and my stepfather went purple with anger, which was an interesting contrast with his red hair." She chuckled to herself and immersed them both in the world of her memories. "I worked down at the market after the war but it was a sorry place then, run mainly by the women of the town. Our men trickled home, injured, broken; not the strong chaps we remembered. My stepfather had a dreadful limp from a lump of shrapnel and he drank for the rest of his days. The sunny red haired man was left in a prisoner of war camp in a foreign land and a tortured monster returned. There were no more babies for my mother, but she wasn't sorry." Freda sighed. "I was working on the vegetable stall in the summer of 1946 and he walked right up to me. I've never forgotten the look on his face when he saw me. '*My goodness*,' he said. '*If it's not little Freda Porter, all grown up and pretty as a daisy.*'

The other girls stared at me, talking so easily to a gentleman but you see, the world was changing."

Emma nodded in sad agreement. Her degree study took her through the post-war miseries of many European countries, a world with very few young men left in it. She understood.

"His eyes were blue, like mine and we played together as children. He cut a handsome figure at the debutante balls of his youth but as we grew, it was forbidden for us to speak. I knew his scent from the shirts I handled as Mother washed them and it felt as though I had loved him forever. There he was, standing in front of me fresh from the war, one of the few young men to return to our town in those early months after the ceasefire." Freda sighed again and as Emma glanced at her, she saw a flush creep up the old lady's neck and into her cheeks like a caress. "I felt dumbstruck. I was just shy of my twenty first birthday, a year younger than him and we hadn't spoken for more than ten years. I gaped like a fish and felt a complete fool." Her fingers fluttered to her mouth and Emma felt alarmed to see a tear drip down onto Freda's skirt.

Emma reached out and gripped the gnarled fingers in hers, squeezing them in an attempt to infuse love. Freda sandwiched Emma's cold hand between hers and lifted it to her lips, placing a gentle kiss on her knuckles. "Bless you, dear," she whispered.

Freda was quiet for the remainder of the journey. Emma found the Common's car park in the west of the town and parked the Mercedes, abandoning it with a shrug of embarrassment at the wonky parking. "I'm so rubbish at driving this car," she muttered as she helped Freda out of the passenger side, frustrated at her complete absence of skill and squeezing between a trolley bay and the side of the car.

They got seated in the busy Baptist Church coffee shop which heaved with mothers and small toddlers. Freda dabbed at her eyes with a spotted handkerchief and watched a little redheaded girl around three years old. Emma smiled at the concentration on the child's face as she poured tea into a china mug from a metal tea pot, pretending to be a big girl in the special moment with her mother. Freda hiccoughed. "She reminds me of one of my sisters. Little Sophia." She smoothed the white tablecloth with a shaking hand and then tapped it smartly. "Memories, memories." With a huge effort, she turned to Emma with a smile plastered on her pink lips.

"Hello, Freda!" A lady in her sixties approached the table, pulling a notepad and pencil from the front pocket of her frilly apron. "Nice to see you out and about." The waitress bent and kissed Freda's sallow cheek and then greeted Emma with a smile and a nod. "What can I get you both?"

Emma's face dropped, remembering her offer and rising from her seat. "I just need to nip back to the car..." she began, mentally adding up the value of Rohan's loose change in the ashtray.

"No, no, dear." Freda placed her fingers over Emma's. "My treat. You did the driving and after all," she wrinkled her nose, "we had immense fun up at the big house."

"Ooh, the big house!" The waitress became animated. "Did you go to the auction?"

"No, just for a nosey. We came away before the auction started. I didn't think I could bear seeing all the Ayers furniture being sold for next to nothing."

"No, you wouldn't, dear, would you?" the waitress sympathised. She took their order, scrawling slowly onto the pad in a neat script reminiscent of the 1950's school taught hand. Emma waited until she was out of earshot before leaning in towards Freda.

"Thank you so much for morning tea," she said, putting her hand over Freda's. "But why is it so cheap? How can a pot of tea and scones for two come to under five pounds? Did she make a mistake?"

"No, dear. It's staffed by volunteers from the church. I did a couple of hours until recently. The doctor wouldn't renew my driving licence so I'm waiting for my mobility scooter to arrive. Then I might come back and do a few hours. It's a great privilege to work here and it makes a cup of tea accessible to some of the families of our town. My husband would have approved." Her eyes misted over again and Emma grew silent. Freda collected herself after a few moments and smiled beneficently at Emma. "I was telling you about him, wasn't I?"

Emma nodded and leaned forward, keen to hear Freda's fascinating story. "Yes, he approached you at the market."

Freda sighed. "Ah, but what I didn't tell you was my John lost an arm in the war and part of his face. Despite all that, he was the handsomest soul I ever met. He approached me, because he knew I wouldn't stare at him and I realised as I watched his beautiful lips move through words filled with bravado, it didn't matter a bit. I loved him then as much as I did when I was ten and he kissed me behind the wall of the coach house during a game of hide and seek."

The tea arrived with a plate of scones and Emma watched while Freda buttered her scone with shaking hands. "You pour please dear," the old lady ordered and Emma obliged, gushing tea into the cups while she waited, desperate for the rest of the tale. She accidentally put in too much sugar in her eagerness, but Freda waited until she'd sampled her scone before resuming.

"John asked my father if he could court me and the bitter old man refused. He threatened to throw me out of the house if we persisted. War is a great leveller of society, Emma and it changed everything. But John was my cousin on Geoffrey Ayers side, the youngest son of Edgar Ayers. Being first cousins and with John a son of the big house, it made our love impossible to sustain." Freda sighed and looked at Emma. "Tell me about your young man, dear."

"No!" Emma's face screwed up in horror. "Don't do that. Don't turn it back on me without telling me what happened!"

"I need you to talk for a while, so I can drink my tea," Freda smiled, with a twinkle in her eye. She raised an eyebrow at Emma and brooked no complaint.

"Fine!" Emma huffed and sipped her tea. "My father married a Russian woman with two sons when I was six. I felt this incredible link to the eldest son, although back then I was too young to know it was attraction; but it never went away. He was three years older than me and he kinda kept his distance until I was older. I became very attached to Anton, his younger brother and we were inseparable. There was a two year gap between us, but it felt like nothing." Emma smiled until she remembered Anton was gone, then her face clouded over with an all-encompassing darkness. Freda reached a hand across and gripped Emma's fingers but didn't interrupt. "When I was twelve, I got into a fight at school with a boy. He was bigger than me and I used dirty tactics to fend him off. A huge crowd gathered and I can't even remember what it was over, but suddenly Rohan waded in and ended it really quickly. He was always tall and strong for his age, blonde and good looking. Something about his Russian accent sounded intimidating and other children didn't mess with him. But the boy cut my lip and ripped my blouse and I knew Ro's mother would go mad when she saw it. Ro said nothing all the way home and it was a pretty decent walk. He strode along next to me and I knew he was angry because he gives off this kind of...angry hum." Emma saw Freda's lips curl in a smile.

"We were almost home and I felt like a coiled spring. I knew I'd be punished for the rip and Ro was the last person I wanted disappointed in me and it all sort of bubbled over. I hurled my school bag on the pavement and threw an almighty tantrum." Emma laughed and covered her mouth. "Anton loved drama class and he would have been impressed. It felt fantastic, just letting off steam." Emma looked down at her uneaten scone. "Rohan just stood there and looked at me, throwing myself around like a maniac and then he laughed. He actually laughed at me. I felt stupid and this rage bubbled up inside. I tried to slap his face and he caught my wrist and...well, he kissed me."

Freda's eyes crinkled in pleasure and she patted Emma's writhing fingers. "And you married when you were sixteen?"

Emma nodded. "Yes. Ro was nineteen and already in the army. We ran away to Gretna Green and married at the blacksmith shop. Ro did all the paperwork and Anton helped with a cover. My stepmother didn't

259

know Rohan was due home on leave. He was at Cottesmore and picked me up on the way through. Anton faked this whole big farce and conned his mother into thinking I went on a school trip. I don't think she ever found out." Emma smirked. "She has no idea we married, or still are."

"What went wrong?" Freda urged, sipping her tea one handed and centring Emma with the other, offering a gentle, intermittent stroke of her fingers.

Emma sighed. "We didn't sleep together until we were married and I fell pregnant straight away. I didn't have a mother to help me so I was naive. I threw up at school every morning for weeks on end and another girl told me what she thought it was. When my stomach started to swell, I knew. After we were married, Rohan was meant to apply for a married quarter on the army base to get me away from his mother, but in the interim, he was deployed to Afghanistan. The last time I saw him, I was meant to tell him about the baby, but all he could talk about was someone else's war. I thought he came to get me, but he didn't. He wanted me to wait for him and live with his mother. He told me to finish school. I was so angry, I walked out and when I cooled down enough to go home; he'd gone."

Emma gave a shuddering breath. "His brother helped me leave Lincoln and took me to a family member in Wales. I had my son and didn't see Rohan again until recently."

"That's so sad." Freda's brow knitted in concern. "Will you get back together?" she asked and Emma shrugged.

"I don't know, Freda. Too much has happened and he has this girlfriend hanging around, so probably not, no."

"We should see her off, for a start!" Freda waved the butter knife threateningly and Emma resisted the urge to laugh.

"Now you finish your story!" Emma insisted. "What happened with you and John?"

"We also ran away, dear, but not so far. We were both over the age of consent and whilst it would have been lovely to have our parents' blessing, we didn't actually need it. John made an honest woman of me and took me home to his parents. It's no surprise we were thrown out, quite dramatically. The words *incest* and *disgusting* were bandied about as they would have been with you, I suppose. Even now, those two words make me cringe. The gates of Wingate Hall closed behind us and John never returned to see his family. We were dead to them, although in my ninetieth year, it all seems so foolish and trivial now. The world has changed such a great deal and illegitimate children and cousins marrying are the very least of society's problems. My John was the love of my life until he died last year. Sixty eight years we were married and I wouldn't change one of them for a different life. God didn't bless us with children, but it was a small price to pay for marrying one's sweetheart, wouldn't you say?" She fixed perceptive eyes on Emma, who nodded in obedience.

"Did you stay in the town?" Emma asked and Freda shook her head.

"No, no, dear. We lived as missionaries in the Philippines and settled there when we retired. But I grew homesick after John's death and wanted to be here to die. I returned a year ago and took an apartment in the flats off the Northampton Road. It'll see me out." She smiled philosophically and started on the uneaten half of Emma's scone.

"What's wrong, dear?" she asked, responding to the paleness of Emma's face.

Emma leaned in close, so only she could hear. "Rohan's mother lives in those apartments. She moved in there a few years ago."

"Oh, I might know her," Freda smiled, pushing her teacup towards Emma so she would pour the last drops into her cup.

"Maybe." Emma became tight lipped and unresponsive, pouring the tea woodenly.

"What's her name?" Freda pushed. "I won't tell," she whispered.

"It's not that; she knows I'm here. We've already had an argument. Rohan banned her from coming round to the house, it's just..." Emma faltered. "I can't let her near my son. Through the kindness of my silly brother-in-law, she now thinks Nicky is his. She bailed me up in the park recently and demanded to see him. All these years, she thought I got knocked up by some spotty teenager in my class but obviously now, the issue of him being her grandson has made her more dogged. I can't let her anywhere near Nicky. She tried to kill him before he was born and I know for a fact she can't be trusted around children; well, around anyone really."

"Oh, that's so sad. We'll just keep our little friendship a secret then, won't we?" Freda beamed. "Who is this terrifying woman?"

"Alanya Harrington," Emma whispered and Freda's eyes bulged like blue marbles.

"The Black Widow!" she breathed. "*She's* your mother-in-law?"

Emma's jaw dropped. "What did you call her?"

Freda grasped both Emma's hands and held them in a vice-like grip. "She befriends the elderly men, silly old fools! We think she kills them but we just haven't worked out how yet."

CHAPTER THIRTY ONE

The next day, Nicky was difficult about getting into the car to go to school, kicking up a fuss on the pavement. "I wanna take Faz," he complained on this particular morning, stamping and posturing. "I wanna run in the park in the snow!"

"Get in the bloody car!" Emma snapped, casting her eyes frantically around the street as she cleared ice off the windscreen. Rohan warned her to be careful and Freda's news about Alanya instilled further fear into Emma's already overloaded brain. She had driven Freda home but refused to go into the flats, fearful of meeting Alanya. Freda wrote her phone number on a napkin and extorted a promise from Emma to have morning tea again sometime.

"Om er! Swearing!" Nicky squeaked, striking a hands on hips pose so much like Anton, it took Emma's breath away. "I'm sick of this! You never walk the dog anymore. It's cruel!" Nicky climbed into the car with genuine reluctance, mollified by his mother's stony glare and the determination in her eyes.

"I already said; I need you to do as you're told for a while," Emma bit, locking the doors and turning to face her son. He stared at her, wide-eyed and fearful at the sudden intensity on her face.

"Is the gang after us?" His mind regressed to the miserable council estate in Lincoln where they lived on their wits and drifted like flotsam with the prevailing tide of trouble.

"No, baby." Emma reached behind her and gripped Nicky's outstretched hand. "But Uncle Rohan asked us to be very careful and we live in his house so have to do what he says."

"Like monsters are chasing us?" Nicky said and Emma sighed.

"Kinda. We just need to do what Rohan said. But Nicky, don't tell anyone please? This isn't exciting or something to tell friends. Ok?" Emma stared at him until she got a crick in her neck, searching for surety he would be wiser than his years.

"Pinky promise, Mummy." The child stretched forward and clasped her baby finger with his, the deal struck easily with a trusting smile and a belief in the impossible. "Harley Man said not to worry. He'll take care of us anyway."

"I thought you grew out of him," Emma said, her voice laced with disappointment.

"No!" Nicky chortled. "How can you grow out of a person, Mummy? I seen him round all the time. He keeps us safe, like always."

"Oh, goody." Emma struggled with the huge vehicle, missing Rohan's capable driving skills with every groan of the engine or jerk of the car body. Nicky sniggered as she almost side swiped another car in the car park. "You don't like this car, do you, Mummy?"

"Not really, Nick. It's too big." Emma glanced in her rear view mirror. "Sorry for swearing at you before. I just feel stressed. Christmas isn't far away and..." Emma stopped and put the hand brake on. Nicky unclipped his seat belt and stood up, reaching forward to hug his mother around the seat. His arms felt tight around her neck.

"Uncle Ro showed me how to get to the money.

You want me to show you tonight?"

"I don't know, babe. We're not really his responsibility, are we?"

"It's not charity. We're looking after his house and his dog and his...well, you're not really looking after his car, are you Mummy? Do you think he'll notice that little scratch on the..."

"Fine! Show me how to get into the safe this weekend, ok?"

"Ok. Oh Mum, I forgot to say, the Christmas nativity is next Friday in the afternoon. I'm gettin' tickets for you and Uncle Ro and Uncle Anton. Can you tell them for me?" He leaned forward and kissed her softly on the cheek and Emma struggled to keep her tears in. Unable to lie any more to her son, Emma kept silent. "I think they'll love how I'm a wise man. I have to wave my telescope and shout, 'This way!' to the other wise men. I'm gonna do it real funny to make Uncle Anton laugh. I love it when he laughs. Do you think he'll laugh at me, Mummy? Do you?"

"I don't know," Emma whispered, barely holding it together.

She returned home after dropping her son at school, avoiding small talk with the other mothers and knocking around the house aimlessly. She avoided the urge to drive to the Northamptonshire border, to the beautiful mansion, which by now would be stripped and empty. She went there so often it was bound to attract attention eventually, if Rohan's fears were real. Emma imagined what it would be like to drive up the long driveway, climbing the gradient through open fields and grazing sheep to a place which looked so much like her perfect home. It called her there like a beacon, promising peace and sanctuary and now she knew its history, Emma found it increasingly hard to stay away. But the petrol gauge on Rohan's car clicked onto a quarter full that morning and Emma dreaded the journey to a tightly structured garage forecourt to fill it up again. She would have to use Rohan's cash from the hiding place under the stairs somewhere and besides, Emma wasn't confident in small spaces with the enormous, imposing vehicle. It wouldn't end well.

When the hammering on the front door came, Emma jumped almost clean out of her skin. Peering through the stained glass at eye level, she saw Felicity.

"Where's Rohan?" The woman pushed past her and stopped in the hallway, casting around and looked at Emma in accusation.

"He's gone away. I'm sure he told you." Emma's impatience was obvious in her voice and she tapped her foot on the floor. Felicity glanced down at the tattered boots which Emma hadn't removed and sneered.

"He's my boyfriend. I don't know what your game is, but you need to back off! It all went wrong when you turned up."

"Why aren't you at work?"

"I'm sick."

"You don't look sick."

"Maybe I'm sick of you!"

Emma smirked at the lame attempt at a threat and opened the door wider. "Go home, Felicity. When Rohan comes back, talk to him. Until then, stay away from me and Nicky."

"I want to wait for my fiancé!" Felicity stood her ground and Emma snapped.

"Well, wait for him then! You're just not doing it here! Get out!"

Felicity moved over the threshold and hovered on the doormat. "I know you're in love with him. As soon as Rohan gets home, we're getting married and there's nothing you can do about it. I'll make sure you're out of this house the second I get that ring on my finger, you make no mistake about that! You're sick if you think he'd ever like you. Alanya says you're a whore and you are. It's incest. It's disgusting. You're disgusting!"

Emma slammed the door in her face and the glass rattled. "Did you see that? I am so tired of being called names! I didn't choose to fall in love with Rohan bloody Andreyev!" Emma clapped her hand over her mouth, too late to stop the declaration spinning out into the open. She'd said it. Farrell gave a woof of approval and wound around her legs like a giant, woolly black cat, getting underfoot. "She's insane!" Emma retorted to cover her embarrassment.

Emma cleaned the house until lunchtime, changing and washing bedding, tumble drying and putting it back on the beds. She killed time, constantly checking her phone for a message from Rohan until the obvious dawned on her and sent her spiralling into distress. "Ro doesn't have my number!" she wailed to the dog. "I never gave him it! He can't even let me know if he's ok!" Emma wrung her hands in desperation, having wasted three weeks in foolish checking and rechecking for an impossibility. He'd been gone such a long time, things must have gone wrong for him. Emma felt worry like a sickness in her heart and no amount of pushing it away seemed to work in the last few days. It felt like an omen.

Finally, rattled beyond belief, she made a foolish decision. "Come on, Faz. We'll go for a really short walk along the street, yeah? I'm sick of being cooped up indoors. I need to get out. *On foot!*"

Even the dog looked doubtful and slouched down in the corner of the kitchen on the cold tiles.

"We won't go far. Just down to the side road half way along Newcombe Street and I'll throw the ball for you on the waste ground behind the house. What do you say?"

Farrell yawned and refused to be drawn, uncharacteristically ignoring Emma as she rattled his leash. "Fine!" she said finally, in irritation. "I'll walk down and see Allaine, without you!"

He stood up at that declaration, allowing Emma to fit the leash onto his collar. He slunk along next to her, stuck to her left leg, so close he almost pitched her over with his inflexibility. At Allaine's gate, Emma sent the dog through first and he sat on the front doormat, waiting for her to follow. Emma watched as his tail thumped a tiny beat, his huge eyes watching as she rang the doorbell.

"Drop the leash, Emma." Christopher's clear voice made her jump and she turned quickly, finding herself up against his chest. "Just do as I say, darlin'. Drop the leash and they'll leave the dog here."

Emma gulped and did as she was told. Christopher smiled at her, an expression which seemed genuine. "How could you? You're a double crossing git! And a pervert!" she hissed at him and his eyes grew wary.

"Just do what they say, Emma," he advised. "They're definitely goin' to kill me, but you might be ok, if you're a good girl for once. And I'm definitely not a pervert, thanks. "

Christopher took her arm after patting the useless dog on the forehead, leading her down the path to the street and clicking the gate shut behind him. "Will your friend take care of the dog?" he asked, sounding concerned.

Emma didn't answer, allowing herself to be pushed towards the road side. Within seconds the dark car with the tinted windows was in front of her, Christopher jabbing her in the back to make her get in. Emma lurched into the back door of the large vehicle, falling face first into the seat. Christopher got in behind her, pushing at her bottom until he was in and the door was closed. The vehicle moved forward even before he managed to secure the door and Emma saw Farrell standing up against the front fence of Allaine's garden, barking his furry head off in distress.

CHAPTER THIRTY TWO

"Get off me, you...you..."

"Shut up, Emma." Christopher's calm, level voice acted as a warning, silencing her immediately. He reached out to take her hand and she took a swipe at him with it. His dark brown eyes flared and a smirk spread across his handsome face. "Feisty! It would've been fun, darlin'." He reached again and successfully pinioned her wrist between vicelike fingers. He kept one eye on the two men in front and when Emma finally stopped wriggling, he looked down at her hand. Prising her fist open, he smoothed long fingers across her palm as though unfolding a piece of paper. The backs of his fingers were dusted with dark hairs as he used them to write something on the soft skin. It tickled and Emma jerked her hand away. Christopher shook his head a fraction and began again.

His long index finger caressed Emma's palm with long sensuous strokes and she grew still.

Keep...quiet...

Emma watched without turning her head. Christopher gave her a sideways glance, waiting for a response. She nodded once and he smoothed her palm again, removing the invisible sentence.

Do...as...I...say...

Emma exhaled in a snuff and rolled her eyes, fear beginning to take hold of her heart and squeeze it until she found it hard to fill her lungs.

You...ok...?

Emma shook her head and bit her lip, seeing Christopher's eyebrows knot together in concern. He stretched his fingers out across her palm and rubbed the back of her hand with his thumb.

"What're you doing back there?"

Emma jumped, embarrassed to hear the whimper escape her lips. For the first time since entering the car, she took note of the driver and passenger. The men from the nightclub sat in front of her, the stockier one of the two looking straight at her, his head twisted round from the passenger seat. His blue eyes bulged and his unshaven face looked flaccid and beefy.

"The wee lass is scared," Christopher answered, sounding bored.

"Yeah, well keep her quiet!" the man spat. "We don't want no trouble."

"That's what I am doing ya wee shite!" Christopher bit back. "Now turn ya fat face round, yer makin' me sick!"

"Can you 'ear this?" The man jabbed his thumb backwards towards the back seat and the driver nodded.

"Yeah. Don't worry about it. Just watch out 'e dun't put 'is hand round yer throat from behind and snap yer neck!"

The passenger screwed his neck round again, turning his eyes on Christopher with suspicion in his face. Christopher rewarded him with a beatific smile in return and the man sat back round, keeping his head well away from the headrest, just in case.

Emma watched her companion smirk so broadly he bit down on his bottom lip to control it. A cute dimple appeared in his right cheek and he glanced at Emma with mischief in his brown eyes. Alarmed, Emma tugged at her hand to release it from his grasp. He tightened his grip and turned his beautiful face to her, his eyes dancing and sparkling in their deep sockets. Christopher raised an eyebrow and winked.

Emma's eyes widened. The man treated everything like a game. Unable to work out which side he was on, she panicked, yanking her hand hard and breaking free. The car moved at a steady pace through traffic on Northampton Road heading south and Emma grappled with the door handle.

The passenger reached around with grasping fingers and snatched hold of Emma's leg, pinching so hard she cried out in pain. "Sit still!" he yelled at her. Emma pulled at the door handle repeatedly, her breath hitching as it refused to open.

"Get hold of 'er!" the driver yelled at Christopher. He turned to his passenger. "I knew you should've sat in the back with 'er!"

"She wouldn't get in for me, would she?" he screeched back, digging his fingers so hard into Emma's thigh, her leg began to go numb.

Christopher sat in the back next to her, separated by the middle seat. His narrowed eyes observed Emma's hysterics with casual interest and she shot a frenzied, horrified look in his direction. Unable to get out of the door, she turned her wasted aggression on him instead. She leaned towards him, bending the passenger's fingers backwards in the movement so he roared in pain and withdrew his hand from her thigh. Then she aimed to thump Christopher hard in the face. His body arched back with amusement in his eyes, lighting the fuse in Emma's sanity and leaving her little choice.

"She bit me!" Christopher sounded so shocked, his

voice rose a few octaves and the two men in front laughed, dispersing the tension. The traffic cleared as Emma made another lurch for his arm, sinking her teeth into the flesh underneath his jacket. "Stop, you little..." Christopher put his palm in front of her face, bending her head up and squashing her nose painfully against hard bone. Undeterred, Emma snapped at the fleshy palm against her lips, securing a thin piece of skin between her two front teeth. Christopher swore like a sailor and the men in the front of the vehicle laughed again, dulling his voice as he leaned down and whispered in Emma's ear. "If you want them to treat you bad, you're goin' the right way about it!"

Emma sat up with a huge inhalation, her anger dissipating with Christopher's warning. "I hate you!" she hissed, shifting her legs across the ridge between their foot wells. She administered a last painful kick at Christopher's calf and he leaned down and pinned her by the shin.

"Enough!" he shouted. Emma felt his breath on her face, stirring the hair which escaped down her cheeks in wispy tendrils. She sat up, her eyes filling with tears and her bottom lip protruding like a child's.

"Don't cry, don't cry," Christopher whispered. He looked genuinely pained as he brushed the hair out of her face with gentle fingers. Emma sniffed, the last of her resolve draining away and Christopher unclipped his seatbelt and shifted over towards her. "Come 'ere." He pulled her stiff body into his kissing the top of her head and wrapping his arms around her. An irritating noise sounded in the front of the car, a persistent bell clanging in warning.

"Put yer seatbelt back on!" the driver shouted, jerking his head backwards.

"Shut it!" Christopher snapped over the top of Emma's head. "She's upset."

"I don't care, get it back on!"

"Stop the car and I'll just shoot him in the legs!" the passenger said to the driver and Emma froze and let out a moan of dismay.

"No, no, I'll stop! I'll behave!" she pleaded, her brown eyes wide and terrified as she looked up at Christopher. His eyes flashed surprise and then pleasure as he scooted round and clipped the centre lap belt across his stomach. His long legs splayed either side of the ridge and he wound a strong, masculine right arm around Emma's shoulders. The alarm on the dashboard ceased. She buried her face in his shoulder and allowed frightened tears to dampen his jacket. Her hand rested gently on his thigh and one handed, Christopher turned it over and flattened her palm out.

Help...will...come...

Emma peered up with trusting brown eyes, praying he was right. She linked her fingers through his and tried to calm down, grounding herself in the safety Christopher gave her. He was a double crossing Irish git, but for now he seemed to be in as much strife as her

"What about Nicky?" she whispered and the passenger immediately turned round and faced her. Emma realised with a jolt, why Christopher kept signing on her hand.

"Who's Nicky?" he asked, bulging eyes red rimmed and unpleasant.

Emma's mouth opened but the look on his face stopped her before she risked her son's safety too.

"The dog," Christopher said. "It's fine. It ran down the road. It'll probably get run over."

"Yeah, well it better," the man growled. "Let's just hope it's not chipped."

The journey took six hours, during which Christopher held Emma's hand and observed the two men up front through cold, expressionless brown eyes. The day disappeared from under them, the last vestiges of daylight claimed by blackness and yellow street lamps. Emma was desperately uncomfortable after the third hour, fighting a need for the toilet which grew overwhelming. They drew up outside a huge house made of red brick, somewhere north of the sign for Falkirk. The sudden lack of engine noise sounded deafening and Emma's ears hummed without its constant buzz.

"I'm busting for the toilet," she complained and Christopher's hand tightened on her wrist.

"We all are!" the passenger snapped. "But we couldn't exactly stop, could we?"

Emma's door was opened and the man put his hand inside. "You get out nice and slow and no stupid moves. Otherwise we just shoot ya and be done with this shit!"

Emma leaned up against the side of the car, clenching her nether regions to prevent an accident. Christopher seemed impossibly long exiting and emerged rubbing his backside. "Geez, my ass has gone to sleep!" he exclaimed.

"Well, nobody told yer to sit in the middle, did they?" the driver remarked grumpily. His bald head glowed in the overhead light from the front door. The building was so huge, it extended either side of the lighted area and rose up before them, an imposing structure in daylight but overbearing at night. Their new prison was to be a Scottish stately home.

Both men pushed Christopher round to face the side of the car, using his temporary weakness to force his hands behind his back and slip handcuffs onto his wrists. He groaned as they tightened them with unnecessary cruelty.

Emma panicked, backing away and shaking her head. "No, no, no! Please don't put any on me. I'm gonna pee myself!" Hysteria laced her voice.

"They won't if yer just do as yer told," Christopher reassured her gently. His dark fringe hung over his eyes and he looked exhausted. Emma hobbled over to his side as the driver pulled him away from the car and pushed him towards the enormous front door.

CHAPTER THIRTY THREE

"We'll be here until yer man gets back from his job," Christopher sighed, snuggling up to Emma's stiff back. He wound his arm over hers and underneath her stomach, pinning his cold hand and splaying his fingers.

"When will that be?" she whispered into the darkness.

"Can't be long if they've taken you now. They wanted to do it weeks ago, before he did the job but I convinced them not to."

"Why? Why would you care?" Emma asked, turning her head so she could sense Christopher's face in the darkness.

"Lotsa reasons." His accent sounded lyrical and comforting in its whispered tones. "I knew the Actuary wouldn't do a convincing enough job of retrieving the drive if he knew they had you. At least this way, he's gone in and out without drawin' attention to himself. To him, it's just a normal job and he won't mess up; apart from the fact I'm not there so it won't be as smooth. The other reasons were personal. I wanted time to tool up because I knew when they took you, it was game over for me as well. I did a little bit of double crossing a while ago, so it was only a matter of time. Their boss doesn't like to lose."

"But you only asked them for another hour, in the nightclub. You said, one hour."

"What yer sayin'?" Christopher sounded genuinely

confused. "Nobody said anything about an hour."

"You did!" Emma hissed. She turned so she was on her back and Christopher stayed leaning half over her body. Emma felt the fabric of his trousers through her socks as she moved her foot sideways. "I read your lips. You said, 'One hour.'" She did a poor impression of his Irish accent and musical tenor voice and he laughed out loud.

"What kinda shite lip readin' school did you go to?" he chuckled. "The one for eejits who haven't a clue what's goin' on?"

"I don't have a clue what's going on!" Emma's voice wobbled and she gave a huge, undignified sniff. "I thought Rohan did maths all day but now I find he's...what is he doing?"

"He assesses risk and then eliminates it. He does the maths and works out projected outcomes with all the other number crunchers. They move on to spreading the cost but he calculates how to solve the problem. Nowadays the risk is stolen information; prototypes, databases or damaging emails, stored on a portable hard drive or some other device. It's Rohan's job to get it back before the thief does anything with it."

Emma stayed eerily silent and Christopher jabbed her lightly in the ribs. He leaned up on one elbow and brushed his other hand lightly across her face. "I told them, *not now*; the guys in the bar. I don't know in what weird Emma world that came out as *one hour*. But I'm guessin' that's why you ran?"

"It's probably your accent," she reasoned with a sigh. "But yes, it's why I ran away from you. I imagined...well, it doesn't matter now." Emma sighed and laid her head back against the mattress.

"You thought I was a weirdo sex predator?"

Christopher stroked the line of Emma's throat, running his finger from underneath her chin to the line of her sweatshirt. She shivered, wondering how terrible it would be to allow him to undress her and enjoy one final moment of pure lust and satiation before she died.

Christopher snuffed once and moved his elbow, laying down flat and pulling Emma into him. She settled with the back of her head on his chest, his arm laid across her stomach. The heat radiating from his body made Emma realise how cold she felt. Christopher sighed. "I had lots of chances to make a move on you, if I'd wanted to," he whispered. "I've been following you on and off for just over four years. I couldn't believe it when the Actuary happened across yer at that weddin'. But then I should've guessed, what with his connections."

"What?" Emma sat up sharply and stared at where she thought his face might be in the darkness. She could almost feel him smiling. "Explain *everything!*" she told him, administering a light slap on his stomach which made him groan.

They snuggled down together on the bare mattress, using Christopher's woollen suit jacket to cover as much of them as possible. The temperature dropped around them as the house failed to protect them against the falling snow outside and the wind pounded the house with what sounded like flurries of ice. "I met Anton through a mutual friend when I came out of the Air Force." Christopher's whispers calmed Emma's fears and offered a soporific effect. "He was friends with someone I knew and gave us tickets to go and see him in this crazy performance he was in. Man, he was just so...so..."

"Full of life?" Emma offered and she heard

Christopher's hair shuffle against the mattress as he nodded.

"Yeah. He was such fun to be with and we knocked around for a year or so before he told me about you. He had me tail you from time to time just so he knew you were ok."

"Was I ok?" Emma asked, hearing the absurdity of the question as it left her lips.

"Aye, mostly," Christopher answered, his smile leaking into his speech. "And sometimes not. Like when ya didn't have enough for the electric bill that time in the post office, or the time that letchy guy from your second year history paper wouldn't leave ya alone."

Emma sat up in astonishment. "Anton sent Lucya money just at the right time and that horrid guy fell down some stairs. He ignored me for the rest of my degree. He wouldn't even look at me!"

"Aye, well I told him not to," Christopher snuffed in the darkness. "Cocky wee shite. But mostly, yeah, I could report to Anton that you were ok."

"So how did you end up working with Rohan?"

"Working *for* him, Emma. It's not a partnership, not really. Well, Anton asked one time if I wanted to meet the Actuary."

"Why do you call him that?"

"That's how I know him. And he knows me as Hack. It's our business arrangement. It was best we knew as little as possible about each other. In case. It was how the Actuary wanted to play so I played along. Ironic really, seeing as I know everything about him, so I do." Christopher didn't offer explanations of what Rohan thought might happen if he revealed himself to this Irishman and Emma chose not to ask, shivering at the possibilities her tired brain conjured up for her. Rohan was right. Christopher *did* know him and had subsequently put him in danger.

Christopher cuddled Emma in closer, over locking his arms behind her back and assuming it was the cold torturing her and not her thoughts. "Anyhoo, Anton said his brother needed some help. He knew I was into writing computer programmes and having great success in the gaming world. He also knew I was military police in the Air Force. It fitted the Actuary's needs and we met and that's how it began, about three years ago. It made Anton feel better about what his brother did for a living and I've worked for him on numerous jobs and made a heap of money at it. But then it started to go wrong." Christopher sighed and Emma waited patiently, allowing him to collect his thoughts.

"We did a job which went bad. The Actuary made the retrieval of a database a guy copied before leaving his job. It contained sensitive information relating to covert military operations by the American government and the guy fancied himself as a whistle blower. The Actuary paid him a visit in the usual style and offered him cash first and then violence second. The guy opted for the cash and handed the drive over but then after the Actuary left, the stupid wee shite tipped himself off a twenty third floor balcony onto a Dubai street."

"Ugh!" The thought made Emma feel sick.

"Oh yeah! Messy! So it opened up a whole big problem with the local cops. Luckily the Actuary always takes precautions and their security cameras and evidence search picked up nothing that could link back to us. But it's when we became aware there was someone goin' behind us; when the cash was never found. There was another job before that; a politician playing heavy on email. He tried to get a government minister to allow a Chinese Triad to immigrate to Britain despite a string of convictions. The minister caved and let him in but someone stole his laptop with the emails on. The ministry wiped the backups and got ready to deny everything but they needed the laptop so they could cover it all up properly. I found the culprit and Rohan paid him off. When we looked back at that, we thought the mark gave it up easily because of the types of others desperate for his information. A skinhead political opponent wanted that laptop very badly and they weren't nice people so we figured it was easier for him to sell to us. But then he went missing and wound up decapitated in the River Thames. We thought initially it was the skinheads but then we literally tripped over the Contessa and her nasty little band of highly paid thugs. They were tailing us and cleaning up afterwards; taking the cash and disposing of the owners. This time, they want the risk itself, as leverage. It's a real juicy one. You're the bait to make the Actuary play the game; kidnap his wee sister. Clever, hey?"

Emma stayed silent. They had scored better than just a stepsister and something told her Christopher was fully aware of Rohan's marital status. He seemed to know everything else; why not that?

Emma made sleepy snuffling noises and pushed her face into Christopher's shirt. Worry about Rohan and Nicky exhausted her emotionally and she no longer knew who to trust. But Christopher was here for the moment and rubbed her back gently, kissing her forehead. "Want me to stop talking?"

"No. It's making me feel safe."

"It's putting you to sleep!"

"Please keep going. I need to hear your voice. How old are you?"

"Ancient, lass. Ok, well, I got word that Anton was sick and went to see him. He asked me to take paid work watching out for you permanently and I didn't feel I could say no."

There came a long pause. Emma put her hands against Christopher's chest and pushed herself back. "It was you in the garden?"

"Aye."

"I only heard the dog bark a couple of times. How come?"

Christopher gave a low chuckle. "I've known that wee fella since he was a pup. We get on just fine, Farrell an' me."

"How often did you tail me?"

"All the time! I don't do a shoddy job, woman! I followed ya everywhere, even to that wedding up north. The car you booked was a heap of crap so I went in behind ya and paid for an upgrade. I couldn't risk you breakin' down on the motorway because I'd have to pull in behind yer." He planted soft lips against Emma's cold forehead. "I knew the minute you clapped eyes on me, you'd want me for yerself and that wasn't part of the deal." He laughed as Emma slapped his chest.

"Well now I *know* you didn't do a proper job!" She heard the smirk in her own voice. "Fat Brian would never let you on the estate. He'd smell you a mile off and...well, you'd end up with broken legs or just plain broke, one of the two."

"Aye, well about that," Rohan chuckled. "I've been

on and off that estate as long as you have, but I usually just intimidated him into letting me move around. After Anton died, I figured I better do a proper job and Fat Brian and his wee flunkeys came to an arrangement with me. Did yer notice how attentive yer man was to you in those last few weeks?"

"Yeah! But I made the mistake of thinking it was because I was kind to him. Ok, so did you hurt him or pay him?"

"I threatened one and did the other. Slimy git! But it meant I could come and go as I wanted. I wanted to help ya, but Anton said I wasn't to let ya see me. So I couldn't."

"Oh." Emma felt small at the thought he'd seen where she lived, her poverty still raw and painful. "You said you were at Susan's wedding? How? All the guests were invited."

"I walked in, bought myself a pint and sat down. A man in a suit with an air of confidence can go anywhere. Your wee boy was very chatty and grown up for his age. I saw you bump into the Actuary and knew the game was up. Anton said you'd run if you saw him so I went outside and waited. Sure enough you came flyin' out and ran for it. I saw his face as he watched you leave and knew he'd find you. He tried to reach out to me even before you were home and I deliberately ignored him, but it wouldn't have been hard to track you down. He has other contacts. A man like him never relies on one source, which has been just as well for him this last few weeks. I haven't been able to help him."

"So it was you the private investigator mentioned when we stopped him following us. He said someone had been following Rohan for a while and he hadn't noticed. But it was you, following me, wasn't it?"

Christopher snorted. "I'm surprised it took him so long to spot that daftie! Having you around put our Russian friend right off his game. He spent more time staring at you than taking notice of his surroundings. I mean, what self-respecting PI tails someone in a white van?"

"I thought it'd be logical. There're white vans everywhere."

"Not driven by pillocks, there aren't!"

"Well, that's actually debatable." Emma grew silent, lulled by the sound of Christopher's regular heartbeat pushing blood through his body. When she spoke, her voice cracked with exhaustion. "I thought his mother put the investigator on him. She said not."

"Na, it wasn't his mother. She's busy doin' other mischief."

"Like what?"

"D'ya know they call her the Black Widow at the residential home?"

"Yeah. I met someone who knows her." Emma pushed herself up on one elbow. "Anton and I were sure she killed his father and mine."

"Aye, I wouldn't be surprised! It'll be somethin' in that herb garden of hers. She plays with it most days like a fanatic. That's where I'd start."

"So who paid...the investigator?" Emma halted half way through her sentence as sleep claimed her and she struggled free.

"Tomorrow, sweetheart," Christopher whispered, stroking her back and resting his chin on the top of her head. "Sleep now. I'm not sure when they'll come. Let me watch over you; like I promised a good friend I would."

CHAPTER THIRTY FOUR

"Get up! Get up!"

Emma jumped awake at the crash of the heavy door opening and groaned. Trouble floated like air scum overhead, creating a milky pall in the light from the hallway. Rough hands grabbed at her shoulders and hauled her to a sitting position.

"Don't touch 'er!" Christopher threatened, already standing. He held his palms outwards in front of him but his eyes flashed dangerously in the semi-darkness. The man next to him jerked the revolver and Christopher shook his head. "No, I'm not turnin' round for yer, ya wee shite. Make me and tell yer buddy to get his hands off her!"

"Let her go!" the bald man told his mate, his cockney accent enhanced by the grogginess of exhaustion. They were tired too. The rough hands released Emma and she slumped face down into the mattress, trying to recapture some of the lingering warmth from it. Failure brought misery and hopelessness.

"Em," Christopher said softly. "Come here, sweetheart." He kept his hands outstretched against the threat of the gun but jerked with his head and encouraged with dark eyes. He smiled, his white teeth incongruous against the blackness of the room. "Come."

With a gargantuan sigh, Emma heaved herself upright and stumbled round the bed, skirting the man who watched her progress with gimlet eyes. She saw his bulging eyes flick towards her breasts and allowed the revulsion to twist her face. He looked away, embarrassed and she knew she read him right in the nightclub, a sex predator. "In your dreams, little man," she muttered as she passed and Christopher shook his head at her.

"Behave, Emma!" he warned and she pouted, falling into his side without coordination and jolting him sideways. Christopher grunted and jerked his head at the aggressor facing him. "The wee girl wants to use the bathroom," he said, his face expressionless.

"No time!" the man protested and Christopher gave him a dirty look.

"She wants the toilet!" Christopher took a step forward and the barrel of the gun touched his shirt.

"Oh let her go for a bloody piss!" the other man shouted.

"You're not coming in!" Emma protested and stood rigid.

"We can't separate them," the man with the gun argued with his friend. "And I'm not looking after him by myself." He waved the revolver towards Christopher and took a step back.

"Fine! Send them in together!" the other man snapped. "But be quick. He's on his way now. This isn't what we were told, it's turnin' into a nightmare."

Christopher smiled, evil undertones in his voice. "Oh yeah! It's gonna be your worst nightmare, for sure. You've made the Actuary angry, how dumb is that? I wouldn't wanna be youse guys in about an hour's time. Nice knowin' ya!"

"Shut up! Move!" Their captors moved the couple down the hallway and stopped outside a wide oak door.

"In!" the bald one ordered. "I'm warnin' ya, no messin' around or I'll just shoot the pair of ya!"

"Whatever!" Christopher pushed the door open and walked inside, pulling Emma behind him.

"Leave the door open!" the bald man shouted and stuck his foot in the gap.

"Pervert!" Emma whined, panicking she wouldn't get her jeans down in time at the inviting sight of the toilet. "Turn around!" she complained to Christopher.

He put his finger to his lips and then waved his hand in a circular motion telling her to keep it going. After a moment of confusion, Emma caught on and began talking in a moderately loud voice, whining and complaining. "I thought you were my friend," she droned on. "How could you do this to me?" She used the toilet while Christopher searched around the room for things he could use as weapons.

"Ach, you mean nothin' to me, ya silly wee girl," he intoned with a wink, flushing the toilet as Emma stood buttoning her jeans. He cast around the small room without success.

"Shut your face!" she yelled, covering the sound of Christopher opening a squeaky vanity cupboard and closing it again. He raised an eyebrow in victory and pushed the long screwdriver down the back of his pants, so the handle nestled against the small of his back.

"Get out here, now!" came a voice from outside. Emma moved towards the door, blocking the view of the bathroom while she sulked and Christopher worked behind her.

"I'm just havin' a piss!" Christopher bit back, urinating into the toilet bowl incredibly loudly.

"I'm sick of this!" Emma worked herself up into a

full blown tantrum, the panic of the situation communicating itself through this play act. Her body occupied the space between the door and the frame, blinding the men to what Christopher was doing. "I want to go home!" she sobbed, finding the tears were real.

"Just shut up!" The bald man grabbed her arm, forcing her out between the gap as Emma felt Christopher's comforting presence behind her. He looked up at the tall Irishman. "You didn't flush, you dirty bugger!"

Christopher slipped next to Emma and took her arm. "Go do it yerself then, eejit!" he offered. The man pulled a face and shook his head.

"It's not like it matters!" the other man complained and they left the bathroom and headed downstairs. Emma glanced back and saw water pouring down the front of the high cistern and flooding the floor. She looked up at Christopher and he winked at her. His hands were wet up to the elbow. He had stood on the seat, hence the loudness of his toilet and broken the ball valve, making the cistern fill endlessly. He was slowly flooding the upstairs. Futility got hold of Emma in a vicelike grip. *Why would these men care about a flooded house? Would it be enough to cause them to divide even momentarily?* Her eyes raked the face of the confident man next to her. Christopher's fingers felt freezing through her jacket sleeve and she laid her hand over his and tried to infuse warmth into him.

The two men forced them down the wide sweeping staircase, pushing until Emma almost fell. Christopher's temper seemed close to snapping and the darkness outside the building fastened around them, oppressive and terrifying. "Touch her again and

I swear, I'll..." Christopher began and received a gun in the back for his pains. He gritted his teeth, his eyes flashing with barely controlled violence.

The air downstairs was stale and damp as the couple were pushed into a room near the front door. The bald man acted as the mouthpiece, telling them what to do and how. "Sit!" he told Emma, indicating a dining chair in the centre of the room. "Put your hands behind you and don't speak."

Emma shivered and shook as she stumbled over to the chair. The frigid air made her blood run cold and it was an effort to place her arms in the right position. She cried out as a pair of metal cuffs were fixed around her wrists and tightly closed.

"You don't need to do that!" Christopher shouted and both man attacked him simultaneously, tripping him and putting him face down on the wooden floor.

"Stop!" Emma begged, unable to leave the chair and help because of how she was restrained. "Leave him alone!" The chair tipped towards her as she tried to stand up, trapping its seat at the back of her legs.

Christopher's nose bled as he was hauled to his feet, his smart shirt stained from filth and his hands wrenched behind his back. The sound of a mobile phone chirped into the room and the men stopped abusing the bound man with their kicks and punches, while the bald man answered the call. He held his index finger up to silence his comrade. "What? He's coming himself? Well, yeah, everything's ready." He sounded pleased and puffed himself up before the assembled party. "Ok. See you soon." He rang off and stuffed the phone back into his inside pocket, punching the air with his fist.

"What?" the other guy asked, looking nervous.

"The Actuary's nearly here but the boss is right behind him!" the man whooped, seeming to forget his role as psychotic kidnapper and prospective killer. "He wants to thank us for bringing the leverage."

"Awesome!" the other man grinned, shoving dark, greasy hair out of his face. He dragged his fingers though his fringe, trying to shove it backwards and flatten it to his head as it was at the nightclub. "We still gonna get paid?"

"Yeah sure!" the bald man reassured him, forgetting his prisoners observing the congratulatory celebration.

Christopher's loud laugh stopped them both in their tracks. "Yeah, sure, you're gonna get paid, so ye are! If yer boss is who I think, you're not leaving here ever!" He snorted and Emma's eyes widened in fear. A strange electrical pulse washed through her body, instantly recognisable as adrenaline. She tried to lift her arms over the high back of the chair and failed, a deadening pain spreading out from her armpits as the cuffs clanked behind her.

"Shut yer face!" the bald cockney retorted. "You don't know nothin', so shut it!"

"Aye, whatever!" Christopher replied and grunted as the revolver was swiped hard across his face. Emma gasped and moaned in misery. She pleaded out loud to Nicky's God, sobbing his name over and over for help, absolution and an end to the terrifying situation.

"Emma! Em!" Christopher saying her name came as a faint prod into her desperation and then louder as she latched onto his voice. He spluttered her name through a cracked lip and Emma took shuddering breaths and listened. "Emma, calm down, sweetheart. Take deep breaths, darlin', hold on, it's gonna be fine."

"Not for you!" The bald man waited until his

companion scraped another chair next to Emma's and then pushed Christopher backwards into it. The tall Irishman folded at the knees and sat down, the chair rocking so violently it almost tipped him over backwards. Emma turned sideways and pushed her face into Christopher's bicep, crying quietly and without shame.

"Hush, hush," he whispered to her, kissing the top of her head with sore, gentle lips. "It's gonna be ok. Just hold on, Em. Calm down and wait."

"What're you sayin' to her?" The bald man slapped Christopher around the head again, drawing a hiss of pain from him and a wail from Emma, who was cruelly jolted in the process. Her arms were dragged sideways, the heavy cuffs pulling them down and a moment of clarity made her realise something. Trying to lift her arms painfully upwards and lean forward had failed to release her. But if she tipped sideways enough, she could lean slightly and allow her arms to move to the right and forward, placing her hands carefully on the seat behind her. The chair back no longer separated them from her body.

She sighed and groaned as her numb bones reacted to the release and looking sideways, she saw a nod of approval from Christopher. "Good gal," he mouthed.

A sudden arc of light flashed through the room, two beams; headlights. Emma's heart stalled in her chest as she sensed the tension in the room hike. Her frantic eyes sought Christopher's and she heard him whisper, "Game on," as much to himself as anyone else. One of the men left the room and Emma held her breath.

The vehicle outside drew to a halt on the loose gravel and a car door slammed. Footsteps ran up the stone steps out front and the front door flew open. A dull light bulb flared in the room as the dark haired man entered and flicked the switch, holding the revolver at Rohan's head. A moan of defeat left Emma's lips.

"We're screwed!" Christopher whispered, observing the Russian through dispassionate eyes. Rohan looked beyond exhausted, a thick covering of beard forming a tight blonde fuzz around the bottom half of his face. His eyes were red rimmed and dull and he held his body in a tight knot of tiredness. He let the dark haired man push him into the room, offering little resistance.

Christopher acknowledged him with a sharp upwards jerk of his head and only Rohan's eyes changed in his still face. Emma watched her husband, refusing to let the tiny bud of hope die in her breast. Rohan's eyes glossed over her as though she were little more than an ornament and she felt her heart clench in disappointment. She hung her head and closed her eyes, not wanting to witness his dismissal of her any further.

"So, this is the famed Actuary, is it?" the bald man postured, enjoying himself thoroughly. "How disappointing. We've been crapping ourselves, certain it would be harder than this." He moved to stand in front of Rohan and eyed the giant of a man from his disadvantaged stature. "So, before my boss gets here, how about you hand the flash drive over to me and save yourself some trouble?" He held his hand out.

Rohan sighed and narrowed his blue eyes. "I apologise for the disappointment, but you'll have to wait." His voice sounded lusciously deep and attractive, laced by his Russian accent. Emma peeked, keeping her head down so as not to draw attention.

Christopher laughed and Rohan's eyes roved to him over the top of the bald man's head. Both men sized Rohan up and in an unspoken agreement decided to leave the frisking of the giant man to someone else.

"Oh. Well, the boss is gonna be stoked with this!" the dark haired man sniggered, waving the gun in Rohan's back. "I can't wait to see him."

Christopher laughed harder and Rohan smirked. The bald man looked from one to the other, realising he was suddenly the butt of an unknown joke. "What?" he asked, moving from foot to foot, unsure of himself. "What's funny?"

Rohan tipped forward slightly, bringing his nose level to the bald man's. "You wanna know?" he asked, his voice hushed. The bald man nodded and looked back at Christopher with doubt standing out in the set of his jaw. In the split second in which he removed his eyes from Rohan's face, the tall Russian flipped his head backwards, catching the dark haired man across his nose. There was a sickening crack as bones gave in his face and Rohan stood upright, faced with the startled eyes of the bald man. Seeing his mate fall to the ground behind Rohan, the bald man aimed the revolver and shot Rohan in the leg. Emma screamed. The shot took Rohan by surprise, but he managed to bend from the waist, snapping up and head butting the bald man in the forehead. His opponent went down with a grunt.

Rohan groaned and grabbed at his knee, releasing a storm of swear words in mixed dialect. He stood up straight, nudging the bald man with his toe as moans and spluttering emerged from the bloodied face. "Your boss is a woman, *durak!*" he hissed. "And now, she's your *palach.*"

"What's that?" the bald man screeched. "What is it?"

"Executioner," Emma said, hopelessness breaking into her words. Christopher looked sideways at her and raised his eyebrow, releasing his wrists easily from the handcuffs. He stood up and eyed Rohan.

"Thanks for nothing!" the Russian spat. "Why this?" He waved his arm around the room in anger. "Seven hours of driving, only to find two half-assed *duraki* and you!" His eyes moved over Emma without interest and her heart sank lower into her stomach, bringing sickness with it.

"He shot you?" Christopher looked concerned and Rohan gritted his teeth.

"Yeah. Nice." He moved his prosthetic leg back and forth and Emma released her breath, realising it took the force of the gunshot.

"My boss is coming!" stammered the bald man and Rohan eyed him with disdain.

"Ooh, goody!" His blue eyes sought Christopher again and hate poured from them. He set off walking, his limp much more pronounced. "You did this on purpose!"

Rohan was half a head taller than the Irishman and furious. It made him appear invincible as they squared off to each other. Christopher placed the redundant handcuffs neatly on his chair seat, making Emma clink hers in case there was a secret switch for removing them easily. She doubted it, even as she felt around the casing.

"They jumped me," Christopher said with a smirk easily discernible in his voice. "It seemed like a good opportunity for catching her out so I bargained with them. I knew she'd come personally for this one. We need to get her off our backs. Sorry about your sister being involved...or should I say, your *wife?*" Christopher cracked his knuckles and Emma looked up at the side of his face, hurt making a dramatic revisit.

"I trusted you!" Emma stood up and forced her way between the men. Her dark eyes were wide with indignation and her arms behind her back forced her to dip slightly forwards. The metal cut into her wrists but anger made her forget to care. "My son's miles away and I've just disappeared! I thought you had no choice but *you* set this up!" Emma rushed Christopher and barged him, using her full body weight. He didn't budge and she only hurt herself, resorting to kicking him hard in the shins. Rohan grabbed her from behind, wordlessly seizing her upper arms and Emma used the leverage to increase her flurry of kicks, landing one on Christopher's knee and an opportune one in his groin. Christopher gasped and bent over double and Emma was thwarted from inflicting further damage by Rohan spinning her around behind him.

"You fool!" he said to Christopher. "Did you think she'd come alone? What's your plan then, mastermind?" He spoke through gritted teeth and Emma writhed, pinned by his painfully strong grip on her arms, grunting as she struggled to break free. The bald man made a grab for her foot so she kicked him instead, getting him in the stomach and glaring at him. The dark haired man lay on the ground behind them, still static.

"I knew you'd bring the crew," Christopher said, standing up gingerly and rubbing at his crotch. He shot Emma a nasty look, smirking at the end in true Christopher style and betraying his admiration. "Someone's telling her what we're working on and she's coming behind us. She's had her fun. We need to take her out!"

"It's you! You're telling her! And that's not how I operate!" Rohan increased his pressure around Emma's shoulders, preventing her movement. Her neck began to ache and she wiggled until he finally let her go. He turned to face his colleague, forgetting about Emma with frightening speed. "She's linked to the Triads. You don't just eliminate people like that; you learn to work around them. You know that! Why now? *Pochemu?* Why the big double cross?"

Emma saw Christopher shrug as she backed slowly away from them, skirting the men on the ground and keeping her footsteps light. "I'm sick of it, right! We case a job, we do the ground work and they turn up hot on our heels with a bigger price. I've had enough! And you know it's not me. We both know who the leak is but you won't sort it out."

"So bail out!" Rohan shouted. "Not this!" Emma saw him run his hands through unruly hair. He reached in his pocket and responded to a quiet vibration from his mobile phone. "I know!" he snapped. "Clean it up and get ready!"

Christopher smirked. "See, you always come equipped. Now we can get rid of a little problem and keep going the way we are."

"You reckon?" Rohan's body language set in a stubborn stance and Emma watched as Rohan lashed out at Christopher, hitting him hard in the jaw. Emma slipped towards a rear wall and leaned against it, feeling sickened.

"Is that because you're pissed or because you realised I dated your wife in that hot, red dress?"

"It was you?" Rohan's eyes strayed to Emma

fractionally. "That's for trying to screw my wife!" Rohan landed another punch, his ego overriding their bizarre surroundings and imminent danger.

"Well, you didn't exactly want her!" Christopher licked at a cut which bled from the corner of his mouth. "I'm not fighting you, you eejit! So back off!" He raised the back of his hand to touch the spot and blood came away on it. He looked at it as though not believing it was his. "Besides, I thought she'd tell you and you'd be sure to come, not her! If you weren't such a dick, and spent less time playin' with that wee school secretary, you'd have asked the right questions and been straight onto it."

"What questions?" Rohan lashed out again and Christopher ducked.

"Like why I used my *real* name, when it was clearly me. We agreed at the start, we don't do that. Working names only! And I used yours, like, fifty million times. You didn't think that was odd?" Christopher shook his head in disbelief. "You didn't even ask her, did ya?"

Rohan took a step back, his shirt untucked and a line of blood running down the front of it. His face had an odd grey tinge and he wavered on his legs while he thought for a second. Then his left fist shot out and put a bone crunching punch into Christopher's right eyebrow. The skin split easily like a sausage and blood spurted. Christopher leaned forward and Rohan pushed him back, like a boxer sizing up for a second go.

"Ah, shite! I never followed through with her." Christopher raised himself to his full height, finding he was a few inches shorter than his opponent. He smirked. "I did have a go with yer wee girlfriend though, so. She wasn't that good. Yer not missin' much. Bet she never told you about that now, did she?"

Rohan's fist shot out again, blocked this time by the side of Christopher's arm. The smaller man bounced back on the balls of his feet and egged Rohan on further in his sense of outrage. "She faked all her orgasms, mate. She's fake right through. See, I've released yer now. You can get rid once and for all. You can do the right thing; before I do it for ya!"

Unguarded, Rohan took a blow to the ribs, collapsing forwards in a spasm of pain, but he managed to stay on his feet. Christopher got into his face, shoving him hard. "Anton said you were an idealist, Andreyev. Yer never saw what was right in front of your bloody big Russian nose. Life happens like that and it's all over that quick!" Christopher clicked his fingers and took a step back. "You know that already, man, so yer do. What's wrong with yer?"

The handcuffs clanked as Emma moved and pain reverberated up her elbows and into her shoulders. Her nose became blocked with the onslaught of her silent tears and breathing got increasingly difficult. She began to gasp as her body hyperventilated, her constriction finally getting the better of her.

"Look at her!" Christopher yelled into Rohan's face. "Look what yer did! You make it right with her or I swear I'll take her and that wee boy of yers and you'll never see them again!"

"Over my dead body!" Rohan shouted and lurched for Christopher again.

Emma stumbled down the hall and into the wide lobby. She almost made it to the front door when a hand snaked around her mouth preventing the inevitable scream of shock. Emma's breath caught in her chest and she looked down at the legs dressed in combat pants and black boots. Another face came into view, a pair of male eyes peering from a black balaclava. He signed something with his hands to the man holding Emma and crept towards the door of the room, where Rohan and Christopher fought. A long, black gun led his way, pointed around the doorframe and he slipped through. Emma squealed a fruitless warning which never made it past the gloved hand. She struggled and the cuffs dug into her flesh. Biting at the heavy gloves over her mouth yielded only empty material between her teeth, which choked and suffocated her. The hand shifted, unscathed and gripped harder over Emma's mouth.

Tears of frustration and fear coursed down her face as she heard no more of Rohan's raised voice and her breath shuddered in and out of her lungs as a gag was fixed over her mouth. She was dragged sideways and handed over to someone else who shoved her over his shoulder, fireman style. The movement was excruciating, her arms behind her back and her shoulders pulled almost out of their sockets as she bounced and shook over the stranger's shoulder. Through the house he ran, exiting into the freezing cold through an open side door. She watched dark tussocks disappear underfoot and lines of straight tree trunks whip past on either side

Finally he set Emma down with care, but she overbalanced and hit her head against the side of a large dark vehicle, gasping with the pain. "Sorry," the man whispered into Emma's face. "You ok?" He turned to the dark shape waiting by the truck, at the same time as releasing the gag. "What's the plan? You hear all that?"

The heavily camouflaged man to Emma's left

nodded once. Over six feet tall, he carried himself like Rohan with an ingrained military bearing. As soon as he spoke, Emma whipped her head round in surprise. "Yep," he said softly in his gentle Yorkshire accent. "We got company about a mile out. Tell the Actuary and let him know it's the Contessa. She's actually come herself."

"So Hack was right?" The man kept his hand on Emma's forearm and looked up at his commanding officer.

"Hack's a dick and he'll get what's coming to him." Frederik nodded at his subordinate. "Plan B and make sure you follow through. The Irishman provided the water so pull the electrics and let's get this done quickly." Susan's husband looked down at Emma, the black smudges under his eyes frightening in the pitch darkness. "If I don't get this lady home safe, the wife will kill me."

The other man sniggered quietly and headed off back towards the building, disappearing into the darkness like a sylph.

Frederik spun Emma round and fiddled with the handcuffs behind her. She heard and felt the click as they fell apart under his ministrations and she turned, falling backwards against the truck again and hitting her head in the same place. "Christopher's got a screwdriver and he's going to hurt Rohan," Emma gasped, struggling to stand upright in the ice underfoot.

"Na, he won't," Frederik replied. "Get in the truck, Emma and shut up. Please," he added. He pressed his ear and listened to something else coming through the curly wire spiralling out of his dark shirt collar. His body tensed and he re-fixed the dark goggles down over his eyes. Holding a radio up to his mouth he whispered instructions into it. Emma heard clicks, whirs and disjointed voices from somewhere.

Frederik trusted Emma to get into the truck and she almost did. He was distracted by a set of vehicles arriving and took his eyes off her. Emma moved around to the driver's side of the truck and waited, listening to the night noises from the dark surrounding forest. The truck was hidden in the trees, camouflaged by its dark matte colour. Emma heard the sound of slamming car doors. She felt insignificant, foolishly inconsequential in the unfolding drama. She helped Christopher get the screwdriver and a sense of responsibility crawled across her flesh. The Irishman set Rohan up and her husband had all the hallmarks of a man who hadn't slept for weeks. Frederik wasn't interested in Emma's opinion and she experienced the overwhelming urge to speak to Rohan, to find out why he disregarded her earlier as though she didn't matter. *Surely she was more than collateral damage to him, wasn't she?*

Emma crept sideways, rubbing the blood back into her arms and keeping level with the vehicle so Frederik didn't pick her up in his strange night-vision goggles, as he watched a car crawl up the driveway with only its side lights showing. She kept low to the ground and used the trees to hide herself, heading back the way she came, slipping in through the side door and navigating her way around the downstairs of the house. Twice she got lost. Her foot bumped a hefty block of wood in a corner, underneath a set of ragged, once ornate curtains and it began to slide down the wall, scraping the plaster as it moved. Emma stilled it with a panicked hand and then wielded it, knowing it could come in handy. She swung it in a couple of practice arcs, wincing at the pain in her arms but certain she could do it.

Creeping closer to the front of the house, Emma heard no sound but saw the occasional flash of metal as one of Frederik's men moved around up ahead. She didn't know how many there were but worked hard to stay out of their way.

Hiding behind a set of display curtains, Emma watched a shape slide past her. He didn't look to be cut from the same scruffy cloth as her wounded kidnappers, more of a snappy dresser, but he carried a lethal looking gun in his outstretched hand. Emma slipped from behind the curtain, hearing her ruined boots squeak against the wooden floor. The man turned in surprise. He was thin and oriental looking and he gaped in surprise at the harpy with the block of wood raised above her head. "Sorry!" Emma whispered as she swiped at his face. The look of amazement stayed fixed to his lips even in sleep as he slid down the wall. Emma struggled to hold onto the wood, imagining the fierce clunk it would make throughout the house if it hit the floor.

With great difficulty, Emma dragged the man into her hiding place and hid him there. Then she snatched up the hand gun from where it bounced, luckily into the folds of the copious curtain. She looked at it in the darkness, working out how to hold it by feel and placing her finger over the trigger. Wrinkling her nose, she shoved it in the pocket of her borrowed jacket and favoured her wooden block, holding it firmly in her right hand and flexing her wrist. She batted it against her left hand a few times to regain balance and crept on.

It felt like a video game Nicky liked to play at Fat Brian's house, sneaking around in the dark and wiping out the enemy. He hated playing Emma because she was far superior with her hand-eye coordination to most of the regular players. Emma hit another man in the hallway, sneaking up behind him with incredible skill and knocking him out with the wooden block. She collected his gun also, switching it to a different pocket when the first gun clanked against the second noisily. She ran out of luck creeping past yet another hall curtain, when a gloved hand shot out and grabbed her around the neck and mouth, pulling her behind the folds of cloth.

"This is not a game!" an aggravated voice breathed in her ear. "Fred told you to get in the truck!" The soldier clearly felt he wasted his time and energy carrying the delicate female out to the vehicle and he pouted under his balaclava, narrowing his eyes in disgust. "Now stay here and shut up!" he demanded. "They've had a good look round and they're coming in."

"I've taken out two," Emma stage whispered and the man shoved his hand over her mouth again.

"I know! Fred told me to watch you so I watched you! Nice technique. Now shut up. It's important!"

Emma exhaled in temper and peered at her wooden block, convinced she saw a dark bloody edge in the growing light.

"Put it down!" the soldier hissed at her and snatched it out of her hand, placing it next to him.

"Don't care. I've got this anyway." Emma yanked the revolver from her pocket and the soldier ducked and pointed it away from his face.

"The bloody safety's off!" he squeaked and confiscated that too. Emma fondled the other gun in her right pocket and pursed her lips like a stroppy teenager.

The sound of the front door slamming made them freeze in place, Emma wishing she'd got comfy instead of engaging in chit chat with her new friend. Her legs ached underneath her and she watched through a chink in the curtains as a tall, elegantly dressed woman clicked past in a set of high heels. She was flanked by two thick set men toting guns. Emma pulled the curtain back at the sides so she could gape some more but her companion nudged her painfully in the leg. She pushed his hand away and admired the cut of the suit drifting elegantly into the room. The woman was beautiful. At the last minute, Emma saw the glint of the metal blade in her manicured right hand.

"Ah, my gorgeous Russian adversary," Emma heard her silky voice intone as she greeted Rohan.

"*Oh shit!*" the soldier mouthed, spotting the knife.

"Why did he just wait there to be killed?" Emma squeaked and the soldier hit her again, harder this time. The dull slap sounded loud in the silent hallway and the gentle hum in the room halted.

"Check it out!" the woman rapped, her oriental tongue making the words sound exotic. Emma experienced a flash of jealousy at the thought Rohan might have actually wanted to see the beautiful woman. Rage lit a fire in her belly. *That's why he's not bothered about me! I've ruined his fun!*

Emma heard the sound of Rohan talking to the woman as quick steps heralded the arrival of the first bodyguard, dispatched to investigate the slap which still stung on Emma's thigh. The soldier stood quietly and curved himself into the corner of the window frame, hearing the big male turning on the spot. He made a small enticing noise and the wide face turned towards them in the half light and held his gun out front in a menacing stance as he searched for the noise. The soldier was slick in his movements, surging forward from the curtains like water as he shoved a metal blade upwards into the man's throat and twisted. Liquid showered Emma and she bit down on the emerging scream as the soldier slithered the body behind the curtain and clamped his hand over her nose and mouth, suppressing breath as well as noise. It was over in seconds without sound but the soldier's glove was wet and Emma's imagination ran wild.

She heard the gentle hum of a woman's unconcerned voice framing her struggle for air and saw in her mind's eye, the slender fingers moving over Rohan's naked body. Her rational mind told her it wasn't real but very little about Emma Harrington-Andreyev was ever completely rational.

"Sorry about this," came the soldier's voice close to her ear. Then Emma felt a sharp spiked prick in the soft flesh of her neck and the world was sucked away from her in a single, ragged flush.

CHAPTER THIRTY FIVE

Emma woke as she was rudely bundled into a vehicle by rough hands. "Gonna kill you," she slurred, unable to work her limbs properly. She flapped a hand and smacked herself in the face.

"Yeah, yeah," came the soldier's voice. "Pretty little girls should stay away from guys like the Actuary. Take that as a word of advice from an old man."

"Old man," Emma repeated, shocked by the excruciating heat coming from behind the soldier as he strapped her into her seat. The whole world felt hot and orange. She couldn't cope with it and closed her eyes. Disjointed voices sounded in her fuddled brain, swirling words which made no sense.

"You need to get that looked at by a doctor."

"I'm fine. I need to get Emma home."

"We didn't expect the Contessa to be tooled up like that. A gun yeah but...sorry mate."

"Yeah well, you live and learn. Clear up here. Make sure nobody gets out."

"What about Hack..."

"Nobody!"

Emma shocked herself awake again as her head hit the side window of the car. Daylight burned her eyelids and she writhed on the seat. A large hand pulled her head sideways and held it there while she drifted off again. "Sleep it off, *dorogaya*," came Rohan's soft voice.

"Cheating bastard, pig, cat, dog! You like her!" Emma heard herself say, realising it didn't make sense but unable to correct it, despite very much wanting to.

She slept deeply without dreams or any sense of time. Daylight hurt her whole face as Rohan stood next to her, shaking her awake. "Time to get out, Em," he said nicely, looking startled at her reply.

"Eff you!" she shouted into his face.

He blinked, dark lashes swishing across a cut under his left eye and he pressed his top teeth down into a swollen bottom lip. "Nice!" he exclaimed. "Someone's never playing with the Irish git again!"

"Effin' effs," Emma groaned, feeling like a rag doll as Rohan's strong arms snaked underneath her and snatched her from the passenger seat like she held no weight. Rohan's body jolted under her as he navigated stairs and balanced her against the wall while he unlocked a door. It banged behind him and Emma felt soft mattress under her back. Thinking she was still in the manor outside Falkirk, Emma tried to stand and make a run for it, lurching into a long desk with a sharp edge and flailing around on the carpet.

"Bloody hell, Em!" Rohan exclaimed. "Just trust me, *dorogaya!* You're safe. We're going home to Nikolai."

"My Nicky! Not yours, *mine!*" Emma sobbed, crawling back onto the bed and burying her face into the pillow. With great relief, she drifted back into the drug induced fog.

When she woke again, it was to find cold water on her face and splattering down her body. She screamed and jerked backwards, finding a hard naked chest against her spine. Emma looked down, horrified to see pink feet coming into focus, followed by pink legs, a pink stomach and some nicely rounded pink breasts. She ran her hands down them, coming to the conclusion they were hers and gasping again as the cold water attacked her face. Turning she found Rohan's firm chest inches away from her nose. So she hit it. "Stop!" he ordered, grasping her painful wrists. "I need you to wake up. I've tried everything else. *Durak* gave you too much. Come, wash the blood off."

Emma looked down, noticing the red splatter in the shower tray beneath her and panicked, letting out a pathetic yelp of fear.

"Not yours," Rohan said urgently. "Don't worry. It's someone else's. Wash it off." He turned the temperature of the water up and squirted a bottle of shower gel into his palm from a tiny motel container, using most of it. He rubbed it over Emma's body as she watched his hands in shock. The memory flashed back of the oriental man's startled face as the soldier stuck the knife through his artery and she jumped. Rohan placed a firm hand on her upper arm, cursing as the soap made getting a grip impossible. "It'll be like that for a while," he said softly. "You'll have flashbacks but they go eventually."

"Get your hands off me!" Emma snapped, taking over the washing of her own body, disconcerted by Rohan's obvious interest. She turned away from his arousal, visible through his tight fitting trousers. Glancing down, Emma saw his socks soaking up water. He didn't realise she knew about his leg and grudgingly she allowed him his privacy, pressing her hands up into her sore neck.

"You need to wash your hair," Rohan stated. "You've got...stuff in it."

Emma ran her wet hands over her curly mop, extracting clots of the man's blood and she shrieked again, almost slipping in her anxiety to get away from herself. Rohan pushed her gently in the back and increased the temperature of the water, soaking her hair and rubbing more motel products into her soft curls. He hissed with annoyance as he rechecked the label on the bottle. "Sorry, I washed it in conditioner. Does it matter?" His accent sounded heavily laden with tiredness and Emma felt a flash of guilt. She turned to look at him, her breasts pressed against his hairy chest in the small space.

"What the hell happened?"

"You don't need to know."

"Of course I do! I was dragged away from my son by thugs connected to a man I thought was a mathematician."

"Nikolai's fine."

"How do you know?"

"I just do, Emma! Why don't you trust me?"

Emma snorted. "I'll never trust you again!"

Rohan spun her around and ran his hands down her slick back. His fingers massaged the knots out of her shoulders as the soap left her body and Emma resisted the urge to groan with pleasure. "My whole body hurts," she moaned.

"I'm sorry. Eddie drugged you."

"Why? I was helping."

Rohan sighed and his fingers ceased their probing of her sore muscles. "He said you were losing the plot and it kicked off right then. He didn't have a choice."

Emma sighed. "I don't understand any of this."

"You don't need to." Rohan's tone was hard and uncompromising. "It's my job, nothing to do with you."

"Fine!" The emotional wall around Emma's heart began to rebuild, brick by solid brick. Rohan's dismissal of her in the ornate room bit at her ego and the way the Chinese woman said his name, pricked at her ready store of jealousy. Alanya and Felicity conspired against her in the deep recesses of her brain and Emma shut down against her husband. Tears welled behind her expressive eyes as her need for self-protection vied with the knowledge this man was her soul-mate. "I want my son."

Rohan nodded. "Yeah, we're going home, as soon as you're dressed."

Emma wrinkled her nose against the thought of underwear she'd slept in. Rohan saw and his lips turned upwards in a tight smile. "I bought clothes."

Emma cocked her head like a small bird and Rohan concentrated on washing conditioner from her fringe. "Clothes?" Emma swiped the back of her hand across her eyes and nose.

"*Da.* Yours were ruined." Rohan bit his lip and focussed on her hair, massaging the water through the curls like his life depended on it.

"So are yours now." Emma placed an index finger on the soaked waistband and felt Rohan shiver at her touch. She saw the concentration in his face as he worked hard not to look down at her luscious body. "Did you have an affair with the Chinese lady?" Emma asked, looking up into his face.

"What?" He looked shocked and stopped, his elbows close to Emma's face as he kept his hands against the side of her head, halted in the rubbing motion. His expression was non-plussed.

Emma shrugged, her voice haughty. "That's why you ignored me, isn't it?"

Rohan's jaw dropped, his patience snapping. "That bitch tried to kill me twice now! And what did you think I'd do, Em? Rush in and twirl you round like in a musical? Did you *want* to die? *Smert'* - so final. No more mother for Nikolai?"

Emma pouted and pushed her bottom lip out and shook her head. "No."

Rohan placed a soapy index finger under Emma's chin and forced her head up to look at him. "Emma Andreyev. You know the safe world Anton Stepanovich created for you in his stories is not real, *da?*"

She let out a laugh, the beginnings of hysteria. "Look at my life!" she stammered. "Of course I know!" Emma heaved in a giant breath and pressed her fingers over her lips, seeing a blob of blood wiggling around the plug hole beneath her. She sniffed and sobbed at the same time, choking on her misery. Rohan wrapped his arms around her, crushing her into him. Her naked legs felt odd against his wet trousers, the material rough against her skin. Rohan hushed her and pressed his lips over hers to prevent her soul escaping through her gut wrenching cries. Emma wrapped her arms around her husband's neck and held onto his strong body. Her emotions seemed to tumble from everywhere, out of sync and nonsensical, but at the same time overwhelmingly real.

The warm water cascaded over them, running down Emma's head in rivulets, deafening her with its hiss and wreathing her in confusion. "Ro, I'm sorry," Emma cried and her lips strayed to his. Rohan gasped as his lips parted and Emma kissed him, wishing things were different and she could go back in time seven years. "I wouldn't leave," she sobbed, "I'd tell you everything. I'm sorry, I'm sorry." Her lips slipped over his slick wet skin and she felt his resistance as his body stiffened.

Rohan hushed her with softly spoken Russian and Emma gulped in sadness, doubting he understood her agonised ramblings anyway. When the shower gave them a startling douse of ice cold water, they both jumped and Rohan laughed. "Time to leave, *dorogaya*." He smiled sadly, pushing dark hair away from her forehead.

Emma looked up at him, her huge brown eyes laced by luscious black eyelashes. "Ro," she whispered. "I can't do this anymore. I'm so confused about everything." Her vision popped out and back again, blurring and then struggling for purchase. Rohan saw. He kissed her gently, his wet lips enticing, offering solace and sanity.

"Talk when we get home, *dorogaya*," he whispered, his eyes filled with hope. "Make decisions then. Get dressed for now and we drive *home*." He turned to open the shower door and Emma shrieked.

"Rohan! You've been stabbed! Did the woman do that?" Bile rose into her throat as she saw the parted oozing skin and exposed fatty layers between his left shoulder and his spine. Her eyes watered and she put her fingers hard to her lips.

Rohan nodded and reached behind him, unable to stretch far enough to touch the wound. Finally his finger pads closed on uppermost edge of the cut and he winced. "Hurts, *da*."

Emma used medical tape from Rohan's small first aid kit to tape up the gaping hole in the muscle above his shoulder blade. Her fingers shook and she felt terrified of hurting him more. "You need a surgeon," she said softly, resting her face against his bicep. "Ro, I can't do this."

He nodded, his eyes shrouded in pain. "*Da*." He

used his right hand to reach up and massage Emma's head through her wet hair. "Sokay, *dorogaya*, I'll sort it when we get home." His fingers snagged in her curls and Emma's brow knitted in irritation, tilting her head backwards and exposing her soft neck. Rohan's guard dropped for just a second and she saw the aching need in him. His eyes strayed to her neck and he lowered his lips, kissing softly in a line up to her jaw. He let go of her hair and tugged at the skimpy towel around her. "Em," he whispered. "Em."

Emma let the towel drop to the bed and kissed his open lips, searching his eyes for anything which might give her a clue of how he really felt. His blue eyes sparkled like an aqua sea in the yellow streetlight from the window and his palms felt rough against her ribs. Rohan pushed her back and lay half across her on the double bed, his trousers still wet from the shower. Emma reached for the button at the waist and instantly he froze. "No." He pushed himself up and stood, his body rigid. "We're leaving soon. I'll dress."

Emma sat on the bed, pulling the scratchy towel around her in embarrassment as Rohan's strong muscles flexed. He snatched clothes from the open bag on the floor and stalked off to the bathroom. Emma dried her tears of humiliation with a corner of the towel, licking her wounds yet again. "I'm so done with this," she whispered to the empty motel room. "You never trusted me, did you, Rohan? Don't worry, now you don't have to."

Emma grappled in the carrier bag laid on the chair, hauling out a pair of expensive jeans and a cute sweater. She snapped the price tags off with her fingers. There was no sign of underwear and she grabbed at her own, lying on the floor next to the bed where Rohan dropped it. Blood stained her faded pink bra and her knickers smelled of smoke. She sniffed the fabric in confusion. A faint memory of fire crossed her consciousness and she grabbed the white blouse and the jeans she arrived in. The distinct scent was released immediately but the sight of the blood spatter on her blouse made her drop it to the floor in fear, stepping back to examine her hand. The stains were dried and crusty, but it was enough to drive her to the small kitchenette to wash her hands frantically with washing up liquid, making them red and sore with her need to clean them thoroughly enough.

Rohan clattered around in the small bathroom and Emma raided his bag while he was busy, stealing a pair of clean boxer shorts to wear under the jeans. It wasn't comfortable but better than nothing. She pulled the sweater over her head, feeling naked without a bra.

When Rohan emerged from the bathroom he looked more composed, smiling in approval at Emma's clothing. "Good." He nodded, "Put the ruined clothes in the black bag. Don't leave anything here!" he warned.

Emma's face fell and the image of the man falling throat first into the soldier's embedded blade coursed before her eyes. She gulped and sat down on the bed. "Are they all dead?" she whispered.

Rohan's eyes flared, warning her and Emma fixed her gaze on the ceiling. "I only hit them over the head. They would have woken up again."

"Not necessarily."

"But..." Emma began and Rohan held a hand up to silence her.

"No more!" he told her and she bit her lip.

"The sooner I leave, the better," she said through

gritted teeth. "Hopefully Felicity's my size and then she can have these." Emma flicked her finger at the sweater covering her naked torso and Rohan's eyes narrowed. As she passed, he reached out and grabbed her wrist. The reddened skin ached and she winced and tried to drag her hand back. "Get off!"

One handed he reeled her in, his brow knitting against the pain in his back. Emma crashed into his chest, her hand outstretched. Rohan tasted of toothpaste as he kissed her, pulling her into him and refusing to let her go, even though she struggled. His tongue was gentle and probing in her mouth and Emma let out a howl of rage and confusion, pushing Rohan away with a huge effort and no longer caring if she hurt him. "Touch me again and I'll kill you!" she threatened.

A sultry look lit her husband's face and the smallest smile turned his lips up at the corners. Emma sat stubbornly on the bed and watched Rohan collect the clothes into a black bin liner. "What about Christopher?" she asked. "Please just tell me about him?"

Rohan's face curled into a sneer and he ignored her as though she hadn't spoken.

"Did you kill him too?" Emma asked. "He didn't deserve that! He was..."

"He was a big Irish *durak!*" Rohan snapped. "We make our own luck in this life. Don't speak of him again!"

Emma hugged herself tightly, drawing her legs up onto the motel bed. "I hate you!" She watched Rohan stuff the rest of her clothing into the bag, but protested when he gathered up the jacket she borrowed from him. "No! Not that! I like it." She stopped when he glared at her. Emma bent forwards and scooped up her old ankle boots. She flung them at him one at a time. "Here, take it all then. I don't bloody care!" She looked down at her bare toes and regretted it.

"I got you some other footwear." Rohan indicated another carrier bag, which Emma hadn't seen next to the door.

She shook her head and buried her face in her knees. "You're taking my old life away. You've no right."

"It's evidence. I forgot to buy socks." Rohan threw a pair of his at Emma and she left them where they lay, resisting the urge to look in the bag as he tossed her holey old boots into the black bin bag.

"What about the gun?" she muttered from between her knees.

Rohan looked up at her startled and his lips parted. "Gun?"

"In the right pocket of your jacket. Why don't you just blow my brains out too? It would definitely be easier for you. Then you could torch this place and wash *my* blood down the shower drain." Nicky's face flashed past her inner vision. He laughed as he rode an old bike which he shared with Mo back on the estate. The tyres were flat and the pedals long gone, but his pink cheeks were flushed with enjoyment as the boys created their own fantasy world. *'Look, Mummy, I'm Harley Man!'* he squealed and Emma gulped. She felt immediate guilt at the thought of leaving him to scratch through a life without her and pressed her eyes to her knees, smelling the newness of the jeans. She heard Rohan sifting through the bag. He swore in Russian as he pulled the revolver from her pocket and held it up to look at. There was a series of clicks as he disarmed it and when Emma peeked he looked back at her, shaking his head in disbelief.

"Bloody safety was off, Em!" he chastised her. "You could have blown us to shit when you were tossing around in your sleep."

"Shame I didn't!" she muttered stubbornly. "And I didn't ask you to nearly get me killed or drug me up to the eyeballs, did I?" She raised her voice to a shout and Rohan decided it was time to leave.

Emma refused to wear the socks or new boots Rohan produced from the bag, skirting round them and waiting outside in the hallway barefoot. A passing couple stared at her pale toes as they walked down the stairs to reception. Emma flounced by, knowing she drew attention to herself and not caring. She cared a great deal once they got outside into the below zero temperatures of a late Friday night. She tiptoed across the freezing car park, the cold concrete burning her feet. Whenever Rohan looked around, she walked normally, cursing her bloody mindedness but determined not to give in.

He dumped his bag and the rubbish bag into the boot, flinging the new boots in on top. Emma noticed a beautiful cashmere coat in another bag, which bulged enough for it to be full length. His hire car was beyond the main car park and rested on gravel, covered in a layer of hard ice. He left the car unlocked and went back to the reception to pay for the room. Emma picked her way across the sharp stones, feeling Rohan's smug eyes on her periodically as he enjoyed her suffering.

He spent time defrosting the car when he returned and Emma shivered in her seat, worrying about what Nicky must be thinking about her absence. "We'll hit the motorway soon and then it won't take long to get home. I'll drop you at the house and return the car," Rohan announced, cranking the gears into reverse. "I'll have a bonfire tomorrow and burn evidence." Tiredness made his speech flip back into broken English.

"Where are we?" Emma asked.

"No matter."

"I want to know how long before we get back!" she snapped. "I just want my son!"

"Another three hours." Rohan clicked a switch on the dashboard to activate the central locking. "Get Nikolai tomorrow."

"Don't tell me what to do!" Emma shouted and lurched at Rohan, slapping him on the arm and causing him to swerve. He set his jaw and ignored her, finally fed up with her antics. Emma felt crushed inside as her whole world came crashing down. She would get Nicky in the morning and do what? *Go where?* She didn't have enough money for a coffee let alone a train ticket.

The sickness in her gut returned and Emma curled up on the seat and went to sleep, her head periodically thudding against the cold glass next to her. She didn't speak to Rohan again, waking groggily when they got back to Market Harborough. He parked in the garage at the bottom of the garden, forcing Emma to walk the length of the gravel and freezing cold grass to the back door. The absence of Farrell's excited tail wagging hit her hard and Emma stumbled up to her room, slamming the door behind her and crawling onto the bed, exhausted.

CHAPTER THIRTY SIX

She woke abruptly, hearing men's voices at two in the morning. Curiosity got the better of her and Emma went out into the lighted hallway, following the sound to Rohan's bedroom. He lay face down on the bed, his head dangling off the edge as a small, skinny man leaned over him, examining the wound on his back. Emma bit her lip. She hadn't even bothered to consider how he felt amidst her own thrashing around. "Can I do anything to help?" she asked groggily, standing in the doorway and watching the doctor's small movements.

When neither of them answered, she ventured into the room and held her breath at what she saw. The fatty tissue was exposed between Rohan's shoulder blade and spine, so deep it oozed a steady flow of liquid. Her ineffectual attempt at first aid lay discarded on the floor. Both men ignored her. "Will there be permanent damage?" she asked softly, edging closer inch by inch. Part of her wanted to witness the tiny man at work and part of her, namely her stomach, definitely didn't. Curiosity drove her on.

Glancing up, the doctor blinked once over his deep brown eyes and glared at Emma. "Don' touch!" he said with a strong Eastern European accent. "Don' wan' infection." He leaned over Rohan so his nose was almost touching the open wound and squirted something from a clear bottle over the raw openness. Rohan swore. Russian, English and what Emma recognised as Spanish came pouring out of his full lips. He sounded more angry than in pain.

"It's ok." Emma patted his good shoulder with gentle fingers, her eyes flickering with pleasure when Rohan reached up and clasped her hand. His vibrant blue eyes glittered in the lamplight with a strange, faraway essence as though his mind was somewhere else altogether.

"Keep still!" The doctor rapped out the order and Rohan breathed through pursed lips which were white around the edges. The doctor took black fibre from a plastic wrapper and a curved, vicious looking needle, already threaded. Rohan closed his eyes as the doctor began to sew through his tender skin, each stitch separately knotted and independent of the others. The wound was over fifteen centimetres long, stretching with a beautiful arch around Rohan's muscular shoulder blade. The man put a stitch every few centimetres, leaving long gaps through which the white fatty layers peeked. Emma rubbed Rohan's sweating fingers and fought waves of nausea.

"Go wash hand!" the doctor snapped at Emma. "Put glove on."

She gaped for a moment, wondering if he meant one hand or both. Jumping into action at his sharp look, she released Rohan's hand and ran into his ensuite, cleaning her hands with soap and watching the bubbles in the water. Last night's shower seemed a long time ago.

With a nod, the doctor indicated a box of disposable gloves poking out of his copious black bag. Emma seized a pair and dragged them onto her hands. The powder inside helped them glide over her still damp fingers.

"Der!" the doctor commanded, pointing to a place next to him. Emma moved into it. "Stitch hold ze vound. You erm...erm..." The man made pincer movements with his fingers and Emma pulled a face.

"Squeeze it?"

"*Da, da!*" he replied, eagerly nodding his head.

Emma took a deep inhale and used both hands to press the flesh together into a line between the first of the rough looking stitches. Her jaw dropped open at the sight of the tube in the doctor's hand. "No! You can't use that!"

"Emma, let him do his job. He knows what he's doing." Rohan spoke through gritted teeth, his pain evident in his slowness of speech and the veiled aggravation in his voice. She exhaled slowly and watched as the tiny, dark haired man squirted the liquid super glue along the seam she created between the folds.

"This is just wrong." she complained. "You should go to a hospital."

"*Nastupnyy!*"

"What? Sorry, what's he saying?" In panic, Emma appealed to Rohan.

"Next," Rohan groaned. "Next bit."

Emma appealed to the doctor. "But it's not dry. It'll bust apart."

"*Nemaye.* Just do!" His reprimand was clear.

Gingerly, Emma released the joined folds of skin, marvelling when already they seemed sealed shut. She moved on with more confidence, closing each area while the doctor spread the glue and waiting a moment for it to seal. In a few minutes the wound looked closed.

"*Vzyaty dva.*" The doctor turned with a pot of pills

in his fingers, dropping the rattling gift into Emma's outstretched palm. He held up two fingers.

"What are they?" Emma asked, rolling the pot in her hand. There was nothing written on it.

"Antibiotics." Rohan groaned as he sat up. "I need to take two a day. They're strong. I've had them before."

"But they could be anything," Emma protested and Rohan's voice grew low with warning.

"Please, Emma! Just take him downstairs while I get his money. Give me a minute."

The doctor flipped his gloves off his hands with expert precision. Emma held her gloved hand out to offer to put them in the dustbin downstairs, but the man shook his head and stuffed them in his pocket inside out. A dusting of powder littered the side of his navy blue suit jacket. In the light from the yellow bulb, the man's head shone like a beacon, strings of dark hair coming loose from their day job of covering his baldness.

Emma followed him downstairs, her footsteps sounding dull on the wooden treads. He knelt down and fiddled in his bag, while Emma stood awkwardly holding onto the banister one handed. "Where are you from?" she ventured, hating the resounding silence.

"Kiev." He rapped out the answer with a flat, disinterested voice.

"Oh, Ukraine?" Emma smiled, trying to impress the doctor with her stunning geographical knowledge. Then the colour drained suddenly from her already washed out face, leaving a grey appearance to her skin. "Ukraine." She repeated the word as realisation hit and she moved back instinctively until her backside touched the cupboard under the stairs. "It was you!"

Panic seized her body, rendering her immobile as the sickness bit at her guts and caused water to spring to her eyes. "You!"

The doctor stood up and eyed Emma through narrowed, half closed eyes. His hooked nose seemed to protrude further as he stared her down. Emma's breath came in sharp heaves as she stared at the face of a murderer.

Rohan's unsteady gait moved around upstairs, reaching the top of the steps and negotiating downwards, a slow, staccato beat of agonising pain. He broached the two bends in the staircase, landing on the parquet floor with a heavy, exhausted tread. His torso was still naked, the wound and its peculiar dressing eerie in the dull light. "*Spasybi.*" The similarity in their languages clanged in Emma's head.

The doctor acknowledged Rohan's thanks and the outstretched hand stuffed with enough cash to have paid Emma's rent for a month. Sickness roiled in her stomach as she pressed herself back against the stairs. At the click of the front door, she exhaled along with a sob.

"Em, what's up? You did good, *doroha*. Real good!"

At Rohan's offered embrace, Emma pushed herself further into the wood, sliding away until she was trapped in the corner between the cupboard and radiator. "You knew! How could you?"

"I didn't really have a choice, Em. I hoped you'd stay asleep."

"He was going to kill your *son!*" Emma screamed, covering her face with her hands and sliding down the wall until her bottom touched the cold floor. "Your mother went to get the money out to take me to him. She said they'd hold me down if they had to!" Hysteria licked at the surface of Emma's sanity, eroding it with each inward breath. "How could you invite him here to stitch you up like it didn't happen?" Emma sniffed and wiped her hand across her nose. "You don't get it. You'll never get it. I just can't do this anymore. None of it!"

Rohan reached down for her and Emma slapped his hand away, irrationally pleased at the wince of pain in his face. He stood up laid his hand down by his side. "I can't go to a hospital, Emma. They automatically call the cops for stab wounds. I have to use back street doctors and I had no idea it was *him!* I'm sorry; I'll never use him again."

"I don't even know if it was him! There could be hundreds just like him but yes you will! Because it's always all about you!" Emma's body stilled with the dawning realisation her words brought. "It was always you first, with me, your mother, everyone. What does *Rohan* want? What's best for *Rohan?* Never what's best for me!" Emma stood up abruptly, feeling the room spin around her. She shook her head slowly. "You're so *selfish!*" Her tears ceased as though a tap was turned off and she stared at Rohan with sudden clarity. She waved her hand at the front door, through which the back street abortionist just left and eyed her husband with something akin to pity. "How can you ever understand? You can't because you don't understand me. You never did. Anton did. *We* were the kindred spirits, him and me. You were no part of that, or of my life for the last seven years. *Or your son's.*"

Emma was calm as she stood and walked past her husband. Rohan seemed diminished somehow, his height bowed and bent and his eyes dull and filled with hurt. She refused to look at him again as she ran up the stairs to her bedroom. She slammed the door and pulled the bedside table in front of it, removing the surgical gloves stained with Rohan's blood and tossing them into the dustbin in the ensuite.

Emma showered again at three in the morning, washing herself clean from the stink of the kidnapping, the death of her assailants and the ruination of the beautiful Scottish mansion. The smoke still hung in her nostrils and felt sooty on the back of her tongue, more psychological than reality. She scrubbed her teeth until her head filled with the stinging scent and taste of mint and the bristles on her brush arced backwards like an old broom. The sickness rose again and she fought it, subduing it by a pure act of will. "Emma Harrington, you're so done," she whispered to herself in the mirror. The staring brown eyes looked back at her with resignation.

CHAPTER THIRTY SEVEN

"I'm getting Nicky." Emma stepped over Rohan's feet as he sat on the sofa in the wide hallway, deliberately blocking her necessary exit. She conceded to wear the new boots but couldn't face the expensive coat, making do with layers of ragged clothing instead against the Saturday morning freeze.

"No!" Rohan stood up, listing to his left, his face a mask of pain. "I mean, not yet. Let's talk. Please. I wanna sort everything out. I don't want Nikolai to come home to this."

"Home?" Emma smiled sadly at him. "This isn't his home. This was a break, a holiday I foolishly tried to make permanent. You have a life which doesn't - and never has - included me or him. Let's just leave it that way, shall we?"

"No! I won't accept that!" Rohan raised his voice. "He's my son. I've been denied him all these years...I..."

"I, I, I!" Emma smiled, her voice cold and level. "See. All about you, just like I said last night. You married me, you got me pregnant and you left. You went off to a war you had no business being in. Then when you came back, you chose to believe lies about me because you wanted to play the hero in other wars that weren't yours. I've seen how Christopher works, Rohan. You could have found me anytime you wanted; I know that now. Something's only lost if you don't care enough to look." She took a step towards him. "Do you realise Christopher's looked out for me for years? He's been pretty much permanently following me ever since your brother died? No? You wouldn't, would you? Anton sent him after me and asked him to keep me safe. Where were you, Rohan? That was your job. Where were *you?*"

Rohan looked agonised, his blue eyes flashing with misery, words seeming to fail him as he opened his mouth and nothing came out. Then his body folded back down onto the sofa, landing with a bump. He ran his hand through his blonde hair and leaned forward, his elbows on his knees. "You're right," he said softly. "Everything you've said is true. She told me you cheated on me and she caught you with him. I believed you ran away and I chose not to come and find you. I was broken outside and in and terrified of being rejected because of...well, I just was. I'm sorry. I've failed you."

"Anton told you to find me. It was his dying wish. But still you didn't."

Rohan shook his head. "No."

"Did you have any intention of fulfilling his wishes or was it pure chance that you ran into me at the wedding?"

"You ran into me." Rohan smiled at the memory and rubbed his eyes. "I knew then, when I held you in my arms what an idiot I'd been. *Durak!*" He thumped his temple with the flat of his hand and shook his head.

Emma watched him for a moment, ruing his failure as a husband and father. Then she left, slipping through the front door and clicking it shut behind her.

Along the street she knocked on Allaine's door, hearing Farrell bark from inside. His eager nose snuffled at the bottom of the door and the barking increased to fever pitch as he recognised Emma's scent. Emma readied her smile as the front door swung open and her friend's concerned face met hers, worried eyes and frown lines betraying a sleepless night.

"Emma!" Allaine embraced her with genuine relief. Emma hugged her tightly and saw over her shoulder, two small pairs of eyes gazing at her with curiosity. Then the dog hit her full in the legs, overbalancing her and causing her to grab at the doorframe. Between them, Allaine and Farrell managed to communicate their concern and Emma's heart sank, knowing Nicky would see straight through her attempts to brush off her disappearance.

"Whoa boy! Steady on there." Emma seized Farrell's collar and forced him to sit down. His tail wagged furiously and he lifted his chin up high, pushing the top of his head repeatedly into Emma's knee.

"You said Mummy went for a little holiday wiv Uncle Rohan," Nicky said accusingly, pursing his lips and putting his hands on his hips. "You was lying, weren't ya, Allaine?" The effect of his reprimand was spoiled by the Spiderman outfit he wore, pulled tightly across his body and cutting him uncomfortably between his legs. Kaylee bounced up and down next to him, clutching a silver wand which blended beautifully with her pink, fluffy fairy outfit.

"Om er!" she interjected. "Lying's naughty, init Mummy?"

Allaine gulped and remained silent, caressing Emma's fingers with affection and struggling to compose herself. Nicky reached behind him and attempted to retrieve the offending seam from between his buttocks, but his face was dark and unforgiving. "You left me," he said to Emma. "You promised you wouldn't ever do that."

Emma studied her son with eyes saddened by exhaustion and a sense of futility. Whatever she did would be wrong. This highly intelligent child with the bright blue eyes would know if she lied and trust her even less. She glanced at Allaine once and then faced Nicky with an injection of fake confidence. "I don't want to lie to you, Nicky. So right now, it's probably best I say nothing. We'll talk later and I'll explain what I can. That will have to be good enough for now."

Nicky studied his mother with Rohan's blue eyes, his head on one side like a little bird. "Ok then," he said. "Do you like my outfit? Allaine got it for me from the Pound Shop. It's a bit small though. There's fifty pence worth of it stuck up my..."

"Nicky!" Emma interrupted him with a speed born of experience. "Maybe go and take it off for now. I'll sit with Allaine for a little while and then we can go."

"Ok. Is Uncle Ro back too?"

Emma nodded, the haunted look returning. "Yeah, sweetheart. He's quite tired and he's got some things to sort out."

"Oh, ok." Nicky smiled and lurched forward, pressing his face into Emma's stomach and wrapping his arms around her waist. "I missed you, Mummy."

"I missed you too," she whispered and leaned down to kiss the top of his head.

The children bounced off to play and Emma sat down at Allaine's kitchen table, laying her face on her forearms. "I suppose you want to hear what happened," she said, sounding tired.

Allaine set the kettle to boil and whirled around. "Of course I do! Every last detail!"

Emma told Allaine some of her story, after exacting

a promise that she would keep it to herself. She left out the bits about the dead kidnappers and the burning of the mansion, but told her most of what Christopher discussed in the eerie darkness.

"So Rohan's not just a number cruncher?" Allaine said with awe. "He takes stuff back? What did you call it? Risk management?"

Emma nodded. "Apparently so. He and Christopher fly all over the world, basically selling their skills to the highest bidder."

"Like a mercenary?"

Emma snuffed and rolled her eyes. "They're certainly that!"

"This is exciting. Tell me something they've done," Allaine begged. "Something else."

"Christopher said there was an employee who stole the blueprints for a type of bomb from a laboratory in Moscow. Ro was paid to find him and eliminate the risk."

"Does he kill people?" Allaine wrinkled her nose. "William would be angry if I knew that and didn't say something."

"I don't believe so." Emma sighed and ran a hand over tired eyes. She remembered Rohan's voice in her drugged state, ordering nobody be allowed out of the burning building. She shivered. "Christopher said they paid for it and destroyed all the copies."

"Did they bring it home?" Allaine asked enthusiastically, her political naivety touching.

"Not sure," Emma lied. "I'm guessing that kind of thing's classified by the government." She swallowed, knowing Allaine would freak out and call her husband if Emma told the truth. Rohan repatriated the bomb design to its rightful owners; the Russian government.

Christopher thought it unlikely the thief got to enjoy the cash once his location was known in certain quarters. It was a bad example and Emma worked to cover up her mistake. "Another case involved a man who stole a database from the bank he worked in. He tried to blackmail account holders who were involved in tax evasion. Rohan found the man and swapped the database for a large amount of money."

"Did he give it back to the bank?" Allaine asked, chewing on a thumb nail in her excitement.

"No. His customer was the British Inland Revenue department and they prosecuted the account holders. Apparently they're still going through the courts."

"I read about that in the news!" Allaine's eyes bugged. "Oh my gosh, how exciting! So the Actuary was behind that too?"

"Please don't repeat any of this; I probably shouldn't be telling you." Emma sank her head into her hands, knowing she needed to shut up.

"I won't." Allaine looked utterly sincere as she laid a comforting hand over Emma's. "I promise. But tell me about Christopher again, your mysterious date."

"Oh, I still need to mend your dress."

"Don't worry about it. So the Irish guy followed you all that time because your dead stepbrother asked him to?" Allaine said in hushed reverence. "How romantic!"

Emma smiled. "Christopher's a complete lush. He's not someone who would ever be satisfied with one woman. I'd never feel completely secure with him. Anyway, it's not really an option." She sighed. "Look, I know Rohan's Nicky's father, but he's shown no interest for the last six years. I'm kidding myself if I think it'll be any different now. I'll let Nicky perform in the Christmas nativity next Friday and then I'll head back up north. Hopefully my council house will still be there. There're people who can help me claim it back, *again*. I need to accept my limits and get on with my life."

Allaine's eyes filled with dark devastation. "So soon? But I'll miss you."

Emma reached across and grabbed her hand, almost knocking over the drinks Allaine had placed between them. "I've so loved your friendship. I've never had a proper friend before."

Allaine looked down and then gasped, pushing Emma's sleeves back to reveal the red wheals from the sharp metallic handcuffs. "It'll fade," Emma said softly. "Compared to dying, it's the least of my worries."

"I think you're wrong," Allaine said.

Emma peeled back her cuffs and examined the swollen skin. "Oh. Don't you think it'll fade?"

"Not that. I think you're wrong about Rohan. He loves you and Nicky; anyone can see that! I wish you'd give him a chance."

Emma shook her head. "Ro doesn't know what love is. I feel like I've loved him forever, this starry eyed schoolgirl crush. We grew up together but we were only man and wife for a short time before he went off to Afghanistan and I fled to Wales. Maybe he was deserving of that kind of adoration once, but I've changed. I need security and a father for Nicky. I'm not going to find that here. But at least I've learned I'm ready for a relationship, maybe even marriage again. I'm lonely. I've spent the last few years since Lucya died, convincing myself I'm not. But I am." Emma smiled. "I'm also unbelievably tired." She put her hand over the escaped yawn. "Sorry."

Nicky opted to stay at Allaine's for another night, insisting he felt ok about it and was having a great time with Kaylee. "It's actually quite nice for me," Allaine insisted. "With my older kids gone, Kaylee gets quite clingy so it's great having someone else to occupy her. Please let him stay just for tonight?"

"And tomorrow morning!" Nicky begged eagerly. "I wanna go to church with you."

Emma wrinkled her nose and shook her head. "If you're happy with that, Allaine, then I'm really grateful. I could use an early night and a very long lie in."

Back at the house Emma let herself in. "Come on, boy, in you go." Farrell ran happily through the front door, inspecting his bowl, his bed and then sniffing frantically around the kitchen. "I think you'd be too much hard work for Allaine if I left you there another night," Emma said to the panting dog. She shook kibbles into his bowl and he sniffed them and then hurled himself into his squashy bed. "Stay here, I'm going for a lie down. No idea where your master's disappeared to."

Upstairs, Emma flopped onto her unmade bed, fully clothed. She yawned, turned over and woke up hours later to the feel of Rohan shaking her shoulder. "Emma wake up. Please Em! I don't know what to do! *Katastrofa!*"

Disaster.

CHAPTER THIRTY EIGHT

"Nicky?" Emma sat up too quickly and her vision spun. She listed, putting her feet on the rug and Rohan took her shoulders in his strong hands.

"Not Nicky, no. Where is he?"

"Allaine's. Is it Christopher then? What's wrong?" Emma rubbed furiously at the tightness of her eyelids.

"No! Why do you care about him?" Rohan let go and stepped back as though Emma was contaminated in some way. She leaned forward for a moment and then exhaled. Rohan looked startled when she turned away from him and lay back down, curling herself up into a ball and dragging the covers back over herself. Her jeans felt crunchy and uncomfortable and she contemplated taking them off, but didn't have the energy. "Emma!" Rohan sounded testy.

"If nothing's wrong with Nicky or Christopher, then there is nobody else I give a damn about anymore. So just go and let me catch up on my sleep." She made contented little moans and pushed her face into the pillow to block out the light. "What time is it?"

"Still Saturday. It's two o'clock."

"Ok." Emma's voice was muffled by the pillow. "Nicky does this play thing on Friday next week and then it's the end of term. We'll head off on Saturday. I checked my bank account earlier and I got a benefits payment so I can afford the train back up to Lincoln. I'll pay you back everything I borrowed so don't worry. You can have your life back..." Emma looked up as the bedroom door clicked shut. She was about to thank Rohan for letting her stay but he didn't give her the chance. She rolled over onto her back for a while and sought to repair the rubbled walls of her heart, building the protective barrier piece by piece. The need to close her battered psyche off from Rohan's charms seemed imperative and Emma's emotional fragility mocked her with the fake bravado she used on him earlier.

After another hour of fitful and unrefreshing sleep, Emma woke and used the bathroom, washing her face in cold water to reduce the puffiness of her eyes and the greyness of her pallor. Downstairs, she ran water into the kettle and stood over it while it boiled. Movement and the scrape of a chair came from across the hallway and the sound of Rohan talking on the telephone in the dining room. Emma steeled herself to behave and keep control of her feelings for just one more week.

The door creaked as Emma poked her head around it, making a 'T' sign with her fingers to ask him if he wanted a drink. He nodded and gave her a small smile and Emma withdrew her head. "But they've charged her. They say there's strong evidence," Rohan said to the person on the other end of the phone call.

Emma raised her eyebrows and shrugged. "Nothing to do with me," she whispered to Farrell as he popped his head up from his paws and thumped his tail on the squashy bed. She made a mug of tea, adding the milk and sugar Rohan liked, taking it to him in a demure waitress style approach. He sat at the dining table with his head in his hands, the silent phone laying on the wooden surface in front of him. His blonde hair stuck up on his head and beard growth pressed through his skin like a covering of bristly grass. He sighed heavily and as Emma laid the mug on the table he grabbed her sore wrist, holding it tightly in his bunched fingers. When he turned his eyes on her they were an odd shade of glittering blue, like a misty morning sky.

"Ow!" Emma tugged at her hand, pain evident in her face. "Get off! That hurts."

Rohan released her and stood, holding her by her forearms and examining her wrists one at a time. "Why didn't you say something?" The bruising was appalling from the handcuffs, comprising every shade of ugly in the colour wheel. A long cut over her left wrist bore testament to their tightness.

Emma snatched her arms back. "Oh, what, so you could get your back street abortionist to take a look after he finished illegally stitching you up?"

Rohan's face fell and he sat down at the table in front of her, the gauze over his wound protruding through his tee shirt and making a jagged line along the ridge of his muscular shoulder. "I'm sorry." His voice was soft and the apology sounded genuine and dripped with inner agony. Emma bit back the spiteful retort, alarmed by the paleness of Rohan's honey coloured skin and the dullness of his eyes. He stroked the handle of his mug with a long forefinger. "I deserved everything you said earlier and I understand you have to leave. I won't ask you for anything, Em; you have every right to refuse. But I would like to make an allowance for you to bring Nicky up. I'd like you to be able to live better than you've been forced to."

Emma took a step back, feeling the sense of being cut off as keenly as if he knifed her. She felt the dreadful searing pain in a heart which had always dreamed of being reunited with her soulmate, accompanied by the dull ache in her stomach. She had lied to herself; nobody else would ever be good enough after Rohan Andreyev. The air in the room was laden with the sorrow of both adults and Emma gulped, reaching out against her better judgement and touching Rohan's arm. He looked down at her fingers and then cupped them with his other hand. Bringing them up to his lips, he kissed them. Then let go.

Emma's heart cracked, causing a physical tearing pain in her chest. She left the room quickly and scooped up her boots, purse and an extra sweater, ignoring the excited dog who wanted to go with her. The front door clicked behind her as the first sob escaped. Emma stood on the doormat undercover of the porch and pushed reluctant arms into her jumper. The mat felt prickly under her socks, the cold seeping immediately into her toes. With an effort of will, Emma squashed her feet into the new boots, expecting to feel the chill entering through the myriad holes. It didn't and it was weird to be able to feel her feet on such a cold day. She let the gate slam behind her as the sickness returned, permeating her spirit as well as her stomach and she used the brisk exercise to alleviate the pain. As she turned once along the street to cross the road, she saw the slender figure of Felicity bounding along towards the house and felt her resolve crumble further. Emma's heart felt shattered, but as always, Rohan would be ok.

Town was busy for late Saturday afternoon and darkness enclosed her as Emma searched for the shop she needed. Her cash card passed through the machine without incident thanks to the small allowance from the government, but she still held her breath as she punched in the numbers and waited for the satisfying beep to confirm it hadn't been declined.

Emma hid the small package in the side pocket of her fleece, feeling the hardness of it against her left breast as she sat on a bench under the protection of St Dionysius Church. "I suppose you've seen many stupid women like me?" she asked the ancient structure under her breath, feeling false warmth from the yellow glow of its floodlit stone. The church remained silent, but Emma drew comfort from its presence, a symbol of sanity in a crazy age.

On her way home she stood under the shelter of the old school house, closing her eyes and taking off her gloves to stroke the solid oak beams. Her archivist's mind sought connection with the citizens of Market Harborough, long since dead and buried in the churchyard or scattered on the green rolling hills of its perimeter. She sought their wisdom, but sensed only emptiness and loss. Emma felt the warm tear run down her freezing cheek as she pressed her lips against the ancient roughness of the wood. "I've allowed him to destroy me again," she whispered to the men and women of old, knowing inwardly that God would never allow them to hear. "I shouldn't have come. Everything's worse. What am I going to do?"

Nobody answered, but Emma's desperate confession didn't feel as though it fell on deaf ears. A fragile thread of inner strength trailed from her heart to her head and gave her a modicum of confidence. A warmth flooded from nowhere and Emma glanced back at the stone of the church behind her. It remained silent, traffic flowing past with glittering headlights, unconcerned for the plight of the woman who loitered under the old school house clutching one of its stilts. But Emma felt the stirring of new life and acceptance; from a God she always believed turned his face away from her in disgust.

With renewed vigour Emma marched home, energy coursing through her body and helping her make plans for the future. *It would be ok. Everything would be ok.*

She fumbled under cover of the porch as a light December rain began. Her woolly gloves made retrieval of the door key impossible and she removed her right one with a sigh of exasperation. Parked cars lined the street on either side, but the one next to Rohan's front gate clicked as though only recently left there.

Emma stepped into the wall of heat from the central heating, the nausea pushing back into her consciousness. The hallway lights were on and the glare hurt her eyes after the darkness of outside. Emma put her boots in the hall cupboard and padded through to the kitchen. Her empty cup stood in the sink, the stain of her cold tea just a patch near the plug hole.

"Hey." Rohan's voice sounded flat as he came up behind her. Emma felt his proximity and stiffened, embarrassed as she realised the presence of the other man who followed him into the kitchen. "This is Craig. He's my lawyer."

Emma nodded to the middle aged man who leaned his backside against the fridge. Her eyes cast around for Felicity, relieved when she didn't appear. Emma allowed her heart to unclench a little. Craig was of average height, coffee skinned and green eyed; handsome in an unusual kind of way. He stepped forward and offered his hand, his mouth giving an upward tilt of approval. "Nice to meet you, Mrs Andreyev."

Emma opened her mouth to contest the title but saw Rohan wince out of the corner of her eye and released the man's hand. "Nice to meet you, Craig. Can I get you some tea?"

"Thank you." Craig gave his order, black hair running to grey in his sideburns as he declared his penchant for sugary tea. Emma went through the machinations of boiling the kettle and preparing the mugs, listening half-heartedly to the conversation which continued behind her.

"So what now?" Rohan asked, accompanied by a sigh as he leaned against the sink, arms folded.

"She already spoke to the police," Craig said. "She never asked for a lawyer so the damage is done. She waived her right to a phone call and the police were uncharacteristically nice to have fetched you. They say they have witness statements and firm evidence she's been doing this for a while. I don't see any way for her to get out of this now; I'm being honest with you. I can challenge the confession on the grounds of her age, possible manipulation of someone for whom English is a second language, but...oh, thank you." Craig took the mug of tea with a nod.

Emma looked to Rohan for clarification, but he kept his head down, chewing on his bottom lip in deep thought. "What is this? What's happened?" Guilt assailed her at the memory of Rohan trying to wake her up earlier. He came to her for genuine help and she pushed him away. Emma squeezed the bridge of her nose with her fingers, her own worries temporarily forgotten. She looked at Rohan until he raised his head and met her brown eyes. "I'm sorry...about before. I'm interested. Tell me."

"My mother's been arrested," Rohan said, the words obviously giving him pain. "She's confessed to murdering my father and..."

"And mine." Emma's statement rapped out like an accusation and she gripped the edge of the counter in an effort not to fall. The room spun like a fairground ride and she heard the tiny moan escape her lips as though it came from someone else. She fixed her eyes on Rohan's, seeking a static point in the room as understanding flooded her. "You're trying to get her off!" Emma let go of the cold surface and stared at her husband, aghast at his misplaced loyalty. "Again, you screw me over because of your mother. Will you never learn, Rohan? She's a murderer. Anton knew it, I know it and even Christopher saw it. Are you really so deluded that you can't?" Emma turned angry eyes on the lawyer, who watched her with his mug half way to his lips. "Have they taken her herb garden from the balcony outside her apartment?"

The lawyer shrugged and looked doubtful, shooting a nervous look towards Rohan before shaking his head in a tiny motion. "They only have her confession but she wisely stopped talking so they have no hard evidence, no."

Emma's husband looked disgusted at her. "Geez, Em! It's just an herb garden, with parsley and stuff she cooks with. I bought her new compost for it a few weeks ago. Did you do this? Did you call the cops on her and finally get your wish?"

Emma's eyes flashed with danger as the lawyer cleared his throat. "Er, no actually. A number of elderly male residents who grew attached to your mother, seem to have died. She cooks for them and looks after them when they get sick. It's the residential home who called the police."

"They're old men!" Rohan roared. "I've met them all, decrepit, elderly men. It's a *residential home!* People buy apartments there so they can enjoy their last few years with help and...and...you know, friendship! They die there because it's their last home."

The lawyer shook his head. "Rohan, the best defence against the murder charge is to plead insanity."

Rohan didn't let him continue. "Are you kidding me?"

Craig sighed and placed his drink on the counter. "I wish I was, my friend. You need to let me intervene and ask for psychological reports, sooner rather than later."

"No, no!" Rohan put the heels of his hands into his eyes and pressed hard. "She wouldn't kill anyone. She's been a good mother. You don't understand. In Russia when I was so sick all the time, she took care of me. She's kind and gentle. Why can't you see that?" He pulled his hands away and begged Emma with his vibrant blue eyes. "I know you felt she didn't like you, Emma, but don't you remember? When you caught all those stomach upsets, she made you nice drinks and bought stuff to help you, didn't she?"

Emma shook her head sadly. "*She* was my stomach upset, Ro. Anton stopped me taking anything from her eventually. He told me about your little sister and her mysterious ailments, undiagnosed by any physician in Russia. He told me how it broke you when she died." Emma moved to his side and put her hand up to Rohan's face, feeling the scratchiness under her fingers. "Remember how clumsy Anton was at meal times when she left us to eat by ourselves? All those drinks of yours he spilled and the plates of food he knocked over and then gave you his? He went without for you, Rohan, for you. He protected us, Ro. We cleaned up the mess because we were terrified of her, yes. But also because she needed to think you ate or drank what she prepared. Because of Anton's incredible sacrifice she decided you were immune and moved her attention to him and me. Anton was a master of deception and I learned to touch nothing she made, but I wasn't as good as him at faking. When you went in the army, we knew you were safe. When Anton left and there was just me and her, it was harder to avoid her potions. She fed me her herbal crap and I was sick a few times. Then I got clever at not taking it. I learned to pretend, just like Anton did."

Emma ran her hand down Rohan's face, agony spilling from her eyes. "We married and I thought you'd take me away from her. I thought you understood, but how could you after all those years of Anton shielding you? You deployed to Afghanistan and I got so sick. Alanya believed my morning sickness was caused by her poisons and she was tender and kind, sitting with me when I couldn't manage school because of the nausea and trying to fill me with her 'cures'. I faked drinking them, but then the bump started to show and she had this dawning realisation. I saw in her eyes how much she'd like my innocent baby to torture and knew I needed to get away. She caught me packing and dragged me to the doctor for an abortion. She's damaged, Ro, crazy. I was waiting for you to come back from this last job and then I intended to leave. Your mother and that witch Felicity are as insane as each other. I can't work at the school or live in this town, I was kidding myself. They've both taken a turn at threatening me. You definitely know how to surround yourself with crazy!"

Emma withdrew her fingers from Rohan's cheek and looked into his brokenness through the sad blue of his eyes. "Anton's no longer here to speak for himself and even when he was, nobody listened. I'm sorry, Ro, but I *will* testify against Alanya for everything she's done. She'll never have access to my son, not as long as I have breath in my body." Emma smiled sadly at the stunned lawyer, extending her hand as she headed towards the door. He took her fingers in his, confusion in his face. "When we meet again, you'll probably be cross examining me in the witness stand," she said with forced politeness. Craig stood up straight and looked down at her, admiration sneaking through his brown eyes. "I've waited years for this and it's been a great weight on my heart." Emma touched her breast bone with fluttering fingers, subconsciously emphasising her point. She smiled at Craig. "I wouldn't take this case, if I were you. There are no winners."

She left then, donning her boots and sweater and heading back out into the cold. Allaine opened the front door on the first knock. "Hey, gorgeous! Oh." She peered at Emma's ashen face in the porch light. "You don't look any better than earlier. Couldn't you sleep?"

Emma removed her outdoor clothing and hurled herself down on the living room sofa, waiting patiently while Allaine made her a drink. "I'm so thirsty," Emma complained, guzzling the hot liquid. "I've wasted two cups of tea this afternoon already. Where are the kids?"

"Will took them to the movies in Leicester. They'll be ages yet. I bet he springs for fast food on the way home too."

"Nicky's never been to the movies," Emma smiled. "And we never afford fast food. He'll think it's Christmas!"

"It nearly is." Allaine settled on the sofa next to

Emma and sat sideways so she could see her. "Will's missing our sons, I think. Having Nicky reminds him of what it was like having little boys to take to soccer games or rough around with. Kaylee's a proper girly girl. That's what happens when an unexpected one pops out. Emma what's wrong?"

Emma told her about Alanya Harrington's arrest and Allaine whistled through her teeth. "Sounds like a form of Munchausen Syndrome by Proxy. The sufferer manufactures ailments for their children but really it's them making the child sick. They commonly use poison, forms of bloodletting, even suffocation in severe cases. It has a high mortality rate for children. It's like child abuse, well, it is literally child abuse. But often undetected. I did heaps of testing in the lab, trying to work out how they'd done it. One woman used to feed her poor toddler salt through a syringe. He died a very painful death."

"Oh, God!" Emma pleaded, putting her hands over her ears. "Please don't tell me anymore. It makes me feel ill."

"Sorry." Allaine pulled Emma's hands down and clasped them in hers. "This must be awful for you. Did you know she was doing it?

Emma nodded. "Rohan's father was some kind of envoy when Britain became more amenable to Russia in the 1990s. From what Anton told me, this posting was meant to be a fresh start for the family after their little sister's death in Russia from some mysterious virus. They came over here and settled in London and then the boys began to get sick; mainly stomach complaints and diarrhoea. Anton had it worse than Rohan but they both had bouts of it. Then the father developed some kind of odd ailment and pulled in every specialist in London. He died with no diagnosis and Alanya received permission to stay here. They shifted north to Lincoln and turned up at our church, where my widowed father was the rector. I never understood why a Russian Orthodox woman would wind up at an Anglican church in the back of beyond, but before my father died, we had this odd conversation. It seems he met her once in St Paul's Cathedral in London when Dad was on business down there. He must have told her enough about himself that she was able to follow him home."

Emma sighed and ran a shaking hand over her face. "My father was a good man, Allaine. He believed only the very best of people. He never saw that side of her which was cruel and unrelenting. My childhood memories are ruined by visions of us avoiding her food, eating sour apples from the garden because we were hungry or groaning in agony when hunger made us give in and eat what she put on the table. Rohan broke his arm and concussed himself once, when she made us pick every damn apple in the tree so she could get rid of our alternative food source."

Allaine stroked a tear from Emma's face. She hadn't even realised it was there. "Was Rohan really so unaware, or do you think he's blocked it out?" she asked.

"Probably both," Emma admitted. "Rohan was the eldest but Anton protected us both from her. He had this larger than life zest for living and such a dramatic personality. He learned to distract us all and hide us under this safe covering of fantasy and idealism. That's the trouble, I think Rohan and I fell in love under the shadow of Anton's wing in a world that didn't really exist. Loving Rohan was like walking through the wardrobe and finding Narnia. Anton would have been the funny little faun creature, with a boy's torso and goat legs." Emma's voice broke. "I miss him so much."

Emma cried until she was spent, grieving for so much stolen life and the people snatched away from her. She felt like a tent, billowing in the wind because its pegs were ripped out of the earth by cruel hands. Allaine let her cry and then led her upstairs to the attic bedroom where her grown sons once rough housed and listened to loud, teenage music. She waited while Emma used the bathroom and helped her remove her jeans, tucking her into the single bed and listening to the exhausted hitches of her chest. "Don't think about anything else tonight," Allaine whispered over her. "We'll talk tomorrow. Things always seem better in the daylight."

CHAPTER THIRTY NINE

Emma woke around five in the morning, confused about where she was. The room smelled masculine and unfamiliar and Emma crept downstairs for a drink of water, barefoot and dressed only in a sweater and knickers. Moonlight lit her way enough and she had moments of stress when a floorboard or stair tread creaked, fearful of meeting Allaine's husband for the first time as a suspected burglar. The long, galley kitchen was at the back of the house and Emma stood at the window and watched the daylight blooming from a far off corner of the earth, not yet reaching its pale fingers far enough to touch Market Harborough. The frost on the ground reflected the full moon outside, twinkling like a carpet of glitter. Emma sipped her water slowly and then she saw him.

He stood like an apparition in the garden, leaned casually against the wooden shed. Emma watched as a red glow from a cigarette flamed and then disappeared. She sat her glass on the counter with precision and carefully unlocked the back door. The blast of wintry English winter air assailed her bare feet and legs as she stepped onto the freezing concrete slabs outside. Clicking the button on the Yale lock so she could get back in again, Emma closed the door quietly and ran across the frozen grass, the prickly stiff blades crunching under her toes.

"Hey there." He blew cigarette smoke over Emma's head and then clasped her to him, the zipper of his coat scratching her face. "So the shit's hit the fan then?" His soft tone accentuated the beauty of his lilting Irish accent as Emma nodded slowly against the front of his coat.

"I thought you died," Emma sniffed into his chest, wrapping her arms around his warm body.

Placing his cigarette between his lips, Christopher bent and seized Emma, hauling her off the cold ground and nestling her in arms that felt reassuringly strong and secure. He carried Emma without great effort, to the very end of the garden furthest from the house. Blessed with the same quarter acre site as Rohan's place further along the street, the long thin garden boasted plenty of places to hide unnoticed in the darkness. In a small orchard crafted by Allaine's green fingers, Christopher sat down on a metal bench which creaked under their combined weight. He shifted Emma so she sat sideways across his thighs and pulled his cigarette from between his lips.

Taking one final drag and exhaling the nicotine laden air, Christopher stubbed it out on the side of the bench and lobbed the dog end backwards into the lane behind. He pulled Emma into his shoulder and cradled her, saying nothing.

It was freezing and the scent of the cigarette got into her stomach. Emma fixed cold fingers across her mouth and heard Christopher chuckle. "Sorry, darlin'. If ya come away with me, I'll give it up."

"Liar," Emma smirked and he laughed.

"Aye, yer probably right. Why give up the things yer enjoy, like sex and smokes. I'll be a long time dead. They seem like a nice family you're with. Interestin' stuff in their bins though. I..."

"Don't!" Emma sat up, her eyes glistening with

moisture in the moonlight. She struggled as though trying to get up.

"It's ok, we won't talk about anything you don't wanna. Just sit with me a while. Yeah?"

Emma nodded and snuggled back down into Christopher's lapel, feeling his rough fingers rubbing warmth into her bare thighs. "I'm glad you're safe," she said, white mist escaping from her lips with her words and leaving a dissipating trail. "I worried about you. You look as banged up as Rohan." Black stitches held his eyebrow together and his lip was swollen on one side. A black eye and another cut across the bridge of his nose evidenced his fight with Rohan, plus whatever happened afterwards.

"Ach! You've enough of your own worries to be goin' on with. Don't be mindin' about me."

A bat soared overhead, visible in Emma's peripheral vision but gone when she tried to focus on it. An owl hooted and she sat up as the cold began to take hold. Christopher stroked her face and pressed their foreheads together. "I'd give ya my coat but I'm not stayin'. I came to say goodbye."

"How did you know I'd see you?" she asked and he smiled, his teeth white against his dark face.

"I didn't. But I'm glad to get the chance to say it to ya."

"How can you do this? Staying out here in the dark." The bat swooped nearer, curiosity driving it to investigate with its sonar. "Don't you get scared?" Emma crouched lower, pushing her face into Christopher's shoulder.

"No. Darkness is a state of mind," he whispered.

"I'm leaving here next weekend," Emma stated, the chattering of her teeth acting as a reminder that she needed to go inside.

"No, you're not. Don't go back to that hole, Emma, I'm tellin' ya. I'll fetch ya and bring ya right back, so don't push me. It'll be a waste of those train tickets in yer coat."

"You don't know I bought train tickets!" Emma complained and her companion chuckled.

"I do, so. And I know what else yer bought too, see."

Emma groaned. "I can't stay here, not with Rohan."

"Aw youse two pair of eejits. You'll work it out. But yer don't have to stay with him if yer don't want to."

"I know. He said today he wanted to give me money to support Nicky but..."

"No, not that, although so he should; the child's his son. *Now he knows about him anyhoo*." Christopher left his reprimand hanging in the air which spangled with floating water molecules.

"It's going to snow, isn't it?" Emma asked, sounding like a child.

"Aye." Christopher kissed her frozen forehead and rested his chin on her hair. "But listen. Just wait a few days. Someone's been lookin' for ya. Let them come and talk to ya."

"No! Who?" Emma looked alarmed.

Christopher smiled. "D'ya trust me, Em?" He waited a heartbeat until she nodded. "Then do as I ask. Wait for him to talk to ya. You've led him a merry dance up and down the country to end up on his own front doorstep. So just give the man a break and wait it out. For me. Please?"

"Is he nice?" Emma asked, turning her bottom lip down in a sulk.

"Who cares?" Christopher snorted. "He's

somethin' to show ya. So you'll wait?" Emma nodded in agreement, although from the set of her shoulders, reluctantly. "Right then. You've to go in before you catch yer death and I've somewhere to be."

Emma stood up and shifted from foot to foot in the icy grass, the biting cold attacking her exposed flesh. Christopher rose from the bench and wrapped his scarf more tightly around his throat. Then he put his hands on Emma's shoulders and observed her one last time. "Goodbye, Emma Andreyev," he breathed, sadness creeping into his dark eyes. "I wish I hadn't fallen in love with ya, but hey, shit happens." He leaned forward and placed soft lips over hers. Her mouth opened in surprise and Christopher flicked his tongue over hers in a tantalisingly short dance of lust and promise. Emma closed her eyes and felt the flare in her stomach, the faint smell of cigarettes wafting round her in a haze.

She opened her eyes the moment he disconnected from her, feeling a cold, numbing emptiness surround her soul. Already he was gone, nothing but a slight movement in the darkness down near the bottom fence. Emma peered, hoping for one last sighting of her handsome Irishman, untameable and unstoppable in his constant questing for something only he understood. She raised her hand in a last wave before she turned, hearing the slightly strange hoot of an owl nearby and wondering if it was him.

CHAPTER FORTY

"You look much better," Allaine told Emma as she served tea and toast at the kitchen table. Her red headed husband smiled nervously at Emma as he got the children ready for church.

Nicky popped up onto Emma's lap, forcing his way into the narrow gap between her stomach and the table. "Come church wiv us, Mummy. Jesus doesn't throw lightning bolts in his church, Will said. He laughed when I told him you said fings like that."

Will bit his lip and looked apologetic, caught in his mocking of Emma's antiquated beliefs. Allaine gave her husband a stern glare before pulling on her boots. Emma kissed her son's rosy lips and smoothed away a smear of chocolate spread from around his mouth. "I just say silly things sometimes." She forced a smile. "My daddy was a good man and he knew Jesus. Don't believe everything I say, Nick. Some of it's just not worth hearing."

Satisfied, Nicky hugged her neck and popped down, wriggling into his school coat over a very old set of trousers and sweatshirt left over from Allaine's boys. Will filed them all into the thin hallway and Allaine pushed a sheaf of papers towards Emma with a slight nod, waiting until her husband was out of earshot. "Don't say anything in front of Will, because he's involved in the case with Rohan's mother. But look at this list of plants. I printed it off the internet. When I worked as a lab technician, these were the most common cause of natural poisoning we came across. Look at the symptoms and see if they match your illnesses and your father's. Then perhaps we can pinpoint which plant causes that. We might be able to go to Will with some hard evidence."

Emma gulped and stared at the white sheets, speckled with writing and colour photos of leaves and blossoms. Allaine rubbed her shoulder with affection. "Have a peaceful morning. Will's promised the kids' lunch out." Allaine rolled her eyes. "I'm not having another baby just to please him, so we'll just keep borrowing Nicky. Well, until you go anyway." Her eyes became shrouded in sadness and regret.

"I don't know if we're leaving immediately. I'm waiting for something." Emma watched the light flick back on in her friend's face. "Not that I can afford to lose a hundred quid on wasted train tickets though. Maybe I can change the date. I'll walk back to the station and ask tomorrow."

"I guess it's a lot of money to waste," Allaine agreed.

"It certainly is where I've come from," Emma snorted, but there was no mirth in the sound, just profound sorrow. "We'll see, anyway. Thanks for everything you've done for me." Emma smiled up at her friend.

"Come on, Alli!" Will shouted from the street. "They'll be singing the last hymn by the time we get there."

Emma went to the front window to drink her tea in the living room and watch the little group bounce down the street past Rohan's house. The children ran ahead in woolly hats and mittens, balls of boundless energy. Allaine and Will followed behind, holding

356

hands and laughing together.

Emma cleared up from her breakfast and set the kitchen to rights. Upstairs she stripped the bed she slept in and loaded up the washing machine, finding the powder and fabric softener and setting a load going. She popped some things from the laundry basket in to make up a full load. The jeans she slipped on for breakfast felt scratchy against her skin and the moment for decision came. Emma stuffed the sheets of information printed from the internet into her pocket, secured the house and closed the front door, posting the spare key through the letterbox after she locked up. With a last wistful look at Allaine's comfortable home, Emma walked down the street to Rohan's front gate, taking in a huge breath as her hand rested on the catch, dreading the reception she would get.

CHAPTER FORTY ONE

"Excuse me, I'm looking for Emma Andreyev." The smart suited man hovered nervously in front of her, a fixed smile on his face. Emma's chest clenched with fear and she grappled at the gate catch, contemplating shouting for Rohan. "No, there's no need to be scared." The man reached a hand out towards her and Emma shied away instinctively. The hand was pudgy, betraying a white collar worker's smooth skin and a fat wedding ring adorned his left ring finger. He looked familiar. "I promise, I mean no harm, Mrs Andreyev. Christopher..." The man glanced down at a notebook on his hand, "Christopher Dolan told me where to find you. He said you'd be scared and I was to explain myself." He bit his lip and Emma visibly relaxed at the mention of Christopher.

"Dolan," she said softly, tasting the name on her tongue. "I didn't know his surname."

"Yes, I asked for his help in finding you. I employed Mr Dolan as a private investigator a while ago after the death of my client."

"Sorry, what? You employed...but I thought Anton asked..."

"Yes! Anton Andreyev." The well-dressed male took another step towards Emma and then thought better of it. "Mr Andreyev was my client. I'm a solicitor. I was *his* solicitor."

Hearing Anton's name spoken so easily by this formal, clearly affluent man, caused Emma to halt. She gripped the wooden top of the gate and studied him, wariness in her brown eyes. The solicitor was of squat build with a black mackintosh over his smart pinstripes. Dark hair stuck up from his head like the down of a baby monkey and blue rimmed spectacles shrouded eyes peering like a mole's. "You're the man, aren't you?" Emma said with resignation. "He said you would be coming."

"Who?" The solicitor looked confused. "Oh, my private investigator." He nodded once and opened his arm, the pudgy forefinger pointing to a black car parked next to the house. "We need to take a small drive. Would you be ok with that?"

Emma glanced back at Rohan's house with doubt in her eyes. As if slamming the door on her heart, she nodded, acknowledging there was no help available there with the tortured Russian. Rohan Andreyev had problems of his own.

The car was posh and the solicitor kind, helping Emma locate her seat belt catch in the centre between them. She felt underdressed and dirty in his opulent vehicle and pushed the ever present feelings of inadequacy back down. They pulled out onto the Northampton Road and headed south, moving quickly past the new housing developments and finding rolling green countryside. Emma watched as it flew past her window at speed. "Not far now," her driver said, smiling sideways at her.

"Am I in trouble? I didn't catch your name," Emma said.

"Gosh, sorry!" The solicitor reached into a clean cigarette tray and pulled out a business card, placing it carefully into Emma's hand. "No, you're not in trouble."

She held onto it with cold fingers and read the embossed wording twice before allowing it to sink into her brain.

Allen, Holdsworth and Bowes, Solicitors.

"Why did you employ somebody to find me?" Emma asked, confusion evident in her troubled eyes.

"You'll see," the man replied. "Two more minutes."

"Which one are you?" Emma asked, glancing back down at the plush card in her fingers. "Allen, Holdsworth or Bowes?"

The solicitor laughed. "None of the above. I'm not a partner. I just work for them as a solicitor. I'd like to be a partner one day, but it's a way off. My name's Kieran Miles, but it will be irrelevant soon. You won't need to remember my name. Any problems, you just deal with the company."

"Nice to meet you, Kieran," Emma said politely, deliberately challenging a statement which rendered him insignificant.

Kieran smiled in acknowledgement as the vehicle sped towards the border between Leicestershire and Northamptonshire. Emma glanced left and spied the beautiful manor house on the hill. The windows looked dark and sad against the watery grey daylight, its red brick taking on a dark sheen as the threatening clouds scudded overhead and threw it into shadow and back out again. An unloved heaviness hung over it, pulling Emma's mood even further into depression. They passed the layby Emma usually parked in to gaze at the stunning building and then Kieran took his foot off the gas slowing the heavy car into a driveway.

Emma tensed, her legs and back locking up. A set of giant iron gates loomed up ahead, shrouded by a stand of trees either side of a long driveway. Kieran leaned out and pressed something into a keypad after opening his window. With a groan, the gates swung open on an automatic system and the car rolled forward. "No!" Emma gasped, memories of her last trip with strangers. "I'm sorry. This is stupid. I shouldn't have come." She grappled for the door handle, pushing with all her might. To her surprise it opened in a rush and she spilled out of the moving vehicle, losing her footing and tumbling onto the hard concrete driveway. The driver looked first astounded and then mortified, his lips opening in an 'o' of shock. Emma heard him put the hand brake on and the engine cut as she used her hands against a nearby tree to push herself upright. Fear made her breathing speed up and the world swam around her head, the trees curving into her vision in threatening arcs.

"Mrs Andreyev, whatever's wrong?" Kieran Miles looked stunned as he rounded the back of the car and slowed down to approach Emma, his mackintosh flapping round his legs. He held his arms out as thought flying, palm upwards like an ungainly blackbird.

Emma wiped her nose on the cuff of her sweater. "I'm so dumb! I got into a car with a complete stranger because I was too proud to just go into the house and ask Rohan for help!"

"I'm not going to hurt you!" Kieran looked horrified. "That's really not why we're here!" He cast around him as though expecting armed policemen to jump out from behind the trees lining the driveway. The overhead branches creaked as though in accusation, bending to the freezing cold wind. "Look," he made a decision. "Let's leave the car parked here and walk up to the house. We can walk on either side of the driveway and I won't come near you but it'll give me an opportunity to explain." He ran his hand through the spiky hair and looked devastated. "I've messed this up. I've messed it totally up."

Emma watched him panic before her, sensing his genuine misery. She still had his business card in her left hand and peered down at it, seeing his name in small type underneath the name of the firm.

Kieran Miles, Legal Consultant.

She hadn't noticed it before and ran her fingers over the deep embossing of the firm's name, feeling the names, Allen, Holdsworth and Bowes rubbing against her skin. Emma studied the man in front of her, aware he was more afraid than her. She straightened her spine. "Tell me why we're here and then I'll decide if I'm going up there with you. I've been here before, anyway." Emma pointed towards the imposing house on the hill and then looked back at Kieran. His brown eyes flickered in panic and he gulped, struggling to get a hold on his fear triggers. He relaxed his body with a huge effort of will.

"I know you have, Mrs Andreyev. The day of the auction I tried to catch you but you left before I got the chance. Ok, I'll start at the beginning. My firm is based up the road in Northampton. The senior partner, Mr Allen is solicitor to Anton Andreyev and handled his affairs for just under a decade. He handled the conveyancing on Mr Andreyev's property purchases and is also listed as the executor of his last and final testament. Mr Andreyev's theatre company is also considered part of his estate."

"Theatre company?" Emma shivered in the biting wind and Kieran waved his arm towards the shelter of the huge house up ahead.

"Can we walk and talk?" he asked, drawing his coat around him.

Emma nodded and stuck to the left of the driveway, forcing Kieran to call across to her. Gradually as the story unfolded, she edged closer without realising it. "So when Mr Andreyev sadly died, Mr Allen was informed as the executor of the will. The address we had for you in Wales was amended a few years ago and the will rewritten to name only you as his sole heir, but the address in Lincoln proved fruitless."

Emma stopped. "You knew about my address in Wales? Anton made his will that long ago?"

Kieran nodded with enthusiasm. "Oh yes! Everyone should have a will, even if they don't have much to leave." He smiled at Emma, confident with talk of his chosen profession. "A Mrs Lucya Andreyev was also an heir but I understand she passed away?"

Emma nodded sadly. "Yes. Lucya died just over two years ago. I moved back to Lincoln then." Emma walked, observing the house ahead. "How long is this driveway?"

"Half a mile exactly." Kieran stated the distance with such precision, Emma wondered if he had the deeds stashed in his copious mackintosh pockets. "So, Mr Allen travelled to Lincoln to visit you and met with...considerable obstacle."

Emma's head whipped round, curiosity blossoming in her face. "What do you mean? Because I was already down here, in Market Harborough?"

"Oh, no!" Kieran looked scandalised, his brown eyes round and staring. "Some thug refused to allow him access to the estate you lived on. Our letters went unanswered and there was no phone number for you. Mr Allen's personal visit was not a positive one! He made a complaint to the local police and they promised to look into it."

"Sounds like you met Fat Brian," Emma mused. "But it's worrying if he was intercepting my post. I never heard anything to suggest he did that kind of thing."

"The letters arrived back in our office as undelivered towards the end of November, by which time we had already engaged Mr Dolan to find you."

"Our estate wasn't very nice and the post office didn't like sending people out there to deliver mail. Things did sometimes take a long time to arrive. I once had this birthday card which Anton sent in June and I didn't get it until..." Emma stopped. "It's hard to believe he won't be sending me any more cards or funny jokes; that he won't just turn up unannounced." Emma sniffed and Kieran poked around in the inside pocket of his jacket. He pulled out a packet of tissues and offered it to Emma. "Thanks."

The first one tore into pieces and parts of it blew away, dancing over the wide expanse of lawn in front of the house like confetti. The wind tore at the next one as Emma lifted it with frozen fingers but she managed to hold on and dab at her eyes. She handed the packet back to Kieran and he wrestled it into his pocket. "Nothing you've said explains why we're here." Emma looked at the solicitor with accusation in her eyes.

Fine pea gravel appeared underfoot, littered with weeds and the brown autumn leaves that hadn't yet blown away on the harsh wind. It crunched under Emma's boot soles and she winced as a tiny nut of gravel spat up and hit her spitefully on the chin. "I've been here," she said to Kieran, rubbing at her sore skin.

"I wandered in and there was this auction. They sold everything."

Kieran looked at Emma with a coy smile. "I know. I saw you. But we didn't sell everything."

Emma shrugged. "Yeah, it seemed such a shame. The auctioneer said the owner died and..." She stopped abruptly. "Who was the owner? Who owned this house? What have I got to do with this?"

Even before the solicitor uttered the name, Emma knew. She paled as the realisation hit her like a force ten gale, shock dilating her pupils until her eyes looked black against her white face.

"This was Mr Andreyev's home." Kieran looked at her with sympathy in his face, his head tilted slightly in a *there-there* posture.

Anton's house rose above Emma, two main floors and the servants' attic. An unexpected shaft of sunlight lit the scene, cheering the red brick and making Emma feel as though Anton's embrace warmed her through the yellow glow. "Why are we here? It's Rohan you need to talk to, not me." Emma grew nervous again as the solicitor stepped up to the front doors and placed a key into the lock. A paper label flapped from it, twisting in the breeze.

"Welcome," Kieran smiled, stepping back to allow Emma entry.

Their footsteps echoed in the cavernous hall and Emma gasped as she looked around. "You lied. It's all gone! They sold everything!" Her eyes sought out Freda's dent in the oak paneling but it was too small to see from a distance and Emma gave up. She rounded on the solicitor. "Why am I here? This is nothing to do with me."

Kieran smiled again and walked down the long

corridor to the sitting room. He pushed open the doors to the huge square room which overlooked Market Harborough from its vantage point. The bare wooden floors creaked under his shiny black shoes. "Please, sit down, Mrs Andreyev." He held his arm outstretched to indicate the window seat. Even the plush cushions were gone, leaving bare, painted wood against cold windows. Emma dragged her feet, not wanting to be confined any further with the stranger.

"Not unless you tell me why. I've got my mobile phone; I can call for help," she lied, remaining standing, her face set stubbornly in a look which resonated of her son's rare petulance.

Kieran sighed and pulled a sheet of paper from his inside pocket, flapping at it gently until it opened into its full A4 size. He directed his voice towards the window seat and began reading as though Emma was already sitting there in abject obedience. She pouted in the doorway at the weird charade. "*This is the last will and testament of I, Anton Stepanovich Andreyev, written in the presence of my executors, Mr David George Allen and Mr Andrew John Holdsworth...*"

CHAPTER FORTY TWO

Emma clung to the edge of the window seat with fingers which were white and aching. She sat rigidly for the reading of Anton's final wishes, her head bowed so her eyes saw only the reddened wood of the floorboards in her immediate vision. Occasionally she saw Anton, his ready smile as he chastised or mocked her for some minor infringement, the intensity of the Andreyev blue eyes and the lightness of spirit which was always his. Emma's tears fell unchecked as Kieran read in a voice which didn't waver in the discharge of his peculiar duty.

"...*I have ordered the house to be stripped and the proceeds from an auction of the minor pieces put into a fund. We never shared artistic taste, Em. Some of it was too good to dispose of...the best furniture will be restored and returned after you take up residence...it's up to you what you do with it.*"

Kieran read on, detailing a trust fund for Nicky to remain untouched until he was twenty-one and numerous investments she would need to learn to manage, a theatre company into which Anton had placed a manager. "...*Henry Macey will contact you at the direction of my solicitor...yours to do what you wish with...*"

"Stop!" Emma held a hand up in front of her eyes and Kieran ceased his monotonous rendition. Her face was streaked and sticky, her dark eyelashes speckled with tear drops which glinted in the light sneaking through the wooden shutters. "I can't do this," Emma begged. "I can't take anymore."

Kieran reached into his pocket for the packet of tissues and then slumped down onto the seat next to her. The vast bay window would have fitted a junior soccer team into it with room to spare. "I'm sorry. It's a lot to take in. Mr Allen was meant to do this part and I would be here in case you fainted or needed clarification. It just took so long to find you and he's not in the country. I have to say though, I love Mr Andreyev's final words to you." The solicitor smiled and looked down at the paper in his hand. "Can I just read this last bit? I really wanted to."

Emma nodded as Kieran handed over a tissue and glanced around the empty room, as though seeking an audience. He puffed up his thin chest and spoke to the empty room. "*To my dearest Printsessa Emma. Everything I have achieved, I lay at your feet. It is all for you; from Russia, with love. Just like her, we will be bent, but never broken.*"

Emma let out a wail and sobbed into her hands. It was Anton's gay joke, bent but never broken. Emma saw his coy, mischievous smile and missed him with a physical, gnawing ache. '*From Russia, with love.* Russia gave Anton to her, but death stole him back. Russia gave her Rohan too, once upon a time, but not to keep. Her gifts were empty gestures.

"Is there someone I can call for you?" Kieran shifted the paper in his hand and flapped it towards Emma. "I think I've read all the parts which required it. I don't wish to cause you any more distress. I have two copies for you to sign to acknowledge receipt, one for you to keep and one for Mr Allen. Then I can leave you to it. It's all yours. Call the number on the business card once you've collected your thoughts and we'll transfer the money from the estate."

"But what am I going to do with all this?" Emma

held her arms out sideways to encompass only a tiny corner of the enormous mansion.

Kieran shrugged, hints of a well disguised Welsh accent sneaking through as an undertone. "Sell it, live in it or restore it properly to its former glory. You've got the money to do any of it." He poked at a fleck of paint on the window seat. "Personally, I'd like to see it restored to how it used to be. But you'd need a historian to know how to do that."

Emma's mouth dropped open in surprise. Kieran looked nervous and shifted around on his bottom. "Bloody hell!" Emma gasped. "Or an archivist. The cunning git!" Then she laughed, shaking her head and giggling at Anton's perfect fix for her life. When the laughter stopped, the tears ran again until Kieran grew eager to leave.

He produced a beautiful ball point pen for Emma to sign her signature on the two sheaves of paper. Then he folded his copy and poked it into his inside jacket pocket. He held out his hand. "Lovely to have met you, Mrs Andreyev. I hope you'll be happy. Please get in touch with us if you require further assistance. Allen, Holdsworth and Bowes have considerable expertise in all legal matters and Mr Bowes deals with investments, covenants and trusts. I'm sure we'll be able to help you."

Emma took his cold fingers in hers and nodded her thanks. "Nice to meet you too," she muttered, stumbling over her words. Kieran placed the key with its paper tag on the seat next to her and left the room after telling her all the other keys were in an envelope on the mantelpiece. Emma nodded woodenly and listened to his footsteps tapping away across the hall and then the slam of the front door. She sat for a while, absorbing the calm of the old building, feeling the stillness comforting her. With everything gone, it was as though Anton had deliberately removed any trace of himself and Emma felt the gnawing grief again. There was no funeral, his will stated that, just a private cremation with nobody invited and his ashes scattered on the grounds of the old house by his solicitor. Kieran didn't know where.

Emma walked slowly over to the huge fireplace, seeking warmth in the cold dark grate and knowing even before she got there, how futile that was. Part of her wanted to revisit the blue room upstairs and see if it was still as Anton left it, but a bigger part feared that it wasn't and Emma's fragile sensibility meant she wouldn't cope. Her fingers reached up and touched the envelope leaning against the wall on the mantel, tutting as it tipped forward with the clang of myriad keys. She experienced a flash of anger. "Why did you do this?" she shouted into the empty room. "I'm an archivist, not an interior designer! I wouldn't know what I was doing!" She imagined Anton's high snort of laughter at her expense. "It's not funny!" she yelled at his ghost.

The sound of a car firing up caught Emma's attention and with a flash of horror she realised her mistake. She rushed to the windows, hauling back the shutter nearest to her and hammering on the glass with the flat of her hand. "Come back! I don't have a ride back into town."

Kieran Miles' car slid out of the gates and indicated left, heading out on the road to Northampton. Emma groaned out loud and sank onto the seat. "Nicky!" She ran her hands through her curls and heaved a huge sigh. "It'll take me ages to walk!" she grumbled and stamped her foot on the floorboards. The old house groaned around her.

"Aye, maybe."

Emma jumped at the sound of Christopher's voice. He leaned against the doorframe with casual ease and acknowledged her with a slight upwards tilt of his head. "Your front door was open."

"I thought you left." Emma stood, wanting to run to him with relief but unsure suddenly.

"Aye. I had a wee job up north with a school teacher who couldn't seem to keep his hands to himself. It's a great pity what a fall down stairs can do to a set of dirty fingers what won't stop touchin' things that don't belong to them."

Emma gulped. "There are no stairs at the school." Her words sounded stupid even to her. Christopher smiled.

"Aye, an' it was my job to be extra inventive, so it was."

"That's terrible." Then Emma smirked. "Do you think I should send him a get well soon card?"

Christopher shook his head. "Na. I'd be stayin' well away from that estate if I was you."

Emma sighed. "I decided to go back there. I thought if I agreed to shag him occasionally he might give me my job back."

"Aye right." Christopher's dark face remained impassive. "Well, I didn't wanna mention the other kind of accident he might also have had."

Emma sat back down and put her face in her hands. "Why is my life so complicated?"

"It's not!" the man scoffed. "You've made it that way. Anton left yer this house and a business. Just fetch yer wee son up here and make somethin' of it - and yerself for that matter."

"Do you think God puts people in your path exactly when you need them?" Emma asked, staring around the room.

"Dunno." Christopher shrugged. "Maybe."

"It's just that the solicitor made an odd comment. He said if I stayed here, I'd need a historian to help renovate this place properly." Her companion raised an eyebrow in question and Emma cocked her head. "I think Anton meant *me* to do it but it's completely out of my league. Then recently I met this elderly lady who's a local historian. She married one of the Ayers sons brought up in this house." Emma bit her lip. "She'd be perfect. Freda would remember the house how it was in the 1920s."

"Well get on with it, then!" Christopher opened his arms wide to take in the surrounding pile.

"I can't!" Emma snapped. "I can't get back into town." She raised her eyes hopefully in Christopher's direction. "Please could you give me a ride?"

Emma locked up the front door and followed Christopher round the side of the house. She looked up at the darkened windows and struggled to deal with the responsibility of it all. Christopher kept his hands in his pockets, trudging along slightly ahead of her. "Oh!" he pulled out a long key ring adorned with silver keys of varying shape. "You'll be wanting these back after."

Emma frowned. "After what? And what are they all for?"

Christopher stopped in front of her and bit his lip. "I came here often so I had my own keys. Anton lent me a room over the old stables and I kept my gear in the shed underneath. I cleared out when the executors came and moved into the motel in Harborough. It's not my proper base but it was somewhere to come when I needed it." He smiled. "It's all yours now."

"You could stay?" Emma said softly, framing the question in her brown eyes.

Christopher laughed and shook his head. "What and cosy up in the middle of you and yer husband? No thanks!" He sounded bitter, striding off towards a long building with an apex roof over the centre of it. He clattered over the cobbles under an archway leading into a stable yard which looked derelict.

"But me and Rohan aren't..." Emma gave up and followed, her mind doing somersaults. Christopher was right. Rohan was Nicky's father and would resent his influence being diluted by the larger than life Irishman. Their enmity was clear. Besides, something told Emma a relationship with Christopher would wield a world of hurt. He was too fly-by-night, definitely not a one-woman-man.

Emma touched a hand to her breast. She didn't need any more heart damage. "Did Anton leave anything for you?" she dared to ask. "You don't have to tell me if you don't want to."

"I wasn't his lover, if that's what yer askin'," Christopher snapped, his dark eyes flashing with injustice.

Emma halted. "I...that never even occurred to me." She tilted her head like a quizzical bird. "I suppose it should have."

"Well, I wasn't! We were just friends. But yes, he did leave me something."

"Oh, good." Emma's eyes filled with curiosity but it felt inappropriate to ask what. Christopher opened one of the stable doors and went inside and she hovered in the courtyard, whirling around and taking in the silent, brooding atmosphere of the place.

"Here!" Christopher thrust the motorbike helmet into Emma's hand and her eyes widened in alarm.

"What? No!"

"It's a fair ole walk back to town. Suit yerself." He disappeared back into the stable. Emma gulped as he pushed the gleaming machine out into the daylight. It glittered like the male equivalent of bling.

"Is this yours?" She reached out and touched the sparkling chrome handlebar.

"T'is now." Christopher grinned like a maniac. "It was the first thing Anton bought when his investments paid off. That's what happens when you've a mathematical genius as a brother; you get to play stockbrokers with the big boys. He got too sick to ride this beauty in the last year so I ran it about, just as a favour you understand." Christopher glowed as he mounted the Harley Davidson and pushed his helmet down over his face. "He left me this and the money for chasin' you indefinitely. It's ironic how his solicitor then engaged me to find you.

"Cunning. Paid twice for the same job." Emma smiled. Any doubts about Christopher as a bed partner evapourated. There was no suggestion he wouldn't invoice the solicitor and Emma knew the payment would come out of Anton's estate, *her* estate. She shook her head.

"You gettin' on or what?" Christopher's voice sounded muffled under the helmet. With great reluctance, she fitted the tight head gear over her delicate ears and brushed her hair out of the front so she could see.

"I thought this was a mid-life-crisis sort of bike," she shouted over the deafening throb of the engine.

Christopher turned his brown eyes on hers and slapped her backside hard as Emma walked past him. "You definitely wanna walk," he yelled, his eyes curving into a smile, his lips hidden behind the bar of his helmet. Emma clambered onto the bike, using Christopher's strong torso to hold onto. She settled herself, the machine vibrating beneath and through her, praying she arrived home before Nicky did and in one piece. Something about the sight of the handsome Irishman in his helmet jarred with Emma's memory and she wrestled to bring it forwards. His brown eyes sparkled as he looked back at her and Emma's brow knitted in confusion.

"Hey!" Christopher turned his head to talk sideways to her and Emma leaned forward, bumping helmets awkwardly. "I'll take care of you," he promised in a half-shout which conveyed his sincerity. He reached behind him with one long arm and wrapped it around Emma, scooting her forward on the seat so her breasts touched the back of his jacket. His fingers lingered on her waist and Emma understood his promise, the weight falling from her chest to her stomach in one fell swoop.

CHAPTER FORTY THREE

Emma tapped Christopher on the shoulder at the end of Granville Street, wanting him to release her there instead of on Newcombe Street. He obliged, pulling the bike over and coming to rest against the curb. Emma struggled from the bike and went to war with her helmet, pulling to no avail.

"Stop, woman!" Christopher batted her hands away and lifted it off easily, leaving Emma panicked and sweating on the footpath. Christopher laid her helmet down on the ground next to his and then began to smooth her frantic hair away from her face. "So, this is goodbye proper then?" A sadness crept into his eyes and Emma felt the hitch in her chest.

"I guess so." She gulped and her eyes filled with tears.

Christopher shook his head. "No more cryin' for you. You've got choices now, so get makin' them." He pressed his forehead to Emma's, curving his neck and spine to reach her. His hands rested either side of her cheeks and he touched his lips to hers, causing the flare of natural passion to spark between them. Too soon, he pulled away, a small smirk touching the corner of his full lips. "Go home to yer husband, beautiful," he said wistfully and let go, leaving Emma standing on the pavement feeling empty.

"Christopher!" Emma's voice sounded panicked and once he turned to look at her, she felt her head empty of all sensible thought. She gulped. "The solicitor couldn't get onto the estate." Christopher looked confused and dismissed the statement with a shrug as he pulled his helmet back on and stowed her redundant one in the cavity under the seat. Emma took a step forward. "Anton did. He came heaps of times. How come?"

Christopher's eyes narrowed into slits of pleasure as his helmet masked the broad smile. Emma mouthed the words even as he said them and shook her head. "Fat Brian." She watched as Christopher started up the engine and pulled out into the traffic. She lifted her hand in acknowledgement of his single left handed salute and then he was gone, blending into the line of lunchtime traffic heading north into town. Emma watched as Christopher plunged through the traffic lights just before they turned red and bit her lip as the memory dislodged itself and flashed before her eyes. The tall motorcyclist stood at the cash register in the service station after Emma's hasty exit from the wedding, his neat backside encased in dark pants and those brown eyes twinkling through the gap in his visor. Nicky waved and Christopher ruffled his hair. *Harley Man.*

'*It was him!*' Nicky argued back in the hire car and Emma had sighed at her child's insistence. But he was right. Harley Man wasn't just a figment of her creative son's imagination. He was real; he was Christopher bloody Dolan.

"Well, looks like everyone knew except me," Emma mused. "And I always deemed it likely anyone with something as expensive as a Harley, would leave that estate in a coffin, robbed for the bike and anything else of value."

'*I chatted to Harley Man today,*' Nicky would tell her and mostly Emma humoured him, not wanting to quash his imagination, even when little Mo nodded enthusiastically and validated Nicky's tale. Now she thought about it, Harley Man often appeared around the same time as one of Anton's surprise visits and more so in the last year. Emma sighed and shook her head. Christopher Dolan would love the nickname and Emma regretted not getting to share it with him. She put her hand into her pocket, feeling the weight of the envelope full of keys. Then she smiled. Christopher hadn't given his back.

With a huge sigh of resignation, Emma trudged up Granville Street with a lightness in her heart. Allaine's God was certainly having a busy morning interceding in her life. The thought wasn't unpleasant and Emma readied herself to see Rohan again after their fight, buoyed up by the knowledge that at least now, she owned somewhere else to go. Realism plucked at her dreams, reminding her how her meagre wage at the school would probably be swallowed up in the power bill for the enormous house. The powerful sense of Rohan which stayed constantly with her, tugged at Emma's heartstrings, fighting with her over her life decisions. Everything about Rohan belonged to her and she squeezed the bridge of her nose as she walked, banishing the love and affection for him which overrode everything else. Allaine's sheets of incriminating plant descriptions nestled against the envelope of keys, daunting and as poisonous as their subject. Rohan would never accept the truth.

Christopher was a gorgeous, dangerous distraction from the reality of her sham marriage and Emma wrinkled her nose in displeasure as she opened the front door, her heart already belonging to the strong Russian but her head convincing her otherwise. The waft of Felicity's overpowering perfume caused a wave of nausea and Emma readied herself for the other woman's spite.

"Em?" Rohan appeared in the doorway from the plush living room they hardly ever used. His eyes were bloodshot and his blonde hair stuck up on end. Yesterday's white shirt listed to one side, untucked from his jeans and he leaned against the doorframe as though afraid he might fall down. Relief flooded his face.

"Hi," Emma replied, shooting a polite smile in his general direction. She slipped her boots off and tutted at the piece of fluff from her tattered sock which floated down onto the wooden floor, ignoring the waft of Rohan's masculine pheromones attacking her hormones with vigour. Emma hung her sweater on its peg and shoved her boots in a cubby hole underneath. Scooping the fluff from the floor, she headed for the dustbin in the kitchen.

Rohan blocked her, putting his body in her way. "Bin!" Emma held the fluff in his face and he snatched it out of her hand.

"I need to talk to you."

Emma tried to turn away in exasperation but found herself pinioned by her shoulders from behind. She resisted the urge to kick out backwards, suspecting Rohan might overbalance. "Em, please?" His voice contained an unfamiliar begging edge as the strong, capable Russian spun her around until her breasts touched his chest. "No more, please," he whispered. "Not just for me, for both of us." His fingers caressed her shoulders and Emma felt herself weakening. Rohan gave her a small shake as though trying to wake her up from some delusional stupor. "Tell me you don't love me and I'll let you go. You can walk away and I'll even give you the money you need. You just have to say the words, Em. Say it."

"We did this already!" Emma stared up into Rohan's deep blue eyes, losing herself like she did when she was a small girl and then a teenager. His soul was as firmly knitted to hers as her own and it would be like admitting she didn't love breathing, or eating or being Nicky's mother. She faltered and her lips moved, wondering if it would be better for all of them if she tried to detach from this beautiful man. The words stuck in her throat, refusing to perjure her heart in the lie.

"I know. But you didn't answer that time." Rohan watched her lips with frightening intensity and the light dulled in his eyes as Emma tried to speak.

Emma shook her head finally. "I can't. I can't do it. I hate you right now, but I can't tell you I don't love you. It wouldn't be true."

Rohan swallowed and wiped Emma's tears away with his thumbs, clasping her face, his fingers moving against the soft skin behind her ears as he pulled her lips towards his, guiding her in to oblivion, just like the first time they kissed, her twelve and him, fifteen. He inhaled and pulled her into him, arching his tall body around hers and making her neck ache with the effort of meeting his lips.

Emma yelped in surprise as Rohan lifted her off her feet, not in a romantic sweep as Christopher had done in the garden but upright, Emma's feet off the floor as Rohan aimed blindly for the living room door, keeping his arms tightly around her body and his lips over hers. He ceased only long enough to lay her on the sofa and strip off his tee shirt. Emma's eyes narrowed as he turned to throw the garment, the long wound on his back protruding from underneath the white gauze. Staining showed through, reminding her of the back street doctor and his unethical practices. Rohan stroked her cheek as he undid his jeans one handed, bringing Emma's focus back to the dark blue pools of his eyes, which fixed on hers as though welded there by an unseen hand. "Look at me," he whispered as he helped her with her zipper. "Don't think about anything else. Just us."

Their lovemaking wasn't a testimony of romance. It was the consummation of an agreement, the resurrection of a covenant made long ago by which each was irrevocably bound. The first time was a rush of explosive passion, a feast for the hungry, but the second time was the love Emma remembered and spent the last seven years craving. Rohan Andreyev was a considerate, attentive lover, leaving Emma moaning, breathless and desperate for more.

When Rohan's feet slipped on the floorboards for the umpteenth time, his foot trapped in the hem of the jeans he resisted pulling down any further than his knees, Emma placed her hand against his chest and turned her face away from his kisses. "Take them off, Ro," she whispered, looking up into his tortured eyes.

"It's fine." He tried to place his lips back over hers, the fire beginning to rage again.

"Ro, I know about your leg. Please, take your jeans off."

His lips parted in futile protest as courage and lust fled. He lay sprawled across her, his skin warm and enticing but the moment ruined. Emma reached up and smoothed the crow's feet next to his eyes, laughter lines no longer used in his present, empty life. "It doesn't matter. It makes no difference to me. Please don't shut me out now. We seem to go forwards making progress and then slip backwards so much further. We need to go forward and keep going, or..."

"No." Rohan placed his lips over Emma's to prevent the threat escaping. "Ok." He kissed her neck and nibbled her ear lobe. "But can we go upstairs to bed? I'm getting too old for shagging on the sofa."

Emma chose her own bed and they snuggled down under the covers, her head tucked tightly in Rohan's armpit and her hand resting on his muscular stomach. They lay for a while as the day waned, not talking but enjoying the sound of each other's heartbeat and the familiarity of being together. The weight of all the things they needed to talk about seemed to hover overhead like a menace.

Emma rolled over onto her stomach and pushed herself up on one elbow, using her other hand to play with the dog tags around Rohan's neck. They clinked in her fingers, a tinny, delicate sound. She pressed her lips against Rohan's service number, punched into the metal. "About Felicity..."

"I don't want you to mention her name ever again!" Rohan wrinkled his face in displeasure. "Especially not in bed with me."

"So can I mention her in bed with someone else?" Emma asked facetiously and Rohan's blue eyes widened.

"No! You won't be in bed with someone else. Felicity was never my girlfriend. She turned up here yesterday and I sent her away after she admitted threatening you. Craig told her he'd call the cops if she didn't leave. But she came again today, just before you got back. I'll just keep sending her away until she gets the message. I think there's something a bit unhinged about her."

"You noticed!" Emma scorned. "It took you long enough!"

"Sorry." Rohan became silent and brooding, smoothing his fingers across a crease in the bedsheet. It occupied all his attention as myriad thoughts coursed through his brain.

Emma sighed and put her fingers over his, stilling their movement. Rohan swallowed, but didn't look up. "You seemed to have a lot to say to me downstairs," she smirked, her lips rising at one corner. Her eyes flickered with mischief as her dark curls tumbled around her face.

"We didn't do much talking," Rohan commented, rewarded by Emma's triumphant smile.

"I didn't mean that kind of talking." She put her lips over his and heard him inhale as her hand wandered below the sheets, exploring forbidden territory. "You seem to have lost your way, Mr Andreyev. Let me help you."

As Emma's soft lips tousled the downy hair on Rohan's chest, he groaned and splayed his fingers across her lower back, grinding her body into his. Emma giggled, sixteen again, as she reached up and bit his full lip, drawing another gasp of pleasure from him. "I forgot what a bad girl you are," he sighed and Emma laughed.

"So did I."

CHAPTER FORTY FOUR

When Nicky hammered on the front door mid-afternoon, Emma opened it and scooped her son up into a bear hug. "Don't you want to come in?" she called to Allaine and Will as they stood outside on the pavement.

"I wanna!" Kaylee squeaked and Will shook his head.

"Thanks, but we've got stuff to do. Have a good weekend."

Emma looked at Allaine and smiled. "Thanks for everything, guys. I really appreciate it."

They waved and proceeded down the street into the growing gloom as daylight withdrew its services from the town early. Emma watched them with confusion in her face at Will's sudden hostility. She feared Allaine might have broken her promise already and winced, hoping the policeman didn't make problems for Rohan.

Nicky was full of where he'd been and what he'd done, chatting non-stop as he shed his outdoor clothes. At the sight of Rohan sitting on the sofa in the living room, Nicky squealed with delight and hurled himself at him. "Uncle Ro! I knowed you'd come back for me. I'm a wise man and I'm gonna make you laugh. Mummy said she didn't knowed if you'd be back in time." He looked accusingly at Emma as though she'd lied to him.

Rohan stayed seated and hauled the small boy onto

his knee, wincing as Nicky's feet caught the prosthetic leg. Emma's brow knitted in concern. Rohan let her touch and kiss every inch of his body earlier as she sought to recapture their former intimacy, everywhere except his right leg. She understood his anxiety about it, but the fact it still hurt to that extent after almost seven years, seemed strange.

Nicky snuggled down into Rohan's body and popped his thumb in his mouth. Emma watched the touching scene with fondness and a sense of disbelief. It was the stuff of her dreams and she waited for it to be ripped from her grasp.

Rohan took his reading glasses off and laid them on the coffee table, putting his energy into holding his son. Nicky's body slumped with exhaustion and Emma smiled as he chatted around his thumb to Rohan. Their voices were a low, comforting hum.

"Hungry Nicky?" Emma asked from the doorway and her son shook his head.

"No fanks. Will fed me till I popped."

"Ok, baby. Why don't you go and have a lie down on Mummy's bed for a while? You look shattered."

"I'm not tired." Nicky punctuated his sentence with a yawn and Emma laughed. "Mum?" Nicky squirmed around on Rohan's knee so he could see his mother. "I'm not getting married ever. Kaylee just talked all night wivout stoppin'. She weared me out."

Emma bit her lip and smirked at Rohan, whose blue eyes danced with laughter. "Know what you mean, mate. Girls wear me out too." He gave Emma a wink which set her heart racing. Thinking about her hunger for Rohan raised another knotty issue and her smile faded from her lips. Rohan saw and his brow knitted. He cocked his head and asked with his face expression what was wrong. Emma shook her head and smiled reassuringly at him.

Later she laid on her bed with Allaine's sheaf of notes, sifting through endless pictures and descriptions of common garden plants and the symptoms resulting from ingestion. Emma jumped at the feel of Rohan's hand on her shoulder. "Budge up," he whispered, sliding onto the bed behind her.

"Where's Nicky?" Emma rolled over onto her back, lifting her head so Rohan could slip his arm under her neck.

"He fell asleep so I laid him on the sofa. Is that ok?"

Emma kissed the underside of Rohan's stubbly jaw. "Of course it is. I knew he was tired, stubborn child."

Rohan's hand slipped underneath Emma's sweatshirt and caressed her stomach. Emma stiffened involuntarily and inhaled. "What's wrong? Are you having regrets?" He shifted so his face was above hers, the dusting of hair on his face adding to his rugged good looks. She shook her head and let her eyes study his, willing him to read in her brown irises what was wrong without her having to tell him. His eyes narrowed as he registered something but Rohan misunderstood, placing his lips over hers and fitting their bodies together like a jigsaw puzzle. Emma breathed out and let him play with her lips, enticing her deeper so she wouldn't be able to back out. His tongue flicked the underside of her top lip and she heard herself moan as Rohan's fingers sneaked higher.

Farrell barked downstairs and they both jumped apart like guilty school children, thrown backwards in time over a decade to another life.

"Gets me every damn time!" Rohan exhaled crossly and Emma giggled.

"Me too. Guilt is an amazing contraceptive."

Rohan tutted and blew a raspberry on Emma's neck and she sniggered and pushed him off. "Don't wake Nicky, please?"

Rohan nodded and rolled off her. "Ok. I'll take your lead, Em. He needs to know I'm his dad and you're my wife though. I can't cope with sleeping next door when you're in here...alone...naked..." He trailed his fingers along the delicate skin of her ribs and Emma squeaked.

"Ok, ok. But if you've got any suggestions about how to drop this all on him, I'm keen to listen." Emma shifted and the papers under her made crinkling sounds as she crumpled and bent them.

"What are you looking at?" Rohan reached under her and grabbed the top piece of paper. Emma stiffened, not quick enough to stop him and it tore, coming away without its heading. "Oh." His face dropped as he read the first paragraph and peered at the picture of the green leaved plant with the vibrant blue flower. Emma tried to struggle away from him, but Rohan increased the pressure around her shoulders, clamping his other arm across her middle and dropping the paper between them. "No! I'm not letting this come between us, Em. It's fine. You do what you think is right."

"Oh, how can I?" Emma sat up and brought her knees to her chest, hugging them and rocking backwards and forwards. "I'm so deluded! There's no way this can work, Ro. You're going to do everything in your power to stop your mother going to prison and I'm doing the exact opposite. We can't possibly build a relationship on that. Besides, today I found out that..."
"

"Oh, no." Rohan leaned up on one elbow, leaving

his arm possessively across Emma's stomach. He sighed and Emma looked down at him. Rohan pointed at the plant half way down the page, tapping the paper. "It's that one. I don't remember it in Russia, but she's grown it since we came to Britain. You must remember." He turned the torn page for Emma to look at. "At your dad's house it was at the bottom of the garden but after he died and we moved out of the vicarage, she kept some in a raised garden. It always looked like a weed to me but she seemed to like it."

"It is a weed. Look." Emma read the description. "Wolfsbane's from the aconite family and can kill within six hours of consumption." Emma peered at the attractive blue flowers and looked up at Rohan, her eyes registering surprise. "I thought they were lupins. But they were this stuff. Ro, look at the symptoms. *Vomiting, diarrhoea, burning and tingling, numbness of the mouth and burning in the stomach.* My father had those symptoms. Severe poisoning can result in motor weakness, what's that?"

"Movement I think," Rohan said, twisting the paper so he could read it too. "Didn't he have problems with dropping things? Oh no, Em, look. *Organ failure leads to death. I'm so sorry!*" Rohan lay on his back and put his hands over his face.

"We all had stomach problems, didn't we?" Emma's voice sounded small. "Wolfsbane. So it was in the garden the whole time."

"But a pathologist would pick it up in a post-mortem wouldn't they? It's a poison so it must linger in the body."

Emma poked through Allaine's notes, trying to remember what her friend told her about the toxins listed in the pages. "No, look. The Greeks called it the

Queen of Poisons because it's hard to detect and can be hidden in food. Anton and I knew it was the food but we never worked out how she did it."

Rohan lay back and held his hand out for the other pages. Emma passed them over and their fingers touched. "I recognise some of these others." He flicked a few of the pictures with his fingernail. "But not in the same way as the Wolfsbane. Mum was quite picky about it. I mowed over some by accident and she gave me the belt across my legs. Your dad pulled her off me."

"What're we going to do?" Emma's face knotted with pain.

"Em, you told me Anton took you to Lucya to have the baby. Would you tell me about her?"

Emma stared at Rohan, her eyes wide with doubt. "Your grandmother, Ro? She was your father's mother. Did you never meet her? She talked of you often. She gave Nicky all his middle names."

"I don't recall her." Rohan sounded unbearably sad, his head low on his chest and his body slumped. "Tell me Nikolai's names?"

Emma knitted her brow and stroked his hair back from his face, keeping her tone light. "Nikolai Rohan Davidovich Andreyev. Nikolai is your handed down name from your father, Rohan is for Nicky's father and Davidovich was your grandfather. Lucya's the reason Nicky knows so much Russian. She spoke it all the time to him. Your father brought her over from Russia and sorted out her residency but after he died, your mother sent her away. She ended up in Wales at the mercy of the state. Lucya was always adamant your mother killed her son, but being a foreigner felt she had no voice. It's maybe why Alanya banished her. Are you sure you don't remember her at all? She was gorgeous and incredibly outspoken; Anton took after her."

"No." Rohan shook his head. "Not one bit." He sat up and leaned forward, mirroring Emma's stance. "What a mess!"

Emma put her arm around his shoulders and kissed his bicep. "I'm sorry. I don't know what to say."

"How come Anton knew all this stuff? How come I didn't?" Rohan shook his head in disgust at himself. "Geez, Em. No wonder you didn't want my mother near Nicky. If we'd stayed together, she would've had access to my son and...I get why you ran now. I've been such a fool."

"I can't argue with that." Emma smirked, realising as the expression lifted her lips, it was inappropriate. Rohan looked irritated and Emma slapped his arm. "We tried so hard to tell you, Ro. In the end you just became a liability so we protected you instead."

"If Anton was such a hero, how come you didn't fall in love with him?" Rohan sulked, his bottom lip protruding slightly.

"Because he was gay, idiot. Otherwise I would have."

Rohan looked horrified and Emma laughed, the tension momentarily dissipating. "He really was like a brother. My love for him was completely different to my hankering after you. Anton was amazing, but apart from not liking girls at all, can you imagine the trouble we'd have caused in the world as a couple? It doesn't bear thinking about." Emma giggled with the memories swimming before her inner vision. In their childhood games, Anton always took the role of leader, directing the mischief in his creative inimitable way. "About Anton, Ro, he..."

"Oh, hell! What are we going to do about my mother?" Rohan closed his eyes and balanced his chin on his wrists, interrupted by the appearance of Nicky, who stumbled through the bedroom doorway rubbing his eyes.

"*Oh no!*" Emma hissed, waiting, her body stiff as her son opened his eyes and observed his mother and uncle sitting on the bed together. She waited for the awkward questions. Then Nicky yawned and the moment passed as he pushed his way in between them, crushing the papers underneath.

"Feel better, baby?" Emma asked, kissing him on his forehead. Nicky nodded.

"Mum, I like how Kaylee has a daddy. She has more fun 'cause she has one. I want a daddy." The child laid between the adults and Emma bit her lip, afraid of the chasm threatening to open up in front of her. Rohan turned towards his son and brushed the baby fine blonde hair from his eyes.

"I could be your daddy," he offered, laying down on his side and leaning up on one elbow. "If you want. You have a think about it."

"No." Nicky took his thumb out of his mouth and Rohan looked devastated. Emma bit back a ready retort at her son's rejection of his father, her heart clenching in agony.

"No?" Rohan's voice wobbled.

"No. I don't need to fink about it," Nicky said. "I want you to be my daddy. I'd like that. Can I call yer *Dad* then?"

"Reckon so." Rohan stroked the boy's soft forehead and smiled at Emma, cuddling Nicky into him as the child popped his thumb back into his mouth. Over the top of the boy's head Rohan spoke to his wife. "I'll sort out that other thing tonight, ok?"

She knitted her brow and looked confused, mouthing, "*What?*" to him. There seemed so many things to still deal with. The threatening notion of Felicity floated across her inner vision, taking pot shots at Emma's fragile happiness. She'd called twice more that afternoon, resulting in a screaming match in the street between Felicity and Rohan's closed front door.

Rohan jerked his head towards the pile of crumpled papers. "That stuff," he said. "I'll sort it out tonight." His eyes strayed to the blonde child cuddled sideways into his chest, sucking his thumb with obvious contentment.

Emma saw the look of determination cross her husband's angular face and sighed, seeing also the level of sacrifice which hid behind it.

His mother in exchange for his son.

CHAPTER FORTY FIVE

Emma arrived back from taking Nicky to school, stamping as she arrived abruptly in the warm hallway to shake warmth into herself. "Eek, it's freezing out there!" she commented, shivering on the mat and doing a funny little dance.

Rohan stepped through the hall doorway and watched her, his eyes dulled by longing. Emma registered his silence and stopped, stripping off her sweater and kicking off her boots. As she opened the cupboard door to put it all away, she felt the air behind her disturb with Rohan's presence. He brushed her long hair off her neck and bent to kiss the soft flesh. Emma exhaled at the welcome feel of his kisses. The night apart after such passionate contact the previous afternoon left them both desperate. "I've been waiting for you," Rohan whispered, teasing her with kisses that ran gently down her neck and onto her shoulder. He pulled her shirt aside and lifted her bra strap, sliding the apologetic grey material down her arm.

"Ro," Emma whispered, sighing at the feel of his lips against the soft skin under her earlobe. "I really need to sit down and talk to you about a couple of things. I..."

"Later." Rohan's kisses were urgent, pressing into Emma's flesh like a brand. She sighed and lifted her lips to his, feeling the plunging sensation behind her navel and giving in to it. His fingers found the gap between her shirt and the waistband of her jeans, lifting the rough material and caressing her cold skin with his warm fingers. "I love you, Emma," he whispered, his eyes glazed with desire as he pressed her backwards against the staircase. The wooden spindles dug into her back and neck as Rohan kept control of her, parting her legs with his thigh and working his magic with his tongue in her mouth.

The sudden hammering on the front door made Emma yelp in fear and Rohan hissed in anger. They jumped apart and Emma felt the arrival of the all too familiar guilt, which settled in her heart again and made her feel dirty. She gulped and pushed herself further into the corner, letting the sharp angles behind her bottom give her a false sense of security.

Rohan strode over to the door and yanked it open. "What?"

Emma feared for the poor postman or some random salesman with his subscription to an unknown magazine. As Felicity stepped over the threshold and into Rohan's hallway, Emma felt her patience snap. "Where have you been?" Felicity screeched into Rohan's face and she prodded his strong chest with a manicured fingernail. "Why didn't you call?"

"Not this again! Working!" Rohan spoke through gritted teeth and Emma winced at the warning in his tone. She edged towards the stairs, snagging her shirt on a loose nail, delayed in the extraction of it. Rohan's words were aimed to hurt. "Same as I was when you bedded that smarmy Irishman!" Rohan took a step back and pointed towards the door. "Yeah, I know about him. But you know what? I actually don't care. I told you countless times I wasn't in the market for anything more than friendship. Now, get out! I don't want you to keep turning up here so please, just leave!

The next time you show up, I'll get the police."

Felicity postured in her high heels, the fluff around her coat collar dancing in the breeze from the open door. "But what about all those times when we nearly..."

"We didn't nearly anything! I wasn't interested and you just wouldn't take no for an answer Felicity!"

The woman's perfect blonde hair fluttered in the breeze from the still open door. "Who's been gossiping, baby? Is it *her*?" She pointed at Emma, pinned to the wooden staircase by the back of her shirt. "She fancies you and it's *gross!* It's *incest*. You're *disgusting!*" Felicity directed her bile at Emma and Alanya's voice came echoing back down the ages. They were her stepmother's words and nausea rose into Emma's throat at their familiar, biting sound, feeling like a physical blow.

Emma pulled and the shirt ripped, the threadbare fabric giving way suddenly. Emma pounded up the stairs, making it only as far as the bathroom on the second level. She locked herself in and only just made it to the toilet in time, as the threatening nausea exploded her nerves and discharged itself into the toilet basin.

The ruckus continued downstairs in the hallway as Emma sat on the floor of the bathroom and cried. She periodically flushed the toilet to mask the sound of the argument, watching copious amounts of toilet paper swilling down its hungry insides. She sniffed and blew her nose again.

"I never proposed to you!" she heard Rohan yell in indignation and leaned her head back against the wall, figuring he just found out first-hand about his impending marriage to Felicity.

Emma splashed water on her face, dried it on the hand towel and headed to her own bedroom to clean her teeth and lie down on the bed.

As Rohan's voice continued downstairs in the hallway, Emma put the pillow over her head and blocked out the noise. Wave after wave of nausea bit her insides and she buried herself further into the bed and tried to distract herself from the overwhelming urge to throw up.

"Em?" Rohan's steady voice disturbed her from a dark fog and Emma struggled free. She sat up in the bed, her hair sticking up on one side and her left eye welded shut with the pressure from the pillow.

"What?" Her voice clanged in the silence, loud to her own ears.

"Your shirt's ripped." Rohan's fingers touched the loose threads and Emma felt the tug.

"Don't care. Go away." She pushed out at him hard, her fingers contacting his right leg just above the knee and she heard a hiss.

Rohan slumped down on the side of Emma's bed, squeezing a section of his leg through his jeans, his face grey with pain. He looked sick, beads of sweat budding on his forehead.

"What did I do?" Emma felt in the wrong, hating the immediate defence mechanism which rose up in her.

"Nothing. It's fine." Rohan exhaled through pursed lips and forced a wooden smile back onto his face. "Did you fall asleep through all that yelling?"

"I put the pillow over my head and it seemed to go away." Emma pushed her unruly hair out of her face. "But the sickness didn't."

"No, *she* went away!" Rohan sounded bitter as he

spat the words. "*Eventually!*"

"I don't care," Emma yawned, covering her mouth with her hand. "I feel really tired of it all."

"She informed me we were apparently engaged, just as my lawyer walked through the gate." Rohan laughed. "He gave her about twelve reasons why he was inclined to go to the cops and file a complaint about her stalking and then he pulled his phone out of his pocket and dialled. She gave in and left."

"You strung her along." Emma sounded grumpy. "You knew how she felt and you did wrong by her. You ate take-away in your bedroom. How could you not think she'd read into that?"

Rohan looked hard at Emma. "There was nothing physical between us, Em. I made it very clear I wasn't interested."

"Well, that's not what she's been telling people, including me! I think you liked the attention and particularly enjoyed how it wound me up."

"*Musor!* Rubbish!"

"Yeah you did. But I really don't need any more of her wacko visits, thanks."

"Geez Em! Don't let her damage what we've got. I'm sick of how she pops up just as its going ok."

"Well, you're the one who allows her to drape herself all over you, like at the school...oh crap!" Nausea gripped Emma's stomach, accompanied by a dull headache. She shoved at Rohan to get past him before she threw up and he groaned in pain as his right knee slipped sideways. Emma slammed the bathroom door behind her, not expecting Rohan to still be there when she emerged, feeling marginally better.

"What's wrong with you?" he asked, perched on her bed looking concerned.

"What's wrong with you?" she retorted rudely. "You jump like a cricket every time you move your leg."

"Nothing. I'm fine."

"Well so am I then," Emma sulked. "But I can't cope with another visit from Cosmopolitan Barbie today so if she turns up, make sure you *do* call the cops. Bloody woman."

"She won't come back. Hack's welcome to her! Looks like he had a grab at everything he thought I valued." Rohan eyed Emma sideways in accusation and she sighed.

"Mmnnnn, I don't think he's interested in Felicity." Emma face planted into her pillow and heaved out a big muffled sigh. "Ro, I really need to talk to you about something. Well, about two things actually." The weight of Anton's legacy pressed down on her chest.

"Yeah, sure, what?" Rohan looked at Emma with concentration etched into his handsome face. She opened her mouth to speak, wondering which particular problem to deal with first, just as his mobile phone rang. Emma groaned.

Rohan lay back against the pillows, keeping his right knee bent and his foot on the floor, the other leg stretched out on the bed. He looked uncomfortable. "Go on. I'll ignore it." He wriggled around, removing the trilling object from his pocket, disconnecting the call and turning the sound down.

Emma pushed her face into his side, smelling his warm, clean scent. "Yesterday, when I was almost home," she began. The phone danced around on top of the bed covers, working itself into a vibrating frenzy. Resignation covered Emma. "Oh, just answer it," she said, laying back on the bed and feeling her stomach churn with the stress.

"Andreyev!" Rohan snapped into the phone. "Oh, hi." His tone changed completely and he limped out into the hallway to finish the call. Memories of his post-coital conversation with Felicity pricked at Emma's security and the nausea flooded her senses and robbed her of practical thought.

"I need to go out." Rohan's voice was low as he re-entered the room and he sounded depressed.

"Who this time? Felicity or your mother?" Emma asked, her face pushed into her pillow.

"Neither. I told you, Felicity's got the message. Mother's been before the magistrates and they're holding her while they get psychology reports. It's more complicated, but that's the gist of it. I handed the printouts to the leading detective last night and pointed out the plant we both recognised. They're checking some stuff with the labs. I saw her for a few minutes, which was nice of them to let me. I er...it was hard. My lawyer's seen her this morning. That's why he popped round. But it's not why I have to go out. I have an appointment, Em. I need to go."

Emma rolled back over to observe her husband, maternal instinct working overtime. His face was locked tight with something other than Felicity's screamed accusations or his mother's plight. It left a residue in his eyes and she recognised it.

"Rohan, what's wrong? Are you in pain?"

The tall, strong Russian bowed his head and looked astounded at Emma's perception, the surprised expression quickly replaced by shame. Then he nodded and ran his hand across his eyes. Emma got shakily up and stood in front of him, her own problems pushed instantly aside. Worry etched lines into her face as

Rohan bit his bottom lip and struggled to form his words. "The *travma* to my leg is painful. The *durak* shot me and shattered part of the prosthesis. Now…" Rohan waved his hand at his knee to accentuate his distress. "My leg bleeds. The call was from my doctor at the clinic. I left a message for him this morning. He wants to see me now."

"Then let's go." Emma strutted from the bedroom and down the stairs, listening to the agonising sound of Rohan limping behind her. "Want me to drive?" she asked, flinging a sweater over her shoulders and pushing her feet into her boots.

"Yes please." Rohan's progress down the long garden to the garage compound at the end of the orchard seemed much slower than usual, but he refused Emma's help, forcing her to walk ahead of him along the crazy paved stones leading to the steps down to the garage. Emma wanted to tell him not to be so foolish but resisted, suppressing her maternal instinct under a need to respect her husband's feelings of protracted uselessness. She beat down the desire to berate him for leaving it a full two days before summoning help, wanting to chastise him like she would her son. But Rohan wasn't six years old. He was a full grown man with an ego that currently stuttered and cringed under her concern. *Leave it*, she told herself.

Emma hopped into the driver's side of the large Mercedes and started the engine, hearing the soft purr as the car vibrated with life underneath her. She eased it out of the garage and Rohan limped over to pull the garage door down after her. Emma put the hand brake on to get out and do it herself, then caught the look of determination and concentration in his face. "Ok," she said to her reflection in the rear view mirror. "This isn't about you. Get it?" Her pale face and messy, dark curls stared back at her, wide brown eyes condemning her for the seven years they'd been apart, leaving Rohan to struggle alone.

Emma rolled the car forward while Rohan opened and closed the huge gate onto the lane behind Newcombe Street. He got into the passenger seat bum first and closed the door behind him, his face flushed from the effort.

"Right then." Emma turned a beautiful hundred watt smile on him. "Tell me where to go and how to get there, and I'll be your chauffeur for this morning."

"Yeah, I've seen your *chauffeuring!*" Rohan snorted. "Just don't take it up professionally."

"That wasn't my fault!" Emma stuck her nose in the air and revved the engine. "I parked near the bushes and the wind blew them and they kinda scratched up and down the side a bit. I moved it as soon as I heard the first screech of the branches on the metal..." Emma turned down the lane and waited at the entrance to Newcombe Street. "It's only a few scratches. Which way?"

"It needs a whole new wing! Left here. Then right onto Nithsdale Avenue, then left at the end."

"No," Emma whinged, "not helpful! Just tell me one instruction at a time. And remind me, which foot do I brake with?"

Rohan looked at her in terror and she saw him grip the door handle, the fingers of his left hand turning white. "What?"

Emma put her head back and laughed, watching the colour flood back into Rohan's rugged features. "Got ya!" she said in an irritating sing-song voice.

"Whatever!" he smirked, realising she had successfully distracted him from the discomfort in his stump. "You wreck it and you'll be off my Christmas card list."

Emma snorted. "I bet you don't even give Christmas cards! You're far too grumpy."

Rohan smiled and leaned his left elbow on the window ledge. "You know me too well." He ran his teeth over his thumbnail and Emma felt his eyes on her. "Em..."

"Which way now?" she interrupted him, not wanting to go where the conversation was bound to take them right then. "Please tell me I don't have to swing this thing round a multi-storey carpark? I don't think either of us will come out unscathed."

"Straight on and no."

"There's other parking then? Thank goodness."

"Yeah." Rohan reached into the glove box and pulled out the orange parking disk. Emma immediately felt terrible about making a big deal of the parking. *You just don't know when to shut up,* she berated herself. She sensed Rohan watching her again, his blue eyes searching for signs of revulsion or diminishing respect. Emma glanced sideways at him, her eyes narrowed and sultry.

"Free parking," she sighed, as though he just donated a month's worth of chocolate ice cream to a diet convention. "Every girl's dream. I think I'll keep you just for that."

She saw Rohan smirk and shake his head. Emma exhaled slowly, controlling the nervous whoosh of air so he couldn't hear her, relieved at having surmounted the obstacle of using the disabled badge. "Saw that," he said without even looking at her. "I'm not fragile.

My ego won't smash into pieces, not today at any rate."

"Liar!" she bit at him and reached across the centre console, laying her hand over his clenched fist. Rohan squeezed her fingers and then put her hand carefully on the steering wheel.

"Two hands in my Merc, woman! *Neposlushnyy!*"

"Naughty yourself!" she commented back and he laughed, his eyes glinting with pleasure at her command of his mother tongue.

"Given half a chance, I will be." Rohan looked more like his old self as he smiled at Emma, his colour returning to normal and the stress leaving his eyes. But as they approached the sprawling city, his body tensed with hidden emotions and the tell-tale vein pulsed in his neck.

"How do I get to the hospital from here?" Emma asked as they whizzed past the city sign.

"You don't need to." Rohan's voice became clipped, issuing orders as he once did, Emma obeying with frustrating slowness. The huge car swung around narrow streets until they came to the clinic Rohan indicated.

"I'm not sure I can squeeze this giant car into that tiny space." Emma's face became pinched with worry. She looked around hopefully. "There aren't any disabled spaces. You lied to me."

"I'll do it. Shift over."

Emma pushed herself over the centre console, banging her backside on the gear lever, hand brake and everything in between. She sat in the passenger seat and rubbed her buttock. Rohan heaved himself into the driver's seat, struggling less as he led with his left side. "Bloody hell, woman!" He cranked the seat back to admit his long body and legs, shooting Emma a look of disbelief. "I was kissing the windscreen!" he exclaimed.

"And you could have been kissing me instead." She smiled and turned her full beauty on him, making Rohan pause as he lifted his painful right leg into place.

"You're very distracting." He cleared his throat and closed the car door.

Emma watched carefully as he backed the huge vehicle into the tiny spot, leaving only enough room for them to squeeze out either side. He did it with practiced skill, but she was fascinated by the use of his left foot on the brake, allowing his prosthetic responsibility only for the accelerator. She marvelled how she failed to notice that before.

The cars either side of them sported orange badges on the dashboard and Emma held Rohan's up with the unspoken question in her face. He nodded and she turned the dial to show their arrival time and slipped it in front of her, face up against the windscreen. They poured themselves out of the tight space, Emma getting her sweater pocket caught around the wing mirror and hearing a foreboding rip as she yanked it off. Rohan fared better, stepping sideways and holding onto the car chassis, fitting his neat butt through a miniscule gap with ease. They met at the bonnet of the car and Rohan caught Emma's arm as she waited for him. "Em." He fought for his words with difficulty. "I...er...I don't know if you'll want to come in with me." He chewed at his upper lip with his teeth. "It's pretty shocking."

"Is that why you never told Felicity?" Emma reached up, feeling the rough stubble of his face under her palm.

Rohan's lips parted in surprise and after a moment's

thought, he nodded. "Yeah."

Emma smiled. "You know she thinks you're impotent, hey?"

Rohan's mouth opened wide in shock. "Really?" He sounded so gutted, Emma laughed. Rohan slapped her on the backside. "Bitch!"

"Don't blame me!" she laughed. "Do you want me to put her straight?"

Rohan sighed and shook his head. "No thanks. I'm fine." He kept his eyes trained on Emma's, his brow knitting slightly as she reached for his hand and joined their fingers.

"Guess what?" she whispered against the cacophony of traffic on the main road. Rohan tilted his head and narrowed his eyes. "You've got a son," Emma said, binding her fingers more tightly around her husband's. "And Nicky loves you, no matter what. So let's go and get this leggy thing fixed up so you can play with him after school."

CHAPTER FORTY SIX

Rohan lay on the bed in the examination room while Emma fanned herself with a leaflet about prosthetic arms. Rohan stretched his head back to look at her. "You ok?"

"No," she admitted, "it's bloody hot in here." She fanned harder, her vision beginning to swim.

Rohan looked devastated. "I know it's ugly and oozing right now, but it doesn't always look this bad. I'm sorry, you should probably have stayed in the waiting room." He sounded depressed, the anticipated rejection surely on its way.

"Nope," Emma insisted. "This was definitely happening out there too. It's not your leg, I promise. I know what it is and it's not that. It's a mixture of things, but your leg is not one of them. I'll get a drink. That should help to cool me off." Emma sipped at the tap where the doctor washed his hands earlier before he lifted the stump sock away from Rohan's leg. The scar tissue where the man's shin once curved was neat and smooth, but a painful ulcer began on the inner part, continuing the line of a deep welt.

Rohan stared at the ceiling, defeat etched in every part of his posture. Emma sipped more water and willed her body to behave, for now at least. Rohan's jeans lay over the back of Emma's chair and he tugged at the white sheet the doctor laid over his thighs, eager to cover himself and avoid further scrutiny. "Ro, stop it." Emma staggered over to the bed, running her hand up Rohan's leg from his knee to the end of his boxer shorts. "I promise it's not that. It's so hot in here. Can't you feel it?" Her vision did a crazy jerk to the right and she gripped his leg too hard.

"Ow!" Rohan put his hand over the fingers, feeling the hardness of her knuckles. "Just sit down, Em." He sounded annoyed. She lurched backwards with a valiant effort and contacted her chair, seating her bum none too carefully. Rohan observed her through eyes filled with hurt. "Emma?" His voice sounded subdued. "When I laid there on the sand...my leg gone and blood everywhere...I thought of you. I regretted going back to the army base without trying harder to...to understand you. I lay there and knew what it would be like to die with that on my conscience." His eyes looked tortured and Emma reached out to him, feeling their connection reviving in her chest. She rubbed her thumb across the flesh above Rohan's top lip, feeling the maleness of his rough skin, shaved just a few hours ago but already budding with stubbly hairs.

Then it came again, the pesky nausea, robbing her of the chance to comfort the man spilling his guts before her. "So hot!" Emma peeled off the sweater and threw it on the ground next to her, quickly adding her sweatshirt to the pile. Sweat seemed to cover her whole body and she stood up again and tugged at the window above her head. "Mind if I have this open? I feel a bit weird." She sat and fanned herself with a whole stack of leaflets to create a decent breeze, slowly losing control of everything as her body violently rebelled. Rohan looked devastated and Emma sought to reassure him. "Lucya was diabetic," she puffed, her breath coming in short bursts. "She had heaps of ulcers constantly over her legs. I used to dress them for her, even the ones with puss and the ones that ate away through the fatty layers. She always said I'd make a superb little *meditsinskaya sestra*."

Emma leaned forward in her seat and concentrated on the swirls in the carpet. Her eyes began following the psychedelic patterns and she realised her mistake as the nausea took a more fairground style hold on her stomach. "Why do you get to come here, instead of the hospital?" she managed to gasp out.

"Agreement with the health service and the army," Rohan stated, not wanting to elabourate.

"Cool," Emma managed, saved from her agonies by the doctor returning. Rohan stared aghast at his empty hands and groaned. Then he swore in Russian and Emma pursed her lips.

The doctor looked nervous. "Sorry, Rohan. Not good news I'm afraid. That jolt you took to the prosthetic leg has knocked the central peg out of alignment as well as shattering the plastic cuff. It's not working properly which is why you've ended up with the pressure sores and cuts, despite using a copious amount of socks." He eyed the stained stocking material forming a cream gauze mountain next to the bed. "We'll throw those away and I'll get you some more. The boys in the workshop think it'll be about a week. They're also quite interested in how you did it. Scorch marks aren't really usual." The doctor looked at Rohan's flushed, angry face and his tone changed. "Look, I get how bad this is for you. It's like going right back to the beginning. I wish there was more I could do."

Every muscle in Rohan's body looked tense, his jaw square and fixed and his fists clenched at his sides. "Yeah, course you do. Because you know what's it's like to look at the car, the toilet, the shower or your trousers and wonder how the hell you're going to tackle every single bloody task with only one leg." He swung himself up using his stomach muscles and glared at the medic. Then he noticed Emma and his jaw dropped, causing the doctor to look over at her too. "Emma!" Rohan sounded shocked.

Emma ignored him, peeling herself out of the flimsy vest which covered her over washed bra. The middle aged doctor watched her unladylike striptease with fascination. Rohan swung his leg over the side of the bed and tried to stand, hobbling on the spot with his arms stretched behind him, grappling for support on the bed. "Emma!" he said again, a tinge of amazement in his voice.

"Sorry!" she gushed, making a dash for it and shoving the prone doctor out of the way. Clasping both hands firmly around the sink, she relaxed like an athlete finding the finish line and hurled straight into the examination room sink.

CHAPTER FORTY SEVEN

"It can be a bit traumatic," the doctor sympathised, handing Emma another Styrofoam cup filled with cold water. Rohan sat on the bed in the corner, cupping his chin in one hand and refusing to catch Emma's eye.

"Oh, will you both stop with the leg stuff?" she exclaimed in frustration. Now she'd purged the last of the morning's cup of tea, her stomach growled in hunger, further irritating her. The breeze from outside caused goose pimples to rise on her bare flesh and she felt like the Elephant Man on a trip to the supermarket. Nurses came and went, mainly out of curiosity and only one of them thought to wrap her in a thin blanket, for which Emma was truly grateful. "It's not the damn leg! I never liked that one anyway. I always preferred your left one with the little mole on your..." She halted her sentence at the look of warning on her husband's face.

Emma stared up at the ceiling, testing the temporary vertigo which could happen again if she stood up too soon. The white plaster rose decorating the centre of the room stayed where it was. *All good*. Emma slipped the blanket from her shoulders, exposing her bra while the doctor watched with interest. She pushed her arms and head through her vest and then added the sweatshirt. *Still ok*. She took another sip of water, deciding the fleece might be a step too far for the moment. She focussed on the ornate architrave around an alcove, testament to the age of the converted old

410

house. Thoughts of Anton's mansion rose to the forefront of her mind, too big to talk about right then. But her other problem pressed on her chest like a concrete block and Emma sighed, feeling as though her head would explode with it all if she didn't confess *something*.

"Please could I have a moment with my husband?" Emma asked the doctor, registering his reluctance to leave. She waited while he messed around with some paperwork and then left, closing the door behind him. Still Rohan said nothing, looking at his hands and adjusting the blanket covering his knees and the scarring below. Emma stood gingerly, finding she felt ok. She walked over to Rohan and tugged at the blanket, engaging in a violent version of the table cloth trick.

"Stop it!" he complained as the blanket fell to the floor, exposing his silky black boxer shorts and the covering of blonde hair on his muscular thighs. He gritted his teeth in irritation.

"Rohan Andreyev, stop being such a big baby." Emma pushed herself between his legs, feeling his thighs part but his chest remained hard, like a wall of muscle. He made no attempt to embrace her. "I'm not sick because of your damn leg." Emma pressed herself closer into her husband and turned her face sideways to snuggle into his warm neck. "It's morning sickness," she whispered. "I've been trying to tell you a few things since yesterday and one of them is that I'm pregnant."

"What?" Rohan's neck crinkled as he craned it to try and see Emma's face. Failing, he grabbed her by the shoulders and sat her up. "What did you just say?"

"You heard. I'm not repeating it," Emma replied stubbornly, watching the myriad of emotions cross

Rohan's handsome face. He worked his way through the full gamut, shock, disbelief, shock and then hope.

"Pregnant?" He bit his lip and tried to hide the smile which threatened at the corners of his mouth, wrenching his lips upwards to reach the ceiling. "Really?"

Emma glared at him. "If you even dare to ask if it's yours, I'll slap your face!"

Rohan shrugged and looked confused. "That never occurred to me. But how can you know already? I mean yesterday..."

"Whoa boy!" Emma's brow knitted in consternation. "Back up a month more like it, to a certain night at the start of November and a nice red dress which *you* ripped and I had to mend!"

Rohan's eyes widened. "Then? Wow!" He swallowed and looked at Emma as though she was made of delicate china. His grip on her upper arms relaxed to a caress. Then his face clouded. "So you were pregnant when they kidnapped you?" His jaw hardened and he swore. "I'll find who started this and make them sorry!" He ran a shaking hand across his face. "Argh! Eddie drugged you. What if it hurts the baby? How can we find out?"

Emma shuddered at the memory of that night and the beautiful, burning mansion. She shook her head and Rohan dismissed the rage, burying it somewhere inside him for another time. Emma pushed herself into her husband's chest and he held her tightly, wrapping his arms around her back and pressing his face into her long dark curls. "What will be, will be," Emma muttered. "We'll deal with it if it happens."

The doctor returned with reinforcements, a white coated gentleman and another nurse. He knocked on the door with a tentative little *rat-tat-tat* and entered despite being ignored. The little group stopped at the sight of the couple entwined around each other. The new doctor stepped forward and offered his outstretched hand to Rohan. "Captain Andreyev, it's a pleasure to meet you."

Emma released herself from Rohan's arms and sat on the bed next to him, keeping hold of his powerful bicep in case the floor began to move in her vision again. Rohan accepted the man's handshake and observed him through blue, dancing eyes filled with life. "I understand you're upset at the length of time it'll take to mend your prosthetic leg," the doctor began, his voice filled with more authority than his colleague. "I've had a word with the boys in the workshop..." he corrected himself. "Laboratory, sorry. They think they could have it ready by this Friday, late afternoon. So you'll have to manage until then but hopefully you'll have it back before Christmas." The man looked nervously for Rohan's approval.

Rohan considered for a moment and then gave it. "Sounds fair. My son's six. I want to be able to play with him on Christmas Day." He looked at Emma and smiled, his face bursting with happiness. He touched her stomach with tender fingers as she balanced on the edge of the bed. "I've already missed far too much," he whispered.

CHAPTER FORTY EIGHT

"Oh my goodness, what a pair of decrepits!" Emma commented as she helped Rohan negotiate the miniscule space between the cars. He swivelled on his only leg and pushed his backside into the car, falling backwards across the gear stick. Emma clanked his crutches and shoved them on the back seat as Rohan managed to get himself seated. In the driving seat, Emma turned to him. "Definitely buckle up. This ain't gonna be pretty. You've only got enough feet to press the brake and I'm working up to another puking session." She exhaled slowly and touched her stomach lightly. "We'll have to have all the windows open."

Rohan snorted. "We don't even make up one decent body between us."

"Speak for your bloody self!" Emma slapped his arm, groaning at the jarring of her body. "Ooh, not good."

It was a slow and painful journey back to Market Harborough and Emma parked out front on the road. "I'm pretending I parked out here for you," Emma grumbled, "but actually it was more for me. I don't think I can make it up the garden without decorating everything on the way."

"It's fine." Rohan spoke softly, stroking Emma's cheek with the backs of his fingers. He glanced up at the house. "Now we just have to work out how to get indoors, seeing as neither of us can help the other."

"If it wasn't so tragic, it'd be funny," Emma

groaned, leaning her head against the headrest.

The neighbours may have been momentarily shocked by the sight of the handsome Russian on crutches with a flapping, empty pants leg blowing in the breeze. But they were far more entertained by Emma's spectacular decoration of the hedge, followed by the pot plants either side of the front porch. "I love how you treat my foliage with scrupulous fairness," Rohan commented as he hopped on one leg, trying to get his key in the lock.

"Hurry up, or the next lot goes in your shoe," Emma threatened as she clutched Rohan's right trainer in her fingers. As the front door opened and Rohan hopped back for her to pass, Emma made a beeline for the downstairs cloakroom, taking her husband's shoe with her.

They snuggled on the couch in a blanket later, Emma clutching a cup of milk which seemed to be miraculously curing her sickness. Rohan sat with his phone in his hand, peering at the tiny writing, his reading glasses in his other hand, resting against his bottom lip. "They work better on your face," Emma sighed, wrinkling her nose as the milk mixed with the taste of toothpaste.

Rohan looked up. "It says here that morning sickness is the stomach's way of telling you it's empty but the hormones mess up the signal. That's why the milk's working. It's satiating the hunger."

"Please don't tell me you plan to Google every sneeze, Ro." Emma stopped herself adding, *I've done this before.* She kept the cruel rejoinder to herself and switched to another knotty issue. "What was that call when I was in the bathroom. Was it about your mother's case? Has she worked out a way to kill her guards yet?"

Rohan shook his head at Emma's jibe and folded his glasses carefully flat, slipping them into the breast pocket of his shirt. "Don't, Em." He glanced at her. "Do you think you'd be alright to light the fire now? I can tell you where everything is."

"Please don't make me?" she groaned. "Why can't you just get a gas fire like normal people? Then you can press a button and heat pops out." Emma silenced herself at the memory of the cold gas fire at her house in Lincoln, which she never afforded to light, even when snow dusted the ground outside. Rohan misinterpreted her silence as a rebuke.

"It's fine. You don't have to." He slipped his arm around her shoulders and Emma snuggled into his chest, the milk tipping dangerously sideways. Rohan took it from her fingers and balanced it on his thigh.

"Stop changing the subject," Emma muttered, pressing her face into his shirt and inhaling his familiar scent. A different feeling began in her stomach, a gentle stirring desire which filtered up through the other signals to her brain. Emma popped one of the buttons and kissed Rohan's blonde chest hair, feeling the fire ignite under her. Rohan's snuff of laughter made her realise her error. Now she was the distraction. "Tell me then? I'll keep quiet, I promise."

Emma shifted position so she faced the back of the sofa and laid across her husband's thighs, her face pushed into his hard stomach. It felt deliciously comfortable and daytime-decadent. She sighed and closed her eyes, feeling Rohan move slightly as he balanced her mug on the arm of the sofa. She sensed his soft breath on her cheek as he looked down at her and his long fingers sifted through her curls, selecting one and then twirling it. The first time he did that, Emma was six and he was nine, lined up in front of the new matriarch in terror as she ranted about some misdemeanour. The tiny Emma was so scared, she almost wet herself.

"Tell me about Alanya." Emma heard the hardness in her voice.

Rohan exhaled, shifting Emma's head as the gush of air left his body. "She's been moved to a secure unit. At the moment she seems like a normal, level headed fifty-six year old woman, but the cops noticed significant agitation when asked about your father, in particular." Rohan paused, his words seeming hard to form. "The detective in charge told the lawyer he didn't believe she was a cold blooded serial killer, but actually someone who has...issues." He swallowed. "She seemed to think she was genuinely helping people, showing them love and nursing them. She'll have a mental health assessment and go back to the court when it's complete. I'm leaving it to the lawyers to sort out."

Emma wrapped her arms securely round Rohan's waist and nestled in, trying to infuse him with love and comfort. The bleakness of her childhood threatened her from its forbidding darkness and Emma squeezed her eyes tightly shut to avoid its onslaught. Alanya affected them all in different ways. Anton became cunning and sly, overtly flamboyant yet protective of his siblings. Rohan switched his mind off and blocked out the bad times, excelling in school and throwing himself into activity and love with Emma. Sighing, Emma reached out with her mind and tried to touch the glowing threads of her stepmother, allowing herself to truly feel her inner emotions about the woman.

For years there was dread and terror but now? Emma stretched her mind to allow Alanya's face to appear, severe, autocratic and dictatorial. She stared into the blue eyes in her imagination and saw something else; a woman haunted by herself, tortured by a spirit of death, always seeking thanks and acclamation but causing only misery and grief. She exhaled and opened her eyes. "Ro?" Emma slid her body up his chest, her breasts banging against every button on the way up until their eyes were level.

Rohan smiled sadly at her and his pupils dilated with attraction, looking huge in his glittering blue eyes. "*Da?*" he replied. Emma reached over and took the remains of her milk from his right hand, sliding the contents down her throat quickly in warning to her delicate stomach not to try any funny business. She put the mug on the floor and putting her arms behind her, seized the edge of the scratchy blanket, pulling it up over her head and Rohan's and sealing them into a grey, secret world.

"I feel better now," she whispered. "Wanna play '*Let's Pretend'* with me?"

Rohan snorted softly. "Hey, I was honourable. I waited until you were sixteen and got the marriage certificate in my hand. I'm a good Russian Orthodox boy."

Emma shifted closer, deliberately pushing herself against him and feeling his arousal under her body. She touched her lips to his and gently nipped his bottom lip. Then in deference to the beautiful Anton, who schooled her in a fake Russian accent until she made him cry with laughter, Emma lowered her voice and said, "But I give you good, strong sons, comrade. And you vill find me very bad Anglican."

It was too hot under the blanket, which became discarded in the freezing living room, but Emma found some creative ways of warming them up. Rohan's shirt buttons were the only casualty fortunately, but as Emma hunted around for them on the floor, shivering and naked, her husband deliberately sent her in the wrong direction so he could ogle her longer. "You're lying!" she complained, snatching at the blanket and meeting the resistance of Rohan's strong fingers. "Count how many are missing. I've got four here."

Rohan ignored his gaping shirt and kept his eyes fixed on Emma as she pouted. "You are *krasivyy*. I've missed you so much," he whispered. His eyes were narrowed and sultry and Emma sat naked on the bare floorboards holding his gaze, wishing she could bottle the moment for harsher times. The buttons clinked in her palm and Rohan's exposed chest was muscular and defined. The blanket covered his modesty, unlike her, and only one sock rested on the cold floor, accentuating the loss of his other foot. Aching for him, Emma kneeled up and tumbled the four tiny buttons onto the blanket, resting her body against his knees.

"You call me *krasivyy*, *beautiful*, Ro. But I have stretch marks from Nicky and I'm bound to get a whole lot more soon. Breastfeeding ruined my boobs and I avoid trying to look at the state of my ass in the mirror." She tugged at the blanket between them, seeing Rohan's fingers clench over the edge in refusal to let go. Emma allowed him to hold on but pushed it aside so his thigh and knee were exposed, Emma's breasts resting against the skin above the gauze stocking. The buttons piled gleefully to the floor again. "You're the sexiest man I've ever met, Ro. Women stare at you and girls like Felicity fixate on you. It drives me crazy and I hate it." She rested her hand on the gauze and felt his muscles tense beneath it. "I love you, Ro. I've never known anyone else and this...doesn't matter." She slipped the top of the stocking back with questing fingers and kissed the exposed space above Rohan's knee. She watched his stomach flex and a storm of emotions dance across his face. Emma pushed the stocking down to his knee cap and kissed the flat bone, careful not to disturb the packing further down which guarded the painful, sensitive wound.

With gentle fingers, Emma replaced the stocking and felt Rohan relax. She laid her chin on his knee and repeated the words of the registrar at Gretna Green a lifetime ago, when presented by two teenagers and a naive and burning love for each other. For some reason on that day, instead of performing his usual speech, he stopped and looked at the kids before him. '*I feel like today, I should say this to you both.*' He smiled, grey hair wafting in a breeze from an open doorway. '*Marriage is for life, a covenant between both of you and God himself. You will be required to love each other through good times and bad, in sickness and in health, in plenty and in poverty. But this is for keeps, no matter what comes your way.*' He smiled at them, a benevolent father approving of a secret marriage known only to Anton.

"Have you ever wondered why he said that?" Rohan asked, his voice hushed with reverence.

Emma nodded, her cheek moving his leg with the motion. "Yeah. I have, often. He was just a registrar and we paid for short and sweet. Well, you paid. But with hindsight, it seems so relevant." She smiled up at him and Rohan stroked her hair back from her face.

"Happiest day of my life," he whispered. "And for the record, I love every one of your stretch marks."

Emma gave him a poignant look and raised one eyebrow. "Yeah, yeah!" He cuffed her lightly on the shoulder.

Emma pressed her lips against her husband's thigh and gave him a beatific smile. "I'm hungry now, Ro. But after we get Nick from school, please can I drive us somewhere special?"

Rohan cocked his head sideways in curiosity and smiled at Emma. She hugged herself like an excited child, although gooseflesh rose on her arms in the cool temperatures. "Do you want to go out for lunch?" he asked, although his jaw tightened in fear of her answer.

"I got the impression you wanted to hide here until your prosthetic was fixed?" Emma asked, laying her cheek back on his knee.

Rohan studied something outside the French doors, his gaze fixed on things Emma couldn't see. He nodded slowly and sighed. "It's what I feel like doing and pretty much what I did when it first happened. But it's not what I should do, is it? I need to face people. Apparently fear is an illusion. But I am scared."

Emma stood up and pushed herself into his lap, covering them both with the blanket and laying her head on his shoulder. "What are you scared most of?"

"*Moy syn.*" Rohan's answer was immediate, listing his son's opinion as his biggest fear. "Him thinking I'm *ne polezno.*"

Emma inhaled and fondled the soft downy hair on Rohan's chest. "He'll never think that, Ro. Not of you. 'Useless' isn't in his vocabulary where you're concerned.

"What do we do? How do we deal with this?" Rohan asked. "I can't stand in the playground with everyone pointing and staring and casually inform him

I've only got one leg."

"No, I know." Emma sat up and looked down at her husband. "How about you let me worry about Nicky?"

Rohan opted bravely to accompany Emma out for lunch. He directed her to a village public house to the west of Market Harborough and sat in the car, twisting his fingers with nerves. "My driving that bad, baby?" Emma asked, putting her fingers over his to stop the writhing.

Rohan looked up and inhaled. "Bloody shocking. Dunno why I let you drive my damn car." His eyes flared and he bit his lip. "Let's get this over with then."

"We can go to the drive through at McDonald's if you'd rather?" Emma offered.

Rohan shook his head. "What, after you helped me dress so beautifully?" He waved a hand at the three quarter pants revealing one, blonde haired leg, its foot stuffed into a trainer. The other pants leg hung over the seat, the absent leg creating a strange illusion.

Emma shrugged. "It looks better than full length jeans. I'm not sure why. But hey, you can wait in the car when I go for Nicky. Then I'll drive you somewhere nice and we'll just hang for a while as a family."

Rohan nodded and Emma got out to hand him the crutches which took up most of the back seat. He used the door to lever himself out, waving away Emma's help with a small look of exasperation. She watched him expertly make his way to the pub door and lower himself down one step and then the next, a look of pride on her face. *This man is truly awesome*, she smiled inwardly, the expression of adoration giving her complexion an ethereal glow.

Emma flanked Rohan to the bar and picked up two

menus, waiting for him to order the drinks. He leaned a crutch against the wooden bar and pulled his wallet awkwardly from his pocket, balancing with enormous skill as he handed over his card in payment for the drinks. Emma wordlessly picked up the soft drinks as the barman handed Rohan the receipt. "Grab a seat over there, mate. Order at the bar when you've decided what food you want. Kitchen closes at two o'clock."

Emma watched her husband struggle over to a small table for two, dropping his crutches down the side next to the wall and shifting into his seat. She felt torn between wanting to smack the barman in the face for his thoughtlessness and kissing him for treating her husband like everyone else. She decided the latter was preferable for Rohan and reached across, taking her husband's fingers in hers. "Want me to order the food?" she asked, trying not to make assumptions about how Rohan might be feeling. He shook his head and smiled up at her, peace beginning to burgeon in his eyes.

"I'll do it. What do you fancy?" Emma shot him a coy look and Rohan squeezed her fingers. "Stop that!" he whispered, biting his bottom lip and looking away. Emma smirked and chose her food, sticking to the soup and some ciabatta bread to help her ailing stomach. Rohan hefted himself to the bar to order and periodically glanced back at Emma, narrowing his eyes at her as she watched his gorgeous bum move across the distance between them. She blew him a sultry kiss, smirking as an elderly lady nearby gave her the thumbs up. Emma snorted out loud and covered it with a fake cough.

Observing the crowd in the snug dining room, Emma watched them glance at Rohan by the bar.

Without exception, they all took a longer look as he balanced on his crutches. Nobody screamed, fainted or ran out. They studied the odd gap at the bottom of his trousers as though processing a complicated jigsaw puzzle, then made the pieces fit and moved on mentally, choosing to look elsewhere without concern. They weren't deliberately cruel, just curious in a human nature sort of way. But for Rohan, it was paralysing.

Emma watched her husband turn and battle his way back to the table, a laminated sign gripped between his lips bearing the number seven. His upper body strength exuded power as he wielded his crutches and his striking good looks drew more than passing glances from all the sexually active women in the room, including the little old lady who winked at Emma through sparkling eyes filled with naughtiness. The pub was olde worlde, dating back hundreds of years. The ceilings were beamed and low and the ambience timeless and calm.

Rohan pushed himself back into the seat and went through the palaver with his crutches again, fitting them back down the side of the table.

"Ro," Emma started and he looked up at her, exhaustion showing in his face already. It was more than just a physical tiredness though, it was mental and emotional fatigue which leached from slightly glazed eyes.

"Yeah?" He sighed and ran a hand over his face.

"Remember that night when I came to you?" Emma fiddled with a packet of sugar between her fingers. Rohan waited for her to go on. "Did you just not want me in bed with you, or was it because you didn't want me to know about your leg?"

"My leg," he replied immediately. "I wasn't ready to

tell you. I heard you bang the crutches by the bed and lost my nerve. I sent you away and spent the whole night regretting it."

"I cried myself to sleep," Emma said, feeling guilty at the look of misery which immediately darkened Rohan's face. She reached across and clasped his fingers. "It's ok," she smirked across at him. "You can make it up to me."

After lunch, Emma drove to the school and parked up on the road. She leaned back in her seat and yawned. Rohan turned sideways and slipped an arm around her shoulders. "Tired, *dorogaya?*"

Emma nodded and he massaged the back of her neck with strong fingers. She sighed with pleasure as he teased the stress knots and aching nerve endings with a firm, kneading action. "I could get used to this," she joked, her energy levels plummeting the nearer it got to meeting Nicky.

Rohan stayed in the car as agreed and Emma walked to the playground to fetch her son. Mel and Allaine stood waiting, tapping their feet on the concrete to keep their toes warm. "How's the job going?" Emma asked Mel, gratified by the happiness which flooded across the beautiful face. Mel's newly beaded affro shimmered and shook in the bland daylight. "It's amazin'!" she gushed. "Such nice people I work for. I'm lovin' it. You should come in for one of ma special coffees," she encouraged. "People are tellin' me how nice ma drinks is."

"I'd like that," Emma smiled, pulling her sweater more snugly round her torso.

"How are you doing?" Allaine asked in a low voice as Mel turned to speak to another parent about a play date for Mo.

"I'm ok," Emma replied and smiled at her friend. "Lots to deal with in the last couple of days but I'm doing alright."

"What about the, *you-know-what?*" Allaine whispered and Emma rolled her eyes in an exaggerated motion.

"Which one?" Emma hissed back. "There's more than one to choose from."

"Oh." Allaine cringed and looked at Emma with concern. "Anything I can do to help?"

Emma leaned in so she could speak without being overheard. "Well, Rohan knows about the baby and is fine, excited actually. His mother's currently undergoing mental health assessments for a form of disorder which leads her to poison people so she can appear to help them get better." Emma paused, not wanting to gossip about Rohan's health issues without his permission.

"Want coffee after this?" Allaine indicated the children bursting from the main door with an outstretched hand

Emma touched her arm in thanks but shook her head. "I've just got something else to deal with, but tomorrow would be good if you're free? Maybe after I drop Nicky in the morning. I wouldn't mind a bit of help with his wise man costume for Friday."

Allaine snorted. "You're lucky. A granny nightie and a tea towel will do Nicky. Pity both of us. Mrs Clarke is gonna regret these particular wise men ever being given air time, let alone a stage!"

"Definitely" Emma agreed. "Well don't lose hope. I think I've just the thing for Kaylee in the suitcase I brought from Lincoln." She smirked. "I've got all Lucya's old nighties."

"Thank goodness for that!" Allaine groaned. I can't

make Kaylee understand the small fact that wise men didn't turn up to see Baby Jesus in fairy outfits!"

Emma laughed, but the happy expression faded from her lips as Nicky's eager face appeared on the steps. "Here goes," she muttered, as much to herself as to Allaine. Her friend looked at her with curiosity, distracted by Kaylee splatting into her stomach armed with several wet paintings. By the time Allaine looked back up, Emma walked slowly towards the play park, her arm around Nicky. Both looked serious.

"Nick, I need to talk to you about some grown up stuff," Emma said, forcing an unthreatening lightness into her voice. Nicky's shoulders automatically drooped as he trudged along next to her. They sat on a wooden bench near the lane out onto Scotland Road and Nicky stared at the floor.

"We're leaving, aren't we?" he asked, sounding far too old for his years.

"No, baby," Emma replied and he looked up at her in confusion.

"Well, what other grown up stuff is there then?"

Emma sighed and bit her lip. "This is to do with Rohan," she began, frustrated by Nicky's interruption.

"Is he leaving?" His eyes widened in horror, tears pricking at the corners.

"No! Nicky, this is important. I need you to listen to me." Emma huffed, wrestling with her exasperation, reminding herself he was only six. "Many years ago, around the time you were born, Rohan had an accident in the army and he lost his leg..."

"Can we help him look for it?" Nicky asked, his little face so sincere, Emma found it hard to be cross.

"There's no point. It was badly damaged so the doctors gave him a special one. Unfortunately it got a bit broken over the weekend and it's gone to the menders." Nicky studied his mother with his full concentration, wide blue eyes boring into her face. "So," Emma bit her lip. "He's only got one leg and he's worried you might not..."

"Might not help 'im up the stairs?"

"No, might not..."

"Might not fetch him fings?"

"No, might not..."

"Might not get 'im cuppa teas?"

"No Nick!" Emma put her head in her hands. "Might not like him!"

"Oh." Nicky seemed genuinely stunned. "Why would I fink that? I love 'im. He's my daddy. Look, I done 'im a picture of us all. That's you, look."

Emma glanced down at the A4 sheet with the stick men splatted on it. There was a tall blue one and a small blue one and a large green one, which Emma assumed was her. In view of her morning sickness, it was an appropriate colour. A black splat sojourning on the bottom of the page denoted Farrell's fuzzy body. He was bigger than everyone else. "Beautiful," Emma smiled. "Well, Ro's in the car so let's go and get him, shall we?"

"Not Ro!" Nicky corrected her. "Daddy!"

Emma opened the door for her son and he slid into the back seat. "Belt up, love," she told him.

"Nice crutches, Daddy!" Nicky complimented Rohan on the metal apparatus straddling the foot well. "These isn't the ones from under your bed, is they?"

Emma shook her head and started the engine, noticing the look of amazement on Rohan's face. She glanced at Nicky in the rear view mirror and saw him rub his eyes and look miserable. "What's the matter,

Nick?"

He shifted in his seat, squirming like he had fleas. "Well, I do walkings about in the night sometimes wiv my pen torch and I seen Daddy's pretend leg in the bathroom in his room. I only touched it though, just a little stroke." Nicky rubbed his eyes again and tears squeezed out and ran down his face. "I didn't mean to break it!"

Rohan peeped through the centre between the two seats offering reassurances and Emma climbed in the back and held her son. "It wasn't you, funny boy," she soothed. "It was a different sort of accident and it broke real good. That's not why I wanted to talk to you. I just wanted you...oh, it doesn't matter." She held her son, glad of the tinted windows as other children filed by on their way home.

Darkness gripped the land in its firm fingers and Emma sighed as all hope of her trip to Anton's place in daylight faded.

CHAPTER FORTY NINE

"I'm not sure if the power will be on," Emma said as she punched in the code written on the paper instructions from the envelope. The keypad beeped and the gates slid apart with a small hiss. Emma closed the passenger window and drove slowly up the driveway, the headlights bouncing yellow orbs onto the concrete ahead. The lights picked out the trees, making them look like forbidding sentries stood to attention.

"Where are we?" Nicky asked.

Emma pulled up next to the front door, trepidation blossoming in her heart at the darkened house and blank, faceless windows. Rohan watched her with the same expectation as his son and Emma took a deep breath. "This was Uncle Anton's house," she said, hearing the waver in her voice. "He's given it to me."

"Wow!" Nicky unclipped his seatbelt and stood in the foot well, tripping and falling over the crutches. "Can I see 'im? I love Uncle Anton!"

Emma's chin wobbled as she glanced sideways at Rohan. He put his hand over hers and turned in his seat to face his son. "Climb through, *syn*." His strong arms caught the boy as Nicky clambered through the gap, turning him to sit sideways on his knee. Nicky looked down at the space where Rohan's leg should be but tactfully said nothing and Emma felt a moment of pride in her son.

Rohan waited patiently for Nicky's attention and then began. "Anton was my *rodnoy brat*, you understand?"

Nicky sniggered and shook his head. "That sounds naughty!" He put his hand up to his mouth to stifle the escaping giggles.

"Brother," Emma whispered, overwhelmed by the moment and Rohan clasped her hand with gratitude.

"*Da*, brother," he repeated. "Nikolai, I was sad when Anton Stepanovich got sick because he was full of life and love and I knew I would miss him. The last thing he said to me was that I must find your mother. *And you.*" Rohan ruffled Nicky's hair with his left hand, keeping Emma's fingers under his right.

Nicky thought for a moment. "So you're a good boy then? You done as you was told?"

"*Da*, kind of." Rohan nodded slowly. The child accepted his answer but his face crumpled with sadness.

"But I want to see 'im now!" His voice hung between them in the darkness.

"He gave me this house," Emma repeated, looking up at the hulk of brick with a feeling of exhaustion lacing her voice. She sighed. "Would you like to look inside?"

They exited from the vehicle into freezing cold darkness and Emma was gratified by the care Nicky gave his father. The small boy fetched the crutches one at a time and made sure Rohan was stable before slamming the car doors. After struggling with the lock, Emma ran her hand along the wall in search of a light switch while the boys waited patiently just inside the door. She found it miles away from where she expected and the click echoed in the empty hallway as light flooded the area from an ornate overhead chandelier.

"Wow!" Nicky squealed.

"*Der'mo!*" Rohan exclaimed and Emma glared at the expletive. Her husband eyed the staircase to the right of them, solid oak and angular as it doglegged twice before sailing to the upstairs level. The balustrade betrayed a gallery over the entrance hall. Rohan glanced down at his crutches and wrinkled his nose.

"Want to look around downstairs?" Emma asked, keeping her tone casual. Rohan nodded and Nicky bounced on the spot with valiantly restrained eagerness.

The little family wandered the many rooms and spaces of the downstairs. The front of the house faced the main road and the back, open fields and what looked like a forest in the distance. A small single storey spur ran off beyond the kitchen with a downstairs bathroom, boot room and empty storage spaces. The light ebbed away, making a trip outside inadvisable but Nicky skipped from room to room with increased excitement. He seemed to be searching for something, spending little time in each space when it failed to reveal the thing he sought. "Upstairs now?" he said, turning hopeful eyes on Emma as she clicked off the last light switch.

"Let's look upstairs tomorrow," she said softly.

Rohan hauled himself along the corridor behind Emma and she glanced back at him, fearing condemnation from his silence. It seemed she was damned no matter what she did. Concentration was etched into his face, growing more pronounced with each click of the rubber pads on the floorboards. "Ro? You wanna head home now?" Emma asked, raising a finger to tell Nicky to wait for her at the end of the hall. "He doesn't get it. I need to actually explain Anton's gone. He's looking for him."

"What, sorry?" he asked, looking up from his task.

"I said did you want to leave now?" Emma asked.

"What about upstairs?"

Emma experienced a flush of awkwardness and deliberately didn't look at Rohan's leg or crutches. "I thought you might be tired."

Rohan's eyes flashed with danger. "I'm not sick, Em. I'm still the same person I was last week. I just took my bloody leg off so life got a whole lot harder. That's all. And I'm trying to work out why my brother lived a few miles away from me and never thought to mention it! He knew everything about me! Pity he never thought to return the favour."

Emma exhaled in frustration, irritated at him but also herself. She recognised the presence of pity in her attitude towards Rohan's disability and understood his resentment. "Sorry," she replied defensively and turned to leave.

There was a crash as Rohan's left crutch hit the floor and he reached out for her, his fingers hard on Emma's shoulders. She thought at first he was falling, until he maneuvered her against the wall with surprising skill. A dado rail dug into Emma's back as Rohan pressed her backwards. Then he bent and kissed her. His lips conveyed passion and hunger and demanded loyalty and healing.

Breathless, Emma pulled away, leaning her head against the wall, her breasts rising and falling against Rohan's hard chest muscles. "Don't leave me, Em." Rohan's whisper was filled with fear and pain and Emma screwed her face up in confusion.

"Leave you?" Emma heard the patter of Nicky's shoes as he skipped round and round the huge entrance hall. She searched Rohan's handsome face for an answer. "Why would I leave you now?"

Rohan's fingers stroked her face as he studied her like an artist about to put brush to canvas. It was as though he read every contour and shadow of her skin so he could do it from memory. "Anton left you this. Why would you want to live with me back in Harborough now? Unless you plan to sell it and I don't believe that was my brother's intention." He looked up at the high ceiling, his blue eyes sparkling in the light from the bulb. Emma wanted to reach up and touch the firm line of his jaw and kiss him until he understood how she felt. When Rohan's glittering eyes settled on her again, he smiled sadly. "You don't remember? All the times we hid from Mama and Anton would make up stories. He would say, '*I buy a big house for us to hide in. And you, dorogaya Emma, you will be printsessa.*' This is it, Em. This is his gift to you and you'll be queen here. You don't need me."

Emma squeezed her eyes shut against the remembered pain. Each beating from the cruel woman, each bout of sickness or diarrhoea, only served to drive the child Emma deeper into a world filled with Anton's ridiculous fantasies. Teenage pregnancy and poverty ensured their illusion never resurfaced. To understand they lived on in Anton's mind and he actively worked to see them happen, was a warped twist of fate, especially as he never survived to see their fruition. This house represented another brick in his fantasy world of endless kindness and joy. Emma felt the impossibility of owning another's dream.

"Emma?" Rohan called her back to him with a stroke of his fingers on her cheek. His warm breath stirred her fringe. "What is it, *dorogaya?*"

"Rohan," Emma swallowed hard. "Do you love

me?"

His eyes crinkled at the corners when he smiled, his dark lashes casting long shadows under his eyes. "*Ya tebya lyublyu.*" His voice came out low and husky. "You know I do. I tell you all the time." His top lip lifted on one side and Emma felt a flush of love which overwhelmed her chest and made her gasp.

"Then stay here with me," she asked him. "Be my *tsar?*"

Rohan ran his thumb under Emma's eye so gently, a sensuous flush embarrassed her and she looked away. He leaned in close so their foreheads touched and whispered, "*Opredelenno,* my *tsarina.* I feared you wouldn't ask."

Emma moaned as Rohan's lips touched hers and she clasped her fingers around his neck, feeling the spiky hair at the back of his head against her palms. His breath came in quick gasps as their passion wound free and he slipped questing fingers inside Emma's sweater, raising her tee shirt from her pants in excitement.

"Oh no!" Nicky's wail of dismay sent them skittering apart, Rohan grabbing at the wall and balancing on one crutch. Emma's heart sank as the words *inappropriate* and *stupid* ran through her mind waving switchblades.

"Er, Nicky, I...Rohan and I...we..." She gulped and collected herself, faced with her son's disapproving eyes. "Nicky, I love Ro...Daddy. I always have and..."

"I know all that!" His small face screwed up and he began to gasp, tears leaking from his eyes and refueling from his clearly broken heart. He rubbed at his face with rough, angry hands, while Rohan leaned against the wall, his fingers white against the handle of the crutch and his eyes dark and unreadable. "But I wanted to be a wise man so bad!" Nicky wailed from the other end of the corridor. "My best friends, Other Mo and Kaylee are wise mens and I wanna be a wise man." His voice hitched and Emma's face turned from rebellious and guilty to mystified in the seconds of silence after Nicky stormed off to the other end of the darkened house.

CHAPTER FIFTY

"What was that about?" Emma's mouth hung slightly open as she stared at the empty corridor. "Did you see where he went?" Panic and annoyance vied for attention as Rohan placed a gentle hand on her shoulder.

"I didn't think he would take it so *plokho!*" Rohan's face looked ashen, the honey colour stripped from his complexion in the bad lighting. He bent and retrieved his other crutch, righting himself but not moving.

"I'll go after him," Emma sighed. "He can't have gone far."

Within minutes she was back, her face a mask of fear. "I can't find him, Ro. I checked all the rooms on that wing and we know he's not on this one." She ran a frantic hand through her hair. "I called and called him and he's not answering." A sob caught in her throat.

Rohan smiled kindly at her and jerked his head towards the centre of the house and the huge hallway. "Go. Sit in the window seat we passed back there. I'll find him."

Emma looked doubtful, trotting to the end of the corridor to the hallway and then casting about her. "I didn't check upstairs." She pointed back behind them at the oak balustrade. Rohan shook his head.

"I know where he is. I heard." He pointed at his ear and then gave Emma a long fortifying kiss before sending her to the square room on the left to wait. Kieran's stumbled will reading came back to Emma.

Rohan stopped in the doorway and fixed his gorgeous blue eyes on her. "I'll bring him back. Trust me, Em. Please? I'll prove I'm worthy of it." Rohan set off towards the stairs and Emma stood in the doorway and watched his laborious progress. Her heart vied with the combined agony of giving up either one of her boys and she fought the urge to cry and beat her fists on the old wooden floor beneath her feet. *Why would Nicky take their relationship so badly?* It seemed unexpected and so unlike his previous overtures.

Rohan turned to the right to face the stairs which led upwards, each dogleg representing a face of Everest to him. Emma crept close and watched as he leaned forward and shoved one of his crutches up onto the fourth step. With huge physical strength, he used the other crutch and the handrail to begin his ascent. He kept the crutch in his right hand, his arm rigid as he hopped up onto the first tread, the handrail to his left taking some of the strain. His shoulder and arm muscles bulged through his jacket and Emma watched him breach the first four steps with apparent ease. Rohan retrieved the dormant crutch and laid it flat along the eighth step, moving upwards again at surprising speed. The stairs punctuated in front of him at the first landing and then Rohan began again. Ceasing to worry, Emma lay her head back against the wall and sighed. When Rohan was finally out of sight, she heard him make his way across the upstairs landing and begin his search of the upstairs. "I'm going to bloody kill you, Nikolai Harrington!" Emma muttered, returning to the empty room. Then she hurled herself onto the window seat to wait.

Half an hour passed. Half an hour of walking to the bottom of the stairs, listening and then walking back to the window seat. At one point, Emma left and wandered to the downstairs cloakroom on the far side of the kitchen, disturbed when the elderly pipes clanged and banged in protest at the toilet flushing.

"This is ridiculous!" she told herself, staring at her foot as it rested on the bottom tread of the stairs. Then she removed it for the hundredth time. Rohan said he would find him and unless he fell into the same peril as Nicky, he must have. Emma listened for movement, holding her breath when she recognised the sound of Rohan's crutches padding along the wing above her. The metal fixings clinked and clanked in the silent house and Emma released the breath with a whoosh as she heard Nicky's level voice.

The boys looked unconcerned as they stood at the top of the stairs. Emma experienced a flash of anger at what they'd put her through in the last half an hour, tempering its effects as irrational and foolish. Emma walked slowly to the bottom of the stairs and watched her men interact. "Hold it like this, Nikolai," Rohan told his son, putting the crutch upright in his small arms and directing him towards the carved oak bannister rail. "Hold on with one hand and carry viz other."

Emma bit back concern as tiredness made Rohan's native accent bleed into his English. She loved it but would never tell him she noticed.

Sinew and muscle stood out on Rohan's neck as he used his upper body strength to negotiate the stairs. The last barrier protecting her heart shattered as an old love flooded through, tightening her chest and causing a pressure to build in her throat. In her memories, Rohan struggled down the stairs at the vicarage, holding onto the wound from his appendectomy. His face registered agony from the cruel staples pressed into his flesh and thirteen year old Emma felt an uncontrollable surge of love for the teenager. Rohan was like a drug to her from before puberty. She needed him as she needed oxygen. He smiled at her back then, pretending like it didn't hurt. He did the same now, brushing off his infirmity against the honesty of her gaze.

"Sorry, Mummy." Nicky pressed his face into her stomach, accidentally bashing her ankles with the crutch. Rohan levered himself down behind the boy and alleviated him of his metal burden.

"I taught you never to run off," Emma said, surprised at the cold element in her voice. "It's dangerous."

Nicky put his head back and Emma looked down into swollen, bloodshot eyes. His chest gave a little hitch which suggested his tears had evolved into full blown hysteria. She caught Rohan's eye and he smiled, a hint of satisfaction in his blue eyes. He dealt with it. She was no longer alone in the parenting game. "Mummy?" Nicky's throat constricted the word as his body rebelled against the gulped air in his lungs. "Mummy, I'm so sad 'bout Uncle Anton. And Daddy said I will be a wise man and the nasty lady can't stop me. I'm sorry I runned away. I didn't want to tell her if you and Daddy did kissing but I saw." The child's whole body shuddered and Rohan laid a strong hand on his tiny shoulder.

"Papa sort it all out. *Zapomnit'*."

"I remember, Dad." Nicky gave another gulping swallow and Rohan shook his head furiously at Emma to warn her to stay quiet.

"Tomorrow, we'll make you a wise man costume,

Nikolai. And we'll practice your words."

"I don't say much," Nicky smiled. He leaned sideways and touched Rohan's thigh with his small hand. "I love you being my dad," he said with genuine affection.

"*Thank you*," Emma mouthed and stroked Rohan's rough cheek with a soft palm. "I feel tired now. I'll look at the upstairs another day."

"I found Uncle Anton's room," Nicky smiled up at her with a tearful hiccough punctuating his sentence. "I smelled his smell in a bedroom. Can we live here and please may I have that blue bedroom to sleep in? It's right next to the massive big room which can be yours. Then I can still hear you when you get scared and cry."

"We'll see, baby," Emma soothed, knitting her brow at the extent of the small boy's understanding. "For now though, let's go home."

Later, after a hastily scratched together dinner of cheese toasted sandwiches, Emma faced Rohan as he lay on her bed. "Are you freaking kidding me? Felicity said *what* to my son?"

"Keep your voice down," Rohan replied, his tone serious. "She said she'd stop him being in the nativity unless he promised to tell her what we were doing. She also told him we were disgusting and she'd get the police involved. From other things Nicky said, she's been feeding him little er..." Rohan struggled with the English word, unusual for him. He spread his hands, asking for help.

"Tidbits? Snippets?"

Rohan shook his head and ran his hands through his hair. "Things to make a small boy scared of her. *Izvergi.*"

"What's that?" Emma scratched her head,

perplexed. "Beast? Monster?"

"*Da!* Fiendish things of the night."

"I'll kill her!" Emma thumped her fist on the bed. "The selfish little...where does she live? I'll go round now and show her what fear is!" Her brown eyes glared in her face and Rohan smirked and dragged her body into his.

"Hush. I said I'd deal with it. He's my son. Let me be his papa."

"I'm trying. It was difficult staying downstairs while you talked to him. I wanted to rush up and make it better. It's how things have been for the last six years; just me and Nicky."

"I know, *dorogaya*. I know." Rohan exhaled and his breath ruffled Emma's hair. His arms felt strong around her and she pushed into his chest. His lips on the top of her head felt safe and comforting, but the sickness had already taken hold in the pit of Emma's stomach. Rohan knew. He stroked her back and whispered gentle Russian words into her ear.

Emma groaned, keeping her voice low. "It's that word, *disgusting*. Your mother called me, *gryaznyy*. Anton said it means filthy. It tainted everything, even Nicky's birth. If it hadn't been for Lucya, I'd be more of a mess than I am already. I always wondered if Alanya suspected the baby was yours; until that bitch kindly informed her Nicky had Anton on his birth certificate. Your mother knew I loved you. I'd like to say that's why she hated me, but I don't feel inclined to make excuses for her."

"I'm not justifying it, but in Russia when we blend families, we accept those new siblings as blood. She saw you as my sister so to her, it was a bad thing. You have to admit, she never treated you any better or worse than she did me and Anton. She was pretty awful to all of us."

Emma grunted and kept silent, not wanting to accede anything to Alanya, least of all fairness in her cruel upbringing. She pressed her face into Rohan's blonde chest, moving his shirt aside with her fingers to touch the muscular chest and feel closer to him. The metal dog tags cut into her cheek and she moved them in frustration before giving up and sitting upright. "Do you think we're disgusting?" she asked, her tone defensive.

"No! Never. We aren't blood and didn't choose to be put together in one family." Rohan ran his hand up Emma's thigh, his grip firm against her jeans. "My love for you was always different to Anton's. He cosseted you like a tiny flower, protecting and nurturing. I battled with my feelings and was shy of you for years. I kept myself separate until I understood what it was and then I kissed you. Remember?"

Emma nodded and allowed a tiny smirk to light her face with pleasure. "I remember."

"Lie down with me?" Rohan's voice sounded seductive and sent a shiver down Emma's spine. His fingers strayed from her thigh to the button at the top of her jeans and she put her hand over his, halting his progress.

"I can't. I'm too angry!" Her tone was huffy with a hint of stubbornness. "And your army tags are getting on my nerves. They keep smacking me in the face."

Rohan hauled himself up to sit next to Emma, punching the pillows behind him to get comfy. Then he undid his shirt buttons one at a time and pulled the fabric slowly from inside his pants. Emma watched in her peripheral vision, ogling the firm abdominal muscles and smooth skin, watching them flex as he moved to slip his shirt off his shoulders. She caught sight of the firm biceps which had bulged through his shirt sleeves as he hauled himself up the long staircase earlier. She couldn't resist turning her head for a sneaky look. Rohan's deft fingers plucked the metal chain and pulled it over his head, dropping it onto the floorboards with a clunk. "I told you I'll deal with school so you don't need to be angry. Now dog tags is all gone."

Emma grinned and turned her face away. "That's bad English and Nicky will hear us. It's embarrassing!"

"*Da*, embarrassing, but not disgusting. Get here woman, I have *zmeya* to show you."

Despite herself, Emma snorted, glancing back at the bedroom door and covering her mouth. "Is this your famous trouser snake? Because I've seen it and I'm not impressed." She squeaked as Rohan grabbed her, hauling her down the bed and biting her neck.

"Too loud!" he chuckled into her soft skin. "My room has more sound proofing. When will you move in there?"

Emma became still. "I don't want to. I have images of Felicity in there with you, giggling up a storm and I can't do it." She sighed, adding, "Sorry. I know you've set that room up to make it easier for you, but I don't think I can. Nicky and I slept in there when you were away and it wasn't a great time for me."

"Ok." Rohan sounded philosophical. "Then I'll move into this room." He worked his fingers under Emma's sweatshirt and laid his palm gently over her stomach. She flinched as his soft movements tickled but another feeling grew, something deeper which emanated from her chest. She waited, allowing it to spread and take hold of her, experiencing the spiritual communion between an excited father and his unborn child filling her heart and soul. It was powerful, breathtaking and full of wonder. Emma choked and spluttered as the nakedness of it overwhelmed her, driving home the emptiness of her pregnancy with Nicky and the months filled with terror and dread. This felt so different and the dismay seeded itself again with phrases like, *it will never last, you'll end up alone again like always*.

"*Chto?*" Rohan's alarm and instant concern was touching and his strong arms around Emma were welcome, shoring her defences against depression and misery. "Don't be afraid," he whispered, holding her tightly. "I'm here."

Emma cried against Rohan's silken skin and breathed in the warm masculine scent. But she had already seen the light in his eyes at the adrenaline rush which came with danger and the sense of aloneness snaked back into her heart. He was here for now maybe, but the Actuary would soon be gone again, roving the world for risks to neutralise, silently, with calculation and skill. Aloneness would take up residence with Emma and stay for good one day.

CHAPTER FIFTY ONE

Rohan looked nervous hauling himself out of the car. Emma left him to negotiate his crutches and slammed the door after him, waiting until he was stable enough to begin the trek up the road and through the school gates. A bitter wind howled around their legs, whipping Emma's new coat around her shins and repeatedly legging her up. Rohan plodded steadily along next to her, smirking from the corner of his mouth. "You're more unsteady on your feet than me," he chuckled.

"It's this gorgeous new coat you bought me." Emma stopped and fixed the bottom button closed. Her cheeks were already a healthy pink from the biting cold and her eyes sparkled. The sumptuous cashmere coat matched her tan boots and Rohan stopped, transfixed. "But I do love it." Emma smiled and her brow knitted at the sultry look on her husband's face. She moved across the footpath and wrapped her arms around his waist, careful not to overbalance him. "I love you," she whispered. "I know how hard this is for you, going public about your leg, but...your son will appreciate your bravery."

Rohan's blue eyes glittered like diamonds in the cold, a tear collecting in objection to the freezing onslaught. But his full lips smiled and his freshly shaven face put his affection on show. "I do it for him." Rohan's eyes roved to Emma's stomach and the smile broadened. "For *them*."

Emma kissed him slowly on the lips, oblivious to

the parents and grandparents navigating around them in the winter blast. "We'll be ok, won't we?" Emma begged, pushing away the dread in her heart.

"Of course!" Rohan looked surprised, kissing away a delicate snowflake which dared to land in Emma's curls. "Let's go in or he'll think I didn't come."

Emma's heart beat a tattoo as they joined the long queue to enter the school hall, displaying tickets and receiving hot coffee and a mince pie from a stand next to the ticket table. Her nerves were partly for Rohan, enduring the stares and curiosity of the school community. She listened to the awkward questions tittering from the mouths of tiny children around them and the well-meant silencing from embarrassed parents.

"Why's that man got one leg?"

"Ssh, I don't know," came the whispered answer.

Emma's back felt rigid and her whole body tense with the force of emotions, wanting so badly to protect the tall Russian from other thoughtless people. It made her feel powerless, wishing with a stab of guilt that she had made excuses for him instead, persuading Nicky not to beg his father to do this public thing.

Part of her nerves were for her son, the familiar dread of a mother anticipating the aftermath of her child making a spectacle of themselves. His line was short and she knew it backwards. Seeing Rohan dart a sideways look at her, Emma leaned towards him and whispered, "I really hope he doesn't forget his line."

Rohan snuffed gently and kissed her on the forehead. "He has nine words to say, *dorogaya*. His address is longer! He doesn't forget that."

Emma nodded, reassured. Then she focussed on the other object of her nerves. Felicity sat behind the ticket table, checking the number on the ticket against the seating plan in front of her. She gave Emma a haughty look and snatched the ticket from her hand, glaring up at Rohan with an acerbic look in her eyes. "You got the wrong tickets," she said in a sing-song voice. "Yours are on the back row." She glared at Emma in challenge and pulled the tickets towards herself, reaching into a biscuit tin and dragging out two replacements. As Emma reached out to take them from her hand, she deliberately dropped them onto the table.

Rohan gave a hiss of displeasure and Felicity looked up at him, her face screwing up in fury. "Thank you," he said politely, his accent sounding sexy in his throat. "Back is fine." He nudged Emma with his crutch, recognising the glint in her eye which signified she was about to jump across the table and rip the other woman's head off. As they moved away, Felicity noticed the crutches and stood up. Her eyes fixed on Rohan's lower half, seeing the right trouser leg neatly pinned up, folded over and over in a garish hem. Emma had struggled with it, knowing Rohan tried so hard not to get frustrated with her fumbling.

"What happened?" Felicity's voice rapped out as a screech amidst the dull hum of adults talking quietly. She pointed at Emma. "What did you do to him?"

Emma's body stiffened as she drew herself up to her full height, hearing the hissed warning from Rohan as she turned back towards the officious secretary. "No!" he told his wife. "Please find a seat for me? I can fight my own battles."

Emma's brown eyes flashed as black as coals in her fury and her jaw worked. The smirk in Rohan's eyes and his dilated pupils told her he found it sexy, infuriating her further. "She menaced my son!" she hissed at him through gritted teeth and Rohan nodded once.

"*My* son," he replied.

Emma walked woodenly to the hall door, aware of hundreds of eyes boring into her back with avid curiosity in an otherwise boring situation. The beam of the headmaster met her and he held out his hand for the tickets, chatting to her with a cheer she no longer felt.

Emma's eyes watched Rohan turn to face Felicity, the crowd around him abruptly silent. He jerked his head towards his missing shin and spoke. "I lost my leg six years ago in Afghanistan serving my chosen country." Felicity gulped and there was an outbreak of interested whispering and acknowledgment from around him. "I came to see my son be a wise man, if that's ok with everyone?" Rohan's hidden temper accentuated his Russian accent as he looked around for approval.

The crowd behind and around him nodded with acceptance and an elderly male voice called, "Bless you for your sacrifice, son."

"Bloody right," another male voice called and Rohan addressed the group with his beautiful smile, flashing his white teeth and gorgeous blue eyes with the skill which made him an officer whom men were willing to follow to their death.

"*Danke*," he said with gratitude.

Felicity sat down with a bump in her seat behind the ticket table, her cheeks flaring red and her lips pressed tightly shut. Emma wondered what backlash the twisted woman would plan as a suitable revenge for her and shuddered. But the way her husband said *thank you*

449

in Russian made Emma's cheeks flush. His whispered words in their shared bed the night before came back to her as a hot memory and she bit her lip against the inappropriate smirk of pleasure.

"I'm so looking forward to you starting here with us," Mr Dalton intoned, oblivious to Emma's absence in the one sided conversation until now. "It's bothered me all our precious photographs shoved in that attic up there." His Welsh accent sparkled through his speech in lyrical bounces, making it feel as though he called to her from a trampoline. "Oh!" he exclaimed. "These aren't your tickets! Staff sit in the front row." He waved a hand to a small child next to him. "Mr and Mrs Andreyev sit on the end, please, Angela."

The child skipped off ahead, her flowing white costume drifting round her legs in an elegant swish of sumptuous net curtain. Emma thanked the headmaster and took a step after her, watching the yellow ponytail swing from side to side as she bounced happily down the centre aisle towards the stage. Emma heard Rohan's crutches behind her and waited, seeing the headmaster grip her husband's right hand without dislodging the metal support. "I dealt with that other little business," Mr Dalton said, leaning in towards Rohan to prevent those bottle necked behind from hearing. "She gave her notice and won't be back next term." He rolled his 'r's,' creating a sound like a purr in his throat. His eye line reached the centre of Rohan's chest but his character rose far above that in stature. He let go of Rohan's hand with a nod and the men parted, Rohan clacking slowly behind his wife.

"I like Nicky," the little girl informed them as Emma held the child sized seat still for Rohan to fold himself into. His leg stuck out forwards for what seemed like miles and he tried to poke his crutches under his own and Emma's miniature seat.

"That's nice," Emma said with a smile, experiencing a maternal flush at hearing her child was accepted.

"Yeah, I like him *a lot*." Angela's blue eyes widened in meaning and Emma gulped as the little girl scratched at an itchy looking lace collar on the front of her angel costume. "I was a sheep," she informed Emma, distracting herself temporarily and staring at Rohan's pinned trouser leg. She turned her huge liquid blue eyes back on the mother of the object of her desire. "Mrs Clarke made me be a sheep but I cried and cried to be an angel. Angels get to sit with the wise men." She scratched again at her neck and extended the movement down her chest to her stomach, her nails making a scritching sound across the starchy cloth. "Do wise men ever marry angels?" she asked pointedly, her confidence ebbing away.

Rohan sat up and slipped his arm around Emma, fixing his handsome smile on the child. "Oh, *da!*" he replied with enthusiasm. "I did."

Angela beamed, showing all the reasons she was easily absorbed into the angel-brigade. She looked up at an agonised shout from her leader. "Where's my angel gone?" Mr Dalton yelled into the darkened hall. "I've lost my angel!" With a cute wave, Angela was gone, skipping off back up the aisle to the teacher.

"Idiot!" Emma snorted, digging Rohan in the ribs. "I'm definitely no angel."

He grunted with the impact of her elbow and kissed her temple. "It's ok. I'm no wise man." His deep voice sounded sexy in the darkness and Emma sighed with contentment.

"I heard what Mr Dalton said at the door," she

whispered. "Thank you for sorting it out."

"It was all my fault," Rohan admitted. "Was my mess to clear up. Loneliness made me unclear so I was wrong." He squeezed her shoulder and then let go as Allaine settled herself in the seat behind them.

"I hope you're ready for this!" she warned. "Why Mrs Clarke would let those three even sit together let alone act together, is beyond me."

"Yeah, I know what you mean," Emma snorted. "They're like the three musketeers."

Rohan shrugged and looked confused. Allaine's husband, Will, leaned forward to shake Rohan's hand. "It sounds ominous, mate. I've no idea what they're talking about. My Kaylee's been practicing with me most days. She's word perfect."

Allaine rolled her eyes and snorted. Her Scottish husband eyed her nervously. "Well, I don't trust those three!" she said sagely with a mother's intuition and Emma nodded in agreement.

The men shrugged and devoured their coffee and mince pies. Rohan ate Emma's too as she rejected it after a single bite. "It's nice," she said apologetically, "I just don't feel so good."

"Ah, poor *devotchka!*" Rohan pulled her chair into his in a single easy movement, not realising they were fixed together. The whole row came scuttling a few inches to the right and an elderly granny squealed at the other end.

Emma heard Allaine burst out laughing behind her, quickly silenced by her husband's muffled rebuke.

The darkness seemed oppressive as silence descended, marred only by the odd shuffle of feet or the loudly whispered question from a bored pre-schooler.

Light burst from a spotlight overhead, blinding the audience as the nativity began, an annual feast of colour, inappropriate behaviour and forgotten lines. It was Rohan's first experience of the fiasco and his eyes shone with a mix of bafflement and hilarity as the disasters unfolded one after another. The first narrator was word perfect and amazing, the second passable but cute and the third, apoplectic. A loud fart issued from the collected menagerie of animals seated in darkness to the right of the stage. There was a lot of shuffling as the animals divided around the offender, leaving a wide area of floorboards for the boy dressed as a chicken to comfortably stretch out in. Assorted sheep, cows and what looked like a gorilla in the gloom, crushed up one end, hugging the stage and forcing it to wobble dangerously.

The narrator giggled and spluttered for three minutes without saying a word before Mrs Clarke's level voice cut through the confusion with, "The inn was full." She rapped it out like an order and the child sniggered his way to the side and flopped down into nothingness.

The light remained trained on centre stage as Mary and Joseph rode a tricycle dressed as a donkey around it for a while. The cardboard donkey head looked sad and Rohan pulled a face at Emma which set her off giggling, exacerbated by her urge for the toilet whenever her stomach constricted. He leaned in close so she felt his breath on her cheek and whispered,

"It's comedy? *Da?*"

Emma caught the sound of Allaine behind, trying to keep it together in the presence of an adoring crowd. She shook her head to tell Rohan, *no*, this was serious stuff.

The donkey's head fell off before it reached the stable and Mary gave birth to Baby Jesus with incredible speed, whipping him out from underneath her skirts with practiced skill.

"Half her luck!" muttered a woman from somewhere in the audience and Emma heard Allaine's muffled squeak from behind. There was a blinding flash as some overenthusiastic parent ignored the no photography rule and snapped themselves a photograph of a bicycle pile-up and a stunned Mary and Joseph with an upside down Cabbage Patch doll falling to the ground.

The chicken farted again, producing a collective groan from the other animals and Mrs Clarke hastily dispatched her classroom assistant. All manner of acceleration was employed to ensure the egg was laid in the appropriate place and the chicken was escorted to the bathrooms.

Emma tensed as the threesome arrived on stage with a fanfare, like a recipe for disaster. The two wise men and one wise woman strode in like something from the Wild West, Mo clutching his trousers in an accurate rendition of a black gun slinger. "Me belt broke!" he announced, peering out into the audience like Long John Silver with his hand shading his eyes. Mel sat in the same row as Allaine and Emma saw her slide down into her tiny seat in an attempt to pretend Mo belonged to someone else. He gave a small, painful squeak as Kaylee hoisted his trousers up from behind and hauled him backwards. In deference to her broad Scots father, she performed her words perfectly, although the forced Scots accent sounded a little weird.

Nicky whipped out a long telescope made from toilet roll holders and held it to his left eye, spinning on the spot to get a good look from every angle. He wavered a bit as he accidentally focussed on the spotlight above the audience and rubbed his eye. "Bloody blinded meself!" he told Mo.

"Oh yeah, it's bright, is that!" Mo agreed, his eyes rolling at the ferocity of Kaylee's grip on his pants. Nicky was taller than his friends, built like his father and with all Rohan's natural Russian beauty. He drew himself up to his full height, his bare toes showing underneath his great grandmother's old dressing gown. "Der is a star, vot shine in de east!" he said, sounding exactly like Rohan, when tiredness reverted his speech into its heavily accented state.

"Ay up! Will us find it then? Is it over Manchester?" Mo asked, a suggestion more than a stage direction. Nicky and Kaylee conferred with him, producing nods of affirmation eventually.

Nicky poked his eye against the end of his wobbly telescope and focussed on Rohan, sitting right at the front. "That's my dad," he announced proudly. "He's a war hero."

There was a muted, impromptu round of applause and Rohan sank down in his seat, cringing. Nicky waved his telescope at his parents and the end flew off and landed amongst the angels. Angela dived for it and had a tug of war with another girl, their scrap divinely lit from above by a spotlight.

Mrs Clarke waved them frantically off the stage from her seating position near the animals, her shoulders slumped as though she had finally reached breaking point. Nicky and Kaylee went one way and Mo the other, meaning he was on his own with his troublesome trousers. There was a whump as his pants hit the wooden stage and a squeal as he pitched off it, followed by a muffled, "I'm ok!"

Everyone worked hard not to look at Mel, who squirmed her way slowly out of a private mortification in her seat and came up smiling. The final bow was loud and raucous, with ample opportunity for parents to photograph the cast.

Emma stood to the side and clicked snaps of the wise men and woman on Rohan's phone, gratified when Nicky threw himself into his father's arms with obvious pleasure. She snapped one of the two of them which they smiled for and one which Rohan wouldn't know about until later. She stroked the screen, seeing two blonde heads close together in conversation, animated blue eyes and the same striking facial structure. *Peas in a pod.*

Needing the toilet urgently, Emma handed the phone back to Rohan and set off in search of the ladies toilets, finding them blessedly empty half way along the wide, brightly lit corridor. Looking up whilst washing her hands, she found herself observed by Felicity. Her heart sank. "You disgust me!" the other woman bit, raising her voice to hysterical proportions. "He was *my* boyfriend! We were getting married!"

"Did Rohan *ever* say that to you?" Emma asked, drying her hands on a paper towel. In her angst, she shredded it and reached for another.

"He didn't have to!" Felicity spat. "We were in love." Her eyes looked crazed and Emma took a step back, shades of Alanya colouring her view.

She shook her head. "I don't think so, Felicity. I think you saw what you wanted." She cast her mind back to Rohan's interactions with the woman, seeing only tolerance and a need for company amidst Felicity's insipid grasping. "If I'm honest, it's not the impression I ever got."

"I'm pregnant!" Felicity snapped, resting a speculative hand over her abdomen.

Emma tutted. "By a man you called impotent?"

Felicity's cheeks flushed harder and Emma took a step towards the doorway. Felicity's eyes snapped in the same direction and she moved slowly sideways, blocking it. "I lied. He...we..."

"Oh come on!" Emma shouted. "You didn't even know about his leg! He didn't trust you. Surely that tells you something? I'm his wife, Felicity. I'm sorry for how this has turned out, but threatening a child? Really? That was sick! You made him terrified of you. It's unforgiveable."

"He's a brat!" Felicity answered, her voice laden with venom. "I knew he was Rohan's son from the start. I've seen pictures of Rohan's brother and that brat is nothing like him. I hate you for what you've done. My life was great until you appeared. You turned it to crap!"

Realisation lit Emma's face with a sneer. "Is that why you hired a private investigator even before I turned up, Felicity? You paid someone to drive up and down the country following my husband to business meetings. It must have cost you a fortune and the silly man didn't even tell you the basics about Rohan Andreyev. You didn't know he'd lost his leg and you still don't know what he does for a living. For goodness sake, Felicity. What is wrong with you?"

Emma took another step towards the open doorway, anger making her eyes flash dangerously. Felicity was unhinged, but nothing compared to some of the women on the estate in Lincoln. Emma braved it out, refusing to show weakness. "Get out of my way!"

She should have seen the slap coming, but wasn't quite quick enough to stop it landing hard on her face. Felicity put her whole grievance into it; her broken hopes and dreams went into the blow and the obsession with Rohan Andreyev which cost her everything. Emma's ears were deafened by the sound of tinkling glass as her head hit the mirror above the sinks and she was showered with sharp debris.

The cunning left hander made her right cheek ring with the vibrations from the blow, but her head smarted above her left ear and blood trickled down her face and onto her new coat. "Damn!" she heard herself say as the word tumbled from her lips and nothingness shrouded her head like a blanket.

Emma felt the soft cushion of Allaine's arms beneath her as she crumpled and Nicky's shrill, hysterical screams overhead as help was summoned,

CHAPTER FIFTY TWO

"Was I a good wise man, Mummy? You didn't fall over because I was rubbish or anyfink?"

"No, baby. You were wonderful. I think maybe I got a bit overexcited." Emma ruffled Nicky's blonde hair and tried not to think about the stitches in the side of her head. They pulled taut and painful, her pregnancy denying her the usual welcome brand of pain relief.

"Why did Kaylee's daddy take the nasty lady off in a police car?" Nicky asked, looking backwards at his wide-eyed friend, who nodded in confirmation. "Is it because she hurt you? Did she make you fall down?" Nicky's words came in short gasps as he panicked. "She said she'd hurt you. Is it my fault? I should've told Daddy she said that." Hysteria picked at the sides of the child's composure and Emma swaddled him in to her breast.

"None of this is your fault, Nick. Forget about it now. Go and see if there's a TV somewhere but don't talk to strangers. Ok? Promise?"

Nicky nodded and Allaine stepped forward to point the way to a room at the end of the hospital ward. She reiterated Emma's warning and watched the children walk away. She turned to Emma with a sigh. "Felicity threatened you?"

"Apparently so." Emma lay back against the pillows and closed her eyes. "I really should have seen that coming. It threw me because she's right handed and she hit me with her left." Emma thumped the sheets in frustration and shook her head, wincing when it hurt.

Allaine sat in the visitor's chair next to the bed, her pretty face paled by the nightmare. "I wasn't quick enough. I saw her follow you out of the hall but Kaylee delayed me. I checked every classroom and then realised you'd probably gone to the toilet. I got there as she hit you and was just in time to stop you falling on the floor and hitting your head again. There was so much blood."

"Nothing you haven't seen before," Emma smiled. "I thought lab technicians were great with bodily fluids."

Allaine nodded. "We don't usually collect it from the scene. Or from people we love." She rubbed a hand across her eyes.

"Thank you." Emma reached out a shaky hand and Allaine took it, holding on firmly.

"How do you feel?" She indicated Emma's stomach with a nod of her head.

Emma shrugged. "I honestly feel fine. It's just my head really. I've asked for a scan, even though the baby won't be much bigger than a walnut yet. I'm just waiting for Rohan." Her face creased in anxiety.

"He's not far now. He's talking to Will." Allaine stroked Emma's fingers, listening to the sound of childish voices from the end of the ward. Nicky and Kaylee sang the theme tune to a popular children's cartoon with sweet clear voices. Emma smiled.

Rohan swung into the room with purpose, his crutches squeaking on the linoleum floor. Will followed him in, telling an eager, uniformed police constable to wait outside. Allaine rose quickly and went to her husband, putting her hands against his strong chest. "Felicity threatened Emma. That makes it different now, doesn't it? She told him she'd hurt her if he didn't do what she wanted. It's why he got so upset in McDonald's that lunchtime when we bumped into her. Don't you remember? Nicky wanted to go home once she arrived."

Will nodded. "Yeah. I do." He looked at Emma in apology. "I thought you'd just muscled in on her boyfriend and the boy was caught in the crossfire. I'm so sorry."

"I kinda did and he kinda was." Emma sounded tired, waving Will's apology away with a flap of her hand. Rohan perched a butt cheek on the side of the bed and held Emma, infusing her with love and strength. "What about getting your prosthetic." She looked up at him, squinting through her tearful left eye. "They close for Christmas today."

"Nothing matters except you and my baby. We're going for a scan soon."

"But what about your leg?" Emma began again and Rohan shook his head.

"It doesn't matter, Em. Believe me, suddenly it just doesn't." Rohan dipped his head but shied off kissing her on the face. Both sides looked pretty messed up. "Just rest."

Will cleared his throat. "It would be good if the officer and I were able to ask Nicky some questions, just preliminary ones. We need to stop this woman just being bailed for giving you a slap and hold her on more serious charges. Would it be ok if Allaine sits in or...what do you want me to do?"

"Allaine can stand in for me," Emma nodded. "If it gives you what you need. But you'd better bring Nicky here first." She sighed, sounding exhausted.

Nicky's feet pattered down the hallway, slapping on the linoleum loudly. "Ssh, Nick. There's sick people here trying to sleep," Emma said calmly. Will sauntered into the room after the child, waiting with interest while Nicky clambered onto the bed.

"Yeah, Mum?" he said, putting his best listening face on.

"Right, baby. Will needs to ask you some quick questions about the lady at school, Miss Robinson. I need you to tell him the truth."

"But he's *police!*" Nicky said the word as though it tasted foul and rolled his eyes at Emma. "Our kind never talks to police."

Emma exhaled. "Nicky, our kind is good, decent, law abiding people. Ok? And we do talk to police, we just haven't needed to."

"But Fat Brian says they take you in a cell and break your arms!" He looked back at Will in the doorway, trying to reconcile Kaylee's fun daddy with his warped image of the police force, courtesy of Fat Brian and Big Jason.

"They don't, Nicky. And this is real important, son. I need you to tell Kaylee's lovely daddy exactly what the lady said to you. I need them to keep her locked up for now. She could have hurt me bad, Nick, so it's important."

"We're ready for you now, Mrs Andreyev." A nurse appeared in the doorway with a porter and Nicky's head swivelled round and back again.

"Where you goin', Mum? Why can't you or Dad be wiv me when Kaylee's daddy talks to me."

Emma looked her son in the eyes, holding him either side of his beautiful face. She couldn't bear to have him in the scan with her, in case it was bad news.

"Nicky, I have a baby in my tummy and the nurse needs to make sure the lady didn't hurt it. Please tell Will everything you know and pray to your God for me, Nick." Emma's voice broke as fear trampled across her heart and Rohan rubbed her back. He smiled at Nicky, not knowing who needed him most, his face a mask of agony.

"We'll be fine," Allaine said, standing up and nodding to her husband. Will scooped the small boy up into his capable arms and held him as Nick wept a river of tears.

"I love you, Mummy," he wailed as Emma was wheeled away down the corridor, to find out the fate of her unborn child.

CHAPTER FIFTY THREE

"It's so beautiful out here," Allaine said, watching Nicky and Kaylee tearing round the front lawn with Farrell barking up a storm. "You're so lucky." The dog herded them like cattle but grew bored as they hurled themselves to the snowy floor giggling.

"I know," Emma agreed, sitting against the side of the window seat and drawing her knees up to her chest.

"How are you?" Allaine asked, and Emma nodded.

"I'm good, thanks. It's a relief the baby was ok. Stupid woman, why would you hit someone that hard over a man?"

"She's done it before, apparently." Allaine lowered her voice. "But please don't tell Will you heard it from me. She gave Mr Dalton one hell of a time at the start of last year and he threatened to sack her when he caught her following his wife around the supermarket. She packed it in and then switched to Rohan when she bumped into him in town. She followed him home and then rented a house round the corner on Granville Street. It was easy after that to keep appearing at his door needing things. She moved here from Nottingham and changed her name after...get this; she was bailed for stalking a local councillor."

"That doesn't make sense." Emma rubbed a hand over her face. "The education department would have paid her wages. They would need to see birth certificates and proof of name and stuff like that, tax number and official stuff. I know because I had to take all that in to Mr Dalton for him to draw up a contract for me for next year."

"She took someone else's identity." Allaine laid a hand on Emma's knee. "Please don't tell anyone. Will would kill me. I just know that you're kind of holding it against Rohan for her behaviour. I wanted you to understand how she worked. It would take nothing for her to be encouraged, believe me."

Emma sighed. "That's partly it. But the other thing I keep asking myself is, how can Rohan not see these strange women attaching themselves to him? I mean, right now, he's visiting his mother who's on remand for murdering vulnerable men and possibly her own child. He shut his mind to her behaviour all those years, Allie. Of course he couldn't see what Felicity...or whatever her name is, was doing. He didn't *want* to see." She dragged a finger down the small rectangular pane of blown glass, leaving a streak in the condensation. "He's like this massive hunk of prime Russian killing machine, who believes anything a manipulative woman says to him. It makes me scared." Emma sighed and stretched her legs out, putting her hand on Allaine's foot as she stretched out next to her. The two of them hardly filled the huge window seat.

"All men have their weaknesses," Allaine said, sounding wise. She watched the children making an igloo in the snow drifts beyond the driveway. "Those kids are gonna be freezing."

Emma watched her friend's face, searching for the wisdom she always managed to produce. Allaine turned back to her and smiled. "Take Will for example. He's handsome, got a great body, still turns me on at forty. He's an incredible father, amazing lover, excellent husband and outstanding police sergeant."

Emma waited patiently for the punch line. Allaine fixed her blue eyes on Emma's brown ones, her face all serious. "The guy can't stand the sight of blood. All that and he's scared of a little bodily fluid! So see, they all have faults."

Emma snorted. "I thought you were going to say something really helpful!" she laughed, holding her sides. "He's squeamish!"

"Hey, what do you usually do for Christmas?" Allaine said suddenly, changing the subject. "It's less than two days away now."

Emma's face took on a haunted, faraway look. "When my father was alive, we did a proper Christmas lunch and gifts. His housekeeper cooked the turkey and ate with us. When he married Alanya, she claimed she couldn't cook such food and the housekeeper was too intimidated to stay and eat with us. My father got sick and it gradually fizzled out. After he died, we didn't do it at all. Lucya and I had no money but it was always happy. We'd save up and buy three chicken drumsticks and watch Christmas movies all afternoon on television. Sometimes the shelters gave food donations and those times were better. There was always a gift for Nicky but she would kiss me on the forehead on Christmas morning and say Nicky was my present to her. After she died, in Lincoln..." Emma sighed. "Nicky knew I had nothing. He drew me a picture and I might write him a story. Once I did it on the computer at work and printed it off. I stitched it into a book and he pretended it was real. We played cards and cuddled. Mostly we listened to the crack addicts next door getting high and the family across the street knocking the snot out of each other. Better than television." Emma inhaled. "I'm not sure about this year. I've promised to visit Freda but I don't know what Rohan has planned. The clinic allowed him to get his leg fitted on Saturday so now there's nothing stopping him. Maybe he'll be away." Emma picked at a piece of loose paint and bit her lip.

"You think he'll still work as the Actuary?" Allaine asked and Emma shrugged.

"I don't know. The night he came for me, he was like a moth to a flame. I'd never seen him more alive. I understood then, once I saw him in action. He won't be honest with me about what actually happened after they drugged me, so I don't even know if she...oh, it doesn't matter. I begged him not to go back to the army all those years ago. He came home on leave and I knew I was pregnant. I was sixteen and terrified and I begged him. He looked me in the eye and said, '*I can't stop, Emma. I love it. I love thinking on my feet and strategising. I work out risks and then walk the paths I map for myself. I love it.*' I asked him, '*Do you love it more than me?*' He couldn't answer." Emma looked at the children rolling in the snow, their bodies covered in icy flakes. She gulped. "I walked out in frustration, he left and I didn't get to tell him about Nicky. He got blown up and I never knew."

Depression settled on her, bringing her very real fears to the surface and ruining her enjoyment of the relaxing afternoon. Emma forced herself to smile at her friend, fixing a false calm over herself to stop her betraying any other deep secrets.

"He might surprise you," Allaine whispered, leaning forward and gripping Emma's cold hand in hers.

"Yeah. And he might not." Emma spread her fingers across the tiny child inside her belly, communicating love through her touch. Her eyes roved again to her son, giggling and hooning around with his friend. "I might just have to accept that I'm on my own again," Emma whispered, extreme sadness penetrating through her words.

"Come to us for Christmas?" Allaine begged, tears in her eyes. "Please? Whether Rohan's here or not, please come and be part of our family. It's crazy busy and there're people everywhere but you'll be so welcome. Think about it, please? Promise me? Freda can come too."

"Thank you." Emma gripped her friend's hand and clung on for dear life, wondering what the future would hold for her and daring to believe it might be good this time.

The women sat in the silence of the ancient house, listening to the boards settling and the old structure giving the occasional involuntary creak. The sound of squeals on the front lawn were joyful and comforting, casting them back to a time when this house was filled with people living their lives, making enemies, making love and rolling around in the winter snow. Emma glanced up with a sigh and raked the garden with her eyes, looking for the children. Nicky heaved his body weight against a round white ball of snow, forcing it uphill with enormous exertion. Kaylee's tiny form lent its help, pushing and making hardly any difference.

The tall, strongly built man squatted down in the snow next to them, a dark jacket protecting his torso. His blonde hair blended with the white snow and his hands were bare. He bent to push the snowball, an awkward movement for him and he shoved one handed from between the children. It crumbled to pieces with the added force and the children stood up and stared at its dilapidated state, their swaddled faces downturned in disappointment. Rohan bent and collected a ball of snow, rolling it in his fingers while the children stared up at him. He set off away from them with long strides and threw the ball backwards with skill, an underarm which caught Nicky on the chest of his duffel coat. With combined squeaks of joy, the children buried their gloves in the snowball, breaking off chunks and rolling them. They pelted Rohan with squeals of delight, running away on small legs as he bent to make sturdy ammunition and advancing with giggles and belly laughs when he ran out.

His car sat idling on the long driveway and he ran towards it with a loping gait and the children pursued, missing him by miles with their hurriedly thrown missiles. The black dog barked and leapt around, trying to catch the balls of flying snow.

Emma watched as Rohan ran to the boot of the car and produced a wide plastic sled with a string attached. The children whooped and screeched, dropping their snowballs and running towards him. Nicky hurled himself at Rohan, hugging his legs and Kaylee took the opportunity to sit herself in the red lid-shaped sled. Rohan bent to kiss Nicky and then stood for a minute, watching as his son hauled his friend around the garden with excitement. Kaylee held on with mittened hands, the bobble on top of her hat wobbling furiously with the action, their laughter carrying back to the women indoors.

Rohan observed for a moment before thrusting cold hands into his jeans pockets and trudging back to the car through the deep snow, his limp barely noticeable in the wide footsteps over the drifts and hidden flower beds.

"It'll be ok, Emma." Allaine's voice was soft as Emma looked up, realising her friend studied her with an intent look on her face. Allaine nudged her shin and Emma nodded and looked away. Rohan's car slid up the driveway, negotiating the pockets of ice and snow with care. He would reach the wide front doors and pillared steps in seconds and Emma's heart gave a lurch of anticipation, which she beat down with a valiant effort.

Emma watched him emerge from the black car and slam the door, walking up the wide front steps and banging his shoes on them to release the clumps of snow. A few days blonde beard growth kissed his angular face and dark lashes framed his expressive marbled blue eyes. He was beautifully made and knitted together and Emma laid her head back against the shutter and closed her eyes. An image of his smiling eyes danced in front of her inner vision, teasing and seductive. She sighed and looked at Allaine, who watched her with concern. "I've loved him since I was not much older than Nicky," Emma said softly. "But I can't own the unpossessable. He's a danger addict. He left once and probably will again. I think that's what this is." Emma looked up at the ceiling rose and the ornate cornering in the huge room. "Anton offered me security in the event of all else failing. He understood. Life as the wife of Rohan Andreyev, the Actuary, has no certainties; he would have known that."

The women jumped at the sound of the front door slamming against the wind. The panes of the inner glass doors shook and they heard Rohan whistling to himself as he wiped his shoes on the doormat. Emma splayed her fingers across her unborn child and stiffened her back as his footsteps echoed down the hallway towards them. A smile sprang to her face as she accepted a kiss from her husband's bitterly cold lips, knowing his love for her burned as fiercely as hers did for him.

Heaven only knew what the future held, but she wouldn't want to face it with anyone else

Dear Reader,

If it were not for you, there would be no point me writing. It's the thought of another's enjoyment and their ability to lay aside their cares in the glorious pastime of reading; which keeps me striving.

I want you to lose yourself, to enter the worlds of others and be released from your own troubles, just for a time.

I hope this novel kept you turning the pages and if it has, I would be grateful if you could leave a review on Goodreads.com and the site where you purchased it from. In the shifting sands of writing and publishing, reviews are the only way of building a reputation and reaching other readers.

Thank you for spending time with the Andreyevs. The Actuary's Wife will be available by the end of 2015.

ABOUT THE AUTHOR

K T Bowes has worked in education for more than a decade, both in New Zealand and the United Kingdom and has been writing since she could first hold a pencil. She is married with four beautiful children who are all now making their own way in the world. She lives in the North Island of New Zealand between the Hakarimata Ranges and the Waikato River with a mad cat and often a few crazy horses. She loves to ride but unfortunately keeps falling off and breaking bones so has gone back to road running instead. She can't be seen pacing the streets of Ngaruawahia because she runs in the dark, convinced people will laugh. Often accompanied by one of her characters complaining about something, the author appears to have mental problems as she frequently answers back, which is another good reason for running under cover of darkness.

Connect with K T Bowes at:
Google+ http://ktbowes.blogspot.co.nz/
Twitter @hanadurose
Facebook www.facebook.com/Author.KTBOWES

She would love to hear from you.

OTHER BOOKS BY THE AUTHOR:
The Hana Du Rose Mysteries:
About Hana
Hana Du Rose
Du Rose Legacy
The New Du Rose Matriarch
One Heartbeat
The Du Rose Prophecy
Du Rose Sons

The Teen Series - Troubled:
Free From the Tracks
Sophia's Dilemma
A Trail of Lies

UK Based Mystery/Romances
Artifact
Demons on Her Shoulder

From Russia, With Love
The Actuary
The Actuary's Wife

41018996R00290

Made in the USA
Columbia, SC
14 December 2018